Nancy Price

*Sleeping with the Enemy*

"TRANSPORTS THE READER . . . Nancy Price is able to sustain the suspense and tautness!"
—*West Coast Review of Books*

"A WELL-PACED THRILLER." —*Boston Herald*

"EFFECTIVE . . . A TRIUMPHANT CONCLU-SION!" —*Publishers Weekly*

"TENSION . . . ROMANCE AND SUSPENSE."
—*Kirkus*

"A SENSITIVE AND HUMANE WRITER OF MERIT." —*The Houston Post*

# NANCY PRICE

# SLEEPING
## with the
# ENEMY

J

JOVE BOOKS, NEW YORK

Grateful acknowledgment is made for permission to reprint
the following:

"The White Mouse" by Nancy Price. Originally published
in *The Virginia Quarterly Review*, Winter 1969 issue (Vol. 45,
No. 1). Copyright © 1969 *The Virginia Quarterly Review*.
Used with permission.

"The Invisible Ones" by Nancy Price. Originally published
in *The Virginia Quarterly Review*, Winter 1968 issue (Vol. 44,
No. 1). Copyright © 1968 *The Virginia Quarterly Review*.
Used with permission.

This Jove book contains the complete
text of the original hardcover edition.
It has been completely reset in a typeface
designed for easy reading, and was printed
from new film.

### SLEEPING WITH THE ENEMY

A Jove Book / published by arrangement with
Simon and Schuster, Inc.

PRINTING HISTORY
Jove edition / June 1988

ISBN: 0-515-09638-5

Jove Books are published by The Berkley Publishing Group,
200 Madison Avenue, New York, New York 10016.
The name "JOVE" and the "J" logo
are trademarks belonging to Jove Publications, Inc.

PRINTED IN THE UNITED STATES OF AMERICA

10  9  8  7  6  5  4  3  2  1

*Gratitude is due*

Howard, David, Catherine and John
and Michael James Carroll, Eleanor Bostwick
Crownfield,
Amy Lockard, Barbara Lounsberry, Clara Southall,
and Evelyn Starkey Wood.

This book was advanced by a stay at the Rockefeller
Foundation Bellagio Study and Conference Center.

# 1

The day before Martin Burney lost his wife Sara, he watched her walk away from him, her long hair lifted at the edges by wind from the Atlantic. A beauty-shop door shut behind her, flashing sun. Martin's eyes were as brown and cold as leftover coffee.

Ocean wind rattled a paper sign on the Beauty Corner window as Martin drove away: MEN WELCOME. Sara said, "Sara Burney," to a woman behind a counter and looked around the new shop; it hadn't been there the summer before.

EMOCLEW NEM the shop sign read from inside, backward; the shop's green floor was scattered with sheared-off hair. Sara walked to shampoo sinks in the wake of the beauty operator whose name tag said, "Carmen."

"Maybe just a little rinse," Carmen said, and put a green plastic cape around Sara's shoulders. Sara leaned back in the shampoo chair and took a deep breath. She could stay there for an hour and a half.

Water rushed behind Sara's ears and down the drain, hissing like waves on sand. She shut her eyes.

"Brings out highlights," Carmen said. She rubbed in shampoo and took a good look at Sara Burney, who had dark circles under her eyes and was so thin she was bony; she wasn't dressed for summer in her jeans and long-sleeved shirt. The back of one of her hands was bruised purple.

A middle-aged woman in the next shampoo chair laughed.

She said to the operator scrubbing her head, "Did you read about this woman in one of those little Southern towns where everybody watches everybody else twenty-five hours a day?" The woman scrubbing her head grunted.

Carmen massaged Sara's scalp. "You here for a vacation, swimming and all?"

"I'm afraid of the water," Sara said. There were no men in the Beauty Corner in spite of the sign rattling in the wind. Perfume and women surrounded Sara. "We're renting on Sand Hook until Saturday."

"They've got nice new docks there," Carmen said. "You got a boat?"

"No. I'm scared of boats too."

"Honest?" Carmen stopped rubbing. "Come to the beach and you're scared of water?"

"I can't help it," Sara said.

"You have kids?"

"No."

"Got to be careful not to scare kids," Carmen said.

Sara shut her eyes again.

"Too bad, being scared." Carmen started rinsing Sara's hair. Sara said nothing against the water-rush.

"Well, at least you can get a nice tan," Carmen said.

There were tears in the corners of Sara's eyes.

"You ever tried getting in the water just a little each day?" Carmen asked.

Sara said yes, she had.

Carmen squeezed water out of Sara's hair, then threw a towel around Sara's head. She held her close against her, rubbing, and Sara took a deep breath in the towel's warm, mothering dark and tried not to cry.

"Now you sit over here," Carmen said. Sara sat down and looked at herself in the mirror: a shapeless mouth and wet blond seaweed for hair. Sara firmed her mouth into a usual expression and blinked a few times.

The middle-aged woman was unwrapped from her towel now; she settled in a chair beside Sara. "The newspaper said it was a little small Southern town that woman moved to." She leaned toward the mirror. "I look like a drowned rat." She stared at herself. "Like a drowned *gray* rat." A row of women along the beauty-shop wall looked at their reflections with serious faces, as if spending time and money every week on the outside of their skulls was necessary and natural, even ordinary. "This woman in the newspaper's a secretary and divorced, and she's got two kids," the middle-aged woman said. "And minding her own business, you know? She joined that church because she wanted the kids to make friends. And of course she had a nice man friend."

"Father for her kids," the operator said.

"Sure—how you going to get one otherwise?" the woman said.

Carmen flipped Sara's long hair around a roller. "Been in Manhasset before?"

"This is our third summer," Sara said.

"Where you from?"

"Near Boston. Montrose." Rollers began to frame Sara's face in pink sausages around empty eyes and a firm mouth.

"Brooke, you got a couple pink rollers I can borrow?" Carmen called, and went off to get them.

"And they saw his car in her drive—isn't that *sinful? His car* in *her driveway?*" the middle-aged woman said.

Sara looked out at a street where people strolled, aimless and free, window shopping, gossiping on the corner.

"And would you believe they got hold of her man friend, and he admitted what *they* called 'fornication,' so she was going to have to stand up in front of the congregation and tell what she'd done and repent and ask for their forgiveness and I don't know what-all. So she sent a letter resigning from the church—then they wouldn't have to feel responsible about how she went about getting the kids a father, you know?"

Carmen came back to finish rolling Sara's hair into pink sausages. "I don't go in the ocean much. It's too cold," Carmen said. "Brooke here, she swims every day in summer. My lord."

"Nope, the church elders told this secretary, they had to kick her out. So they got the congregation together—it was about half the town—and told everybody what she'd done, and that nobody should talk to her or anything. And she was mad as hell. She went to a lawyer and sued the church and two elders, said it was an invasion of privacy.''

''Imagine that,'' the operator said.

Carmen pulled a net over Sara's rollers.

''And would you believe—that secretary's going to own that church? Graveyard, parking lot, and all?''

Carmen led Sara to a dryer and gave her a woman's magazine. ''Here's the control,'' Carmen said. ''Turn it down if it gets too hot.''

Warm, rushing air surrounded Sara. Her glossy magazine fell open to an ad—a woman with blue eyelids above a pouty mouth.

The dryer's flow of air, minute after minute, closed Sara in a soft curtain. She shut her eyes and dozed a little in that soft cave of sound. But time was going fast. Her hair was drying; she couldn't stop that. She jerked and opened her eyes to look at lovers kissing passionately in a magazine illustration. The paragraph under the picture began, ''His mouth swooped down on hers, and he took his time, as determined to undermine her resistance as she was to maintain it. He forced her backward, and made her stirringly aware of the dominating need of his hard male body.''

Sara watched women yawning under dryers. The magazine had a quiz about your love life and tips for sexual satisfaction and ways to please your husband or handle children's problems at school. Sara shut it and stared at operators walking through tufts of drifting hair. She watched their calm shoes side by side, and the placid busyness of their hands.

Sara's hair was drying; Carmen came every now and then to feel it, and finally she turned off the dryer. Its rush drained away. Sara saw Martin drive up to park beyond EMOCLEW NEM.

Carmen led Sara to a chair in front of the mirrors. A small girl sat next to Sara. The child's hair was plastered wet to her scalp and her face was grim. ''You're going to look *so pretty*,'' an operator crooned to her. The small girl said nothing.

"You a teacher?" Carmen asked Sara after a while. She had all the curlers out. She swept Sara's hair overhead with a big hairbrush. "Reason I say that, you talk very nice, and I said to Brooke, she's a teacher."

"I work in a library," Sara said, not looking at Martin waiting in the car. "Part-time."

"Thought so." Carmen smoothed Sara's hair around her face. "Thought you had something to do with teaching—education—you know. I got a feeling about people."

Sara stared at the mirrored blonde, who was dried out now. She closed her eyes, smelling alcohol and peroxide. "How'd your hubby like that new tint we used on you?" an operator asked an old lady. Equipment glittered in the big room, white and chrome, cold as a hospital. Women were having their cuticles pushed back; their hair was being bleached or dyed and crimped with chemicals.

"How's that?" Carmen held out a mirror, and Sara twisted around to look at the sides and back of her head.

"Fine," Sara said. "That's the way my husband likes it." She rubbed her forehead with the heel of her hand, her eyes shut, then gave the mirror back. Martin was opening the shop door.

"That him?" Carmen asked. "Nice-looking guy. Both of you blond and all. Make a nice pair." She took the green cape from Sara's shoulders.

Sara walked to Martin and the cash register. She paid and gave Carmen her tip, and glanced back once at women in chairs and under dryers. The small girl still stared straight ahead, tight curlers yanking her eyebrows out of line. Then Martin opened the door. Ocean breeze surrounded Sara, a last breath of perfume was gone, and she had to walk across the street with Martin, making a nice pair.

# 2

Wind blew from the water. Martin said nothing. Sara went around to her side of the car, squeezing in beside sacks of groceries. As Martin drove out of town she watched families with children . . . two women talking on a corner . . . a child on a tricycle. Policemen sat in a cruiser at a last intersection. Then Manhasset was gone. There was nothing but Martin's profile against the long blue haze of the bay.

Sara shut her eyes in the car's silence. A sack of wine bottles was almost hidden by groceries. Carrot and celery tops blew in wind that rushed through the car.

They passed the Blue Lobster and rounded a hook on a sandy road. Wind lifted blond strands from thin spots in Martin's hair. They drove along a shallow bay beyond Manhasset. Sara glanced at Martin. His mouth looked small and clamped-down from the side.

Grass and scrub hid the water, and then Martin turned into their drive, where two beach houses stood by themselves between a pine grove and the bay.

Martin had forgotten the front-door key; they had to go down a steep bank beside the house and climb beach stairs where they'd made love, giggling and methodical, on every step. Sara's two sacks were heavy. When Martin went in the bathroom Sara eased wine bottles out of a sack. One bottle of port was almost empty.

She put canned food on cupboard shelves, labels to the front and one can high the way Martin liked them. Martin hated to see vegetables put away before they were cleaned. She began picking off outside lettuce leaves and saw Martin check to be sure she was doing it when he came out.

The beach house was small and furnished with mistakes: chairs with lumps in the middle of their backs, lamps that fell over, a table with legs where you wanted to put yours. On their honeymoon they'd made love on every piece of furniture that was big enough.

Sara listened as she washed celery. Martin was sitting on the living-room couch; she heard him rattle his newspaper.

"M-m-m-m," Martin said, coming behind Sara while she scraped carrots. He ran his hands under her clean hair and kissed the back of her neck and she shivered, so he laughed and did it again. She twisted around to kiss him the way he liked to kiss. His breath was plummy with port wine. Then he slapped her hard, almost before they'd stopped kissing; she was slammed against the table, and her newspaper and carrot scrapings fell to the floor.

"Make me wait while you're at Boston U.— no supper ready!" Martin yelled. "Hell! You came home almost an hour late Thursday!"

Sara touched her hot, stinging cheek and watched Martin's hands that were fists now—he hit her in the stomach and Sara doubled over, sucking her breath with pain, but he pulled her face against his by her hair. "Just you wait," Martin whispered in her ear. His tongue sounded too big for his mouth.

Martin let her get away. Sara knelt to clean up the carrots, her tears dripping on old linoleum. He shouted, "Stop that blubbering!" and kicked the backs of her legs where she already had bruises.

Sara pulled herself up from the floor on the side of the table away from Martin.

Martin poured himself more wine, then came to watch her finish scraping and slicing.

Sara didn't meet his eyes. Her stomach hurt; she could breathe only a little at a time. Waves broke below the house as the tide crept in to fill the kitchen with pounding and hissing. Martin watched Sara.

She kept her eyes down and scraped each carrot raw, then sliced it thin with a sharp knife.

Martin emptied a wineglass and came to Sara so suddenly that she dropped the knife to dodge, her hands flung out. He held her tight. She could only move slowly to put carrots on the stove and start hamburgers.

Sara kept quiet, moved quietly. She wasn't wearing a bra because he didn't like bras. She had on his favorite bikini pants under her jeans, and he pulled both down; she made a sound that was supposed to be a giggle, and kept on slicing potatoes very thin. He kissed her again. She hobbled to the stove with her pants and jeans around her knees to turn the hamburgers.

When he was in the living room pouring more wine, Sara pulled up her clothes and finished the potatoes. It was almost dark outside; the bay had turned from lavender to dead gray.

"C'mon," Martin said, trying to unbutton her shirt.

"Supper's almost ready," she said, but she smiled and put her arms around his neck.

"Wh' about me?" Martin said. " 'M ready—what if I get cold?" He pulled her jean zipper down again. She unbuttoned her shirt the rest of the way quick. While he shucked his pants and turned down the heat under potatoes and carrots, she put her clothes in a neat pile by the door, wincing with pain as she leaned over.

Their bed squeaked its three familiar notes—C, A-flat, F. Sara made her usual noises, too, doing what Martin liked best, not forgetting anything. The kitchen light was on. Her clothes were by the door. Martin's sweet alcohol breath panted in her face, and he fumbled. When he was through she lay looking at a mirror that was losing its silver.

Sara woke to Martin's heavy arm and leg pressing her down, and the smell of wine. He began to snore.

Sara slid slowly from beneath him; the bed hardly sprang back when she left it. Her clothes waited in their neat pile.

The bathroom door didn't squeak if she closed it slowly. Bruises on her legs were dark red now. She hadn't been able to jog for a week when he'd kicked her before, and now her legs were bruised again; she couldn't run along the beach at dawn, quiet and alone. She rubbed her stomach where he'd hit her, rubbed it and rubbed it.

The bathroom mirror seemed to be left over from their honeymoon: it showed red marks on her breasts and skinny neck, and she might have been another Sara, a newlywed Sara smiling after love, not wanting the marks to go away. But the bruises on the backs of her legs were turning red-purple. Her stomach ached. There were blue patches on the wrist that he'd broken once.

Dressed again, Sara shut the kitchen door. Carrots and potatoes were done. She dished up both dinner plates, not forgetting parsley garnish, or a bowl of salad dressing, or the pitcher of cream for his coffee.

Then the telephone rang; Sara sprang to catch it almost before it sounded. She knelt beside the couch, then stretched her stiff legs out. "Hello?" she whispered, and muffled her whispering with dusty couch cushions. Steady snores came from the bedroom.

"Sara?" It was Joan Pagent. "I got your vacation number from Marie. Did I get you at dinnertime? We had our lunch today. Everybody was there but you. I said I'd call and find out if you'd be able to come to Cristine's a week from Monday."

Sara's eyes were shut tight. "A week from Monday will be fine for me," she whispered. "Martin's asleep. That's why I'm whispering."

"You having a good vacation? Did you know Karen's got a job at Humbert Associates?"

"No," Sara said. Martin's snores kept their steady rhythm.

"Are you okay?" Joan's voice changed. "It looked like Martin was mad at you at the picnic Friday."

"He was upset," Sara said, with a poinsettia in her mind suddenly—on Christmas Eve Martin had yanked it out of her hand and smashed it in a snowbank because it cost too much.

"Upset!" Joan echoed, and Sara heard the word and saw Martin in snow, broken and red like her poinsettia he'd thrown out. "Your face was so white."

"I hadn't come home when I said I would, that's all," Sara said. "I was ashamed, I guess—all the fuss we were making. I'm sorry." She was sorry until she cried under hot, stale cushions.

"Well, we couldn't believe it," Joan said.

"I know," Sara whispered from her hole. "Thanks for calling. Good-bye." Joan went on talking, but Sara closed the sound of Joan's voice away slowly until it was gone with one last click.

Sara sat by the couch for a while and rubbed between her eyes with the heel of her hand as if, rubbing hard enough, she could think of something useful or comforting. Then she got up sidewise, stiff-legged. There were sailboats for rent; Martin had rented one before. She took a deep breath, rubbed her stomach and ribs, and thought of a sailboat. The beach house flickered around her. Martin snored and sighed in their dark bedroom.

It was a good dinner: juicy hamburgers with onions still faintly crunchy. Real butter on the potatoes, so Martin could dip each mouthful in a golden puddle; the carrots were sweet and not too soft. If he woke, his dinner would be ready. If he slept all night, he'd find his plate on the kitchen table in the morning.

Sara's throat closed as if she were sobbing, but she wasn't crying; she made no sound. The cherry cake had her best custard frosting, and almonds scattered over it. She dumped her dinner and piece of cake in the garbage can, and got ready for bed quietly, very quietly.

Light from a small kitchen lamp showed Martin asleep, his mouth open, his arms flung above his head. Sara watched him for a long time. Then she turned out the light and slipped into dark sheets beside him, biting her lip when she straightened her legs out.

Her clothes were in the same neat pile by the door.

There was a twenty-four-hour Laundromat a mile away at Grenville, and scrub trees to hide in along the road. At home there was money buried in a plastic pill bottle in the back hedge, and a nearby bus-station bathroom with a chair in it; the station was open all night.

She had until the next Saturday. Waves pounded in. The beach house jutted from hill and pine grove; their bed was high above the surf.

When she was in Montrose she stayed late at the library to study drama, her project for the year. Now line after line of the plays came into her head. She could remember the speech of the Shrew, leading apes in hell. She had memorized whole scenes—Linda at her salesman's grave, free and clear. Waves broke one after another on the beach below, until their rhythm sounded like a door blown back and forth by the wind, and Sara fell asleep.

# 3

Waves still foamed on hard beach when Sara woke. Sun striped the bed. Martin swore in the kitchen, and a garbage-can lid clanged; china clattered.

Martin shut the bathroom door, and it squeaked. Sara got up, hobbling on sore legs to get her slacks and long-sleeved shirt. She made their bed, put eggs on to boil, set the table. Bacon sizzled in a pan when Martin came; he had a towel around his neck and walked barefoot on scarred linoleum. He didn't look at his dirty dishes from the night before, but they sat between him and Sara on the table.

"Breakfast ready?" Martin asked.

"Yes," Sara said. She finished the bacon and put it, just the way he liked it, on a plate beside his boiled eggs. Her own breakfast sat across from him beside the dirty dishes. She went to the bathroom, then started down the long flight of beach steps into warm sun step by step, stiff-legged.

She stopped, holding her breath, and stared—there was a sailboat next door. Tied to the dock, it bobbed softly over its rippling shadow.

Sara felt cold in the sunshine. Manhasset Bay lay shallow and blue before her—she had sailed there—she knew how the bay was fed by creeks and river, its narrow mouth to the east. The town of Bankton flashed specks of light far away. A few buoys marked where tidal currents began to be strong and deadly off a sandbar hook where she stood staring at a sailboat, morning, and the sea.

Sara picked her way through beach grass and stepped over a low wall to the neighboring stretch of sand, her eyes never leaving the sailboat. A man squatted on the dock, his back turned to her, his brief shorts bright gold in the sun.

"Hi," the man said, getting up and wiping his hands on his shorts.

"Hello," Sara said. "You renting from the Driscolls? I'm Sara Burney."

"John Fleishman. Just for two weeks." He was young and skinny, and held his chin high to look down at her with glittering, long-lashed eyes.

"You're a sailor," Sara said.

"My girl's at Bankton. I'll sail over there every day."

"Isn't that a pretty big boat for one man?"

"Not really. She usually sails with at least one hand crewing, plus a skipper, but you leave the jib sheet a little slack and you can handle the main and tiller all right. You a native?"

"I lived in Manhasset for a couple of years when I was growing up. We've come here every summer since we got married," Sara said.

"Boston?"

"Montrose."

"Waltham," John said, and laughed. "I've got to be there today—drive back tonight. Could you keep an eye on the place?"

"Sure," Sara said again, and smiled. John's eyes were on her as she walked stiffly to the low beach wall and stepped over, watching the tide come in. She knew exactly how tides flowed in that shallow bay, how winds blew, the lee of the hook. Sand at her feet sifted with sea breeze, blowing away through beach grass.

Martin had finished eating. He'd been standing at the door, watching her talk to John Fleishman. Her breakfast was getting cold across from him.

"How about a swim?" he said, smiling.

Sara sat down and began to eat her cold breakfast.

"We got a new neighbor? Better go over and be neighborly," Martin said. Sara watched him pull his stomach in as he went downstairs; he hit the steps hard with his heels the way he always did, and smoothed his hair as he went toward Fleishman.

Sara saw Martin and John shake hands. One sailboat, far beyond scattered swimming buoys, skimmed toward Bankton across the bay.

She washed dishes. Martin had bought cooking apples. She began mixing piecrust.

Halfway through rolling out dough, she heard Martin's voice rise, saying good-bye. He came upstairs, slammed the screen door, and went to the stove. She'd made fresh coffee.

Sara put her floury hands on her bare arms, looked at a boat in the bay. "How can they stand going out in waves like that!" she said.

Martin's lips turned down; he looked like his father. "Hell! Scared of water!"

Sara rolled dough, lined a pie pan, and started paring apples.

Martin sat down and watched her. Sara's knife slipped under apple skin.

Martin watched her. She watched the apples.

Clink-clink-clink went metal against metal at the dock next door. Martin's chair scraped sharply on linoleum as he got up and went out.

He was going to talk to John again. She peeled apples steadily and finished them.

Then John called, "See you!" A car door slammed, and gravel spit under wheels. Their only neighbor was gone for the day.

She was about to roll a top crust when Martin came back. His hair was ruffled and his bald spots showed. He ran his hands through his hair, sat down, watched Sara.

Sara rolled crust in a circle. Silence between them got thinner and thinner, like the piecrust.

"Nice little boat he's got," Martin said. "I wish one came with this place."

Sara kept her eyes on the piecrust.

"Not too thin," Martin said, looking at it. "Having steaks tonight?"

Sara nodded.

"Nice little boat," Martin said.

Sara covered the apples neatly. She pressed crust around the pan rim and listened to the silence.

"We ought to go out, just for a little sail," Martin said. "Do it every year, don't we?"

Sara picked up the pan and cut dangling bits of crust off one by one, the pie pan balanced on her palm.

"Get you over being so scared," Martin said.

Piecrust bits fell to the table. The pan was steady in Sara's grasp.

"Think so?" Martin said, smiling. Her hands shook a little now. "Just a short trip tonight with the fellow next door. Across the bay to Bankton, that's all. He's going to need help. There and back."

"I'd rather not," Sara said.

"That brother Joe of yours bragged about how you were like one of the boys—said you could do anything? Like hell! And he let you be scared of water? Every year!"

"We lived here only two years!"

"Tonight," Martin said. "When it gets dark enough so the town lights look pretty. Nice little sail across the bay. This time you're going to enjoy it."

"You know how I feel," Sara said, raising her chin and scowling at him. Martin stamped out, jamming his heels into the old living-room rug, slamming the front door. In a moment she heard him slam the door of the car. He'd go swimming and then to some bar, and wouldn't come back until dinnertime; she heard him driving away down the beach road.

Sara leaned to see waves beating beneath their windows and began to tremble. Over there, almost out of sight, a shelf of rock and sand hung over surf. That rock had held sun's heat under her hand once . . . she remembered that heat and was back in the dark with her brother Joe, twelve years old to his sixteen, and out on a dare—beat you across the bay to Bankton!

Joe's bare shoulders had gleamed in moonlight that turned his red curls black. He'd had pneumonia and shouldn't have tried that race, but who could have stopped him? He'd have gone without her if she'd said no.

Sara pressed the backs of her floury hands to her eyes, then stared at little rooms furnished with mistakes.

"A boat," she said aloud.

Sara went back to the kitchen table. Sugar trickled fine as sand from her measuring cup to smooth piecrust. When the pie was in the oven she went to look a long time at the blue gap in Manhasset Bay where the ocean began.

Then she turned to squint at their beach house and Fleishman's next door to it. They stood far from other houses and were the cheapest rentals on Sand Hook. The beach house oven had to be propped shut with a yardstick; pans in the cupboards were crusted with other people's burned food.

Sara shut her eyes against warm sun and listened to the stillness between wave surges.

But the beach house had a wide view of the ocean. The roof didn't leak. They could afford it. At home in Montrose, their little Cape Cod house was the cheapest on their block, but she had her new refrigerator and stove, and her desk at the library.

When the pie was done Sara watched houses and ocean for a long time. She sat on the low stone wall between cottages, and walked stiffly up and down the beach. There were no boats sailing near. Nobody strolled beside foaming surf. Martin was gone, and John Fleishman.

The sailboat tapped, tapped, tapped against the dock in noon sun.

Sara stood by the wall for a long time, rubbing her forehead with the heel of her hand while she looked into the distance, farther than a gap in the bay, far away to a distant haze that was the ocean.

Then she hunted for stones, scrabbled for them in coarse grass until she had a handful. Squinting against the sun, she aimed at two beach lights on their poles and hurled stones the way Joe had taught her, her lips drawn back in a kind of smile at the smash and glitter of falling glass.

# 4

Martin came home just before dark. Sara didn't ask where he'd been. Her eyes were red and full of tears from onions she'd peeled, and Martin was drunk enough to be sorry. "I hit you," he crooned in her ear. "But you know I love you, don't you? You didn't come home on time from Boston U., and you make me so *angry* when you don't *think*." He had a big bunch of roses behind his back, and when he gave them to her and kissed her, she smelled their delicate scent and closed her eyes to pretend, the way she sometimes did, that this was her marriage.

"And look here," Martin said, grinning. "Something for you to wear just for me!"

Sara opened the box while Martin still had his arms around her and was kissing the back of her neck. "Sexy!" he said when she lifted out a black silk teddy.

A tear from the onions ran down Sara's cheek. "Don't cry!" Martin said. "Hey—put it on." He unzipped her jeans; she unbuttoned her shirt and pushed off her sneakers. Sara got her legs through the teddy pants and pulled the top up; it stretched to fit her and was made to show her nipples through the top lace and her pubic hair through the bottom.

"Wow!" Martin said. "The blonde in black! Walk around and give us a fashion show."

Sara stood in the kitchen doorway and turned slowly to show the teddy's lace and black silk and the red-blue bruises on her hand and down the backs of her legs, the yellow-green ones on her arms and breasts.

"Great!" Martin said, and went to get a glass for his wine. Sara pulled on her shirt and jeans over the teddy. There wasn't a vase in the beach house; she had to put the roses in a pickle bottle.

Martin relaxed and drank wine in the living room, waiting for dinner. He'd given her a present. Her red kitchen had been a present after he broke her toe. Red rose scent hung over their dinner; they kept the radio on to fill the silence while Martin ate steak and potatoes and creamed onions and salad and apple pie. Sara ate hardly anything. They heard John Fleishman drive in next door.

"More wine?" Sara said.

"After we come back." He finished his coffee. "C'mon. It's dark now. He said to come over when it was dark."

"Let me do the dishes. You hate to come back to dirty dishes."

"Later. We'll just sail to Bankton and see the town lights in the water—remember how pretty it was last year? —and then come right back and you can do all the dishes you want to." He came over to her and nuzzled her neck. "If that's what you want to do when you come home."

"Let me just rinse them off."

Martin laughed. "Come on. Better put on a jacket. And sneakers."

"I wonder—can't we go some other time? He'll be there with the boat all week." Sara's voice was quivery, like a little girl's. She stopped at the bedroom door.

"You want to be scared of water all your life?" Martin said, his voice rising. Then it turned coaxing. "You should see the full moon out there! Get in that big boat in the dark, you won't even know you're on the water. That's the whole idea. It'll be over before you've got time to be afraid. C'mon."

She stood looking at him.

"Hell, you're not going *swimming!*" Martin yelled. Sara backed up when she saw him coming. She put her arms over her face, but he hit her at the side of one breast, and when she curled away from him against the door-frame, slapped her head so that it whacked against wood. "He said to come over at dark. Five minutes and I want to see you in that boat!" He grabbed his jacket, slammed the screen door, flipped a light switch outside, and swore.

Sara put both hands on her breast, gasping, trying to keep from crying as she went to get her jacket and sneakers. Her head was bleeding, but not much. She had to go to the toilet twice. John's beach light wasn't working either; she heard Martin come back to rummage in the storage compartment for a flashlight.

Sara shut the door behind her and started downstairs, walking stiffly, feeling sharp step edges through her sneakers.

The full moon gleamed; waves below Sara had little silver edges, pounding in. Then the moon went under.

Two flashlights bobbed on John's dock. "Sara?" Martin called. His voice was polite, so she knew John was with him. "Both the beach lights are out—some damn kids throwing stones again, I guess." He was only a shape against silvery water, but she could see John's white jacket.

Martin moved toward her with his flashlight. "Come on," he said behind the light, his voice almost gentle. "You'll like it." He took her hand and half pulled her over the low stone wall. "I guarantee you'll like it so much you'll want to sail every night." His voice got louder and more jovial as they came closer to John. "I'll end up having to buy you a boat!"

Sara pulled her hand away, but Martin caught it again and made her follow him along the dock. Then she clung to him as he half pushed her into the boat's rocking shell.

"Sit right there," John said, and turned away to check that the main sheet was clear in the block, but Sara didn't sit. She stood with both hands clamped around a shroud, her head filled with the snap and pop of the luffing main.

"You want to fall in?" Martin yelled. He turned around to push her down, and she crouched there. "She's a little afraid of the water," Martin had to tell John.

"We'll go slow," John said. His voice wasn't loud like

Martin's. "This boat's big. She's got so much beam she can't do anything but float. You don't even have to change sides when we tack. Barely enough breeze for a good heel." His white jacket, lit by the flashlight, reflected his serious face, his blown, dark hair. "You sure don't *have* to go. My sister's afraid of the water, so I know—"

"She's all right now," Martin said. "She's fine. Once she gets in the boat, she's fine."

"Onshore wind, so we'll be on a close reach until we clear the hook. Probably only have to tack once with the tide going out," John said. "And the moon's up and full now—nice."

But the moon slid under thick clouds. Sara gripped the boat's edge. Flashlights cast a few straws of light through blackness; the dock slid away, disappeared. Land sank beneath them. Buoys were ahead. From where she was on the lee side of the cockpit, Sara saw Martin and John as headless, because the boom was close-hauled in the light air and showed them only from the chest down. John's hand was on the tiller; Martin held the main sheet just behind the cleat. With each gust of wind the boat heeled obediently, and Sara heard gurgling water inch close to her back.

Her breast ached. The lump on her head was sticky with blood.

When the full moon shone again stars powdered the sky, and Sara looked back at beach houses and Sand Hook. The tide was going out. Sand Hook made calm water, cutting the force of currents that would pull a corpse out to sea and never give it back, not even as a heap of flesh rotting in seaweed on some beach. The water would be as cold as a pistol against her head: *I'll kill you if you ever leave me again.*

"Isn't that pretty? Look at the Bankton lights!" Martin called to Sara.

Sara didn't answer. For a moment the moon slid behind clouds. Water, sky, and air darkened as if she sailed only into night and sleep.

The full moon broke free. "You all right?" John called,

glancing back at Sara. She didn't answer. The whisper of the wake underscored her silence.

"We can go back if you're not."

"I'm all right," Sara said, a small sob in her voice.

The ocean heaved only a foot away through the boat's thin shell, then sank, then heaved again like deeper and deeper breathing.

John glanced at Sara crouched there, gripping the boat's side. He looked uncomfortable and eased the boat a point or two closer to the wind. There was no sound but wave-slap and faint music from a dance pavilion across the water. "Music would unground us best" . . . the full moon sailed free, and Sara's cheeks shone with tears. She had been reading *The Dark Is Light Enough* the day before they left for the beach house. She stared at heaving waves.

Were they staying still, rising and falling forever in the same billowing patch in that bay? Sara shifted her cramped, stiff legs. Why did you drown, Joe Gray? Her brother Joe had made her yell "Kill!" and run at a stuffed gunny sack he had tied to their tree swing. She had to jab it in the middle with their mother's favorite butcher knife tied to a rake handle. Their mother didn't know half of what they did. They grew up in a world of strangers. It was always another town, another school, another old house, while their father sold another kind of fertilizer, a sensational ironing board, a magic cream to erase face wrinkles.

Why did you drown, Joe Gray? When she read about Tom Sawyer and Huck Finn, she thought of creeping behind Joe along their porch roof in Fredsburg at night. They had climbed into a maple tree above the living-room window and looked in at their mother bent over her mending there. Rough bark had scratched Sara's hands as she crawled down to explore the night with Joe.

Sara wiped tears from her cheeks and watched the moon. She said she'd been afraid of water all her life. Martin knew that. Her friends knew that. Even the beauty-shop operator knew that.

Suddenly the moon went into a thick cloud.

The tide was going out.

Sara gripped the boat's edge, her stiff legs jammed against wood. The lump on her head ached, and so did her bruised breast.

Both men looked up to where a full moon had been. Sara sat in blackness. One flashlight sent its tiny rays into the dark behind the boat; the other flashlight rolled under Martin's sweater.

They had cleared buoys now. To the east was the mouth of Manhasset Bay and the black of open sea.

Sara crouched in the lee and was only a dark shape against shore lights when John Fleishman looked under the boom. "Wish that moon would come out," he said to Martin

Wind whipped Sara's long hair behind her. She looked back. There was Sand Hook, still across heaving waves. Other beach-house lights were on, but two houses standing by themselves were dark. They made a black hole in a sand bar's bright curve: a smile with two teeth punched out.

"Sure is dark, but look at those lights!" Martin called to Sara without looking at her. "Aren't you glad you came?"

The first of the big swells hammered the side. Sara had seen them coming, knew they would come—tide ran with the wind against it over the shallow bay. Their boat heeled crazily in darkness with no moon. John shoved the tiller hard to starboard. Martin ripped the main sheet from its cleat and let it go.

The boom swept across the lee of the cockpit like a scythe—swept across water that poured over the coaming and an empty seat.

# 5

"**H**ell!" Martin kept saying. It was after midnight. His clothes were wet and his hands were bleeding. "It was such a nice night, full moon and all." He was hoarse with shouting, and so was John.

"Just past the buoys and then the moon went under," John said. His legs wobbled; he dragged a chair away from a police desk and sat down.

The policeman and a scribbling clerk looked tired too. "You've got to write everything," the policeman said to the clerk. "The bay's shallow, so waves get high, and the pull of the tide going out is awfully strong. Put that in."

"They were out maybe an hour," the man from the harbor patrol said. "We could go out, but what chance is there?" He stared at the two office types from Boston.

"We were just sailing to Bankton," Martin said. "Hell!"

"Write down that they had lights on board." The policeman watched the clerk scribble.

"She was a little afraid of the water." Martin kept running his hands through his hair as if he could find Sara that way.

"I'd just looked back at her. She was okay," John said. "A little upset, maybe." He didn't look at Martin; he remembered Sara's long, shining blond hair, and how thin and tired-looking she was.

"You'd never met Mr. and Mrs. Burney before today?" the policeman asked John.

"The moon went under and it was awfully dark, and then came that first big swell," Martin said.

"No," John told the policeman. "Just met them this morning."

"Why don't you go on home, Roy," the policeman said to the man from harbor patrol. "Nobody expects you to go out there looking for bodies in the ocean—" He realized that Martin was staring at him. "Sorry," he said. "We do all we can in these cases, and then we just have to wait and see if the person is found someplace, and whether they can be identified."

"She was a little scared of the water," Martin said, crying again. "She wouldn't go swimming. Never would. My boss threw a beach party, and everybody where I work saw how she wouldn't even put her toe in the ocean. It made my boss kind of mad. But she was doing real well in the boat."

"She was crying a little, that's all," John said. He tried not to look at Martin crying. "It took a while to get turned, but we yelled and crossed back and forth . . ."

"I think she stood up. Neither of us saw her," Martin sobbed.

"Didn't hear anything. She was just gone," John said.

"She was sitting there looking at the nice view . . ." Martin took deep breaths as he tried to stop crying. The clerk had finished scribbling; the policeman had a public-service look on his face. You had to let people talk it out.

"Martin here jumped in after her, and I tried to get him back in. And then we yelled and sailed around in the dark and found a buoy and got our bearings, and looked some more," John said.

The policeman said they'd bring the boat back to John's dock in the morning. He drove the men home after they had both signed a statement that Sara Gray Burney had stood up in the sailboat before it left the dock, that she had not appeared to realize the danger, that no one had been near Sara Gray Burney when she had jumped or fallen or was knocked by a boom in to Manhasset Bay.

The policeman went with Martin and John to check their houses and the docks and beach. There was no sign of footprints in the sand or wet prints anywhere, and nothing seemed to be missing in Martin's house.

"Check the nearest bus and train stations," the tired sergeant told the clerk. "Just in case this Mrs. Burney decided to make Mr. Burney sweat a little, you know? Wanted a fur coat or a trip to New York, maybe, or found out he was having a little skirt on the side, so she's going to scare him." But no blonde had been seen at any station. The clerk yawned.

"You going to be okay?" John said. He was in Martin's kitchen having a beer at a table full of dirty dishes and red roses. "All alone?"

"I guess so," Martin said, looking at Sara's plate. She had eaten hardly any of the good steak or potatoes. "I'll try to sleep."

But he couldn't sleep. Sara's clothes had smelled like her perfume when he checked them for the police. He turned on the kitchen light and looked at her plate of food every now and then, and the vase of roses. He sat for hours on their bed, holding her clothes.

After a while all he could hear was waves coming up, going out again. He sat at the top of the beach stairs with tears running down his face and remembered Sara falling backward with a scream, hitting stairs on the way down, spread-eagled in sand, and him at the top. He'd been punching her as hard as he could, and yet now he'd forgotten what she'd done.

When he put his hands to his face hot tears ran through his fingers. The doctor had said, "She has a ruptured spleen—we think we can patch it for her—and a broken right wrist. Must have been quite a fall." And why had he dragged her away from the picnic the week before and hit her and kicked her? Because she'd come home late from her class at Boston U.

When he couldn't cry any more he looked up and saw blue sky—it was morning. Beach stairs led down to the same sand and water. The same tides came in, went out.

Everything was the same, except his life. His parents were the same when they came to stay in a motel near town for a day or two. His father used phrases like "buck up" and "take it on the chin." His mother put her arms around him and let him cry and said Sara had been a perfect wife and daughter-in-law . . . couldn't have asked for better . . . so kind and pretty, and such a good housekeeper. "An awful tragedy for you, my dear . . . for all of us," she said, and didn't care if he cried, and patted his back, and came to the beach house early to give him breakfast in bed.

Martin didn't have any good picture of Sara by herself, so newspapers had to use their wedding photo with both of them grinning under the headline WIFE DROWNS AS HUSBAND TRIES RESCUE. The patrol went out next morning, but they didn't expect to find the body, and they didn't. It had gone out for good.

Martin drove to Manhasset nearly every day; there were details to take care of, papers to sign. Sara's plate of steak and potatoes was in the refrigerator yet. The roses wilted to purplish blobs on the kitchen table. He thought people stared at him in the street.

"He looks just awful, even if he is a big guy," Brooke said, watching Martin Burney through the Beauty Corner window under the sign that said EMOCLEW NEM. "Nice build. Strong and all."

"Ought to be in jail," Carmen said. They were through for the day, and she had her shoes off and her feet on a dryer chair. "She sat right here and said how afraid of water she was—right in that very chair. Wasn't even thirty, and so awful thin—remember?"

"Maybe she killed herself," Brooke said. "Maybe he'll go crazy with grief. Poor guy."

"When she sat right there and told me she was so scared. He ought to be put in jail."

"He's got kind of a craggy face, like those cowboy ads for cigarettes," Brooke said. "But they won't find the body—they never do when the tide's going out. At least you told the police what she said."

"Huh. Sure," Carmen said. "So I'm going to get my picture in the paper, maybe?" She had the article propped on a chair seat; Martin and Sara Burney smiled at her from their picture while she rubbed her ankles with liniment. Sara wasn't thin in the picture.

"That Fleishman guy was with them in the sailboat and saw it all, so her husband couldn't have killed her." Brooke sighed and looked at an innocent, baby-blue ocean between buildings across the street. She watched Martin Burney walk away, then pulled down the Beauty Corner shade.

Martin turned a corner in the hot sun.

"Dollar, mister?" somebody whined. Martin turned around. A dirty young woman held her hand out. She had a baby in a pouch on her back.

"What for?" Martin said.

"To raise the next generation here—whaddya think? You ever bought a box of diapers?" The filthy young woman was yelling now, and her baby began to make sounds like a chicken cackling; he guessed it was crying. "Jesus! He asks what the dollar's fucking *for!*"

Martin thought he could smell the baby. "Here," he said, and gave her a dollar, and got in his hot car.

He had to drive back and forth from the beach house to Manhasset and Bankton every day. He shouldn't expect the body to be found, they told him, but of course there was always a chance, so he went every morning to check, and lived at the beach house, and drank wine. At last his vacation was over. He had to pack Sara's clothes.

Suitcases stood by the front door the last morning— Sara's case, his case. Martin opened the refrigerator and looked at her last meal: dried-up steak and potatoes. He threw it in the garbage can. He drove to Boston and went back to work at Rambaugh Computer Sales and Service.

"Martin Burney. Poor guy. He can't believe it," Chuck Jenner said during coffee break at Rambaugh. He handed a cup to Al Surrino, who was new. "It hit him so hard. Nice-looking couple, no real worries, no kids to get sick or need college educations.'' Chuck could see Martin through the salesroom doorway. ''Her mother's in a nursing home in Nebraska. That's all the family she's got. They had to tell her.''

''He doesn't think she's dead?'' Al Surrino asked. They were drinking too much coffee in the back room at Rambaugh's, as usual, and Chuck flirted with by-the-hour secretaries, especially the one with the boobs.

''He's shook up. Keeps telling you details over and over. She was a blonde, awfully skinny. Never played around that I know of. Maybe even kind of shy. House-wife type. Always brought real good food to the potlucks. One of those extra-money jobs in a library in Montrose part-time. Poor guy.''

''McManus is sure keeping an eye on him,'' Al said.

''He had a chance for manager once,'' Chuck said. ''Hell—I'm betting on you.''

''Maybe we both got a chance now,'' Al said. ''Or we get sent to New York, maybe? Florida?''

Chuck looked at Martin sitting in the showroom. ''A good chance.''

Martin sat and scowled at Rambaugh Computer Sales and Service: the paper shuffling, schoolteacher work, men in coats and ties standing around talking, talking, talking.

Sara's clothes hung in their closet. Not that she had a lot to wear—he'd kept at her and kept at her about money. Now all the money they'd saved was in their bank account, and she was gone. Her clothes had the scent of her hair; he always wanted her to go to the beauty shop—no woman in curlers for him. The black silk teddy . . . she was drowned somewhere, rotting in black silk and lace, his last nice present to her.

Rambaugh salesrooms, expanses of glass, faced the high-way. Machines he had to sell stood on wall-to-wall carpet-ing. He talked all day about k's and rams and menus and bytes as if he really knew how computers were built. Machines copied and printed and stored and stapled paper, and so did he. Maybe he got a hangnail doing that kind of work. Maybe he got ink on his finger. Huge machines stood in neatly ruled blocks of sunshine that fell through plate glass.

Smash it. Smash it all. Smash Chuck and Al, talking about him in the back room. Did they think he didn't know? He went in the back room to the files, and Chuck was saying, "The wife's got to have two weeks in Vegas. 'Whose vacation is it, anyway?' I told her. 'We'll go to Maine and fish like always. That's it.' "

"Right," Al said.

"Not like that Dressler," Chuck said. "Bought his wife a new house! Because she said she'd leave him otherwise!" He saw Martin coming. "Hi, Martin, fella."

Martin said, "Hi," and went back to the salesroom. Gossip and double-dealing and one-upmanship all day, all week—years—the rest of his life. He'd gone home every day and there was Sara so nice and quiet and safe and lazy, just keeping house.

He went on selling machines that copied and printed and counted and sorted paper. When the day was finally over he had to drive through miles of traffic to an empty house. He didn't know how Sara cleaned the place—he just swiped at dust with a kitchen towel now and then. The rooms were small and smelled stale.

He picked up a hamburger if he felt hungry. Mostly he drank the wines he liked: port, sherry. He took guns out of his gun case and worked on them and put them back, and started crying when he picked up the pistol. It had eagles on the grips, their claws spread sharp. He'd jammed that against her head often enough, threatening to kill her, and the man, too, if she ever left him again. And he would have. Hell. She'd never been unfaithful, not that he knew of—there hadn't been any other man. She just didn't want to get beaten up any more, so sometimes she ran off, but he found her.

Oh, hell, the sissy, paper-pushing work, always the same. He'd do it for the rest of his life, nine to five, and two weeks vacation. His old school-principal dad at least had summers off, and he got to make decisions, even if they were only about whether to pay bus fare for the debate team or how to keep kids from smoking pot in the johns.

Jockeying for position all day, that's what he did—wasting time and money, nobody caring, the whole business like a fancy wrapped-up present with its guts dribbling out the bottom.

Sara couldn't see through Rambaugh's pretty outside. She kept saying he was doing so well, advancing so fast; she was building him up—nice of her.

He banged his head against a wall. He'd throw her on their bed, screw her, beat her—she didn't dare leave him. If she divorced him, he'd follow her anywhere. She was his wife. You didn't just let them walk away, say bye-bye. But then he remembered—she was drowned.

He went through drawers in her dresser and drawers in her desk. She was gone without a sound and not one word, down in the bay and gone, just like the time when she left him and took a bus all the way to Nebraska, limping because he'd broken her toe.

Some janitor guy brought Sara's personal belongings from the library and said they'd send her office things when they'd been sorted. At the bottom of the box of notebooks and a makeup kit and raincoat and umbrella Martin found two little black books that were locked. They said "Diary" on their covers. He walked from room to room wondering if he should send them to her mother in Nebraska. But she was blind and couldn't even sit up, stuck in that nursing home.

The bathroom door had long cracks in it. Sara had locked it once when he was hitting her, and he had smashed it open with his fists, so they had to patch it with wood putty. He went in the bathroom and shut the door and tried to imagine what it would be like, trapped there with somebody smashing a door to get at you. Hell. What had they been fighting about?

Because she wanted to work part-time at the library.

He looked at the two small books in his hand, then

yanked their locks off. They were diaries, all right, written in Sara's neat handwriting—ten years of days, five years in each book, five days on every page. Nobody could imagine a man fitting years of his life into neat little lined spaces. He looked at the bathroom door. Women were different from men. Painted their faces. Liked to be bossed. Twitched the asses and tits around and didn't look you in the eye. Mysteries.

# 6

For a moment Sara's eyes widened. Then she shut them, took a deep breath, and waited. As the first swell struck John Fleishman's boat, a black, cold Atlantic swallowed her with nothing more than one momentary scar in a wave's trough.

Sara dived deep, stiff-legged. She had waded into the YWCA pool step by step, her eyes shut. Now she sank with open eyes into Manhasset Bay.

Bitter cold salt water closed over her head, and suddenly she dropped into the past, drowned in it, twelve years old and swimming with her brother Joe. Their parents were home in bed. Moonlight glittered on Joe's wet face. He screamed that he couldn't go on, couldn't get his breath— she saw his twisted face.

Her body acted for itself—it shed sneakers and jacket and kicked her down, shocked with cold.

Now her head rang with Joe's yell. Her brother's wild face in the moonlight was printed inside her head with the sound of his scream as he went down. As she went down.

Sara struggled to find him, diving deep. Then the memory of Joe's loved hands fastened on her.

*Give up!* She was running out of air; her lungs were screaming too. *Give up!* It would be simple to go down. She sank, locked to Joe, deeper and deeper.

And then her body began to fight—it kicked, bit at

her brother's strangling hands, beat Joe's face with its fists.

Her back arched. She was going up.

Sara beat and kicked and bit her way free of Joe, her lungs howling for air. She came up from the memory of her brother; her body saved her again without thought.

The feel of Joe's cold flesh, the sound of his scream sank in black water.

Now wind blew in Sara's face, and she wasn't twelve any more. Manhasset Bay spread wide around her—an immense, clouded night sky and a heaving floor of water she rode like a fish, her long hair spread on it. She gulped air into her lungs and sobbed. Waves slapped at her.

The tide was going out and the current pulled her with it, but wind blew waves back into the bay.

Bitter cold water lifted her, dropped her in a hollow, lifted her again. Martin yelled, "Sara!" far away by a bobbing light. "Sara!"

Sara dived away from Martin's scream.

Her aim was good—she came up by a slippery swimming buoy and grabbed it, panting, grinning through salt water. She got her breath and turned on her back to float under a wide, clearing sky and look for the small flicker of a flashlight as a boat moved closer.

"Sara!" Martin yelled.

Sara watched one small sailboat under a sky full of gauzy clouds, a high-riding moon, and fields of stars in space.

"Sara!" Sara opened her mouth once as if to answer, but what could she have said except good-bye?

Martin jumped overboard. Just before Sara dived again, she saw John hauling him over the boat's side. The boat drew nearer and nearer. "Sara!" She heard Martin, but she had her breath back; she could dive away from the sound and sink from sight, her long hair eddying for a second in yellow moonlight.

When she came up she was almost warm in water that cradled her. She swam to another buoy, salt water in her mouth.

Now Sara was in the lee of Sand Hook. Another buoy rose before her, and she clung to it, panting, listening, floating in gentler waves.

The boat was much farther away now; Martin and John sailed toward the bay mouth. Someone fallen overboard would be pulled there, drowning in outgoing tide.

But she floated in the full moon's light.

"Sara!" Martin's far-off shout died in sounds of water. She had time to rest and stretch herself in all that space of sea and sky.

After a while Sara swam slowly to a buoy nearest the beach house, then aimed for the gap in the shore, a black spot that was two lights smashed.

Her feet touched bottom in the dark. She pushed forward. "Sara!" echoed in her head. Wet jeans and shirt dragged her thin body down, heavy in surf.

*You bastard!* she wanted to yell over her shoulder at a moonlit bay. Lighted houses stood too far to hear her over pounding water, but she kept her mouth shut. Wet clothes stuck to her; she waded through the suck and shove of waves. Two beach houses were black shapes above her, empty and still.

Sara tore off her wet shirt, stripped off her jeans. "Beat me up when I tell the truth!" she whispered fiercely, a shining-wet blonde in black silk and lace, stamping through foam.

Water hissed at her feet. She yanked down the lace teddy. *I'm through! I'm free! Follow me—go on! Drown!* The teddy rolled into a wet pair of nooses and tripped her; she sat down hard on her bare bottom and wanted to shout, *Make me beg you for money for your own meals, you bastard!*

Her clothes slid out to sea with the water-rush, but she grabbed them and splashed to her feet, gleaming naked in moonlight. *Beg and cheat and steal because of you!*

Two houses watched a small, thin, naked figure slosh back and forth, jerking, punching at air with wet clothes in both hands. *Never talk any more! Never read books to-*

*gether or listen to music or go to a play! Just watch me, hate me when I have a little two-bit job!*

Skinny and slick with water, a small figure smashed at waves with its feet, breasts bouncing. *Sneak money out of your billfold! I've got a soul! Lie about taking your suit to the cleaners!* The little naked figure jumped up and down. *Lie—cheat—steal—or I get beaten up!* It dropped wet clothes and snatched handfuls of sand to throw them at the sea. *I don't know you! I never did! You corrupter!*

Sara sank to her knees in foaming water. *Beat me up!* she yelled inside her head, her face contorted. *Stamp on my toe and break it! B-b-break my wrist. . . .* She put her head on her skinny knees and cried. Her long, wet hair streamed out with the waves, streamed back.

Then she crawled to her feet, looking at her thin arms and legs covered with goose pimples and bruises. A few tendrils of her hair began to dry a little, raveling along her bare shoulder.

There was a piece of driftwood by the wall. "I loved you," she whispered, wet clothes in one hand, driftwood in the other. A small light almost too far away to see bobbed near the bay mouth. She scraped out her footprints fast with the knotted stick as she hurried across sand. The memory of their happy shouts rang around her, thin as moonlight, and she remembered lying in waves there, laughing and bare and wet under Martin's wet bareness.

She was dry enough now; she walked on top of the wall as far as she could, sobbing softly, then wound her shirt around one foot and her jeans around the other to work her way through beach grass. No footsteps showed—only smudges in sand. Stairs that stretched above Sara were beach stairs that somebody else had run up and down a thousand times in sea wind and sunlight, or made love on in the dark. When she climbed them in a hurry, stiff-legged, she remembered those sharp stair edges biting into her, and a slow-motion fall.

Sara opened the kitchen door. Her eyes were used to darkness. She saw Martin's empty plate, and the piece of steak she had hardly touched, and smelled the bunch of red roses on the table.

She poked their bed once to hear a three-note honeymoon squeak, dry as an old snake skin.

Far back in the corner under the couch was a plastic bag full of all she would need. She wrapped her wet clothes in plastic—she had to take them with her. Hurrying, hurrying, she dressed in new clothes from the bag: panties, bra, a long-sleeved shirt, slacks, sandals.

Secret money had been sewed in her raincoat's lining—months of cheating and sneaking. She couldn't take the coat. He'd miss it. She had ripped out the money that afternoon and put it in an old wallet in the plastic bag.

The bag had cheese in it too; Sarah had hidden it under carrots in the refrigerator drawer. There was bread in the bag, and powdered milk, and coffee and peanut butter she'd brought from Montrose. There was an old knife, too, and a spoon and cup.

Standing in darkness and the sound of waves, Sara braided her long hair with shaking hands. A car motor could cut off in the pines. There might be a knock at the door.

Her left hand flashed in the dark bathroom mirror. She stopped to pull her rings off, tie them in plastic, and drop them in the bag. When she pinned braids tight to her head, no rings scraped against her fingers.

Moonlight streamed through bedroom windows now. She found makeup in the plastic bag and could see well enough to put on black eyebrows, thick and heavy, and a bright red mouth.

The bag had a short, wavy brunette wig in it, too, and a pair of tinted glasses. Sara pulled the wig over her braids, put on the glasses, and looked at the stranger in the mirror.

Somebody new hurried past chairs with lumps in the middle of their backs, and lamps that tipped. The woman wearing glasses looked the house over, room by room. She looked at Manhasset Bay from a bedroom window. Cold waves pounded and foamed below.

There was time to shut the front door softly, though no one was there to hear it. But a car could pull up, someone might be walking along the road . . .

Sara ran away from the beach houses, stiff-legged in her low-heeled sandals. Sidewalk and road showed no footprints. Joe Gray. Joe Gray. The full moon slid under clouds. Sara never looked back.

# 7

The woman wearing black-rimmed glasses walked fast now; her road was striped with pine shade and moonlight. Under the wig her heavy, wet braids were salty with ocean, and so was she.

Wind sang in scrub trees. When a car's lights warned her the woman stepped into pines beside the road, but tears weren't blinding her this time; she smelled pines and new clothes and perfume in her wig. Sand and pebbles made a sharp, real crackle under her shoes. A glow in the sky ahead was Grenville.

After a while she began to walk faster away from waves pounding on a beach just out of sight. There were a few lights far out on the water. Telephone lines ran over her head against stars. She began to run in spite of her aching legs, and didn't slow until she passed the first cars in driveways, and living rooms blue with television light.

Only a few people waited in the small bus station. They watched the skinny brunette buy a ticket, then they yawned, drank coffee, rattled newspapers, stared at yellow walls.

Suddenly Sara was hungry—she went in the women's rest room to mix herself coffee. She made a cheese sandwich for herself and ate it sitting on a chair by the sinks.

When she came back to the waiting room somebody had left a magazine on an empty seat; she kept her face down, reading it page by page, her plastic bag between her feet.

"Bus for Boston," a man called.

*Act ordinary*, Sara told herself, and made herself read a

magazine paragraph three times before she gave the driver her ticket and climbed bus stairs. She turned away from the window, rummaging in her plastic bag. An old lady sat down beside her, and the bus drew away from the curb. They passed the outskirts of Grenville and were on the dark highway.

Manhasset Bay glimmered through trees under the full moon. Sliding over the bay was a woman reflected in a bus window. She stared at Sara through black-rimmed glasses; her hair was a short, dark, wavy cap. Sara stared back at a spectacled face that was her own.

"Nice weather," said a small, dry voice.

Sara turned to an old woman beside her who was so bent in her bus seat that she looked like the letter C.

"Very nice," Sara said.

"Visited my son in Hadley," said the old lady.

Sara stared at the woman's gnarled hands fiddling with each other, smoothing and resmoothing a paper sack. *I'm dead.*

"Hadley, Massachusetts," the old lady said.

A young woman reflected in a bus window began to smile. She was alive: blood pulsed in her body; her breath moved steadily in and out; she was dry and warm. She curled her toes. "That's nice," Sara said.

A mile stretched between Sara and the ocean now. Sara said, "My mother's all by herself in a nursing home." Her throat tightened around the words.

Other people were talking in the warm, dark bus. Now and then Sara saw the ocean shining through trees, a slick silver far away.

"Nursing homes," the old woman said. "Stuck away like that."

"Mother was awfully old when I was born, and we moved around so much she doesn't have friends left who come. She hadn't been in town long before my dad died and she had a stroke."

The little old lady beside her looked like somebody's grandmother, a scarf tied around her dried-apple face.

Tears filled Sara's eyes. Her voice went on in a dull monotone: "She doesn't have any relatives but me, and I can't go see her. I don't have enough money. But I'll get there." Sara licked her wrist that had been broken, tasting salt. "She had two friends, but both of them moved away, and Mom's blind, and can't sit up or walk."

The bent little grandmother in the seat beside her stared straight ahead.

The two of them were nested in their dark double seat under luggage racks. Sara's throat ached with all she didn't dare tell anyone. She said, "I've been to see . . . my sister who's having such an unhappy marriage. Her husband started hurting her on their honeymoon, and she fought back. She says she'd never been treated like that, just because she didn't want to go somewhere with him, or forgot to tighten the cap on the toothpaste."

The bus roared and rattled. "At first he swore he didn't mean to hurt her and was sorry and wouldn't do it again," Sara said. "And he made her read a book called *The Fulfilled Woman*. It said that a wife could be happy only if she obeyed her husband at all times."

Sara sobbed too softly to be heard and imagined she was shocking the old lady, but she couldn't seem to stop talking. "My sister ran to a home for battered women, but she didn't want to lose her job. She told me that when you go back to a husband like that, the police and the courts won't do anything much—they have so many cases—and she went back to him."

Sara licked her wrist again, watching the old, dried-up face beside her. "And my sister *loved* him! She thought they liked the same things—music and books and talking to each other. She says she changed all her habits she could—always had boiled eggs for breakfast and folded the blankets in thirds. . . ." Sara heard her voice telling her own story as if she had died. "My sister started to lie and cheat and steal money from his billfold just to keep from being hit. All her life she said she'd never do that. She says she gets so mad she wonders if she forgets to do what he wants on purpose. And he said she could divorce him if she wanted, but he'd track her down wherever she went, whatever she did. She was his forever.''

The dried-apple face looked straight ahead.

Miles between Sara and the ocean now. Her voice told about a woman who was not Sara Burney. Sara listened as if she were outside looking in while she jerked with a sob here and there. ''The police couldn't stay in my sister's house with her, and she couldn't live forever in a battered-women shelter. She had her job, and she loved it. She told me that sometimes she thought *she* was wrong . . . she should stop being such a bad wife and stay home and have a baby. A baby! Two of them in his house then, and what would he—'' Sara stopped, tears running down her face. The old lady was probably too shocked to speak.

Then the dried-up face turned to her, its wrinkled mouth lit with red neon from a passing town. ''Nasty little boys,'' it said. ''Most of them. They beat up their wives, give them orders, make them wash their underwear when those men never wipe themselves—pee everywhere but the toilet. My first husband died, and my friends said wasn't I going to get married again, and how would I get along without a man? And I said, 'Now, who would put beans up their noses twice?' So I lived by myself with my own clean toilet and my own underwear to wash. Don't suppose it sounds like much fun to you, but it was. Still is.''

Sara stretched her arms and legs and felt the rough bus seat under her hands. She bared her teeth against her salty wrist in a sudden, silent laugh. ''Yes!'' she said.

Their bus gathered speed. The highway ran dry and wide before it in yellow moonlight. She wanted to tell the old lady, *I'm going to live in a town I haven't seen since my college roommate invited me to her home there.*

A tree limb scraped the roof as the bus lurched along a detour. *Three years married,* Sara wanted to say, *and no social security number I can use. No driver's license or recommendations. No decent job—not for years—because I have to hide.*

The bus rattled in a loose-jointed rhythm. Sara shut her eyes.

"I got this dog next door," the old lady cackled in Sara's ear after a while. "Darn thing howled all day, and the old poop next door never heard it. He was off playing bingo."

"M-m-m," Sara said.

The ocean disappeared and was only a layer of salt on her skin now. Towns passed. Passengers got on and off. "Hi!" a young girl cried to another, hanging over a seat ahead of Sara. "You go to summer school?"

Her friend groaned! "Two months. Math. It's hell."

Two women came down the aisle. "I don't know what he's going to do," one of them said. "Sell his house, I suppose, and store all that rosewood furniture."

Sara closed her eyes and thought she could clean houses or baby-sit—she wouldn't need a social security number for jobs like that.

"I sure fixed that old poop," her seatmate cackled in her ear.

"You did?" Sara said.

"They never think old ladies know anything. Never think an old body like me can work my son's tape recorder."

"No?" Sara said.

"No," the old lady said.

They were coming into Boston. Sara wasn't going to sleep at home that night; she gritted her teeth. She'd sleep in the bus station.

"No. The old poop," the grandma said.

Shop windows lit the bus after a while. *Nobody except my mother will know I'm alive*, Sara told herself. *If I can get a master's degree in library science . . .* She remembered her desk at the Montrose library. Under the blotter were lists of books she'd read, hundreds of them, with some of their words in her head for good. She saw her name on the desk, and her African violets.

Neon turned bus passengers red, green, blue. After a while the old lady said, "No, he did not."

"M-m-m," Sara said, thinking of a headline: WOMAN DROWNED IN BAY.

"He certainly did not! Until he got woke up at four o'clock every morning."

Sara remembered car keys that had to be kept in a dish on Martin's desk when she wasn't using them. He made fun of her books . . . books bored him, he said, and always had. He left television blatting, hour after hour, with its canned giggles and jokes. He had twisted her arm because she had paid too much for a pillowcase. She remembered the .25 pistol pressed against her temple until she could see the circle on her skin afterward and hear the click of its hammer against her skull.

"Woke him with his own mutt's yips and howls and whine-whine-whine. Four o'clock in the morning. Right in his bedroom window. I turned it on and slept on t'other side of my house, so I didn't hear a thing."

Passengers stirred in their seats now, finding their parcels, pulling on coats.

Sara said, "What did the old poop do?"

"Told me I was ruining his health. I said I was doing no such thing. It was just his own dog and he bought it and tied it up in his backyard, didn't he? So he must've wanted to hear it."

"Good for you," Sara said.

"It was good for him," the old lady said. "Brought him down to us lesser mortals. Sold the dog and got a cat."

The bus swung to the curb and passengers crowded the aisle. "Dumb cat kills the birds at my feeder," the old lady said, getting up and out in the aisle little by little, hanging on to the seat ahead of her. "But I'll fool that old poop." The dried-apple face grinned at Sara. "Again."

"Good for you," Sara said. "Good-bye."

"Poops," the old lady said as she went down the aisle. "Who needs 'em?"

Sara's bruised legs were stiff; she climbed down the stairs step by step and went to ask about buses to Iowa.

The man behind the counter said that she could leave

Boston the next morning, be out of New York the next night for Chicago, and would arrive in Waterloo, Iowa, the following evening.

Sara heard him, but her mouth was too dry to answer. Suddenly she said to herself, *I'll never see Cristine again, will I?* Cristine Weidin had three children whose pajamas she washed every morning. She waxed her furniture every Friday. She wailed about her weight. And there was Karen Fairchild with her Southern accent and her little presents: a rose in a wineglass on Sara's doorstep or a mug with a silly cartoon pasted on it . . .

People waited in a line behind Sara. "You want the ticket?" the man asked her.

Sara's heart was beating so fast it filled her ears. All her friends were only a few miles away now, but she'd never see them again. She'd never finish reading *Ulysses* with Joan Pagent or play again with Marie O'Brien's children, who were as beautiful as those in fairy-tale books. She'd never see Pam at the library.

"You want it?" the man asked. Sara looked at the money in her hand. She was in Boston yet. It was still the same evening. The day wasn't over. She backed away from the counter, shaking her head, and found a chair and sat on it, her plastic bag at her feet, her hands cold and trembling.

What was the matter with her? She saw Martin crying her name, tears falling down his face.

It was still the same evening. It hadn't been more than a few hours.

She jumped up and ran from the station into brightly lit streets she hardly knew. Evening surrounded her like a bubble she could break—there was so little between her and the bay, the beach house, Martin.

She walked block after block, her plastic bag dangling from her hand and Martin running beside her along the beach on their honeymoon, his kind voice in her ears, his eyes shining. They danced in their little Cape Cod house the night they bought it, their footsteps clattering in empty rooms. She smelled his hair and his skin, and walls of their house rose around her—it was so close, just a bus and subway ride away.

Sara passed a street-corner telephone. She stopped, went back.

Cars shifted gears at the corner. A truck belched exhaust. Sara crept into the telephone booth, shut the door behind her, and stood in the yellow light looking at the receiver on its hook.

He hadn't thought she was dead for more than a few hours. Their dinner dishes were probably on the kitchen table yet. She knew the beach-house telephone number. "I'm in Boston," she could say. "I'm alive."

A black telephone receiver hung before her, but she was in a sailboat with Martin as he yelled in the dark. She was at a police station with him, but he didn't know it; he ran his fingers through his hair and cried and explained and signed papers.

Martin climbed the beach-house stairs; she followed him into the dark kitchen. He would see the roses and her plate of food. It wasn't far to that kitchen. She was there with him as he looked around it. If she called, the telephone would ring through smells of steak and onions and apple pie from the dinner she'd cooked.

A black telephone receiver hung waiting. Her bedroom slippers were under their dresser yet; she saw them. She saw Martin finding them and looking at her clothes in the closet, tears running down his face. . . .

The black receiver was in her hand before she realized it. She had dialed the beach-house number. Martin was at the other end of a black cord. His words would pour from the black hole: *Where are you?*

The receiver in Sara's hand had one ear and one mouth and waited to shout at her, scream at her.

Sara slammed it back on the wall, trembling. When she leaned her head against the booth the lump on her head hurt.

She stared at a telephone that might have let Martin's

voice out to scream and yell. Then she backed out of the booth and the light went off.

Sara looked through the window. The telephone hung silent and black behind the glass, shutting Martin up with the night and Manhasset Bay forever, like a ship in a bottle. She turned her back. She walked away.

Sara passed blocks of shops that were shut, with one or two lights inside, sentinels. It was growing late. Her stiff legs hurried her up and down curbs as if she had a destination. She passed another telephone booth without a glance.

Where was she going? Waiting on a corner for a light to turn green, she forgot the light and looked at a tree beside her. The tree was small and had a few leaves that stirred in summer night breeze. Beyond the tree's highest branch a full moon sailed between buildings. Sidewalk pavement left the tree only a very small circle of earth, air, and water, and that circle was drifted almost over with empty cigarette packs, newspaper, soft-drink cups, gum wrappers.

Sara blinked her tired eyes and looked around her, as if she were waking to find herself on a lonely street corner beside closed shops.

She rubbed her eyes. Her head ached; she felt the lump in her hair and the scab on it. Her breast hurt when she took a breath, and the backs of her legs were so sore she couldn't touch them.

A clock against the sky said it was after midnight. Another day.

Sara walked back to the bus station. A few lonely people slumped in chairs; a radio talked busily somewhere. Sara sat down in a corner and put her rings in her wallet and the plastic bag between her feet. She unzipped her slacks enough to pull out her long shirttail and stuff her wallet under the waistband beneath her arm.

Now she was drowsy. She leaned back and found that her eyes would close. Her body hurt, it was so tired. Her hands were trembling.

Sara fell asleep in her chair, her mouth open, her long eyelashes fluttering now and then. Sometimes her bruised hand felt for her wallet or twitched.

A clock ticked through the night on the bus-station wall.

A man swept station floors when dawn came. Now and then the door opened and shut behind a paperboy or some early traveler.

At seven o'clock a middle-aged woman came in and sat down beside Sara. Sara woke with a start and looked around her, not finding the bedroom of the Cape Cod house or the beach house. She blinked and stared at a bus station, seeing that it wasn't a dream. Its ordinary lights and colors were so real that she looked at the clock, looked for the plastic bag between her feet and the wallet under her arm, and was in a new day that she couldn't have believed without the smell of coffee, somebody's newspaper rattling, cars glittering along a street outside in early light.

The middle-aged woman next to Sara opened a huge pocketbook and rummaged through it. She sighed and gripped paper sacks firmly in her lap. "My feet," she said to Sara. "I was on the go all yesterday."

Sara's mouth was dry. She wanted some coffee.

"Getting ready for my husband's birthday tomorrow. We're having it at my sister's. Jimmy's going to be so surprised when he gets there—he thinks we're just going to see my sister because she's got a broken leg. She got it selling popcorn," the woman said.

Sara sat up straight in her chair, blinking.

"At a Little League game, climbing in the bleachers, you know."

Sara looked out the bus-station windows. The woman said nothing more. Sara shut her eyes and dozed and fell into black water. She was trying to save Martin, but he pulled her down, and she bit his hands, kicked him, smashed at his face to break his grip—

"About the second inning," the woman said. Sara opened her eyes. The woman got a better grip on her two paper sacks and smiled at Sara.

"Yes," Sara said.

The woman opened one of her sacks and pawed to the bottom of it. "Broke it in two places," she said, but found she was talking to Sara's empty chair. Sara had left her seat to buy herself a ticket to Waterloo, Iowa.

No one was in the women's rest room. Sara ran water until it was hot and mixed herself a cup of coffee, then a cup of milk. She leaned against the wall, sipping it.

It was morning of another day.

She was stiff, and her legs and head and breast were sore. But she hunched her shoulders and smiled a little, leaning against the wall, loving the taste of her own food she had made for herself when the night was gone.

# 8

Rain, blowing across dark Iowa miles, ruled off the sweep of the Greyhound's headlights in narrow silver lines and flooded down the windshield. Sara sat almost at the front across from two children. An old farmer leaned on the back of the white-haired bus driver's seat, and two men a few rows back were still awake. The rest of the passengers were dark mounds huddled in sleep above an empty soft-drink can that trundled back and forth, forth and back along the floor.

Sara shut her eyes, her head aching. Her wig was tight and clamped to her braids with bobby pins, and she'd worn it more than forty-eight hours.

She touched the wig's springy, safe cap and yawned. Two nights sleeping in bus stations. Two days napping in a bus seat. She swayed and jiggled through a slow, ordinary world where tickets had to be bought, buses had to be waited for, and wheels had to turn, turn, turn.

"Didn't hear a thing," the old farmer said. His bony nose was yellow with the dashboard glow.

"Sound sleeper," the driver said.

Forth and back, back-forth, back and forth—the bus windshield wipers never moved together. Sara watched them swing loose-jointed and at odds, but they kept the glass clear in wide arcs. The farmer stared through them as if he had seen many haphazard, unsynchronized things work in his day. "Straight stretch of road, too, a bit east of Solon."

Sara sat alone in her shadowed window seat, jiggling, smelling damp clothes. The two children sitting across from her were brilliantly spotlit; they had turned their reading lights on. Sara could hear what people were saying over the motor, the sticky swish of tires passing, the rattle of wiper blades.

Sara watched rain angle down the window—real rain in a real world where people had real names. She looked real enough herself. She clamped her teeth together and watched the children and she was hungry. She had only enough bread and cheese for supper. She had to save the money she had left. There was no one in the world to help her, feed her, give her a place to sleep, because she was dead.

Rain streamed along the wiper blades. Their crazy dance seemed to amuse the old man and the driver; they were both grinning. "No kidding?" asked the driver.

The farmer sat back, smiling; Sara watched his smile cut across his seamed face unexpectedly, as if it surprised even himself. "Right off the straight road and into Clay's farmyard and around and around right under Clay's bedroom window at two A.M., and Clay says he never heard the car even hit a fence he's got by his feed lot. Took out a twelve-foot section. I said to Clay, like you said, what the heck did he do at night to be so deaf?"

A semi passed. The white-haired driver raised his left hand a few inches above the wheel. Mile after mile Sara had seen him salute each truck or bus that way, his hand lifting in the few seconds before two heavy loads missed each other by a foot or two of violently churned air.

There was salt from the ocean on Sara's skin yet; her hair was sticky with it. She could sit in a Waterloo park or station until morning, then get a bus for Cedar Falls and hunt for a cheap room somewhere. Go to the university and ask. Summer school was probably over, but the offices might be open.

Sara watched the driver raise his hand, let it fall. Nobody could ever un-live what they'd done, like a movie run backward. They couldn't ever shoot out of the ocean feetfirst, sail backward in a boat to a dock, and back up beach stairs step by step to be where they'd been. They couldn't have a name and a life back. They could only be shut out, hurting people by being dead.

Iowa rain ran down the window. Sara watched the children across from her. The older boy's hair under the light was the color of popcorn, white, with a buttery sheen to it and bright glints like light on crystals. "You talk?" he asked the smaller boy beside him. Getting no answer, he sat back and slid down until his eyes were level with those of the child beside him. "You talk?" he growled in mock fury.

The mouth in the small, impassive face finally opened and said, "Yeh." The child jammed his fists tightly together. "I got eight baby mice. I got one's named Minerva."

"Where?"

"At home. But I got one here, buttoned in my pocket."

The Greyhound rounded a curve. Sara imagined small mistakes: one wet footprint on a floor . . . someone swimming at night who saw a blonde come from the water on a beach by two dark houses. She watched a car on the road ahead leave momentary streaks behind it on a wet highway.

The old farmer kept his face straight. "Got two of Clay's apple trees next and made a wreck of his rotary hoe and cultivator he had standing out there. Then the corn crib. Pushed the hayrick right out of it. Darned if the fool didn't stop then. Then he started up again and backed into an old outhouse Clay's still got. And then revved up and shot off down a cow path into a fresh-plowed field for near a mile till he got stuck."

"Drunk," said the driver.

"Sure," said the farmer.

Forth and back, back-forth, forth-back and back and forth. The highway slid under Sara, a stripe down its back. In the diamond-studded blaze of rain and headlights the driver's hand lifted, fell. Dense, dark cornfields drank rain on both sides of the road. Each time Sara had climbed out to walk and stretch at bus stops, she'd smelled that black earth.

The older boy stroked a mouse's moon-white fur. The

mouse sat in his hat, cleaning her face and ears with bare pink claws like hands. "Why was you in the hospital?" the younger child asked.

"I was in a accident," the older boy said. "Me and my kid brother. He got thrown out of the car. He was just in kindergarten." He curled his hand around the mouse and held her close to his eyes. Her cobwebby whiskers were in constant motion. "She's awfully small," he said.

"What happened to your brother?"

"He died."

Sara watched the wet highway. It had rained her last afternoon in Montrose, and she had roamed the small Cape Cod house without stopping, wild with the chances she had to take: if Martin took a boat out, and if she could dive, and if she could make it to shore, and if no one saw her, and if she could get to Boston, and if . . .

All those ifs. She remembered standing by the light table in their bedroom where her African violets were nosegays of brilliant pink, white, blue, purple. If she meant to do the almost impossible things she planned, she might never see that house again. The violets would die. Martin would never notice them or water them. They would shrivel to nothing but brown heaps in dirt.

Leaves spread green rosettes beneath glowing violets. Each plant was perfect; for months she had trained their leaves in circles around mounds of flowers.

Rain had streamed down the bedroom window.

She hadn't known what she would do, could do.

Then she had reached out and broken one leaf from one perfect circle.

If the plant had cried as it broke, she wouldn't have been surprised. She heard only rain on the window and the low hum of the lights.

She broke the circle of the next plant, and the next. She cut each leaf stem with a razor and wrapped it in wet cotton in plastic and then packed them with the razor blade in a small box. She filled two sacks with potting soil and vermiculite and put leaves and sacks at the bottom of her suitcase under her clothes, hiding a small, secret garden.

Wherever she found a home, new plants would grow from each leaf.

That night when she got into bed with Martin, the last thing she saw were the shelves of violets. Their broken rosettes told her she would leave if she could, that she meant to try, that it might not be a dream.

Now their leaves lay in a plastic bag in her lap.

Rain streaked sidewise across bus windows, blown by wind. There had been nothing said in the front of the bus for five miles. The old man peered over the driver's shoulder; the driver stared at the road. Finally the driver asked, "When did Clay notice something was wrong?"

"Five A.M." The farmer's face drew crosswise in a grin again. "Clay woke up and saw a hole in his fence and the hayrick out in the yard. When he was milking, an hour later, up comes the kid and wonders if Clay will pull him out of that field."

Now the two men behind Sara laughed out loud. The farmer looked over his shoulder as if noticing for the first time that they were there. His eyes sparkled with the dashboard lights. "Yep," he said, leaning back and folding his arms. "Said he was lost." The men shouted with laughter this time. The old man threw a quick look at them and settled deeper in his seat.

The small boy said, "You can get cages in the dime store. She just needs a little one with a wheel to run around on and a cardboard roll from toilet paper to sleep in. Don't use newspaper in the cage. She tears it up and gets dirty and cleans herself too much and gets sick."

"You sure you got more mice? You sure you won't miss this one?" the older boy asked.

His seatmate nodded gravely. "I've got a safety pin. Pin her in your pocket." He stared at the boy beside him. "Did they put your brother in the ground?"

"Yes."

The mouse kept trying to climb out of the older boy's shirt pocket.

"In the rain?" The small boy's eyes were wide open.

The older boy pushed the mouse down each time she

reached the top of the pocket. His seatmate stopped staring to work the hinge of a big safety pin out of the edge of his jean pocket. "No," the older boy said after a while. "It was a nice sunny day."

The lights of the bus went on. Streetlights winked in and out of the wet windows. "Waterloo," the driver chanted as he drove.

The farmer still leaned over the driver's seat. "When the sheriff came to Clay's place about eight o'clock the next morning, you know what he charged that kid with?"

"No. What?" said the driver, swinging the Greyhound around a corner, pulling it up to the curb. He opened the door, then swung around to the old man.

"Reckless driving and failure to have his car under control." In the burst of laughter even the bus driver grinned broadly. "Couldn't find any sign of liquor on him by then."

The old man blocked the way out, pausing as if he were delivering a punch line. "Took Clay a month to get his farm back into shape. But the kid claimed he couldn't remember a thing happened that night. If it hadn't been for the mess that farm was in and the mess his car was in, nobody'd know anything happened at all." He stepped off the bus to laughter, grinning, holding his shoulders straight and his chin out.

It had almost stopped raining. Pavements shone with the upside-down neon of Bar and Coffee Shop. Sara climbed down to wet pavement and followed the driver into the station. He carried a load of boxes and backed through the door, saying, "Hi, George" to the yawning man at the desk.

"P.R. ride with you?" George said. He was a fat man and got his paunch as close as he could to the window to look out.

"Yep. How long has he got, you know?"

"Two–three months, last I heard."

"Anyone to go?"

"Nope," the fat man said. "He tell his story about the drunk driver at Clay's farm?"

"Never misses a cue," the white-haired bus driver said. "Ought to've been on the stage." He went out past P.R. and clapped him on the back, climbed the bus steps, and pulled the door shut.

Sara looked through the bus-station window. The old farmer watched the bus as it pulled out, and faces in it slid past above the only one left on the street. The bus streaked wet pavement with warm yellow window light, but the lean, loping greyhound painted on the side turned his muzzle toward distances, his rib cage swollen with deep breath, his belly sucked in.

The old man stood where he was, watching the bus as long as he could. It turned a far corner; its last back window blinked and was gone. Sara heard the far-off sound of gears shifting through to high.

The old man was alone then on a long, glistening street that stood, light by light, in silence.

# 9

The next afternoon Ben Woodward watched her come across Seerley Boulevard under crab apple trees, walking a little stiff-legged in shade, then in sun, then in maple shade down Ben's street, a brunette carrying a big plastic bag. She had nice breasts, but the rest of her was all bones. Sunlight glinted on her short hair.

When she saw Ben she looked away. He pushed his lawn mower up his bank; it was a noisy Sears monster.

The brunette looked at the number of the house next to his, then went up steps to ring the bell by Mrs. Nepper's battered screen door.

Ben went on mowing; he didn't notice he was doing the same grass twice. There was a yellowed, rolled Cedar Falls *Citizen* in his bridal wreath bushes. Ben picked it out and started to read Iowa news that was two months old.

Mrs. Nepper came to the door of her screened front porch and said, "You come in, you just come right in," to the brunette.

When he had his front yard mowed Ben went into his house and looked at dirty clothes in a living-room chair. He'd left an empty beer can on the bust of Shakespeare. After a while he noticed he was cruising from window to open window on his side of the house, watching the place next door. Mrs. Nepper kept her junk stored upstairs and rented the downstairs.

Finally Mrs. Nepper came out and stood on her front

steps, talking through the porch screen. "Then that's all settled," she said. "Keep the telephone in my name and you won't have to pay to change it. You can pay me every month. They pick the trash up in the alley. And there's a bus down College Street to the shopping centers." Mrs. Nepper repeated herself like a cuckoo in a clock and had a tuft of white hair waving above her wood-brown old face. Ben could hear her saying "trash in the alley" and "down College Street" as she went off to her own house three blocks away.

Ben couldn't settle down. He went to his kitchen after a while when he heard the brunette's back-porch door screech. She was going toward the alley. He could wash sweat off his face and go out, say hello.

He watched her come back along her overgrown walk. She looked half starved, but her eyes were very blue. Her upper lip was fuller than her lower one. He heard her back-porch door screech again.

Ben looked in his kitchen mirror. He could say, *I'll tell you what—how about seeing a play at the Old Creamery Theatre? Next week? Dinner first?*

He ran his fingers through curls over his eyes. He had to check the costumes for *Candide* and sketch some set changes. He sat down at his study desk and listened to his air conditioner going pft-pft-pft.

Mrs. Nepper's back porch sloped toward a backyard overgrown with day lilies, phlox, grass tops, and green fans of funkia. Its door was walled around with lilac bushes. When Sara came out, hidden in that green, she noticed a narrow path through the lilacs. They grew against a redwood fence to an old house like hers next door. Children played in that secret path; there was a set of acorn dishes beside the dusty track.

The old house next door had a barn for a garage, and her house had no garage at all. A city block of backyards merged their lawns and gardens companionably. Her yard was the only overgrown one. The corner house faced Seerley Boulevard and its back door overlooked her yard. The door had an arch above it like one white-painted eyebrow. Smooth grass before the door surrounded a flower bed full of chrysanthemums.

Sara went back to her kitchen, feeling light-headed, grinning foolishly at old kitchen cabinets, refrigerator, stove. A whole apartment! She couldn't have afforded it, but Mrs. Nepper said, "I'll cut the rent because you're willing to paint." She'd make the kitchen walls orange and the woodwork all cream, and the table and chairs too. There were so many ferns in the yard. She could plant some in empty flowerpots she'd seen on the back porch and hang them in her long kitchen window.

Stove and sink and refrigerator were caked with lime and grease. She found cleanser and steel wool and three half bottles of shampoo under the sink with a pile of rags and a pair of cotton gloves that fit her. She could get to work right away.

Her bedroom had once been a dining room, she supposed. A small bathroom had been walled off at one end. She'd paint the bathroom cream-colored and the bedroom yellow and the living room gold. How many families had wondered what to do with such a big, useless front hall? She'd make it her study. Oak steps turned at a landing and ended upstairs at a locked door.

Sara saw Mrs. Nepper coming up the walk of the old house next door. "Hello," a man's voice said after she'd rung the bell. A man's arm opened the screen door for Mrs. Nepper, "Won't you come in?"

"Just can't. In such a hurry," Mrs. Nepper said. "Went and forgot it when I rented my apartment next door. I've got an invitation for you." She was waving an envelope. "In such a hurry. My niece's wedding." Her sharp voice traveled through Sara's open window.

Sara walked away, not eavesdropping. She picked at a piece of sticky tape on a wall; college students always hung posters everywhere, Mrs. Nepper said. When Sara peeled off the crackling yellowed paper it left a brown rectangle. Every room was nicked and scratched and dirty, but she had time, and the rent was so low, she'd paid a month in advance. All the rooms were hers. "Oh!" she said once to her four-rooms-and-bath, and grinned, and stretched her arms out wide.

She'd have a yellow bedroom. The sheets on her brass double bed were worn but clean, and so were the bathroom towels. Every drawer in an empty dresser was hers and so was a closet full of hangers. She took her wig off at last, unbraided her sticky, salty hair, and scratched her head luxuriously, smiling even when she felt the scab where her head had struck the beach-house door.

Her bathtub was on claw feet and had a peculiar shower: a ring of metal at the ceiling and a circling curtain. It was all dirty, but it worked. The toilet flushed with a business-like gurgle. Faucets delivered hot and cold. You could wash clothes and take baths with shampoo.

She heard Mrs. Nepper say, "You remember her, don't you? In your Human Communications course last fall? Karen Birtch?"

The man's voice said, "Yes, but I don't think I—"

"You've got to come. They're new in town and haven't made a lot of friends yet—not enough to fill a church— and we don't have many relatives. My bridge circle is coming, and Laura Pray, the new girl. You've seen her? She just rented my apartment next door. And I want you to come too."

"Well," the man said.

"They're new in town and they don't know a lot of people, and we don't—"

"Yes," he said. "Yes, I'll be glad to come."

"I always do think weddings are neighborly, don't you? It's at ten-thirty in the morning, to keep away from the hot part of the day." Mrs. Nepper said good-bye twice and repeated "neighborly" and "ten-thirty" as she went down the street.

Clean the bathroom first. Sara tied her hair back with a rag from the kitchen and put the shower curtain to soak in the tub. Down on her knees scrubbing the floor, Sara remembered urine splattered on a toilet's rim or over the sides, little yellow puddles.

Then Sara laughed, there on her knees. *My first husband*

*died, and my friends said wasn't I going to get married
again, and I said, "Now, who would put beans up their
noses twice?"*

Sara backed out of the bathroom door at last. Her legs
were so sore, she grabbed the doorknob to pull herself to
her feet. Steel wool had taken yellowed wax off the linoleum's crisp black and cream squares. Her shower curtain
was clean and drying, and so was her sink and toilet and
tub—nobody's dirt to clean up but her own now.

Sara walked back and forth in her quiet rooms. Paint
brushes . . . a roller . . . Spackle . . . sandpaper . . . if she
could find a job, get some money of her own. Mrs.
Nepper would buy the paint. She looked out the window at
her front-porch swing that hung on chains. There were
ferns and bridal wreath and lily of the valley around her
front porch. Nobody lived upstairs. She had a beautiful
city block of green park for her front yard.

Curtains in her windows were cheap net that stirred a
little, moving in late afternoon breeze. Ben looked in the
mirror again, then started walking from window to window. He took a shower, had a beer, and found he was
cruising from window to window again.

Sara walked back and forth, back and forth, then stopped
and danced on her living-room rug, laughing to herself.
She grabbed her plastic bag and spilled it out on her bed.
Sunday night she'd dived in the bay. Now it was Wednesday and she was unpacking in Cedar Falls, Iowa, putting
her eyebrow pencil and lipstick in one drawer, her wig in
another, her violet leaves and potting supplies in the kitchen,
her wet clothes in the bathroom. She poured shampoo in
the bathroom sink and washed salt water from Manhasset
Bay out of shirt and slacks and a black silk teddy.

"Don't!" a child yelled under her bedroom window.
Sara couldn't see through a thick roof of lilac leaves, but
she heard a scuffle and cries. "I'm the mother!" somebody said indignantly.

Cicadas were zing-zinging in high, hot trees. Maybe
Laura Pray was getting her dinner, Ben thought, and put

his own in the microwave. Maybe she'd take out garbage afterward.

Ben ate in the kitchen where he could listen for her back-porch door's gliding screech. About seven o'clock he heard it and rinsed dishwater off his hands, checked how his hair looked in the kitchen mirror. "Welcome to the neighborhood," he could say. "I'm Ben Woodward. Teach at the university."

He watched her walk around her jungle of a backyard with the trash pile in it. Her skin wasn't deep tan, and in the winter it would be so fair it would look almost blue. Maybe her nose was too long to be pretty, and her mouth was small, but all together she was beautiful, or could be if she weren't so thin and tired-looking. "Thank you for the welcome," she might tell him. "I'd love to go to dinner with you and see a play."

Her door shut behind her.

Ben scowled into the mirror over the sink, finished dinner dishes, did some exercises, and went to his study to work on *Candide*.

He was alone in his own house. It wasn't so bad. It was good. It was enough for him. A university job, tenure track, money in the bank, and no woman saying "No. Not now. Not yet."

Ben watched net curtains blowing in what must be her living-room window.

Sara slipped off her sandals and lay on her bed, stretching arms and legs to the four corners.

She stared up the way a body might stare, rotting on a beach. Tears came to her eyes. Her mother would think she had no children left . . . no one to call her at four o'clock every Saturday afternoon. Sara's lies, huge and cruel as waves in a bay, towered over her. People were crying because she was dead. They were mourning and lonely and hunted for her.

"You're mean!" somebody yelled under Sara's bedroom window. "I'm going home!"

Sara looked at her ceiling. It had spots on it. So did her arms and legs and breasts. She gritted her teeth. When her bruises were gone there wouldn't be any more, and she could wear shorts and a short-sleeved shirt.

Three nights without a bed. She was still coated with salt, and her hair was sticky with it, but she could wash her own hair now—no more beauty shops.

"Who could help me?" she said out loud. She put her clothes on her bed and crawled into her clean little shower tent in the bathtub.

"The best I could," she said, and soaped herself all over with shampoo, so that the last of the Atlantic went down the drain in a swirl of white. She had stepped into the YWCA pool trembling all over. Women had comforted her, encouraged her to take just one step, and then another. She'd gotten sick at first; Joe sank beneath that swimming pool's surface every day, screaming.

But she forced herself in three times a week, sick and shaking but going deeper and deeper. One day her fear melted away; the blue water held her in its arms and she swam the length of the pool over and over like a wild machine while everybody cheered and clapped.

Braiding her wet hair, Sara looked at cleaning supplies under the sink. She had only a little money left; she'd get the most nourishing and cheapest food, oatmeal and dry beans. Sometimes her family had lived on those for weeks when she was little. There was a bottle of catsup in the refrigerator and a carton of salt in the cupboard. She didn't have to beg anybody for money. Nobody would look in the grocery bag when she got home.

She had unpacked her African violet leaves; they were still alive and green, but they wouldn't last much longer. She was almost sick with hunger now. She spread her dollar bills on the table, and her change.

College Square shopping center was only a mile down University Avenue. Sara pulled the wig over her wet braids and fluffed it up. She was a brunette. Her name was Laura Pray. It sounded enough like Sara Gray so that she would pay attention when she heard it, without thinking.

Laura Pray took what money she had and went down her sidewalk that had grass growing in every crack. She stopped to look at the whole house she had to herself, when she'd imagined living in one room, cooking on a hot plate.

Her house was square, with a big screened porch across the front; it stood high on its bank overlooking the park, shadowed and partly hidden by tall trees. It had a brick house on one side. On the other a red-painted home crowded the corner lot, its front door on Seerley Boulevard, its back to her. It blocked traffic noise from Seerley, but made noise of its own—wild modern music blared from an upstairs window as she went by.

Ben watched her go. Laura Pray. Short, dark hair. He liked blondes. He saw Deborah's shining hair before he could turn the memory off.

Long, clinging, silvery hair. Ben stared at Laura walking away. He'd never get that close again or feel that blow in the gut when a woman turns her back, says *Not you. Somebody else*.

Laura Pray. He watched her disappear around the Seerley Boulevard corner. Her bottom was hardly there under her slacks. Somebody should feed her good, fattening meals. He sighed and looked at the sketch of the old woman in *Candide* who had only one buttock. Somebody had cut off her other buttock when she was young and food was scarce. Nobody ever forgot that detail in Voltaire, so her costume should have a bulge on one side in back.

He had his own house, his own good job.

The brunette's curtains stirred in the evening breeze.

# 10

The next day Sara saw a man mowing the backyard of the old brick and shingle house next door. "Ben Woodward," Mrs. Nepper had told her. "A professor at the university." He had red hair like Joe's and golden-red hair on his bare chest, too, and long legs in tight jeans.

Sara stayed behind her curtains. She wore only her bra and some bikini underpants to wash the kitchen ceiling because she had to save her clothes and it was so hot. Ben Woodward was tall and looked like a lumberjack, not a professor. He was squarish, and stumped through his yard with big feet. Now he was standing under a tree, his shoulders hunched, turning his head this way and that as if he had a stiff neck. Sara watched him, thinking of big fists, of being pinned down. . . .

She looked at his apple tree too. Ben Woodward was kicking at the apples on the ground; she thought she heard him swear. He wanted to mow the grass, she supposed, and the fallen apples were in his way.

Sara's mouth watered. Applesauce. Baked apples.

She gritted her teeth and concentrated on his house next door. It wasn't as old as hers, but old enough. It had a gambrel roof, and its red shingle and brick front was outlined in white, so that it looked like a child's crayon drawing of a barn. Maybe, Sara thought hungrily, it was more like a reddish-brown chocolate layer cake with white frosting oozing out between stories. . . .

She hadn't seen any woman go in or out.

Sara roamed from window to window. Maybe Ben Woodward had the whole house, up and down. Did he live alone? She'd stay out of sight as much as she could. Leaning on her front windowsill, she looked through net curtains at green Seerley Park.

"Beat you home!" yelled a small girl, running up Sara's bank.

"Chicken!" yelled another child. A toddler followed her, his shorts sagging with wet diapers.

Sara sighed and wondered if Ben Woodward had air-conditioning. She didn't even have a fan. Sweat dripped down her face.

She went back to wash grease off the kitchen ceiling until her wrist hurt too much. She got off the stepladder Mrs. Nepper had loaned her and walked up and down her living room. People in houses around the park were cooking their good dinners now. She saw the pink juiciness of a steak . . . a fat baked potato with sour cream melting into its mealy and steaming insides . . . a chocolate sundae whose thick hot fudge hardened and shone as it ran down scoops of ice cream. . . .

No money. No food but oatmeal and beans.

She grabbed a kitchen knife and began to scrape burned food off her oven with her left hand, remembering Martin's big hands changing to hard fists, only the bones touching her, not the caressing fingers . . . his wineglasses that were sticky with sherry he couldn't see to pour. The man next door would have plenty to eat when he finished mowing his lawn. . . .

She had no house of her own, no driver's license, no social security number. Tears ran into the corners of her mouth. She smeared the sticky brown grease from the oven on an old newspaper; the broiler wouldn't swing out unless she could find a piece of wire to fasten it to its frame.

Children were calling to each other in a block of green park.

She heard Ben Woodward start his car in his old barn.

Maybe he was going out to a good dinner with his friends or his lover. They'd look at a menu. . . .

Sara scraped grease from the oven, and then used cleanser on it. It began to look almost new. Sneezing with cleanser dust, she got up to rest in her living room. Net curtains and tree shadow gave it an underwater look, shifting and cool. The table was old, but she'd put a jelly glass of daisies on it.

She began to wash the kitchen ceiling again. Climbing on and off the ladder, she heard Ben Woodward drive into his barn and thought that perhaps she should make herself homelier so no man would get killed because of her. She was carrying death around with her like a blonde in some old movie who pulled out the pin of a hand grenade, put it inside her unbuttoned blouse, and walked toward the enemy.

Sara sighed and scrubbed paint until her wrist ached and the ceiling was done. She took a shower then and sat on her front-porch swing, its chains creaking softly. She tried not to think of steak or pie or chicken and watched cars go along Seerley toward the university, a few blocks away. She could walk to the shopping center and the post office and library and university lectures and concerts and plays; she didn't need a car.

She didn't need a post office.

She was cut off. Her mother was lying alone, thinking she had no children any more, no one would call her Saturday afternoons. Sara found herself staring at twigs and maple seeds that had drifted into corners outside the porch screen.

She sighed and looked at beautiful green Seerley Park. Nobody was watching her, waiting to catch her doing something wrong. She wouldn't be kicked out of her own bed that night because someone was mad and drunk. So she stretched her stiff legs, swinging on a porch overlooking green grass and trees. She went to see the row of lilacs making a tunnel of heart-shaped leaves along Ben Woodward's fence. Two squirrels lived in a towering evergreen beside her porch. At night there was an owl.

Now there was the beat-beat-beat of wild music from

the old red house facing Seerley. Sara closed her kitchen door to shut away the racket. Her dinner was waiting for her; she dished up beans with catsup on them. She'd found some candle ends, so she ate her beans with candlelight flickering and no sound but the steady rhythm of park swings, and now and then a spurt of children's voices or the rush of tires as a car went by.

Sara left her dinner plate in the sink, pulled on her wig, turned out her lights, and didn't have to tell anybody at all where she was going or when she would come back. Night was coming, damp and sweet under the trees. Her stiff legs weren't so sore now, but it would be a while before she could run, and she didn't have any running shoes. Sara walked as fast as if she were keeping up with Joe, stride for stride.

Helen Tyler and Edna Grant, standing under a streetlight on Seerley Boulevard, watched Sara walking fast across the street under the park trees.

"Laura Pray, her name is," Edna said. "She paid in advance, Grace Nepper says. Got Grace's name from the university. Real quiet and nice."

Helen watched her spaniel sniff Edna's poodle. "Looks like she's on one of those crazy diets—all bones. She have a job?"

"Doesn't look that way. Grace said she asked if there was anyone Grace knew who would pay to have her come in and cook for them, clean, that sort of thing. Or maybe baby-sit. Kind of shy and jumpy, Grace says. Maybe she's got a broken marriage."

"How about her working for Hazel George Channing? On her back with that awful accident. Can't even feed herself, and she won't talk. It's hard to find people to come in part of a day."

"Needs somebody," Helen said, jerking Brownie's leash to make him quit that nasty sniffing.

"I'll tell Grace, or maybe she thought of it."

"Muriel Braun's dying, they tell me."

"Jack Shaeffer's got diabetes. All those doughnuts he had every morning at the Eagle Grill."

"Mary's still eating three pounds of butter a week, and her legs like sacks full of cement."

Edna's poodle wound his leash around her legs; she had to bat him with her purse to get unwound. "This Laura Pray said she'd like to paint all the rooms, just wants to do it. Ceilings too. Grace'll give her money for paint when she gets her monthly check."

"She's so lucky with her renters," Helen said. Both dogs had smelled the streetlight pole all they wanted. "I better go on home."

Katydids twanged like shrill banjos from darkening trees above. Children bicycled along Seerley from the Ray Edwards Pool. Sara found Mrs. Nepper's house and rang the bell, and Mrs. Nepper came in a short housecoat, a towel around her head, and said she'd just washed her hair.

"I won't come in, you're busy," Sara said. "I wondered if you'd heard of any job for me."

"I have, yes, I have. Just washed my hair—come right in," Mrs. Nepper said, beaming and holding the screen door open for Sara. The small living room was clean but crowded with menageries of china. There was a vase of dusty everlastings, and framed and everlasting smiles of big-eyed children and hoop-skirted maidens. "Just the job for you. I have, yes, I have."

She waved skinny Sara to a chair festooned with starched doilies and asked wouldn't she like some ice cream and cookies? Sara said, "Oh, yes, thanks!" Mrs. Nepper said she'd go put something better on her head and get their little snack.

Mrs. Nepper's cookies were oatmeal, but Mrs. Nepper piled three scoops of ice cream in Sara's dish. "I didn't have any dessert for dinner," Sara said, and that was true.

"Just the job for you," Mrs. Nepper said. She had a flowered scarf around her head now and waved a piece of paper. "It's Hazel George Channing. She was an English professor at the university all her life and just retired and had this awful car accident out west of Minona. Hazel George Channing. Never married, but she's got a student, Ellen Garner, living with her—Ellen Garner—nice, plain sort of girl. Hazel just retired and was an English professor. Needs somebody to come in at noon every day and clean a little, do washing, get her lunch and dinner and feed her. Twelve to six, and she's paying real well.''

"Just the kind of job I need!" Sara cried, and Mrs. Nepper saw her smile for the first time. "When do I start?"

"A week from Monday at four. The visiting nurse'll be there when you come, and she'll explain things. Clean, do washing, get her dinner, work twelve to six—you can't hardly find anyone who wants that kind of work. Awful car accident. Then you'll meet Ellen and she'll talk about the money. Here's the address. I said I'd call Ellen if it wasn't all right with you.''

The ice cream and cookies were gone. "I'm so grateful," Sara said. "I don't know how to thank—"

"Don't you try," Mrs. Nepper said. "Where did you say you come from? Are you married? I didn't know quite what to tell Ellen.''

The sweet taste of ice cream and cookies was still in Sara's mouth, and of course Mrs. Nepper had a right to ask, but Sara felt sick just the same. "I'm from Nebraska, originally, and I'm not married. I want to go back to college for a master's degree when I can.''

"That's nice, and you'll enjoy your job, I hope," Mrs. Nepper said, taking both Sara's hands and shaking them.

Sara said, "Thanks so much for all your trouble, and for that nice snack too." She went to the door with the ice-cream-and-lies taste in her mouth and the false hair on her head.

Mrs. Nepper's eyes were blue and guileless. "Awful car accident," she said. "Here's the address. I suppose you've found the town map in the phone book." She stood in her lighted doorway smiling as Sara went down her walk.

Sara had seen the town map, a grid of named streets running north and south, numbered streets running east and west, the grid's corner poked into the looping Cedar River at Main and First Street. She walked away from the

sound of her voice lying—walked down Clay Street to
Eleventh to find Dr. Channing's house.

For a few blocks Sara had a lump in her throat, but the
steady pound of her shoes on concrete said she had to be
solidly at home somewhere. The air smelled of farm fields—
earth still warm from the sun. Sara passed new ranch-style
homes, but one had a lawn swing in the front yard.
Another had a flag over the front door. They shared blocks
with old frame houses that spread their white porches front
and side like setting hens. Sometimes the old ones had a
solar collector beside a Victorian bay window or a row of
motorcycles under a front porch's wooden gingerbread.

Dr. Hazel George Channing's house, high on a slope
above the street, was even older than Sara's and as ugly as
it was interesting. Its great porch ran across its dark green
face and arched over the front door like an upside-down
smile; two holes beside the arch were its eyes. The second
story had another arch above its bay and little side windows wearing witch's-hat roofs.

Sara walked by its lighted windows. Next door children
were catching fireflies in jars; a small boy clapped a lid
tight and stared at Sara as she went by, the insects glowing
through his fingers.

Sara walked home again and was sweaty when she
closed her front door behind her. She took off her wet
clothes and crawled into the shower curtain's small circle.
Cool water ran over her face, into her hot mouth, down
her back. She soaped her hair and said softly to herself,
"Orange kitchen. Gold living room. Yellow bedroom."
When she dried herself she was cool in the breeze from her
open windows. She turned out the lights and rubbed her
hair dry in her dark living room.

Her mother was always in darkness. Now there were no
telephone calls for Chloe Gray on Saturdays—there couldn't
be. If anyone called her mother, Martin would suspect . . .
Sara bit her lip. Her mother lay with her blind eyes turned
to the ceiling, knowing that both her children were dead.

Sara rubbed between her eyes, rubbed tears away. She'd
get money and go to Fredsburg. Her mother would be the

only one to know Sara had come up from the ocean alive—she existed, she was as real as anybody else. . . .

But Martin knew she would go to Fredsburg.

Children played on park swings and slides until dark, their voices as bright as the colors of their sneakers and flying hair. At night couples came.

Sara's eyes were used to the darkness now. Her living room had a soft glow. After a while she got up. A shaft of light came from the professor's house next door. Some piece of furniture blocked part of a lighted window there, and a shade blocked most of the rest.

Sara knelt on her couch, its rough hide scratching her breasts as she leaned against the back. She could rest her head on her arms and see a painting of a bullfight and a shadow moving on a white wall. The bull was glazed with blood and stuck with pics. The bullfighter balanced on muscled legs.

There was a shadow on the wall; it seemed to be a naked man stretching his arms over his head. But he wasn't naked, for as she watched he peeled off a shirt, and then his shorts, and began to dance.

Sara drew back, cupping her breasts in her hands, and didn't look any more, because it was sneaky and she didn't have to do it. She crawled into bed, remembering red hair, long legs—Ben Woodward. She'd never seen a woman going in or out next door.

Then she got out of bed fast and threw on her shirt and slacks, pulled on her sandals. Ben Woodward was dancing in his living room. She knew where he was.

When she tiptoed down her creaking back-porch stairs, the night cheeped and chirred and creaked with insects. Her overgrown backyard stopped at Ben Woodward's mowed grass; she took only a moment to dart across his lawn to the apple tree. Down on her knees in the grass, she stuffed fallen apples into her plastic bag as fast as she could, then hoisted the bag in her arms and ran.

Apples! She dumped then in her kitchen sink. Some were rotten and most of them had been chewed by insects or pecked by birds, but they were good food. She could have an apple for breakfast and applesauce for lunch.

Sara hung her clothes up, then leaned against her closet door in the dark. She had stolen the apples. Stealing. Cheating. Lies.

Someone began to giggle and squeal in the park where lights threw shadows of swing-set poles toward her house— long spider legs. In the web of swing chains one swing dangled back and forth. A man started to push it higher and higher. Someone in a long skirt rushed through dark air, squealing.

Sara stood by her telephone, listening to the giggles from the park. The telephone squatted in her house, day after day, waiting for her to come back from the dead, tell her mother she had not drowned, say, "Martin? It's Sara. . . ."

Soft summer air blew along Sara's skin as she stood in darkness at her screen door. She felt the night breeze lift hair at the back of her neck a little, and shivered, and went to kneel on her couch again.

She couldn't see the bullfighter or the bull. There was no shadow on the wall. The narrow crack into the next house was as dark as an animal's hole, and quiet

# 11

The next Monday morning something yowled and yowled outside Sara's bedroom window. It was a cat. Sara was sure of it after a while.

She ate her breakfast—an apple and a little oatmeal with hot water on it. For lunch she'd have catsup mixed with hot water and salt. Just applesauce for dinner. She didn't have enough food, not even apples; they were about gone and she hadn't stolen any more. Her job began in a week.

The cat yowled. Sara looked at her dirty kitchen walls. They'd have to be washed, too, before she painted; paint wouldn't stick to grease. She sighed.

A cardinal in backyard trees scolded with short, clucking notes. That yowling cat—where was it? She pulled on her wig and went out to see. There it was, stuck in a fork of a maple between her house and the old one next door, a kitten making all that noise, the mouth in its three-cornered face wide open.

"What we need is a ladder," a male voice said behind her. "Mrs. Nepper and I bought one together. We can use my half." Sara turned to see Ben Woodward. He grinned and rubbed gold-red hair on his chest and looked sleepy.

"Hello," Sara said. It was hot already. Her house's shadow, a cool blue, fell across the street to the park. The kitten mewed.

"The name's Ben Woodward," he said, and smelled good when he came close to Sara. "I teach in the drama department of Communication and Theatre Arts at U.N.I. Welcome to the neighborhood.''

"Thanks. I'm Laura Pray," she said, and followed him to his backyard in the corridor of his perfume. There was an extension ladder tied to the ground with a grape vine; they yanked together until they broke it loose.

"This is *not* the best of all possible worlds," Ben said, swinging the ladder against the maple. "If the Lord had meant for kittens to climb, He'd have put their heads on the other end."

The kitten was small and white, with brown spots here and there. "It looks like a bruised banana," Sara said. She had slacks and a long-sleeved shirt on, hot as it was. Ben wore shorts, and he was hairy all over, and curly, like Joe. Ben got the kitten in one big hand, but couldn't unhook it, and the kitten's high-pitched mews were as monotonous as a squeaking door. "It's put down roots," he said. "Thinks it's ivy."

Sara climbed behind Ben on the ladder and tried to loosen a dozen claws. No sooner did one set let go than three others sank in against gravity. She didn't want to pull them out of the small paws. The kitten yowled. Sara was plastered against Ben's hot back as she tried to help, and morning mosquitoes had found them and were humming along.

"All right!" Ben said as Sara pried the hind feet away and held them while he got the front ones loose. He gave the small, distressed ball to Sara and put the ladder back while she stroked the kitten and murmured to it.

"I'll tell you what—we'll take that cat to my place, and I'll report it missing tomorrow," Ben said. "Talk to the kids in the park. Probably belongs around here somewhere."

"I wonder if you can take it . . ." Sara began, but Ben was leading the way next door, and the kitten had hooked itself to Sara's damp shirtfront. By the time Ben opened his door Sara had worked two paws out of the cloth without snagging it.

Ben grabbed some dirty cups and a pile of clothes from an upholstered chair and said, "Sit down, won't you?"

Sara sat down beneath a bust of Shakespeare, grateful for Ben's air-conditioning, and worked the last two sets of kitten claws loose. Then she looked around her. A worn couch, chairs, and the Shakespeare bust tried to fill an old living room like hers. It smelled interesting, like hers—a mix of dust and old wood. But there was a bacon smell, too, that made her mouth water. She could see part of her house through a small window, a strange view of a familiar screened porch, mailbox, bridal wreath bush. She sighed, smelling the bacon; she was light-headed with not enough to eat.

Ben came through his dining room, where there was a dark oak table and chairs. He was grinning. "You thought of a good name for that cat—Banana." He had two streaks across his clean white shorts from the dirty ladder. "Would you like some coffee?"

"Yes, I would," Sara said, and put the kitten down on a thin rug that had some fringe left on it. The kitten toddled toward Ben when he came back in. Maybe he'd bring something to eat with the coffee.

"Guess kittens are like children," Ben said, watching Banana sniff his sandal and handing Sara a gold-rimmed mug. He sat down and didn't look as if he'd bring anything else and hunched his shoulders, turning his head this way and that. "Develop from the brain down, looks like—feet last and back feet last of all."

The coffee was hot and good and would go right to her head, thanks to her almost empty stomach. She hadn't had any coffee for days. "It's so wonderfully cool in here," she said. Shakespeare watched them with his almond-shaped eyes.

"You're a librarian?" Ben asked.

Sara swallowed her coffee wrong and coughed and had time to think. "What makes you say that?"

"Saw you come out of the downtown library last Saturday," Ben said.

"I like to read," Sara said, and shivered. Her shirt was sticking to her back, and she could smell bacon and maybe eggs. She emptied her cup fast and said, "Thanks for the coffee," and got up. "I hope you find whose kitten Banana is." Now she could see a corner of his kitchen—old cupboards like hers, a microwave. "I've been washing ceilings and walls for days. I'd better get back to work."

"I'll tell you what—let's have dinner together tonight," Ben said, leaping up. Banana swiped at his bare toes and missed. "Maybe at six? Seven? Go someplace cool and nice?"

"I'm sorry," Sara said. "I'm better off alone."

"Show you the whole Strayer-Wood Theatre afterward," Ben said. "Catwalks to the greenroom."

Sara hugged herself with her cold arms and shook her head and smiled and wanted to run from his closeness, his hairy, muscled legs.

"Being alone all day is fine for a while," Ben said. "But you start going shopping so you can talk to the checkout clerk."

Sara turned toward the door, away from his smile, his deep voice saying ordinary words, expected words.

"Maybe you're a Martian librarian? FBI? Don't want to be seen with a redheaded gent?"

Sara had opened his door to a street in morning-blue shadows. She turned around and looked at him, rubbing her forehead with the heel of her hand as if trying to knead the right answer out of her eyebrows.

"Tell you what," Ben said. "If you don't mind frozen dinners right out of the microwave, how about dinner at eight, my place, come as you are?"

Sara hesitated, glancing around Ben's living room at nothing more threatening than battered oak woodwork, lumpy window seats, chintz pillows without their shine.

"You've noticed that there's a line of lilacs from your back door to my place along the fence?" Ben's hair curled with the heat and hung over his eyes. "Secret route."

Still she said nothing, but Ben thought he saw her lips curve upward a little.

"Not a fancy dinner, I admit," Ben said. "Just lasagna and a salad. But I've got some fresh rolls and a cake."

He saw her swallow and press her lips hard together. "Yes," she said.

"Yes, you'll come?"

"Yes." She took a last look at him, her eyes moving over his glistening red curls, his face. "I'll come the back way," she said. "Through the lilacs." Now she almost smiled for the first time and was gone, shutting the door behind her.

The first woman in his house. But only for one dinner, just a microwave dinner. His old apartment had been full of Deborah's ghosts: Deborah cooking in the kitchen, Deborah letting him kiss her—but they were just friends, she said. She was trying to be honest, she said. She didn't want to get married, she was going on to graduate work. She didn't want to be seen with a faculty member, even a lowly instructor. She didn't want to sleep with him or marry him—

Ben hit a doorframe with his fist, but after a while he smiled to himself. He thought he might dance a little. With the first leap he almost stepped on Banana, but he missed the kitten with a sidewise jump and went to open a can of tuna fish, a whole can of tuna fish, the kitten at his heels.

He watched Banana eat, thinking that Laura was hiding something. She was wearing a wig; nobody could fool him with wigs. For a minute he'd thought she was scared—of what? Her full, small lips were almost as expressive as her eyes, and her skin was only a little tan; blue veins showed under it here and there. What was her real hair like— maybe light brown? Blond? She had dark mascara on, but he'd seen the light roots of her lashes. She was so thin.

Maybe she had a past . . . maybe she was being hunted by the Mafia. He didn't care. He wasn't going to get involved. She looked hungry. She looked tired.

She was coming. He did a Greek dance around his dining-room table. That was the shadow Sara saw when she let herself into her house, knelt on her couch, and looked through the crack left by his half-drawn shade and bookcase.

She was hungry. She was running out of beans and apples and oatmeal, with a whole week left and no money.

She'd said yes to dinner with him because she smelled the bacon he'd had for breakfast and imagined it bubbling in its bright grease and turning slowly from white to golden brown, its edges crinkling, the brown streaks ready to crackle in her mouth. . . . Sara's eyes filled with tears. When she blinked his shadow leapt on the wall.

# 12

Every day Martin worked at Rambaugh Computer Sales and Service. Every night he sat in his little Cape Cod house. He left Sara's clothes in closets and drawers. He read her diaries, starting before Sara met him, when she got a scholarship from Boston U. and came from Nebraska. She was dating somebody named Chris Petersen, who was a graduate student at Boston U., and somebody named Russ.

"I want to put down things I wonder about and things I want to change in myself," Sara wrote. Martin made himself follow the months, day after day, and didn't skip to the years after she met him.

Sara read so much! She copied long paragraphs from books he'd never heard of, and argued with the authors, and made lists of characters and "issues" and "themes" and "literary periods."

She wrote about memories of her brother Joe. "I wonder if the reason that neither of us wanted to get married was because Mom and Dad were so unhappy. Joe blamed Mom. Joe didn't make sense—he wanted me to be strong, but he blamed Mom because she was. *She was*. She had to raise us and train us and punish us all those years. We hardly knew Dad. We hardly ever saw him."

Each year she studied some new subject for herself. One year it was geography. Another year it was literature by black authors. You'd think she'd have had enough studying at school.

Joe had drowned when he was only sixteen. Sara never told how it happened. She wrote about her folks moving back to Fredsburg, Nebraska, and staying there when her dad retired, and how she'd come to Boston U. to be independent and get good library science training.

Martin wandered around the house at night, jabbing his heels into carpeting they'd bought cheap; it was already wearing out. He drank port or sherry from the bottle and looked from his windows at lighted homes—husbands and wives and children. He stared at himself in a hall mirror. He'd knocked Sara against the mirror, and when he got the glass replaced it didn't have a beveled edge and etched flowers any more. Sara missed the old mirror glass because she'd played games with her brother in rainbows the mirror made when sun hit it. She missed Joe, her diary said. He waited for her to write about how Joe drowned. She never did.

Sometimes he looked at all her dead violets on light tables. He didn't know what to do with them; they shriveled day by day and turned brown and wadded up. Sara wrote about wanting a husband and children and whether she could raise children so they wouldn't hate her. She got a part-time job to pay her tuition at B.U.

"I want to be honest and strong and kind." Such a pretty blonde with that face and body—who'd imagine she ever worried about lying or cheating? She'd written two papers on the same subject for different classes at the university and worried about it—it didn't seem honest to do just half the work, she said.

Sometimes she had to fib to get out of dates with Chris or Russ or a new man, Fred Trillin. She wrote how awful she felt, lying.

Martin skipped most of the book stuff—pages and pages of quotes from people named Cleaver and Malcolm X and Proust and Buber. He got to the day when she went to church and met Martin Burney. He was a man she felt she could talk to, Sara wrote. She thought he was kind and thoughtful: he called her when he'd be late and seemed to like his mother and father. He had a steady job, and was ambitious, and made her heart beat fast just by helping her with her coat or touching her hand. "Physical attraction is important," she wrote. "It holds marriages together."

She dreamed about being married to him. She'd cook the food he especially liked and make him so comfortable—clean clothes and a clean house. She'd try to be a good wife and make him happy and wouldn't do anything in the world to hurt him. She wrote "Sara Burney" and "Sara Gray Burney" on a back page of her diary to see how the names looked.

Martin snapped on the television and stared at late-night programs for a while. The ads had pretty women talking about soap and cleaning their kitchen floors and waxing tables. That was all he'd ever wanted—a wife to be there when he got home, like his mother. Look at all the women doing it on television.

"I wonder why men and women are always expected to be so different in the way they look and act," Sara's diary read. "What good does it do?"

All the original thoughts she'd had.

Maybe she was drifting somewhere, rotting in a black silk teddy that had showed all the bruises—

Martin grabbed one of her shriveled brown plants in each hand and whacked the pot on the toilet seat and flushed dead things down until the toilet stopped up, and then he sat on the seat and cried. They hadn't even had a baby so he could have a part of her still alive. She'd always wanted one.

He read all night. She'd loved him. He could see that. He sat and sobbed when he got to wonderful days before they got married, and then through the beach-house honeymoon. She had written "Joy" across some of those days. Just "Joy."

# 13

Sara took a shower, washed and dried her hair, and stood before her speckled bedroom mirror. A date with a man, after all these years. When she was touching wineglasses with Martin in some restaurant before they were even engaged, he'd said, "If you were my wife and left me, I'd kill you, and the man too."

"Martin's so romantic," she had told the roommate who ate popcorn for breakfast.

She walked around her house. The bedroom walls were cracked, but they were clean now. She'd been in Cedar Falls not quite six days, and she was more than half done washing walls and woodwork, happy to be working, happy in her rooms of solitude. When she had some money she'd buy Spackle, a putty knife, and brushes, and Mrs. Nepper would pay for the paint.

Sara had cut her violet leaf stems with the razor blade, then stuck the stems in soil mixed with vermiculite. She smiled to see them marching along her kitchen windowsill like hairy green ears all listening one way.

Sara yearned suddenly for Karen Fairchild's soft Southern voice. Karen was a national African violet judge and taught Sara how to slice the bottom inch of roots from a violet that had a "neck" and was lanky. "Sink it to the bottom of the pot and put new dirt around its bare neck. Some plants are a hundred years old, honey," she said. "They're just the bloomin' tops of somethin' that could be high as a house, maybe, by now."

Sara remembered burying her head beneath dusty couch cushions at the beach house, listening to Joan's voice on the phone. Today . . . just about now . . . Cristine and Karen and Joan and Marie were meeting at Cristine's house. Sara stared at the violet leaves on the sill. *They think I'm dead. They're crying together and talking about how I drowned eight days ago.*

Tears came to her eyes. The violet leaves seemed to be listening with her to the echo of all that had happened in eight days. She was a long way from her life, too, and had to put new roots down.

Sara swallowed hard, blinked tears back, and tried to think of something pleasant: food. She hadn't had anything that day except oatmeal with water on it, and an apple. But when she reminded herself she was going to Ben Woodward's, she felt ashamed.

Sighing, she put on her slacks and a clean long-sleeved shirt and sandals. A real dinner. Her mouth watered for browned and steaming meat to chew . . . the crunch of vegetables . . . butter melting on hot bread. She had learned to walk early or late enough to miss coffee and food smells wafting from open kitchen windows.

When she stopped thinking of a glass of wine sparkling with light and bubbles, or chicken in brown juice puddled with gold fat, she found she was beginning to put on lipstick. She gave a low cry and ran to wash her face clean and put on no makeup but dark mascara and dark eyebrows to match her wig.

Sara eased her kitchen door open. It was almost dark. She pushed through the lilac path toward food and found she came out at Ben's back door. No one could see her knock there.

"Come on in," Ben said, holding his kitchen door open. Sara went through the kitchen fast, trying not to look at a bowl of salad, a plate of rolls.

The house was cool. Sara's damp skin began to dry and her hunger was sharper. There was wine on the living-room window seat, and some potato chips. Ben held the tray out to Sara. She bit her lip and took a wineglass and a few chips as if her mouth weren't watering almost too much to talk.

Cool air and white wine, frothy with bubbles . . . the crunch of potato chips against her tongue . . . Sara sighed. Ben Woodward lived here and wasn't afraid and thought she was crazy. For a moment she felt safe with him—a stupid feeling for someone carrying danger with her like a secret disease. He had dressed up for dinner: cream-colored slacks and shirt.

She wouldn't come here again. Ben was watching her, never thinking that she could be dangerous. Martin kept his guns in a gun rack in their den. The .25 pistol gleamed in her memory, its grips decorated with eagles in bas-relief, their claws spread, sharp. Martin held it against her temple. The hammer click echoed through her skull. *I'll kill you, and the man too.*

"Hope you like fresh tomatoes," Ben said. Sara said yes, she certainly did, and he sat down beside her on the lumpy couch with his glass of wine. He was tall and broad-shouldered and looked a little like Joe would have looked, perhaps. She could have hidden with Joe. She wouldn't have wanted to move away from Joe to the other end of a couch.

"Banana prowls the house," Ben said. "Knows it better than I do already." Banana rubbed against Sara's foot, purring.

Sara felt thin as empty china. She was eating all the potato chips while Ben talked about growing up near Chicago. His father was a deliveryman, he said, and he was the only one of five children who'd gone to college, let alone had a Ph.D. Some of his relatives thought he was pretty dumb to have to go to school so long.

Sara sipped her wine and imagined Mrs. Nepper saying to a stranger in town who asked about Laura Pray—a stranger who was Martin Burney—"She had dinner with Professor Woodward. Such a nice young man—lives right next door."

"I got scholarships and worked summers in construction, and made it through my Ph.D in less than three years,'' Ben said, pouring more wine for them. He'd been lucky to fall into this position at the university, he said, and find a house he could afford to buy near the campus, on the park. He'd never been married, never found just the right woman. Not much of a housekeeper. Sara drank her wine, stroking Banana's spotted fur, and waited for him to start asking her questions, polite, ordinary questions that she couldn't answer.

Ben asked nothing at all, not even when they were sitting at his old oak dining-room table. The lasagna was hot and gilded with melted cheese. Ben's tossed salad had Iowa summer tomatoes in it, thick crimson chunks drizzled with French dressing. Every hot roll crunched brown and crusty at the edges. Red wine sent lazy bubbles up the sides of Sara's glass.

Sara tried not to eat too fast or too much, polite as a stray cat that explores a house hesitantly, delicately, as if it does not need a home and may not come again.

By the time her plate was empty, Sara could begin to think, begin to talk about books and plays. By the time she helped Ben carry dishes to his kitchen, she had shifted them from the small, ordinary furnished rooms of sport talk, news talk, or weather talk. Now they were in outer landscapes where they met now and then in a clump of ideas, surprised, or found themselves taking the same narrow road, side by side.

Sara scraped dishes at an old sink like hers. The drainboard needed bleaching. Ben was talking about Dickens: ''Just a little? Don't you think so? That's what makes him great theater.'' He brought a chocolate cake from a cupboard. Sara tried not to look greedily at his knife cutting through swirled, dappled frosting.

*''Nicholas Nickelby?''* Sara said. All evening Ben had left her free, asked no questions; she felt that as keenly as she'd felt her hunger. ''When all's said and done, Dickens lets you think there might be a happy ending for you, too, if you live virtuously and wait in hope.''

The knife cut through moist layers, leaving a light brown fringe of frosting at each level. The tops of Ben's hands were bright with red-gold hairs. "And life's not like that," Ben said.

"No," Sara said, seeing those hands as fists, feeling Ben look down at her, the smaller one. Coffee glittered golden-brown into white cups, and its rich steam hung above it.

They brought coffee and cake to the dining-room table and sat down. "Fellini writes about what he wants to do with his films," Sara said, waiting for Ben to take up his fork. "He says he never wants to make a film with a happy ending, because then people will go home and never change their lives. On a subconscious level, happy endings fool us. We think our lives will turn out nicely without our help, like the movie."

Ben had seen most of Fellini's films. So had she. They argued about Zampano buying Gelsomina from her mother—the Beast buying Beauty—and about the sex goddess in *La Dolce Vita*.

Sara was full now, and a little dreamy with wine. She roamed Ben's house with him, listening to what he was going to do when he had more money. There were three bedrooms upstairs, and a little room off the living room downstairs that had been a sun room but was his study now, except when it got too cold in winter. She looked at his house hesitantly and walked softly in her one pair of shoes, hearing Ben Woodward not asking for anything he thought she didn't want to give.

She settled on a living-room chair, the sleeping kitten in her lap, but in her mind she walked from one end of Ben's reticence to the other; she examined it, tried its length. She stroked the kitten. "If nobody claims Banana, I wonder if I could have her—him? If Banana doesn't belong anywhere?"

"Sure," Ben said. "I tell you what—I'll find out if it's one of the Granger kittens. They give them away, glad to."

"In a day or two you might know," Sara said. "Can you keep it till then?" She couldn't feed a cat; she didn't want to lie. "I'm going to have wet paint in almost every room. No place for a kitten."

"Just tell me when the paint's dry. I've got cans of tuna fish, and that's what it seems to like."

"I've got a job starting a week from today," Sara said. "Mrs. Nepper found the job for me, taking care of a Dr. Channing on Clay Street. She was in a terrible automobile accident."

"Hazel George Channing," Ben said. "Taught English forty years at the university, Henry James scholar. We used to argue about why he was so wordy. She fought for every one of those words. For Henry James."

"That's more than most people did when he was alive, I guess," Sara said. "I'd better go home now if you won't even let me wash dishes to pay you back."

"Pay me back by coming to dinner again. Sunday night? Same time, same station, will Laura Pray solve the mystery of why Ben Woodward's dinners always taste like cardboard?"

"All right," she said, because that next Monday she would start work, with only oatmeal to eat, if she had any left by then. "And I wonder . . . do you have any use for the apples under your tree?"

"Them?" Ben laughed. "Anybody who wants them can have them—they're nothing but a nuisance. Help yourself anytime. Pick them, don't pick them up. The best ones are on the tree yet."

"I like applesauce," Sara said. "I'll bring you some."

"Great." Ben leaned against his kitchen door and hunched his shoulders, turning his head back and forth to look at his dim kitchen as if pleased that they were in it together. When she wished him good-night he smiled as though they had plenty of time, and he was happy and satisfied with whatever she had brought and whatever she would bring again.

So Sara stood closer to him in the doorway and smiled at him in the almost-dark. He didn't try to touch her, but she didn't step away, and when she went through rustling lilacs she was smiling. He was smiling, too, when he closed his kitchen door and stood alone where candles still burned.

# 14

When Sara's drowned body hadn't been found after more than a week, Martin's parents called and said perhaps he ought to have a memorial service for Sara. Would he like them to come and help? Should the service be in Montrose where his friends were?

He said he supposed so. After the call he wandered around the house and looked at the red kitchen. That kitchen had cost him plenty, and so had their pine furniture.

He looked at the diary in his hand; he'd been reading it for hours: "I wonder why Martin has such a passion about window shades. I must keep them pulled down one foot from the top. He's very neat. I found that out at the beach house. He hasn't slapped me again. I try to forget it ever happened."

Now the shades were always pulled down a foot from the top. He had to get his own dinners when he'd been working all day, and it made him mad at Sara—dead Sara. On Saturdays he shopped, and put canned food in neat rows in the cupboard, only one can high, all labels to the front. Now his car was always in the garage, and both sets of keys were in a dish on his desk where he wanted them.

"I will try to be as neat as Martin wants, but I wonder why *things* are more important to him than me. He slaps *me* because *objects* aren't arranged right."

She wrote about her father's death, and taking care of her mother when she had the stroke and was blind and couldn't walk. Martin didn't want her to bring her mother to Massachusetts, and Sara wrote that she understood, but she'd never showed him how bad she felt, leaving her mother alone.

"Today I forgot to sweep the garage, and Martin kicked me after he came from work and drank wine."

She wrote about their kitchen. She hadn't wanted a red one. He'd forgotten that.

She wrote about how ashamed she was: "It's like hanging on with just the tips of your fingers, trying not to fall. I can feel one finger slip off, and then another. Last Monday I needed new panty hose, but Martin always makes me ask him for money. Supermarkets sell them, so I just put some in my cart and ran them through with the groceries, and Martin didn't notice, but *I* noticed.

"I've started to lie. He didn't hit me when I forgot the magazine he wanted. I told him the drugstore didn't have any more copies. Just to keep from being hurt, I lied!"

She wrote about the time he stamped on her foot and broke her toe, and how she didn't think it was hate. He was just worried about his work.

"I lied again. I made love to Martin when I didn't want to—I did it because I was afraid. He couldn't tell. He saw bruises on my breast and thigh, not the bruises in my heart.

"I'm too ashamed to tell anyone. I wonder why. Because I lie and cheat and steal? Because he hurts me? Should I be ashamed of these things?

"I lied to Martin. I said the Montrose library called me because they needed someone part-time. Martin wouldn't have liked it if he'd known I looked for a job. And before I told him I got him a special dinner, and made love to him, too, just the way he likes it, and then I mentioned it. I've got the job! Maybe I can stop being dishonest and a prostitute."

He'd beaten her up. Drunk wine by the bottle, then gone at her. She put it all down. "I'm trying to be honest. It isn't really me he hates," she wrote. "It's something he thinks I am—I'm different from him. He really believes that.'' Sometimes she was hurt and stiff for weeks. "Martin looks ashamed when he sees me walking so slowly.''

A little black book with five years in it, and her small, neat writing going through each day, trying to understand what was happening. "I never felt different from Joe. But I knew boys didn't like girls, right from the beginning. No. It was something more than that. They didn't ever want to be like a girl—but I wanted to be like Joe.''

And then she was really afraid. He didn't recognize himself, but he was all through that little book—bits of him, like his face reflected in their hall mirror after he smashed it again. He did it one night because he was crying, all alone . . . no Sara in his lonely house. After he'd smashed it he stood and scowled at his bloody knuckles.

"I wonder if maybe it's my fault,'' she wrote. "But I don't see why, unless I'm weaker than he is, and that makes it easier for him to hit me. What would he do if we had a baby?''

Then she ran away the first time, and went to see her mother in Nebraska, limping because he'd broken her toe, and he went after her on the weekend, dragged her back to the beach house on Sand Hook, and knocked her down the stairs.

"I should have acted like another man from the very beginning,'' she wrote when she could write again. Her writing was a scrawl now because her wrist was in a cast. "The minute you act like a woman you're not like them, and they can hit you because you're different. If you sleep with them, you're the Lay, Cunt, Slut. If you won't, you're the Ball-breaker, the Bitch. No such names for men.''

She wrote about how he knocked her down the beach stairs—ruptured her spleen and broke her wrist so it would always be ten degrees crooked. She'd gone to the battered-woman shelter, but she didn't want to lose her library job; she came back home. And then the police wouldn't help her any more because they were busy, and the courts were busy, and she'd gone back to him. He made himself read her cramped and painful writing. He had broken her wrist.

He read it all. "I wonder if Martin is the one I should hate, or is there something out there making him do it, making me get hurt?"

He read it all to the last day before she drowned, then put the little black books in her desk again, but they made him madder and madder, just thinking about them. He yelled in the silent house, "It wasn't *fun* to organize things around here! You want to live in a mess? And what kind of a woman just pretends she's happy in bed? You sneak— you liar—marriage promises and then you leave me, want a divorce—like hell! You don't leave me! Should have broken your neck—" And then he remembered she was dead.

His parents came and planned a memorial service at the Melrose church, and friends stood around afterward and patted Martin on the back when he cried. Some of their best friends—Cristine and Roger Weidin and the Fairchilds and Joan and Jim Pagent and Sam and Marie O'Brien— didn't say much. Some of the women wouldn't look at him. He noticed that. He was glad when it was over.

His parents came home with him after the service and stayed overnight. His father, a prim little dried-up stick, sat down before dinner and watched football heroes on television. He'd gone to every high school game when he was a high school principal and yelled and cheered and lost his voice and gotten colds.

Martin's mother was cleaning the house and starting dinner. She came to the living-room door and looked at Martin's father until he had to look at her. "Why don't you spend a little time with Martin?" she said when the announcer stopped talking for a minute. Her voice was soft and gentle, just like Sara's had been when she didn't know whether Martin was going to hit her or not. The soft voice was part of her lying and cheating, Sara wrote in her diary.

Martin's father didn't answer for a while. Then he said, "Don't be silly, Martha. Can't you see we're watching the final play?"

"I just thought—"

"Well, Martha, don't," his father said. "Don't start trying to think this late in life."

"Martin would appreciate a little talk—"

"The hell I would!" Martin yelled. His father turned off the television set when he heard Martin swear and looked at Martin with his pursed-up little mouth. "Go on—say it!" Martin shouted at him. "Tell Mother how stupid she is—you've done it for years!"

His father said, "Martin—"

"You were the boss!" Martin yelled. "You could come home and do anything you wanted! Isn't that right, Mom? *We* were the ones who had to lie and cheat and steal so I could have a Boy Scout uniform—remember? Or that one new bike? Didn't we have the secrets, huh, Mom? And that's still going on all over town, all the time! Hell!"

His father pursed his mouth and said nothing; he was tuning Martin out the way he'd tuned out hippie high school students in the sixties. Martin could tell. His father's face puckered like an old balloon. He didn't look at either Martin or Martha.

"He's upset," his mother said to his father. "Of course he's upset." She was watching Martin, a look on her face he hadn't seen before.

"I do not approve of swear—" his father began.

"What if you and I had to live like Mom does!" Martin yelled at his father. "I'd rather be dead!"

Martin went into the kitchen, jabbing his heels in scarred linoleum. His mother had been mopping the floor. He stepped over puddles and sat at the table and sobbed, thinking of that—that he'd rather be dead than live like his mother did.

# 15

"Nice," Ben's brother Rod said. He had parked his semi near Ben's house Saturday on his way to Texas. "Nice. Maybe a little thin." He was squinting through Sunday morning sunshine at Sara in her backyard. "Right next door too."

"I'll tell you what—she's hard to know," Ben said, opening two more beers. "Laura Pray. She came to dinner Monday night, and she's coming again tonight, but she won't go out in public except by herself. Says she's better off that way."

"Better off?" Rod said.

Ben didn't want to talk about her. Rod was like the rest of his family—hard-boiled with working for the paycheck. Fun was what you did when you were through work. None of them could understand somebody who had fun working at a university, for God's sake, even if he did make a decent salary.

Rod was talking about his kids, and Laura Pray was calling the kitten. Ben listened to her voice. That first night he'd known she didn't want to talk about herself, so he said U.N.I. might put on a Christopher Fry play in the spring.

"Christopher Fry," Laura said. "He translated *The Trojan War Will Not Take Place*. I've read his *Can You Find Me?*"

"So have I," Ben said, looking at her, and after a while she looked away. He turned on the radio, and a Bach fugue surrounded them.

" 'Music would unground us best, as a tide in the dark comes to boats at anchor, and they begin to dance,' " she said. "From Fry's *The Dark Is Light Enough.*"

And he thought of that in his house, watching her come down her overgrown garden walk, wishing he could hear her talk like that again, the way he loved to talk. Music. A beautiful woman in his house —no curves, all bones, but beautiful.

Nobody knew what women were thinking; they were mysteries from another world. Deborah's fair, long, clinging hair she'd let him brush and comb and braid . . . above her shoulders and breasts that someday . . .

Deborah's old apartment house had its rows of student names on mailboxes yet, and porch paint was still peeling above baby strollers and an old mattress. He passed the house nearly every day. He knew she was married and gone, sleeping with some guy the way she wouldn't sleep with him, that pale, slippery hair beneath somebody, somebody's mouth on those breasts.

Rod was talking about their father's rheumatism. Ben felt the way you do when you ring a doorbell and nobody answers, but you know somebody's there and you can't do anything but look at the blank door. Laura Pray was a blank door. She didn't want him to ask her any questions . . . but why? He heard Laura climb her back steps and disappear.

It made him mad, as if she were only teasing him, as if she could tell him where she came from. Was she married? Why was she doing housework in Cedar Falls, Iowa, educated as she obviously was? She didn't want to tell him.

What did she think she was doing? Playing hard to get?

"Have a nice evening," Rod said, and grinned.

"She's hard to know," Ben said, and walked up and down his kitchen while Rod talked, and looked at Sara's curtains moving a little in the breeze.

Sara lay down on her bed; her wrist ached. All week she had washed walls and woodwork and thought about food. Her lonely rooms seemed to echo; she longed for her sewing machine and her ironing board. She longed for a hamburger and french fries.

There were old, favorite books on her bookshelves in Montrose . . . she turned their pages in her dreams. She smelled fried chicken.

Sometimes she saw a parade of her friends' faces and heard their voices. They thought she was dead. She'd never see them again. She had never told them how she loved them.

She missed her big frying pan; she didn't know why. What would she put in it? She thought of her mother's dried-up, bony hands that had planted so many seeds in so many gardens and dragged pails of water to make them sprout and keep them alive. Her mother was uprooted from all she remembered, and so was Sara. Sara woke with the smell of frying pork in her memory and the rich milk taste of pork-chop gravy or corn on the cob, steaming.

But when she wasn't washing walls and woodwork, she forgot what she had lost, or what she yearned to eat, because books were free. She carried home as many as she could from the city library. When she dumped them on her battered living-room table, she knew what they could do. She opened one and crawled out of its dream hours later. As she sat blinking at her lumpy couch and chairs and a rug with a hole in it, she felt like a dream in a dream. The world she believed was the world in the book.

One evening Sara found she was reading in the very last of the light. She turned on a lamp, still holding her book; the people in it seemed more solid than she was. She went to look at herself in the hall mirror. "You don't exist, even in a book," she said to herself. "You're dead."

Sara hardly noticed the monotony of oatmeal, beans, apples, beans, oatmeal, apples when she read. Hours and hours to read—her days were as wide and long and deep as a child's. She had forgotten what joy that was.

On Sunday Sara had an apple and the last of her beans for breakfast. She kept what oatmeal she had left; she'd eat it before she went to her job the next afternoon. She mixed hot water and catsup to make soup and had applesauce with it for lunch. Her refrigerator was bare and clean and white inside, except for some apples.

She heard Ben and another man walk down his front sidewalk, talking while wild music blatted from an upstairs window of the old red house next door. Ben was carrying the kitten. They strolled through park trees to a semi parked on Seerley Boulevard.

Sara watched through her net curtains as the truck pulled away and Ben walked back. He strode along, sunlight catching browns and reds in his curly hair and the silvery white of the kitten he carried. She knew what his hands looked like—big hands with long fingers and freckles among gold hairs on the back. Wrinkles were beginning at the corners of his eyes. He hunched his shoulders, then turned his head back and forth, as if uncertain what to do next.

Sara walked from room to room. She'd have to patch with Spackle twice and sand, then roll on a coat of primer, and then a coat of color.

Woodwork in every room was chipped and full of nail holes. She'd have to fill holes with wood putty and then sand it. But her kitchen would be soft orange, and her living room and front hall would be gold, and her bedroom light yellow. Sunlight would seem to shine everywhere. She was the only one who'd still see shadows of patched places under paint; she'd know where they had been.

Sara ran her finger over cracks in her bedroom wall. Ben had a refrigerator full of food and all those dinners in a freezer. . . . Stop that, she said to herself. She watched Ben talk to children on a jungle gym, squatting down to show the cat to two small girls who had jumped off swings. She saw him throw his head back and laugh.

Pretend you're dieting, she said to herself. Go to bed and forget it and save your energy. She went to bed and thought about Martin eating in their red kitchen, or taking some woman out for dinner, perhaps, or visiting his parents. "Don't be silly," she said out loud to her dim bedroom. She'd only been drowned two weeks; he couldn't find another woman that quick.

Another woman in the Montrose house. It had been a mess when they moved in, but she could patch walls and sand and paint, and make curtains from sheets, and refinish secondhand furniture; she'd done it with Joe and her mother, over and over. But a red kitchen! Martin had said it had to be tomato-red.

Her new refrigerator was far away in Montrose, and her stove. Every pot and pan and favorite spoon, and even her glass nut chopper and plastic butter dish—she saw them as if they were deserters gone over to the enemy. There were two new pairs of blue top sheets in the Montrose linen closet, and flowered fitted ones to match, and pillowcases too. She'd found them on sale. She'd made curtains for every window and slipcovered their couch, and none of it was hers any more.

She prowled the small Cape Cod house in her mind. Bedroom windows had needed washing when she left; nobody would think she'd left that house suspiciously neat and clean. And there had to be nothing missing except her.

She was almost asleep when she dreamed of a YWCA pool freezing her with fear—blue ice. Fat women and thin women clustered around her with soft, soothing voices while she moaned and hung on to any warm hand or arm, her eyes shut, trembling. They wouldn't know she'd drowned, and she was glad. They didn't know her real name.

She had no real name now. Floating out of sleep, she knew she was drifting outside ordinary places where people answered to their names and didn't lie.

Sara lay in her dim bedroom without any books to read; she'd finished all she had brought from the library. And she was hungry.

Apples . . . Sara could hardly bear the thought of them. She paced her house, tears in her eyes. At last she grabbed an apple, cut it in slices, and went out to the afternoon sunshine of her backyard.

She sat down in a weed patch, her elbows on her knees, and kept her eyes on the small, mysterious world of the ground. In the shade and sun of grass blade forests, small living things had their metropolis.

Afternoon simmered around her with insect voices. The sun was hot on her shoulders and wig. Slowly she relaxed, feeling nothing but sun and breeze, seeing nothing but the small world of pebbles, sand grains, and dead leaves.

She broke slices of apple in tiny pieces and played the game she'd loved as a little girl: feeding the ants. Bent double in the hot sun, she was a great god dropping manna from heaven with no more reason and logic than any human could ever discover.

The ants stopped in their tracks before such food from paradise, showing their astonishment with agitated feelers at first. Then, human as people, they put such amazing gifts to practical use—they picked up the food and headed for home. If they met other ants at the corner or down the block, the word went out in Formic, and the newcomers came looking for manna too.

Sun-warm and drowsy, Sara was half asleep in the sun as she watched a line of ants waving bits of her apple in the air. When she got up at last and went in, she fell asleep at once in her bed, with no dreams.

Cicadas strummed in high summer trees. Leaves brushed against her roof. A siren howled down Main Street. Sara woke just in time to shower and put on the same shirt and slacks again. She didn't have an iron or ironing board. She washed her clothes in shampoo, and they dripped dry overnight without too many wrinkles. Her bruises still showed a little. But when she went through the lilac tunnel with some applesauce in a bowl, Ben was wearing the same cream-colored shirt and pants too.

Ben said he liked applesauce, and thanks, and stood back to let Sara go into his living room. Banana was asleep, all four paws in the air, on the swaybacked couch in candlelight. Sara sat down, weak with lovely cooking smells. There was wine again, and crackers and cheese and olives. Banana woke up beside Sara on the couch and batted at food Sara hoped she wasn't stuffing into her mouth.

"You said you'd read Maeterlinck," Ben said.

Wine warmed Sara; cheese played against red wine in

her mouth, sour and subtle. "Only in a collection," she said. " 'The Tragic in Daily Life.' " Ben didn't turn music on the minute they were together, and Sara liked that. "I'm glad you don't play music all the time," she told him.

"I'll tell you what—I've lived in cities." Ben narrowed his eyes when he was thinking. They were gray-blue and fringed with blond lashes that glistened, framing them in light. "In cities you want to drown out machines and motors, night and day." He smiled. "But here you've got crickets. Owls. Cat fights at night. Your back-porch door—I ought to oil that."

"I wonder if I can help you with dinner tonight," Sara said, putting Banana on the rug and getting up. "I feel lazy and no-good, and I like to cook."

"I don't," Ben said. "For myself, I mean."

"But it's nice for two to work together on something they can sit down afterward and eat."

"Well, then, there's salad to cut up," Ben said at his kitchen counter. "You take lettuce and I'll take tomatoes."

They chopped for a while in silence at both ends of a kitchen table covered with tacked-down plastic. Sara knew she'd been saying what she thought, not putting on a woman act. No one would hit her or yell. She had hardly any makeup on, and she wasn't being coy or twitchy or different. She was cutting up lettuce. "I like the sound cars make going by in the rain," she said.

"Or in snow, when it's very cold and crunches," Ben said. She was as cool as the lettuce she was cutting up—so touch-me-not.

"Ugh," Sara said. "I've been too *cold* in the snow."

"Smells of a summer shower?" Ben dumped sliced tomatoes in a wooden bowl. "A train going through town?"

Sara took a deep breath, relaxing, and smiled. "Imagine when there were no cars to hear, only horse hooves or wagon wheels or feet."

"You'd go to the window and look, because there couldn't have been so many people passing," Ben said, mad inside—she wanted to play a game. He didn't even know what her real hair looked like, but he knew wigs. Did she think she could fool him?

"Folks sat out on these big front porches at night, watching carriages and horses."

"Strolled in our park. They had band concerts there once, and there was a fountain in the middle, before kids wrecked it. After that there was a drinking fountain there, until kids wrecked it." Ben dumped lettuce she'd cut in with the tomatoes. He didn't look at her. He didn't understand women, no matter what they did. "Hope you like turkey tetrazzini, whatever that really is. Turkey and noodles." Ben felt the wall between them, even if he wanted her and she knew it. Games.

"Um," Sara said. "Smells good." But what she was sensing like a fragrance was the courtesy that almost-strangers pay to each other.

"Maeterlinck talks about ordinary life in that piece, doesn't he?"

Sara held a plate over the casserole for Ben. "He says that all he gets in modern plays, and even in some of Shakespeare's plays, is people doing violent things he has never done and so can't share. But many of the great Greek tragedies, and Ibsen's plays, are 'motionless,' he says, so we can feel the way magnificent and horrible things hover over us all the time."

"Lots of green beans?" Ben asked.

"Please," Sara said.

"Hungry?"

"Hungry."

"There's yours, and I'll carry mine and then get the rolls in the oven."

"Butter go in?"

"Yes, and do you like jam?"

Sara said she did and sat down in a room that wasn't strange now. Even the bull stuck with pics glared at her as if he recognized, in his agony, that she belonged there. Wine had gone to her head a little, so that emeralds and jades of tossed salad, golden, buttery rolls, the cream and brown casserole steaming on her plate were as brilliant as stained glass in the sun.

Banana yowled. Sara lifted the kitten to her lap, where it curled up.

"I asked kids in the park." Ben held a plate of rolls out to Sara. "They said it was a kitten from the Grangers, so I called them, and they said they were glad it was going to have a good home."

"Thanks," Sara said. "I'll take it off your hands later when the paint's all dry." She had to stop talking because her mouth was watering. There was hot meat to chew, and sauce that tasted of onions and garlic, a little. Green beans shone in their butter. Sara tried not to eat too fast and watched Ben rub his eyes with his big hands. "A hard day?"

"Yes. And a student of mine didn't like his grade last semester, so he's been phoning me in the middle of the night, calling me names."

"What can you do?" she asked.

"I'll tell you what—he's one of the gay ones. I get that kind sometimes," Ben said. "Good actors. They can let the woman in them out—makes them complex. And sometimes the women can show their male side, like Shakespeare's heroines."

"Or Antigone?"

"How about another roll?" Ben said.

Sara took another roll and more butter, and brown crust crunched deliciously against her tongue. Banana had been lying in a half-moon shape like one of the croissants, but now the kitten climbed Sara's shirtfront with sharp claws, smelling Sara's mouth, its whiskers a soft tickle against her chin. Sara gave the cat a bit of buttered and crusty moon. "Cat?" Sara said to a pair of yellow eyes. "I wonder if you're male or female?"

"Can't tell sometimes until kittens show up," Ben said.

"It'll get its own food and find its own home, no matter which it is," Sara said.

Ben watched lines around her mouth and a thin hand running over spotted fur. She wasn't telling what she was and looked at him with eyes as opaque as the cat's. What was he supposed to do—play games, too, and rip her defenses off, the way Victorian men had taken half an hour to strip off their women's corsets, unhook buttoned boots, unfasten rows of little pearl buttons?

She smiled at him above the kitten's fuzzy head. It wasn't a flirting smile; she kept her head level and her chin up and helped carry dishes into his kitchen and cut an apple pie. She was so thin her hip bones showed through her slacks.

"What classes will you teach this fall?" she asked, and he said he was stuck with Beginning Makeup and Introduction to Theatre: " 'The place of theatre and drama in the life of man.' Not many upper-class courses for a lowly instructor." He made her laugh by describing freshmen in makeup lab, and felt there was a part of her that never laughed, but stood aside and watched him.

Sara listened while he told about the President's TV press conference. She rinsed plates, he put food away, and then they washed dishes. She said she hadn't watched the talk; she didn't say she had no television.

Ben asked no questions at all. They talked and laughed and watched a British drama on TV, but she felt his reserve. He would not pry.

But she didn't stand close to Ben, saying good-bye. She was bruised from big hands like his. She only told him how much the meals meant to her and what a friend he was.

"Glad to help," Ben said. She hadn't asked many questions or tried to worm into his life. "Good luck with your new job tomorrow." He watched Laura go through the tunnel of rustling lilac leaves.

# 16

It rained in Massachusetts. Boston streets were lonely with umbrellas in the noon rush, and lonely with reflected neon when Martin drove home to Montrose every night.

Martin watched streets for Sara. He couldn't stop. He searched the crowds on Boylston Street, at Filene's, and passing the Montrose library. He sat in front of the library sometimes because she'd been there once, working.

There were blondes with long hair flying behind them. Blue eyes met Martin's as he stopped for a light. He'd see a small mouth . . . the profile of a narrow nose. Not one of them was Sara. Martin drove back and forth to his job, searching, and the searching was the most important thing. At Rambaugh Computer Sales and Service, Al Surrino got the manager's job and the private office and his private secretary. Martin didn't care. He knew the staff was watching him to see how he'd take it and whether he'd snap out of it. He didn't care.

"We think you need to be alone to sort your life out," his father said, so his parents didn't come to visit often, thank God. Martin sat for hours every evening reading Sara's papers and books. She had so many books. She hid books everywhere. He lifted a bed ruffle or moved a stack of towels and there her books were with their damn closed-up look like his father when he talked about "the masters of prose." Years of schoolbooks were enough for most people—you never dared make a sales brochure look like a book, and you never called it a book or you'd turn buyers off. Sara had read a couple of books out loud on their honeymoon.

He could call the Salvation Army and they'd come get every book Sara spent good money on. Every now and then he took one out of her dressing table or from high shelves in the kitchen behind boxes of cereal. He looked for the sexy parts. She underlined words and wrote in the margins: "Yes!" "Male chauvinist." "Drivel!" "Who says?"

He'd hit her with his fists because she spent her own money on books, but she stood up to him the way a man would, even when he hit her. Hell! What would a man do if you told him he couldn't spend his own money?

"Hell!" he shouted, and sat in their little second bedroom they'd never used for a baby, staring at dead violets in rows.

They sent the rest of Sara's stuff home from her library office. Pam Fitzer came with it: a little brunette who said she'd been Sara's best friend at the library. She looked Martin and the house over while he carried boxes into the bedroom. "You're so lonely," she said every time he went by her with another load. "I can just tell how lonely and *desolate* you must feel."

Finally Pam went away and he could open the boxes. "You're nothing more than a checkout girl," he'd told Sara, making fun of her part-time job. "Just stamp books in, stamp books out."

Pam Fitzer came back the next night and asked if he wouldn't like a real home-cooked meal, and he could hardly say no, he wouldn't. So she came in and poked around in his cupboards and refrigerator and brought back stuff from the store. He paid her for it.

There she was, rattling around at his kitchen sink and stove, sounding like Sara. Of course he was lonesome—he started talking to her and couldn't stop. He told her how his friends and teachers and coaches treated him because his father was the high school principal; he never knew if he'd deserved his good grades or really made the football team until he got to college and had a hard time.

They drank plenty of wine before dinner, so maybe he shocked Pam with some of the things he said—that he always thought God was like his own son-of-a-bitch father, puckering up his mouth if you said "Hell" or "Damn" and letting his own son get crucified. Pam said she'd never really thought of it that way.

Ambitious, he told Pam. He was really ambitious. His father had that sour look on his face watching Martin graduate without getting a prize for this-or-that like some of the guys did. What did prizes matter? He could talk and impress people; he got a good job at Rambaugh right away. Pam said education wasn't everything.

You bet the hell not, Martin said, but she should have gone to his family reunions. His dad was about the only one who'd finished college. Most of their slew of relatives were farmers or salesmen or mechanics; they thought a high school principal was big potatoes, and his mother would smile and nod until it made him sick. Everything was the show you could put on. But when his father went after him, his mother told Martin not to let it bother him; he was going to amount to something. Pam said his mother must be a nice person, and she'd like to meet her.

Martin was glad for somebody to talk to, so Pam Fitzer came back the next night and cooked dinner. Martin went through Sara's boxes from the library, reading everything. Now he found out how much money she spent in a year for books. She'd tried to be "fair" to everybody's interests, even when she didn't approve of them. She had the public on her back every minute, and not enough money, and the schoolchildren to take care of.

Sometimes he almost smiled. She gave people names in her private record of arguments and fights and struggles to keep the library "balanced." "Mrs. Nuthatch" had torn up a *Ms.* magazine before her face. "Mr. Double-breasted" paid his son's fines in twenty-five dollars worth of pennies because he was mad. "Miss Heavenly" wanted a Bible put on every rack of paperback books.

The names were funny, but he saw right away how much responsibility she'd had compared to him. She'd never talked about it. He'd never tried to find out. She met him at the door and asked him about his day, brought him a drink and listened, got dinner, washed dishes. . . .

His doorbell rang the next night when he was watching some sexy women detectives on television and drinking wine from a bottle. Pam was standing outside; she slid through the half-open door and stood too close to him and said she'd been thinking about poor Martin.

Well, that was nice, Martin said. She had on plenty of perfume, and when she pressed herself against him and put her arms around his neck, he could feel she was wearing a lot more perfume than clothes. "I've been thinking about you so much, so much," Pam crooned. "How you must be suffering."

Tears rose in Martin's eyes while he was wondering how to get rid of her. She rubbed the back of his neck and he felt a sob in his throat. "I left her to eat her good dinners alone—did that lots of times because she hated it when I wouldn't eat with her and food got cold," he said.

Pam wanted to hear all about it, and about how his work was going . . . she was a good listener, she said. She sat down and listened, nodding her head and playing with her hair and her necklace and squirming around on the couch. He didn't mind the work, Martin said. He had a lot of responsibility. It kept him from thinking.

"And you've got a nice new car," Pam said. "That should cheer you up a little." He looked at her. "I saw you parked by the library last week," she said, and got red in the face.

Nosy women, Martin thought, and said he had some money in the bank and it was about time for him to move up to a better car.

Would he like a cup of coffee? It was pretty late. Had he eaten any dinner? He said he hadn't, so she scrambled him some eggs and said she'd just straighten up his kitchen a little. He got tears in his eyes again, listening to her rattling dishes and silverware while he sat at the dining-room table pretending she was Sara.

Martin brought his dirty dishes to the kitchen, and Pam washed them and wiped them and put them away while he explained what he did at Rambaugh Computer Sales and Service. He hadn't told her much about it before. He had to understand very sophisticated machinery, he said—office equipment that sold for more than houses. He was always exhausted when he got home, but he couldn't stop thinking how he'd left Sara alone their last day together. She'd sat at the beach house and cried all those hours; he could tell.

"I know," Pam crooned, coming over to where he was standing by the stove. She put an arm around his neck and stuffed one of his hands into her low neckline.

"If Sara could only come back!" Martin sobbed. He didn't want to take his hand out of the front of Pam's dress because he might hurt her feelings. So he left it there, and she wiggled around against it, then slid his other hand up her thigh and under whatever she was wearing, which wasn't much, and lacy.

"I'd be kind the rest of my life if she could be here again!" Martin sobbed.

Pam didn't feel like Sara or smell like Sara. She started taking her clothes off and Martin didn't think he ought to stop her—she'd gotten his dinner for him. She was just being friendly. She had a red lace teddy on; Martin didn't want to think about it.

When she was standing by the stove naked, she started taking off his shirt. He tried not to look at her standing like that beside the wet dish towels and a pan he'd burned baked beans in.

She got his shirt off and started on his pants, and he wondered if it was going to work. He was full of scrambled eggs and toast, and he couldn't stop having tears in his eyes even while he wished she'd put her clothes on and go home.

All he could do was shut his eyes and pretend she was Sara. At least she wasn't fat, and she smelled all right. She made funny noises on the bed and kept talking, and she didn't know what he liked. He remembered the bed at the beach house that squeaked, and Sara under him crying, "Oh!"

He wished Pam would stop whispering after he got on top of her. He didn't listen; he was concentrating on Sara's big breasts and soft hair until he thought she was under him and went off like July 4—he must have given that librarian a paragraph or two more than she expected.

"Now you just go right to sleep," Pam said when she finally got up and went to get her clothes off the kitchen floor. She came back to the bedroom and stepped into her lacy red teddy, pulling it up to fit her the way Sara had. She smiled at Martin, who was wrapped in a sheet, but he shut his eyes until she had dressed and was gone out his front door.

# 17

"**I**'m married," Pam Fitzer whispered to herself after she'd smiled at Martin in bed all happy and relaxed and let herself out his front door. She ran blocks and blocks in the rain, not caring now what it did to her hair or her mascara.

"And at home they won't know." Thinking of that, she stopped to let the drops fall on her face, and thought she was brave and would be true until she died, and it hadn't hurt very much. "I did it right!" she whispered to the rain, and her heart blew up like a balloon under her new emerald-green raincoat with real pearl buttons. But her mother would take one look at her . . .

She ran on. So that was what people did. Thank God for books at the library she could read anytime because they were on special shelves nobody remembered were there, locked away. She'd done it right—shown him how much she loved him by asking about his grief and his work, and listening, listening. Poor soul. Poor, naked soul, lonely and heartbroken, missing Sara.

Everything in the right order, even when she'd been so scared that he'd think she was silly and pushy and unfeminine. But he'd cried in her arms. She was sweeter than candy at the very thought, melting in the rain. Scrambled eggs. She'd burned the first batch of toast, but he hadn't noticed the smell.

She knew exactly how to make scrambled eggs—not too wet, not too dry. And tomorrow he'd find sandwiches she'd made while he was talking about Rambaugh Computer Sales and Service—nice chicken ones with mayonnaise. She'd brought the chicken from home.

Pam stopped under a streetlight and put her wet hands to her wet face. Sometimes he looked like a little boy with his round forehead that was already getting wrinkled, and his round chin, and the full lips that didn't have any color. You couldn't even see his eyebrows unless you were close; then you saw how the fine hairs lay flat in a pattern, like part of a fan.

She started walking again. It would show. Her mother would take one look at her.

She closed her front door softly. Her mother didn't look at her; she was reading a book when Pam turned out the porch light and came through the hall. Her father and mother sat under two living-room lamps reading. "You got wet, I suppose," her mother said without looking up. "In that new coat. And gone four evenings now. Your friends are certainly gadabouts."

"It's waterproof," Pam said, not really listening, looking at her mother and father. So that was how they did it, if they ever did. They must have. No matter how much you read, you couldn't be sure of how they found the place, with legs in the way and all. With a big, fat paunch, or skinny legs in black oxfords?

She'd have a diamond on her finger. Shelving books at the library with a flash on her finger every time.

"How was the movie?" her mother asked, still not looking up.

"Cowboys," Pam said. "All getting together to save their ranch, but they lose it." The living room looked different to Pam; the house looked different. That was because she was different. So it was that big and could be pushed—that made sense. It all made sense now.

"Tell your father he didn't take the trash out, and I suppose he'll say it's raining again, and he can't, and they pick it up tomorrow morning before he's even awake, though God knows *I'm* awake," her mother said.

"All right," Pam said, thinking how it went on behind

dark windows up and down streets in Montrose—every night! Wetness and bleeding a little, but tissues and pins she'd found in his bathroom. No bath. Not as long as she could stand it. To wash the smell of him away?

"Dad?" Pam said, and he looked up. "Mom says you didn't take the trash out, and now you'll say it's raining again and you can't, and they pick it up tomorrow before you wake up, but she's always awake." Her beautiful red underwear with the black roses on it—he'd seen it. He'd seen how beautiful it was.

"Tell your mother I took it out," her father said, and laughed and laughed. He rattled his newspaper, laughing, and got up and went into the kitchen, still laughing.

"He took it out, Mom," Pam said, and hung her coat on a hall hook to dry out, and went upstairs with her new body that felt opened and handled and used and knowing how the world was. It climbed stairs with its blood beating through it, beautiful and functional like a curving stair rail, like a wandering Jew, green and growing under her parents' wedding picture.

Pam stopped to look at that pair. They stood as tightly against each other as possible, her mother's roses bent slightly against her father's sleeve, his white shirt collar melting, white against white, into her bridal veil.

Taking your clothes off. She thought she couldn't do it, but she had, because all she thought of was him, standing there sobbing that he'd be kind the rest of his life if he had Sara back.

Pam shut her bedroom door and locked it and took off all her clothes. Not much blood. And there were red marks on her yet. They hadn't gone away too fast—there they were. Finger marks. They weren't hers. They weren't hers. She felt her heart blow up like a balloon again. She could never be any happier than she was now, not even when she was married in a beautiful white wedding gown at their church. Pamela Burney. Mrs. Martin Burney. She couldn't hurt Sara. Sara was drowned.

She had told Sara everything—about her parents, and the way other girls had treated her in high school, and not

having a boyfriend. Sara listened to her, the first one who
ever had. She thought Sara looked sad and lonely. "Sometimes," Sara told her, "I see the world from out in space
somewhere, and it's so arbitrary—it's nothing but choices
we make. We choose to have concrete streets with curbs,
and we choose to make children go to school, and we
choose to have men and women living together in houses,
'married.' It doesn't have to be that way at all. You don't
have to have a boyfriend or sex or children to be happy.
Who told you so?"

Pam put on her nightgown, thinking of Martin. He
ripped his fingernail edges off while he talked and kept his
shoulders hunched—it made him look a little top-heavy,
along with his thick neck. He didn't like his father, but he
was fond of his mother; that was nice. He toed in when he
walked and jabbed his heels down first as he strode along—
she'd watched him from a library window—and swung his
arms hard, as if he were rowing himself through water.

She wouldn't ever be as smart as Sara had been. Sara
studied a different subject every month or two, and read
and read and read. She could recite poems by new poets
Pam never heard of, and when she was reading drama she
ordered tapes from other libraries and listened to plays
after work.

Pam sighed. When she married Martin her parents could
have a cat. Her mother could say, "Kitty (or whatever the
cat's name was), I don't think he's put the trash out, and
the men come to pick it up first thing tomorrow, and he
won't be up, but you and I will, Kitty."

Pam leaned toward her face in the mirror. She'd whispered, "Don't hurt me. This is my first time." But he was
so passionate. He couldn't stop by that time. It must be a
little bit like having to throw up or cough. He had broad
cheekbones and ears close to his head, and thumbs that
were always bent at the knuckles. She had whispered her
deepest thoughts to him while he was so busy down there
getting what he wanted.

Every night, when she could, she'd stand around the
corner and watch to see if Martin's lights were on, and

then knock and get him his dinner. Every night. Until he'd miss her when she couldn't come and say, "I waited for you all night last night. I can't live without you. Marry me."

She wrote "Pamela Burney" on her mirror in very light lipstick. There she was behind the words, the one he would love—not as beautiful as Sara, but loving. Hot meals when he came home, and everything mended and clean, because he'd be her reason for living, and she wouldn't work at the library if he didn't want her to—she wouldn't do anything in the world to hurt him.

"Pamela Burney." She looked at herself for a long time, smiling, pushing her nightgown down and turning to see the red marks before she wiped the mirror clean.

# 18

Sara had what oatmeal was left for Monday morning breakfast, and the last tomato catsup with hot water for lunch. She had applesauce at three-thirty, then went out in hot afternoon air.

She passed Ben's barn-shaped house. Its grassy bank sloped gently like hers and lifted their houses almost to the level of the park across the street. He had a cracked sidewalk with a half-moon out of it where a vanished tree had once grown. Trees made a roof above her house and Ben's; they darkened his red bricks and shingles and dappled her white walls with blue shade.

Sara walked halfway downtown and rang the doorbell at Dr. Channing's. The woman who answered the bell was so skinny that she looked as if her bones were working out of her body. "You're Laura Pray?" she said, leading the way into the dim house. "I'm Mrs. Baker, the practical nurse. Dr. Channing has two mornings a week to give her a bath. She's got a student staying nights, but she needs somebody to fill in days, get lunch and dinner for her, clean up a little—that kind of thing."

"I've taken care of my mother," Sara said, looking around her. The cool plainness of Dr. Channing's living room set forth an inlaid desk for her inspection and two prints that looked like Hogarths. A cast of a Greek head watched Sara with eyes as blank as grapes. "She's blind, and in bed all the time."

"Dr. Channing's not blind, but she's lost interest, won't let us put her in a chair, won't talk," Mrs. Eaker said. "A bad car accident, you know. Do sit down. And here's Ellen to talk to you. Ellen Garner, Laura Pray."

The fat young woman in the doorway looked at Sara for only a fraction of a second, then looked anywhere else the rest of the time. She bulged under her shirt and over her jeans, and when Mrs. Eaker left she settled awkwardly on a creaking chair.

Sara heard the front door close. After a moment or two Ellen said in a flat voice, "Mostly she just needs somebody to be here, and she has to be fed, and you can do dishes and the washing."

"Yes," Sara said. "I wonder if I can start this afternoon."

"I'll show you the kitchen," Ellen said. The house was cool and airy; they passed a flight of stairs to a second floor. Windows on the landing were moon-white with organdy curtains and red with sunlit geraniums.

"The washer and dryer are off the kitchen here. I bring groceries home." Ellen's eyes, brown and beautifully fringed with dark lashes, stared into the refrigerator she opened, as blank as if food did not interest her.

Sara's mouth watered at the sight of milk and cheese and eggs and fruit. "You can get her dinner tonight. She needs her food chopped pretty fine but she can eat most things," Ellen said. "Just tell her what there is, and she'll nod if she wants it. She can move her head. She's not interested in eating and hates to be fed, but she's got to be. She can't feed herself, and she won't talk."

"Yes," Sara said. She could watch Ellen, for Ellen's eyes never met hers; they stayed on the floor, a kitchen table and chairs, a row of earthenware jars, pots of green herbs.

"I give her breakfast and go to my afternoon classes when you come at twelve," Ellen said, looking at brilliant linen towels on the wall. Elizabeth I and Henry VIII stared down from the towels at Ellen; their printed faces seemed more alive than hers. "So she eats lunch at about twelve-fifteen and dinner at five, and I come at six, and then you can go home. She doesn't need a bedpan often, but ask her every now and then and keep checking on her."

Sara thought that Ellen Garner couldn't be more than eighteen; she lived with a woman who would not speak a word. The house surrounded them with a cool silence like Ellen's.

"You can come meet her," Ellen said.

Pearly light through glass curtains whitened a large bedroom at the back of the house and silvered a ruddy face on the pillow. Brass lamps and pulls of a walnut dresser and highboy gleamed against blue draperies and spread and rug.

"Here's Laura Pray," Ellen said tonelessly to a head propped on a pillow. The face was old and homely; its brown eyes stared at Sara, alert, watchful. "Mrs. Nepper's friend. She says she can come at noon and wash and clean and feed you lunch and dinner."

Deep brown eyes looked at them both. A neat braid of gray hair surrounded the head on the pillow.

"I'm glad for the job," Sara said to Dr. Channing after a pause. "You must let me know if I do anything wrong. Shake your head at me. Wink." Sara thought she saw a little light in the brown eyes for a moment.

Ellen's face was blank; her eyes ran around the room as if she were looking for something. "Well, I'm going shopping. Mrs. Eaker's telephone number and the doctor's number are on the refrigerator."

What could be said to either of them? Sara watched Ellen waddle out and was left with coolness and silence and two brown eyes watching her from the bed. She moved closer and smiled. "I wonder what you'd like for dinner? Meat? Are you hungry?"

The pillowed head moved back and forth.

"Scrambled eggs, maybe?" Sara smiled into alert eyes that seemed wounded and grieving even as they watched her closely. The face had never been beautiful—a large nose over an overblown mouth and big teeth. The body under the sheet looked substantial yet, even heavy. The head moved up and down.

"I'll look in the refrigerator and cupboards to see what else there is," Sara said, and patted one still hand on the sheet. Only the hum of air-conditioning answered her.

Sara went to the kitchen to move briskly back and forth, filling the air with sounds of doors opened and shut, ringing of pans against pan lids. There were plenty of eggs, and a good skillet, and peas in the freezer, and apples. "Would frozen green peas taste good?" she went back to ask the sad brown eyes. "And maybe a fresh apple cut in small pieces?" The head on the pillow moved up and down. Sara smiled and went back to the kitchen.

Eggs, milk, salt. The sight of food made her weak. If she could have a glass of milk . . . who would see her? She picked up a milk carton and took a step toward the dish cupboard, then stopped in mid-step, a look of horror on her face.

Sara almost ran through the hall to the bedroom, standing where Dr. Channing could see her. "I wonder if you'd mind if I had a glass of milk while I'm getting dinner."

The head moved back and forth.

"Thank you so much," Sara said, and went to pour cold, rich milk. Her stomach eased its cramping; she could hum a little bit as she worked.

There was a row of parsley and chive plants on the sill. Sara looked at the new, shining stove, refrigerator, microwave. A linen towel on the wall showed a portly Henry VIII, fat and dreamy, but his daughter's sharp black eyes stared from her portrait and seemed to follow Sara from table to stove to sink. Maybe Dr. Channing would pay her something tonight. She could buy groceries.

Sara heard faint children's calls from next door. Then the dumb, sullen quiet of two women closed around her. But eggs plopped into a bowl, a mixer purred. Sara put Dr. Channing's dinner on a tray and found a napkin in a drawer.

"Now," Sara said, coming to spread the napkin under Dr. Channing's chin. "We'll enjoy dinner and a chat. I'm afraid you'll have to listen to me, because your mouth will be full." The brown eyes seemed to smile a little.

"I'll never do it just right," Sara said, bringing egg to the woman's mouth. "Nobody can ever feed anyone the way they'd do it themselves, but I'll try." A skinny brunette was feeding an old woman in the mirror above a dresser, and the brunette looked happy, Sara thought—she had a job. She rubbed her forehead with the heel of her hand and smiled at Dr. Channing.

How awkward it was, trying to gauge when someone else would swallow or what she would want to eat next. A crumb of egg was on Dr. Channing's chin, and Sara didn't want to scrape it off with the spoon. "That's pretty dry stuff," Sara said. "Would you like something to drink? Milk?" The woman shook her head. "Coffee? Tea?" This time the head nodded. "I'll go put some water on."

There were tea bags in the cupboard; Sara finally found them. "Sugar in your tea?" she asked when she came back to pick up the spoon again. "Lemon?" The head said no twice.

A bite of egg. A spoonful of peas. The room and its silence surrounded them like a cocoon; sounds were swallowed by the soft rush of air-conditioning. Only light muted by curtains reached them. "I'm twenty-five years old and I live in Mrs. Nepper's house on Seerley Park," Sara said. "I was raised in different towns in Nebraska—except when we lived awhile in Massachusetts—so I'm a Middle Westerner. I love Cedar Falls, especially because it's a university town."

Some apple pieces. A bite of egg. "You have so many books. Maybe tomorrow you'd like me to read to you?" The brown eyes grew warmer. "You would? I love to read, but I may not do it well enough for a university professor."

Dr. Channing's eyes looked away with that depth of sadness in them again, far away from the large lips and chewing teeth.

"I wonder if you'd like me to read Henry James," Sara said, pushing peas against scrambled eggs to get them on the spoon.

A clock ticked in the hall.

"You've studied him all your life, haven't you?" Sara said in a little while. "If you'd enjoy that, I would too. I've never been able to get through any of his novels but *The Turn of the Screw*. I get wound up in all those words like a cat with a ball of yarn."

Air-conditioning hummed softly, constantly.

Sara's mind left Henry James and remembered, all by itself, that Martin wanted every towel folded in thirds on the bathroom rods, and his underwear folded in thirds, and all blankets folded in thirds on closet shelves. Suddenly she wanted to laugh, but instead she told the face on the pillow, "I don't want to chatter at you all the time. Maybe we can play music on the radio sometimes while you eat."

The head nodded.

At last Sara said, "There. We're through," and went to get the tea. Dr. Channing sipped it through a plastic straw.

"Would you like anything more?" Sara asked. The head wound with braids moved back and forth. "Then I'll go do the dishes. Ellen will be here in a little while. I'll come every now and then to see if you need anything."

Sara Burney, trained to be a librarian, put dirty dishes in a dishpan, found dish soap, and met Queen Elizabeth's black, intense gaze from a towel on the wall. Elizabeth had been hidden away and scared for her life too—afraid of her own father. (Now Henry VIII looked at them both over his cock-pheasant paunch.)

When Dr. Channing needed a bedpan, Sara rolled the old, heavy body on its side, rolled it back. Its lumpy, loose flesh was like her mother's. She touched it carefully, gently, and circled Dr. Channing with her thin arms, smiling into brown eyes that were deep and hurt and still.

Sara was in the kitchen when the door rattled and Ellen

came in with sacks of groceries. She looked once at Sara, then kept busy unloading cans and bottles and boxes. "Hello," Sara said.

"Hello," Ellen said flatly. Her fat arms bulged between elbow and wrist as if they were tied at those two places—fleshy balloons.

To look like that, Sara thought . . . to roll your immense thighs around each other, walking from cupboard to cupboard, and peer over and around that huge belly to find the right low drawer.

"Dr. Channing's had her dinner," Sara said. "Scrambled eggs and peas and an apple and tea."

Ellen's mouth hung open a minute. "She hasn't eaten that much since her accident." Her face was expressionless under wispy brown hair, but her brown eyes were like Dr. Channing's when Sara caught a glimpse of them—alert, withdrawn.

Sara wiped dishes and put them away. Ellen folded paper bags. "I'm supposed to pay you for the first two weeks," Ellen said in a little while and held out an envelope.

"Thanks," Sara said. "Do you want me to come every day from noon until six?"

"Yes," Ellen said. "And maybe you could come in the morning sometimes so I can work in the library? I'm trying to read for my classes."

"I can come anytime," Sara said. "Just let me know a little ahead. And whenever you want me to wash or clean—"

"Could you come tomorrow morning at eight? We've got a cleaning lady who comes in Friday mornings, so I go to the library then," Ellen said. "You can have lunch here." Her tone was practical now, as if she were used to planning.

"All right," Sara said. The kitchen clock said it was after six, and Ellen seemed to be waiting for her to leave. "Good-bye."

Sara walked for a block before she opened the envelope

and looked at enough money to pay her next rent and buy
groceries and some Spackle and a putty knife, at least,
and some running shoes. She almost danced along the
sidewalk—a job, and they hadn't asked any questions she
couldn't answer! She put the money in her pocket and felt
it there as she walked shady streets and then a hot dirt path
along Highway 218.

College Square had a supermarket with a cheap delicatessen; Sara peered through slanted glass to pick this meat
and those vegetables and that dessert like jewels from
velvet, and ate slowly at a table in the corner, dollars and
dollars still in her pocket. If she only had Cristine Weiden
across from her. Cristine loved to eat in a delicatessen in
Montrose. She'd eat everything on her plate, finish anything Sara didn't want and then go back for more, rolling
her eyes and saying, "Diet's first three letters are a warning, that's what they are! Don't tell me those letters don't
mean anything!"

Now Sara Burney was drowned. She'd never see Cristine
again, or Karen or Joan or Pam or Marie. Sara Burney was
dead, they thought. She could never go back to tell them
she wasn't.

When Sara had eaten her dinner she pushed a cart
slowly, luxuriously, and never stopped at oatmeal or beans
or catsup. Her bag of groceries was heavy, but she bought
some good running shoes, then stopped at a hardware
store. Mrs. Nepper had promised to buy the paint; Sara
bought a brush, primer, Spackle, putty knife, and sandpaper, and caught a bus that went down College Street.

When Sara dumped bags on her kitchen table and opened
her clean, white, empty refrigerator, she laughed out loud
in delight. Breakfast would be waiting in the morning. She
could have a glass of milk before she went to bed. Tomorrow she could begin to fill wall cracks and holes. She
could run in her new shoes.

She could buy a diary—she'd written in a diary as long
as she could remember . . . no. She couldn't keep a diary.
She was Laura Pray, who would leave no tracks at all.

Sara took a bath and had her milk and lay in bed thinking of Dr. Channing, who stared at a ceiling all day. She thought of Ellen Garner, talking about Dr. Channing.

"She got paralyzed in the accident last summer," Ellen had said. "She doesn't want to live any more, that's all."

Sara saw Ellen's eyes for a moment before they dropped. They looked as if Ellen were quietly observing a woman who wanted to die, as a college student might look at a classroom, or an assignment, or a library shelf full of books.

# 19

Ellen Garner looked up from washing dishes as Laura Pray knocked at the kitchen door. When Laura came in sun set tendrils of her shiny, dark hair on fire. Ellen looked at Laura and felt herself bulge shapelessly like a beach ball with a hole in it.

"Good morning," Laura said. "It's a beautiful morning. How's Dr. Channing?"

"All right," Ellen said.

"I'll wipe," Laura said, and took up a dish towel. "Not much point in using the dishwasher when there are so few of us."

"No," Ellen said, scraping at an eggy pan with her thumbnail.

Clinking dishes and rushing water were the only sounds for a while. Summer seemed to stop at Dr. Channing's doors. Sara wiped dishes and remembered some poem by James Russell Lowell—was it?—about a castle like an outpost of winter. "Summer besieged it on every side," da-da, da-dum, da-da. . . . "It could not scale that chilly wall, but around it for leagues its pavilions tall stretched left and right," da-dum-dum-dum. She didn't think she remembered it correctly. "Green and broad was every tent and out of each a murmur went till the breeze fell off at night." Leaves fluttered outside kitchen windows. "I hope I'm putting things where they belong," she said to Ellen.

Ellen said nothing, only glanced at cupboards, not Sara. Her eyes were liquid brown and very still. She stood at the sink showing nothing but her surface, like a bulging earthenware jar she was washing. The kitchen might have been empty around her, her body said.

"Where do you hang dish towels?" Sara asked.

"You can do that one with the rest of the laundry today, I guess," Ellen said. "There's a hamperful by the washer." She dumped soapsuds, wiped the pan out with her sponge, and put it under the sink by slowly lowering her weight and sticking her behind out as she stooped. She pushed her wispy hair off her forehead. Sara would have liked to put her hand on her shoulder and say something kind, but what was there to say?

"Good-bye," Sara said when Ellen let herself out the kitchen door with some notebooks in her arms.

The hamper was full of sheets and towels and nightgowns. Sara sorted them in piles and sang as she worked—an old folk song about careless love. The clear sound filtered through a hall to a still face on a pillow.

The sun had gone under, and it smelled like rain, but it was hot, though it was only eight-thirty. El Garner was wet with sweat by the time she got to the university library.

Not many students there. El could sit down in her favorite upholstered chair in a corner, pull her skirt straight under her, and wrap her old raincoat around her. If anybody noticed her, they'd never think she was pregnant—she was just another fat girl, a farm girl, one of the invisible ones the university turned out as teachers every year.

It wasn't long before a summer storm streaked rain down a library window near El. She had run through a winter downpour to Beeley's Drive Inn last winter, but Jerry's trailer was gone. No one knew where he'd headed for (or much about where he came from, for that matter). El had found only a yellow rectangle of dead grass and some whiskey bottles in the trash can.

El opened her Humanities notebook; it began with her notes for the first semester. *Don't Think of Unpleasant*

*Things*. That had been her first rule. There it was on the second page: *Don't Think of Unpleasant Things,* underlined in red. She leafed through "The Otherworldly Cults of Persia."

Bright red and blue upholstered chairs surrounded El. Sometimes she looked out windows at rain and her lips moved. When she got to "Hebrew Origins" in her notes, El saw she had added *Don't Take Chances* at the top of her notes and underlined it to match her first rule. In "The Early Middle Ages" she had printed *Watch Your Health.* No more Cokes and a hot dog for lunch. Those were the three rules she had thought of that first semester. Maybe there should have been others, like *Learn From Your Mistakes* or even *Repent of Your Sins,* but somehow those three had kept her going.

Yike, I'm lucky I'm fat, El thought, looking at her notes on the rise of medieval abbeys but remembering Laura Pray's skinny figure and the shine of her ruffly hair. El was fat and ordinary-looking, lost in crowds of students. At home she was Pete Garner's oldest, who never dated, got top grades, worked at the Drive Inn every summer, and was always dragging her little brothers and sisters around. At the university people's glances slid over her like rain down a window. She could be no one in Cedar Falls—a pair of eyes watching.

In February she had been sick still, and scared, and she had stared out classroom windows wondering what she could do. Class hours were the only places (except toilet stalls) where she could be alone to think.

All the students her own age—she hadn't dreamed there were so many like herself. In September she'd walked lost in crowds of them in big, frightening buildings. She sat in a corner and watched them eating from trays like hers. At night a hundred girls slept under the same roof she did, like bees in cells, their hair full of curlers and pins, smelling of perfume. She loved to see them go by her dorm-room door. She'd sit on a corner of somebody's bed and watch girls lounging close to her, their pretty mouths laughing, their curving legs and breasts so beautiful, like

Laura Pray. And she, too, had been beautiful to someone, and was a woman, and belonged.

In March she moved into Dr. Channing's house. By then she could let herself remember lying close to Jerry, her face in the warm place between his neck and shoulder.

El leafed through "The Achievement of the Egyptians." About the time they got to Egypt, she'd been able to think ahead. The campus was four feet deep in snow, and she felt buried too. She'd cried all she was going to and had all the thoughts of jumping out windows she supposed were normal.

Hadn't she been a sick little chicken then, hanging on to the place where she knew she had to stay, creeping around edges, scared of not getting her work done on time—yike!

Pig feeders would be banging this morning at home. Fields outside her bedroom window would be thick with green corn. If it were raining there, too, their house would smell like animals and barn-lot dirt, and farm buildings would be gray-streaked with wet. Her father's pickup truck would churn mud by their back door. When the children came in there'd be a row of dirty boots along the back hall.

El sighed and turned to notes on hieroglyphics. Her mother would be tired of mud and just tired, and scared she might be left alone. Pete Garner had just gotten tired of farming somebody else's land and gone away for a while when El was fourteen. "Just one thing too much and Dad'll leave," El said under her breath, watching the rain. El wasn't going to be that one thing too much. She wasn't costing him a thing, with her scholarship and her job at Dr. Channing's.

El smelled fried eggs bubbling on the grill at Beeley's Drive Inn. She stood there with a broken-handled spatula, waiting to turn them over. When she was hungry (which was most of the time), the Drive Inn was what she thought of. Three summers of rolling up faded bamboo blinds, lifting out storms in two doors, and putting in screens every morning at seven, when the world smelled green and clean.

By this time gas would be on under the carbonated water, trays would be full of frozen french fries, the grill and deep-fat fryer would be hot, and she'd be filling napkin dispensers, or washing booth tables, or turning eggs over on the grill. She saw the broken-handled spatula with a kind of glory to it, because Jerry had been there the third summer, coming in from his trailer to lift her hair from the back of her neck and kiss the place beneath it that he said was the softest place on her.

Her suitcase was packed at the back of her closet. She was working ahead on her fall classes just in case something happened and she was sick and couldn't keep up with the others. She had money for a taxi and a note telling Dr. Channing she had to go to her Aunt Marcella's to take care of her for a few weeks—an emergency. Aunt Marcella would take care of that, and Dr. Channing had Laura Pray now. "Mrs. Marcella Dehlstrom, 109 Fourth Street, Waterloo, Iowa" was typed on a card, all ready, with Aunt Marcella's telephone number.

Two men students came along a row of chairs near El, laughing at some joke. El watched their big, awkward hands swinging back and forth and thought she'd call a taxi down at the hotel and take it to Waterloo. Then she'd just walk into the hospital with the card in her hand and say, "I'm Eleanor Dehlstrom. Will you call my aunt for me and tell her where I am? She'll want to come." And that was all they'd get her to say.

El watched rain running down the window like clear veins, joining and rejoining. What if Jerry had really been laughing at her and marking her down as "easy" on his list of women? He'd told her a little about others, but he said none of them had been as good as she was, and she'd been so proud, even when she was tired and sweaty, driving down to the creamery to get two five-gallon cans of ice-cream mix for the after-the-movies rush. He said he'd never forget her.

*Don't Think of Unpleasant*—she thought of that Summer instead. She always spelled it with a capital S in her mind. She could smell the alfalfa and clover of it sometimes before she went to sleep at Dr. Channing's. Rain clouds had heaped up behind red barns. Then salty, buttery August sun had poured down again. The smell of that Summer's sun had been in the children's hair when she tucked them in. When she'd gone to sleep the feeling of Jerry had been with her still, and her sheets had that airy smell in the dark, like white clouds.

She could go home when she left the hospital. The house would be littered with toys and dirty clothes and her mother would be pale and tired all the time. El would try to sort and clean before she went back to classes. And she could pick up a little one, Beverly or Art, and cuddle them. She'd been so sad at Christmas; she'd rocked them for hours. When she packed up to go back to the university, wondering how she could ever do it, they had been so excited, jumping in her piles of clothes, bouncing on her old bed.

Tenderness flowed through El, a hot sweetness she could almost taste. Jerry's head bent over bills in the Drive Inn at night had given her that same melted feeling. His wife would come in from the trailer and yell something at him, a whiskey smell always hanging around her like her chenille bathrobe, and El would melt in tenderness to see thin places in Jerry's hair, deep lines across his forehead, sweat patches under his arms.

Egyptian hieroglyphics were dotted with small, plump birds and crouching lions. El had sketched a few in her notes and they watched her now. Jerry hadn't wanted to know about her feelings; if she showed them, he told her dirty stories about what he had taught her to do. When he stopped the loving part he told her she improved his health, like exercises he did with weights behind the Drive Inn. They were just good friends, he said, and had such a great thing going.

Someone behind a shelf of magazines dropped a book flat on the floor. The slam of it woke up the baby. El felt what she thought was a little rubbery foot thrust her skin out; there was a hard knob of him under her arm against her side. She slid her hand under her raincoat and softly rubbed until little unborn Em pulled back his elbow or knee or foot or whatever it was.

"El and Em." Their private joke. They had been studying Machiavelli the day she first felt him move and she thought of calling him "Mac," or "Wren" for "Renaissance," because he fluttered at first, just like a bird, and was so tiny. But he turned out to be "Em" for "Embryo." Day or night, there he was, secret and alive under her coat or sweater or her old raincoat. A fat girl getting fatter—that was all anyone saw. Even her mother never noticed at spring vacation, except to say once that El should go on a diet again, shouldn't she? When El watched students dancing in the Union, Em thumped around under her coat, a little nut in her shell. Yike! He loved the bass beat, that little invisible one!

Aunt Marcella's long yellow face wouldn't change as she listened to the hospital calling. She wouldn't say "I don't know any Ellen Dehlstrom," because Dehlstrom had been her maiden name. She'd figure out that it was El and why El couldn't use her own name; she'd "save face for the family," as she said she was always having to do.

Yes, she would say, she was glad to know about Ellen Dehlstrom and was she all right? And yes, she would get there as soon as she could. Then she would drive out to the farm and get El's mother alone and tell her coldly that another of her mistakes had come home to roost—Ellen had evidently had a baby in a hospital in Waterloo. Good old Aunt Marcella would be expected, she supposed, to take care of the mess, because they couldn't leave the farm and all those children they'd seen fit to have.

A student sat down at a table near El and put his head on his arms. The back of his neck looked like a little boy's, the way Em's would look someday. Aunt Marcella would find out how to give Em up for adoption and she'd take El home. She'd see to it the university never heard of it, or the neighbors, or El's father. Ann Olson, one of the girls from home, had done the same thing when El was in junior high. Ann had gotten scared, though, when pains began and she told her roommate at the university. Her roommate never told anybody in Cedar Falls, but she told somebody, and somebody told somebody, and everybody in town knew it pretty soon. Aunt Marcella would die before she'd tell. And she'd have to admit El had handled it well. Just once El would know Aunt Marcella approved.

El turned over the last page of her Egyptian notes. Someday Aunt Marcella would come to visit El at a grade school where El would be a teacher. Children would be busy at their desks, and sun would come through windows on cowlicks and curls, and an aquarium, and rows of plants and books. El would be at her own desk, her eyes going from one child to another, knowing what each one needed. She would ask Aunt Marcella to sit in the back of the room and watch.

Rain was still streaming down library windows. El ran her hand along her chair's arm. There was a heart scratched into it with two initials inside the heart (neither of them hers).

She shut her eyes, trying to imagine herself sitting there a month from then. Em would be gone—somebody else's baby. She would be in her old black coat again, empty, a single life like all the others in the library.

El did something silly. She reached down and stuck her chewing gum to the bottom of the chair, right behind where the arm was screwed on. When she came back to the library in September, it would be there, like a letter. A love letter from "El and Em" to the empty one she would be.

# 20

Sara sang before dawn the next morning, putting on her wig. Bruises on the backs of her legs were only a faint yellow now. When they were gone she'd promised herself a new pair of shorts and a short-sleeved shirt.

She ran down Main Street. She'd read about the town when it was called Sturgis Falls, and the Cedar River turned a grist mill. "Elms on Main Street made a perfect green tunnel when I came here," Mrs. Nepper had said. "Green. Met overhead for miles. A perfect green tunnel." To Sara the town seemed friendly now, its new trees rooted and standing firm the way she was—Laura Pray, who washed Dr. Channing's sheets and nightgowns and got her lunch and dinner, put her on the bedpan and emptied it, turned her in bed, read her Henry James.

Sara ran on campus, her running shoes hardly making a sound as she passed from one round island of light to another. Ten thousand students were still in bed; the modern fountain outside the education center dropped its shining sheet of water, a lonely, constant sound. Rabbits ran before her near the campanile. She smelled petunias in huge flower beds; archery targets sat back on their heels, moon-round in rows; Prexy's Pond gleamed here and there beside the power plant and its streaking smoke.

Ben's house was still dark when she came back to strip and take a shower. Bruises on her breasts and arms were almost gone. She dozed naked in her tumbled bed until the telephone startled her.

"I'll tell you what—come over for breakfast," Ben said in her ear. "Come through the lilacs. My treat."

Sara's mouth formed no, but she never said it, because Ben's voice was so light, so offhand. He stood back. He asked no questions.

The sun was up now. She put on a shirt and jeans and was glad of the dense tunnel of lilac to Ben's kitchen door. Now she knew how to squeeze her back-porch door shut; it didn't make a sound.

Ben stood scrambling eggs at his funny old stove, whose oven stood beside the burners. He was dressed for work: nice slacks, a short-sleeved shirt and tie that made him look older, different, a workingman, a young professor, except for the plastic apron.

Ben had heard rustling lilac leaves and watched Laura slip in his door, graceful, light-fingered, easing it shut behind her. She came close to him, barefooted and thin, and Banana yowled and twined around her ankle.

"Hi," he said. Only two weeks since he first saw her walking down his street, but already she was smoothing out, losing her thin, tired look. Now she sat at his kitchen table with a quiet smile and put bread in his toaster; you had to watch it or it would burn every piece of toast. She said it wasn't going to be so hot that day and did he by any chance have a copy of Shakespeare's plays?

Ben wondered about her real hair under the shiny wig. He wondered who she was hiding from, and why, and for how long. "I'll tell you what," he said, setting plates of scrambled eggs and bacon before them and sitting down. "Why should you be stuck in that place of yours all morning every day with no books or TV or radio, and no air-conditioning, either? Stay here. Keep Banana company. Nobody ever comes but the meter man, and in this town he knocks and comes right in, goes to the basement, and leaves. Let the telephone ring. And you can get to your house in a second if you need to."

Laura didn't answer right away. He saw her glance

through his living-room door at his bookshelves. "It would be nice to do that sometimes," she said, thinking of how hot her rooms were and how many books Ben had. "You come home for lunch," she said finally.

"There's only a greasy hamburger joint in the university Union or some crowded places on College Hill."

"I'll get your lunch today before I go to work," she said. "And leave your dinner ready. To pay you back."

"And eat it with me," Ben said.

Laura said, "I wonder . . ." then stopped. All at once Ben held his breath, felt cold.

"Can I pay my half?" Laura asked.

Ben's laugh sounded happy, relieved. "Sure," he said.

She was playing with a bit of toast on her plate. "But you've got your own friends. You don't want to be stuck with me every night."

"Join us," Ben said, and the old scared look changed her whole expression. Her fingers tightened on the bit of toast on her plate. "If you want to," he added lamely.

"I can't," she said softly. "Of course I want to, but I can't. I have to stay by myself."

"Why?" he asked before he thought.

She got up to stack dirty plates, not looking at him, but he didn't stop, couldn't stop: "Are you married? Are you afraid of someone?" He heard his half-angry tone and knew it was all wrong, all—

"I have to stay by myself," she said again.

Silence lengthened between them, the first such stillness since he had said "Don't want to be seen with a redheaded gent?"

Laura scraped plates at the sink. Ben went to his study for papers, seating charts, notes. He listened to the clatter of dishes.

"Do you like dark or light bread?" Laura called.

"Dark," Ben called back.

"When do you want dinner?" she asked after a while. Light and lovely, a woman's voice from his kitchen asked such an ordinary question, as if he didn't live alone, as if there would be someone here in his house always, busy with sandwiches and dinners, washing, putting ironing away, getting cleaning picked up. The gnawing of a thousand little details would stop. He could write that book about experimental theater. "How about seven?" he asked.

Laura came from the kitchen when he called good-bye. She stood well back from the front door as he opened it, and Ben shut her smiling face away in his house as if she were a wife, someone who belonged to him.

Seerley Park was green and fresh. One small child sat on a swing by herself. "Want a push?" he asked her, surprised at his happy voice, surprised at the beauty of speckled shade on child and grass as she flew higher and higher, giggling.

Children, Ben thought. He passed the university president's big, square house that watched lawns and trees, College Street and the campus beneath its overhanging eaves. He took deep breaths of morning air. Not September yet—only a leaf or two had fallen. A few years before, bulldozers had pulled down the old Administration Building's turreted towers and double brick walls, but he still expected to see them blocking his way, ugly, endearing.

"Dr. Woodward?"

Ben stopped. Annie Frazer caught up with him, clunking along in her high-heeled shoes and too-tight pants and batting her confused, mascara rimmed eyes.

"I can't *understand* the assignment for the fifteenth!" she said. "We can write only ten pages? But I have so much to *say* about Eugene O'Neill!"

"Ten pages," Ben said, and opened the Union door for Annie. She stood at the top of the inner stairs fluttering her mascara at him, but he went past her and downstairs. "See you in class."

He was noticing familiar things in a strange way this morning. The Maucker Union had concrete and brick terraces on top; its rooms were underground . . . a hole in the center of the campus, a pit full of young people yelling and reading and eating and drinking. It was, Ben suddenly realized, like the boys' burrow in *Peter Pan*. Instead of a tree above it, there were concrete trunks for air and some little round amphitheaters of seats to delude Captain Hook.

Ben bought coffee with cream, sat down at a crumb-covered table, and saw that the Union had been built to be full of boys and girls forever. It served the fast food they loved, and music blatted from rooms even deeper underground.

His coffee tasted like the cup's Styrofoam. He would walk into this *Peter Pan* burrow for more than thirty years, maybe, growing older, grayer, bald, but he'd never find anything underground in that Union but the young, eating what the young liked in each succeeding decade, wearing their current uniform, thinking they'd never grow up.

Ben hunched his shoulders, looked around the Union and left half his coffee. When he climbed out of Peter Pan's hideout he thought he heard the campanile clock ticking—the voice of Old Crocodile Time. But Ben was in fine fettle, and Cedar Falls, Iowa, looked new, strange, lovely this September morning because—was he?—in love?

Red-brick campus buildings glowed in morning sun. Ben passed students playing tennis on the courts. None of the women were as thin as Laura or had her ruffled, glossy cap of false hair.

The staff room smelled like stale cigarette smoke, as usual. Ben listened to Gene Moser's sad story of a jammed projector and looked over the mail from his slot: ads for texts, United Faculty minutes, a questionnaire about his opinion of the graduate program.

"We're counting paper clips again," Alice Spicer said.

"Saving paper too," Ben said, and showed her copies of his Introduction to Theatre exam—it had out-of-date parking regulations on the reverse.

"How about some beer tonight at Pour Richards?" Hal Esterbrook called from the corner of the staff room.

"Working on that play," Ben said. "Take a rain check?"

He had two morning classes, two hours full of blank young faces in rows; they stared at him like the living dead. What *did* those eyes light up for? Keggers? X-rated movies?

Ben joked. Ben grinned. He knew already where a few faces were that he could talk to, faces that would smile or frown or look confused. He was sure that hacks of old vaudeville stages, doing a last turn from their graves, would recognize those classrooms full of coughers and shufflers who had paid their money and taken their choice. You sold the tickets and then you put on the show, with no applause when the bell rang.

But he did it and didn't really mind, thinking of all the jobs that were worse. He'd go home, and there would be Laura's lunch ready for him on his dining-room table. She was there, thinking of him. So let Peter and Wendy clone themselves forever. Let the crocodile tick. News of two afternoon committee meetings couldn't even bother him—he thought about Laura's lips and breasts and wondered about her hair.

Ben's office was small and windowless. Freshmen were already coming in wanting to know, as usual, whether he was going to nurse them the way their high school teachers had: Could they miss a class or would it hurt their grade? Could they take the first exam on another day? He answered them gently. His lunch would be on the table when he got home, and she would have put it there.

And the lunch was there. At noon he hurried home and found sandwiches and salad and fruit and cookies laid out on one of his good linen place mats with a small bouquet of daisies in a vase. He took one from the water and held it for a moment where her hands must have been on its stem.

Cedar Falls was hot in noon sun. The Parkade wound through downtown storefronts; students crowded the cool Maucker Union. Sara, walking to Dr. Channing's house, thought how ordinary and beautiful Cedar Falls looked in its summer-heavy leaves. Children playing in the Clay Street park watched her pass; dogs barked at a bus. The bus driver opened his door and yelled, "Hey, Merv, how was the fishin'?"

"Got a couple cat!" an old man on Clay Street yelled back.

When Sara let herself in at Dr. Channing's kitchen door,

a small thought was weaving through Ben Woodward's blue eyes in her mind. She heard him saying "Join us," and at the same time had the small idea, bright as flakes of sunlight falling on Dr. Channing's kitchen table.

Ellen Garner stood by that table, and there was no more expression on her fat face than on the face of the kitchen clock above her. She didn't look at Sara; she said goodbye and shut the door behind her, going off to her classes. Sara watched Ellen's silhouette against a sunny sidewalk: Ellen swayed slightly from side to side, waddling away in her hot, dark raincoat when the kitchen-window thermometer said it was eighty degrees at noon.

Dr. Channing was having her bath. Mrs. Eaker came into the kitchen after a while, her skull-face cheerful. "She looks so much better!" she said. "We couldn't get her interested in a blessed thing before, but now she's eating. Building up her strength."

"I wonder if it's the books," Sara said. "When I'm upset or worried all I have to do is open Jane Austen, and then, well, I'm safe."

"It's so much *work* with 'the classics,' " Mrs. Eaker said. "I like easy books—escape in them, you know? Murder mysteries. Historical romances."

"Do you really escape into them?" Sara asked. "Or are you just watching the characters do this or that, but when you're through the world hasn't changed at all for you?" She smiled. "The classics are the books people have loved and kept alive—but I'm a book lover. I gnaw on books like bones."

"So does Dr. Channing," Mrs. Eaker said. "You're two of a kind."

The odd thought wriggled in Sara's mind again, just out of reach. She went in to feed Dr. Channing. They were reading short stories now.

Perhaps Dr. Channing's eyes lost their withdrawn look a little when she saw Sara. Sara couldn't tell. "Good morning," Sara said. "What a beautiful day." She looked, Dr. Channing thought, as if she had been kissed, perhaps, or her name had been said by someone with a certain inflection.

Sara spread a napkin under Dr. Channing's chin and went to get the book of James stories, passing through cool rooms that showed what Dr. Channing had loved once: rich objects and colors, walls of books. But Dr. Channing had stayed in dimness and silence since they brought her home. She would not be moved. She lay at the back of her house like an animal that had crawled into a discarded shell.

Sara began to spoon meatballs and spaghetti into Dr. Channing's mouth and opened the book of stories where she'd stuck a bit of newspaper. She was conscious again of the small thought just out of reach in her head. "Your house is perfect," she said. "It looks as if you've worked on it all your life, so that it will look very rich but not overdone, and plain but not bare, and like nobody's house but yours."

By now Sara was used to talking to Dr. Channing's silence. She sighed. "If I could, I'd buy an older house and do the very same thing, my whole life long. When I retired I'd have a place exactly my own size and shape, with just as many books too."

Sara began to read as she spooned. They were finishing *The Aspern Papers* and were at the place where Miss Tita offered herself (and the precious author's papers) to the hero, who would not marry a "ridiculous, pathetic, provincial old woman" even to get those papers he prized.

Sara began the last few pages and fed Dr. Channing spaghetti, which seemed right because the story was laid in Venice. But she didn't notice what she was spooning after a while, and Dr. Channing didn't seem to notice either. She simply ate and listened as the hero wandered about Venice, followed by his mystified gondolier. He almost decided to marry the "poor lady" to get the papers.

Sara's voice hardly faltered, but she knew Henry James saw all the ways that lies smashed lives. Behind her, suddenly, the bulk of her own great lie rose and crested, unforgivable. Her mother lay on her back, blind, knowing she would never hear Sara's voice again. And if ever, once, Martin suspected . . . Sara read on.

Sara read well; the "splendid common domicile" of Venice seemed to surround the two of them just beyond the hum of the air-conditioning.

But the lady burned the papers. The gentleman, back at home without them, found the loss of the papers "almost intolerable."

Sara closed the book. A sharp, precise agony seemed to leak out of it even after it was shut.

Sara sat silent, looking at the small blue book. That was when the thought, the plan she'd been searching for, came as delicately to her mind as a sentence from the story.

Sara looked at Dr. Channing. "What a pair of insane ladies!" she said, and caught, for a second, a kind of horror in Dr. Channing's eyes. So she smiled.

# 21

Rains made the last August days cool and green—high Iowa summer, hardly a yellow leaf yet.

Sara smashed loose plaster from her walls with the putty knife; rough chunks thudded to the floor. Gray lath showed like bones in the deepest cracks. Then patches and veins of Spackle dried on her walls and ceilings. She walked on newspapers and sneezed with plaster dust.

Every morning she was up before dawn to work on rooms that weren't even hers. She rolled thin skins of paint over plaster and old varnish, wanting yellow and gold and orange, wanting her own warm nest. When her living room and kitchen were primed and painted at last, she got Ben a dinner at her house. Sometimes she came through the lilac tunnel for breakfast with him, Banana jumping around her bare feet.

Ben thought about her when he wasn't teaching his first classes or going to committee meetings that multiplied like rabbits, reproducing their kind in every gap of his day.

He'd known Laura Pray two weeks, and she hadn't told him a thing about herself. He had a good imagination; he wove stories around the scared look she sometimes gave him, the way she kept out of reach, the breathless way she seemed to wait, afraid he would ask a question. "She's obviously a criminal on the run," he'd said to Banana the day after Laura had come for that first microwave dinner.

The kitten had its face and one paw in a tuna can and wasn't listening.

"Tell you what—she went into a fancy jewelry store in New York or L.A. or somewhere," Ben told Banana, "and she fainted dead away. While they were calling a doctor she swallowed a few diamonds, sniffed the doctor's smelling salts, and then came here to the Midwest to digest the whole thing."

The kitten licked its face with an amazingly long, cat-size tongue.

"I'm such a 'good friend,' that's what she tells me," Ben said. He supposed she saw the look on his face. He felt played with; women were always on-again-off-again, keeping you guessing.

Laura wore the same few clothes and hardly any makeup. She helped him with breakfast and didn't make coy jokes or give him sweet, lingering glances like some women did. Ben talked more than he ever could remember talking to anyone, lonely for the sound of their voices together.

"What's she so jumpy for?" he asked Banana later in the week. Banana didn't know. "I've got a theory," he told the cat. "She's so jumpy because she's the leader of a conspiracy dedicated to playing boys' *and* girls' teams in every high school football and basketball match, and then averaging each school's score. Manufacturers of jockstraps are on her trail." Banana scratched fleas.

Only once in a while did Laura have the pinched, scared look he remembered from those first days. Counting out money to pay for her share of their groceries, she said softly, "Not to be corrupted. My own money. I say how to spend it, and never, never have to lie or cheat or steal." So she hadn't had her own money. Whose then? And why had she been "corrupted"?

She laughed, saying that "never, never." Ben liked to watch her laugh—she tossed her head back a little as if she were tossing long hair over her shoulder. Breaking eggs into a bowl, Laura said she admired Hemingway's style. It sounded as if it had been translated from an older, simpler language. She found the egg beater and smiled at Ben.

"His women?" Ben said, turning bacon; it was almost done.

"He thought they were different, not like men—didn't see that we aren't born 'women.' Hey, how about a slice?" Laura leaned close to Ben to break off a bit of bacon, her full, small lips pulled back from her white teeth. She could have looked at him. She didn't. "Love bacon."

"More?" he said, holding out another slice.

She took it and put it on the stove edge. "Watch the eggs, will you? I want you to hear something funny." She came back from her house with a small journal she'd found in the library. An Imitation Hemingway Contest, she said, and began to read while Ben watched the eggs, until they were both laughing so hard at the parody (making love on the pool table at Harry's Bar & American Grill with balls flying in all directions) that Ben had to take the eggs off the burner and lean against the wall.

The bartender at Harry's (Laura read) asked if they'd made the table move, and when they said yes, he said they must move it back. Her voice went up at the end in a kind of squeak.

"Ah, ah, ah," was all Ben could say, folding his arms against his stomach because it hurt so much; tears ran down his cheeks to his full, red mouth.

Laura's face was flushed, and she rubbed her eyes and made little strangled sounds.

"That's great," Ben said when both of them could talk again. Laura said if you won the prize, you got a flight to Venice and back, and a dinner for two at Harry's Bar. They didn't look at each other.

"We laughed pretty hard," Ben said after a while.

"Yes," Laura said. "Good for us."

"We need it," Ben said.

"Yes." And then they both laughed because they sounded like Hemingway. Laura got silverware out of a drawer. Watching her, Ben thought he knew so little about her. Had she ever been married? Was she married now?

Maybe he looked mad; he didn't know. Laura said she'd make his lunch for him, and after breakfast she sang softly in his kitchen, where slatted blinds were closed against the sun. He shut his eyes before the bathroom mirror, listening to a woman singing in his house.

She was still singing when he came to the kitchen door, his hair wet—it never would lie down. She was going to be beautiful when she was plump enough. Two weeks and he hadn't even touched her.

Ben came close to Laura, who was scraping plates at his sink. He looked down at her false hair. He'd seen it was a wig the first day. Part of her damned mystery business.

Ben came just a little too close, barely crossed the invisible line in the air where friendship ends, judging it with the instinct of skin and hair tips. He was only a little beyond friendship. She knew it immediately and turned her profile, which was ugly, yet so beautiful—the long, bony nose, the flower-mouth.

He said nothing, didn't need to. She moved the few inches it took to make them nothing but friends again who laughed at somebody else making love on a pool table. Only a step. Anger suddenly made his fingers curl and cut off his breath.

"Do you like chop suey?" Laura asked. He said he did and went to get his briefcase. Nobody knew what women were thinking; they were mysteries from another world. He snapped his briefcase shut and caught his finger in the lock.

"Serves you right," he said to himself, sucking blood off the finger. Laura was singing again in the kitchen. He hunched his shoulders and looked around his living room, where drapes were still drawn, thinking maybe he wouldn't even say good-bye, mad at everybody and everything.

But Laura followed him as if she were his wife seeing him off to work. Just before he opened the door she reached out to straighten his collar a little, crossing the invisible line for that second.

Ben went through Seerley Park sucking his hurt finger, tasting blood but walking all the way to the Communications Arts building with a little smile on his face.

Summer morning in Cedar Falls pulsed with birdsong.

A leaf or two fell from trees in Ben's backyard. Sara thought of the wedding. What could she wear? She took the bus to College Square and got off at Walmart.

Sara felt warm and dreamy with the sound of Ben's laughter still in her head. She wandered down aisles in the store looking at cheap clothes that wouldn't last long. But she could afford a dress, and she didn't have to hide bruises any more.

Marie O'Brien would like Walmart, Sara thought wistfully. "Expensive stores make me jumpy," Marie had said once. "Things seem to stare back at me. Clerks are right there when I take one step inside. They hide all the price tags—the bad news is always down a neck or up a sleeve."

A stab of longing for Marie went through Sara. Here at Walmart prices could be read across the aisle. She passed rack after rack of identical dresses: no clerks were visible for half a city block in any direction.

There was a row of green dresses with low necks and wide, short sleeves. And she had promised herself that when her bruises were gone, she'd buy shorts and a short-sleeved shirt. She picked out a few.

"You got how many garmints?" asked a bored woman in a little booth. She gave Sara a card marked "5." The trying-on booths were closets with one shelf and no mirror. Each had a curtain on sagging string that blew in and out with a floor fan's blast of air.

Of course the dress was cheap, but it was the green of first leaves in May, and fit Sara exactly, and so did some white shorts with a white and black belt, and a white T-shirt trimmed in black. When they lay on the checkout counter, tags fluttering, Sara glowed as she counted out change and carried her new dress and shirt and shorts away in their crackling plastic bag, her prizes.

Ben's house was quiet and dim when she opened the door; small straws of sunlight fell through kitchen blinds. Sara washed dishes; she picked, peeled, and sliced apples from Ben's tree. She mixed her own good piecrust, found a rolling pin, spread flour on the table, and suddenly began to tremble. "Not too thin," she heard Martin say. "Having steak tonight?"

"Cedar Falls," Sara whispered to herself, trying to hear sounds of a small Iowa town: creak of swing chains in a park, leaves rustling at windowsills. She shut her eyes, trembling, but all she heard was the clink-clink-clink of metal at a dock.

"Nice little boat." Sara covered the apples with crust, pressed it around the pan rim with a fork, her hands shaking. "Nice little sail across the bay."

"Scared of water!" Martin's narrowed eyes . . . she had been so careful. Sara cut dangling bits of crust from a pan edge and remembered her piece of pie on a table with dirty dishes, heard waves slap. She had thought of everything. Hadn't she?

Sara wiped the pie pan's bottom, put it in Ben's oven, and leaned against a wall below two actors' masks, one grieving, one grinning. Trembling, she saw chairs with knobs in the middle of their backs and heard a squeaking bed.

Hardly knowing what she was doing, Sara went upstairs to Ben's bedroom, passing a battered walnut bed with bunches of grapes on the headboard. An old rocking chair spread its arms beside it. She went to Ben's closet and hid her face in his clothes, her floury hands clenched before her. She smelled the scent that was only his, mixed, one-of-a-kind. She felt safe.

And yet he was, after all, bigger, stronger. Sometimes she saw a look of his, an angry look that seemed to say she shouldn't have secrets and was a tease. He'd never look at a man that way. What was she doing in a house that belonged to a man?

After a while she wiped her eyes and went downstairs to wash her hands and look at the pie. She must never touch Ben Woodward. She couldn't even look at him too much.

Spicy apples began to fill the kitchen with their rich smell. If she got too close to Ben Woodward, she might kill him with no more than an apple pie, or a smile, or a green dress. If Martin found her.

Cutting up meat for chop suey, she saw her hands trembling. The meat's red juice leaked out.

Ben would protect her, and she could hide. . . .

"Oh!" Sara yelled in the empty kitchen. Her knife skittered from her hand and across Ben's plastic-covered table, she was so ashamed.

# 22

August was hot in Boston. New England beaches were clogged with bare bodies. Montrose, Massachusetts, had "Montrose in History Days," with a parade and craft booths along Atlantic Street.

Pam Fitzer stood on a dark street corner and cried.

Martin drove back and forth to work. The house was so quiet, Martin said to himself. Every day when he came back in the heat from Boston, it was so quiet.

He looked at the bathroom door and the broken hall mirror. He read Sara's diaries over again. She wrote so well. They ought to be published. Everybody ought to know what he'd done to her.

There were some chicken sandwiches in the refrigerator; he didn't know how they got there. He threw them out and went through cupboards thinking how Sara's hands had opened this crackerbox and that package of half-used coconut; he sat down at the kitchen table and cried.

He'd never paid much attention to the kitchen cupboards, except for the cans. Now he took everything out and found a package of birth-control pills in a canister marked "Sugar."

"Oh, hell!" he shouted. There were no pills in the box; he threw it across the kitchen. The doorbell rang.

Sara's lying and cheating and stealing. Saying she wanted a baby because he wanted one, and all the time not wanting one. Not with him. Not with somebody who beat you up and broke mirrors and busted doors in and knocked you downstairs. "Yes!" he yelled, running to the door but not opening it.

"It's Pam."

"Go away!" he shouted. "Go away!"

He sat down on their rumpled bed. Dragged her out of Cristine and Roger's house at the picnic before they went to the beach house. Of course she was scared. Of course she thought there wasn't any way out and wouldn't ever want a baby of his.

Martin jumped up and paced the house, jabbing his heels in ratty old rugs. She went to the police . . . but she didn't want to get him in trouble and make him lose his job. McManus wanted happy families working for him, he said, and he was up for promotion and McManus—oh, hell.

Jumped in the bay. Wiped herself out for him.

And he'd slept with another woman right in their bed.

He ought to get Sara's diaries printed. They were all that was left of her.

He felt as if people were talking about him at Rambaugh and watching him in Montrose. So he stopped shopping in Montrose and started going to new supermarkets.

Sometimes he saw women who looked a little like Sara. Sometimes they had children with them. Sara had wanted a baby, until she got so frightened of him.

He went home and put cans of food on shelves with all the labels facing out, and cried.

He began to read Sara's diaries again. Then he started a fire in a metal wastebasket set on bricks and ripped out and burned every page as he finished it. When only the covers of the books were left, he burned them, too, and the house stank of plastic. She was his. He wasn't going to share her with anybody.

Martin went to a new supermarket in Waltham the last day of August. He had to hunt and hunt for what he wanted, and after a while he noticed that a woman seemed to be following him; she turned up around ends of aisles and kept staring. She was the stringy type nobody looks at twice. She finally came up to him in front of sacks of potatoes.

"Pardon me," she said. "I hate to intrude, but could you be Sara Langer's husband?" She didn't have any makeup on. He said he was Martin Burney.

"Oh, yes—I meant Burney. She told us her name was Langer. I thought maybe it was her maiden name," she said. "You don't know me. I'm Vanessa Shelly. But I met your wife at the YWCA . . . got to know her quite well. She was such a nice person and so pretty." Martin looked at her, and she got a little flustered. "I don't want to rake up all your sorrow. I just wanted to say how much courage she had—she was so afraid of that water! We all worked to get her into that pool every Monday, Wednesday, and Friday, and then we worked to make her stay there. And then she got to be a better swimmer than any of the rest of us!"

He stared at her.

"I wouldn't have known that Sara Langer was Sara Burney, except for the picture of you two," Vanessa said. "But I'm just babbling along. I'm sorry. I saw an article in the paper last month, and I meant to write and tell you how sorry we all felt. . . ."

Martin said nothing. Vanessa fiddled with a bag of bread on her cart. "She got to be a real good swimmer." If Vanessa noticed she was talking to Martin's blank face and eyes, she seemed too embarrassed to stop. "Saw both of you in the paper and knew Sara right away, and then I recognized you tonight. From the picture. I should have written you. I'm so sorry. . . ."

Martin left his cart where it was. His face was very blank and very white.

"She was such a good swimmer," Vanessa said. "Probably just dived in and didn't realize . . ." Vanessa followed Martin. He went out the supermarket door, and Vanessa said, "I'm really so sorry!" to nothing but plate glass sliding shut behind him.

# 23

The last day of August, and hot. Ben's cool house felt good, and so did a shower. A wedding on a morning like that? He heard Laura Pray close her front door and go off to catch the bus. She wouldn't ride with him, go out with him, be seen with him. Like Deborah. At least Deborah had given a reason—she was a student and he was a teacher, she said.

What did you wear to a wedding in August? Something too hot—that was about it. Ben pawed through his closet and talked to Banana, who swiped at his ties if he let them dangle too low. "Why doesn't she want to be seen with me?" Ben said to the cat. "Tell you what—she's got a rich, elderly lover who pursues her all over the country. He's into spreading expensive gourmet foods on her skin and putting mustard in her navel, and she's fed up. He's vowed to kill any man who says a word to her or—God forbid—eats a dinner with her, right?"

Ben got dressed and found the church, a brick barn with four pillars hitched to the sidewalk. A tumor of concrete bricks had grown out of its side and was labeled "Christian School."

It was already hot inside, and stained glass let in a gravy-brown and pea-soup-green light. Lower parts of windows were pushed up, so that green and brown saints and kings and angels were jackknifed into dwarves who stared solemnly over their knees at the sanctuary.

Ben saw Laura Pray before she saw him. She was with

Mrs. Nepper about halfway back, and a youngish man beside her grinned and whispered to her. Laura had a green dress on—she'd never worn it for him—and it made her seem cool and very beautiful; some early asters from her garden were pinned at the neck of it.

"Hello," Mrs. Nepper whispered when she saw him. "Glad you could come. Have a seat. Glad you could come."

Laura turned her head, saw Ben sitting on the other side of Mrs. Nepper from her, and smiled. "You two know each other by now," Mrs. Nepper said, her old brown face nodding from one to the other.

"We've met in the backyard and gotten a kitten out of a tree," Laura said.

"Yes," Ben said.

He heard Laura's soft, low voice answer a question from the man with blond hair and a striped tie.

So Laura Pray liked strange men but didn't want anyone to connect her with Ben Woodward—maybe ashamed she'd eaten breakfasts and dinners with him? Anger made Ben hotter yet.

Ben could lean out a little once in a while and look at Laura's asters across Mrs. Nepper's flowered ruffles—the asters had the best place in church.

Bits of sun fell over Laura as she talked to whoever-it-was in the fancy suit and tie. Ben wished Mrs. Nepper weren't there and he could sit next to Laura. He wished he'd worn a fancier suit and tie. Then it made him mad that he wished he'd worn a fancier suit and tie.

A kid in a wrinkled sport jacket kept leading people up the aisle, then brought in what looked like the mother of the bride—she had the right overdressed, flowered, frantic look. She kept trying to glance at the back of the church without being able to turn enough to do it. She was worried about something important, Ben supposed, like whether the veil would stay on, or if the cake frosting would get sticky, or whether the bride had taken her birth-control pills.

Laura whispered now and then to the brown-haired fellow with classy clothes. She hung mystery around her like the black widow's veil in nineteenth-century plays. You could hardly see through it. It had a sexy charm.

He watched her from the corner of his eye. Weeks, and he hadn't even kissed her. Alone with her in his own house.

"Craig Miller," Mrs. Nepper said.

"Who?" Ben whispered.

"Sitting with us," Mrs. Nepper said. "His father owns the People's Bank."

A middle-aged woman played a violin solo. Flesh on her arms hung and shook like loose chicken skin with every stroke of the bow.

"Craig Miller," Mrs. Nepper whispered. "Bank in Waterloo. Assistant manager already. Smart. Went to Ames. I'll introduce you later. Bank in Waterloo."

So Laura was all dressed up and sitting with an assistant bank manager, and hadn't told Ben where she came from, whether she was married or not . . . a splotch of pea-soup green fell on Ben's shoe. A pretty young girl got up and sang about a love that would be true always.

Miller whispered to Laura again, and she smiled, then turned her head fast and caught Ben looking around Mrs. Nepper. He thought she blushed a trifle, maybe, and looked a little ashamed.

Ben scowled at a stained-glass saint with knees under his chin and a key as big as he was. Women like to play around. You think they enjoy your company, then off they go with somebody new. Ben hunched his shoulders and looked around the church as organ music wandered through it.

The groom came in and stood with another guy, looking pinned down to the whole affair with his white carnation. Imagine everybody dressed up and hot, sitting in rows to watch two other people announce in public that they were going to sleep together for the rest of their lives. You'd think they'd want to keep it quiet.

But the organ started the wedding march, thundering, and here came the bride looking twice as big as the groom with her Southern-belle hoopskirt and veil halfway down the aisle behind her, being given away by her father in a voice nobody could hear.

Ben sneaked a look at Laura. He thought she was crying; there seemed to be spots on the front of her green dress and she wasn't watching the groom put the ring on or the pair kneeling at the altar. He didn't even know her well enough to guess why she was crying. But then, women were sentimental; they always cried at weddings. Sweat was glistening on Mrs. Nepper's nose. Weddings were women's business. Women loved this kind of stuff. There were stores devoted to it, whole magazines.

Bride and groom kissed with quick embarrassment and then rushed down the aisle—an odd pair, one swathed in white cloth with flowers in her hands and flowers in her long, hot hair, and the other in practical clothes, free arms and legs, short hair, nothing to carry. Wet spots widened on Sara's green dress; her throat ached. "Asunder." Who ever used that word except at weddings?

"I've got to get to my job," Sara whispered to Mrs. Nepper as wedding guests began to rise and leave. She slipped past Craig Miller, saying she was glad she'd met him, and managed to get out through the crowd. Ben hadn't even been able to remind her she was meeting him for an after-hours tour of the theater that night.

Birds sang in hot summer trees. Sara wiped her eyes as she hurried to Main Street. It was almost eleven forty-five and a bus waited in front of the Black Hawk Hotel. Three men on the bus looked Sara over as she climbed in and sat down.

So hot. She got off the bus at Dr. Channing's corner. Ben couldn't hide his angry eyes, his stiff back, the edge in his voice, his glances at a woman who wouldn't be seen with him.

The tear spots on her dress were drying. Move. Go to another town. Not before she had done one thing, if she could. She let herself into Dr. Channing's house, shutting the heat out.

A stylish woman stood in the kitchen doorway. "There

you are!'' she said. "Laura Pray? I'm Georgia Parrish.
I've heard about you—helping Haze, reading Henry James.''
Her slate-gray hair was a silver helmet; she wore makeup
that looked almost natural, a setting for her slate-gray
eyes.

"Yes," Sara said, feeling herself wince away from
knowing another person. When she dreamed of Cedar
Falls she'd seen herself alone, always alone.

"Haze and I traveled together sometimes—France, the
Greek Isles, and to see her now''—Georgia dropped her
gray eyes—"refusing to talk, refusing to be moved, refusing to go on . . .'' She stopped and picked at the corner of
a kitchen towel with her long red nails. "She won't even
talk to *me*.''

Ellen Garner came with an armful of books, said good-
bye, and closed the door behind her. Georgia watched her
with preoccupied eyes. "To lie in this house of hers and
rot. You never knew her. You can't imagine.''

"They told me the accident paralyzed her. I wonder if
she doesn't want to live any more,'' Sara said.

"You're educated—that's obvious. You love books and
music and thinking and talking . . . reading Henry James
so well. Henry James! And she gives that all up, just tries
to die?'' Georgia Parrish was talking about Hazel Channing, but her gray eyes were going over Laura Pray now:
discount-house dress, pretty, thin as a piece of paper but
clever, quiet, a presence in the kitchen, very sad.

Watching Laura, Georgia said she'd be back when she
could get to Cedar Falls again. She was an architect, with
a project shaping up in Des Moines. She said good-bye
and, going out, smiled and put one red-tipped hand on
Laura's arm in a gesture that seemed meant to comfort.

Sara watched Georgia Parrish get in her new car, her
linen suit the palest gold, her rings a momentary flash at
the steering wheel.

A hot breeze came in the open door. Sara shut it out.

Noon sun lost its damp heat at the windows of Dr.
Channing's room. Outside it pulled the corn higher and
higher and made Iowa soil and grass fill a hot noon with

their scent, but here it fell thin and pale, a white glow edging wood and china and brass.

"Hello," Laura said. "I've been talking to your friend. And I went to a wedding this morning—Karen Ann Birtch and Judson Barker." She spread a napkin under Dr. Channing's chin. Asters were wilted at the neckline of her dress; she put them in water on the dresser.

Hazel's brown eyes were on Laura as she came and went. Laura moved against pale window light, a woman who kept herself to herself, would not be touched. Hazel Channing understood the not-being-touched, never again.

But experienced, yes. Hazel thought so. Laura's body said that; Hazel didn't know how. Laura's lips and thin neck said "hurt." Her gestures said she wasn't staying anywhere for any longer than she could manage. The rest of her, sitting beside Hazel now, was glad with its full breasts and bony hips that the old body in the bed would not ask a single question. And it would not.

So Hazel stared at Laura Pray. Who cared any more what happened, whether friends came or not, what day it was, what year, or whose beautiful old age had been smashed in a ditch with a car?

Hazel's eyes met Laura Pray's. Hazel would die in silence, a homely old woman stuck in a ruined life like an animal stuck in a dried-up water hole. She had seen African animals trapped in mud, jaws wide open above bunched bones.

But she opened her mouth for the spoon and began to eat her lunch. Laura, turned golden by a bedside lamp, opened the Henry James they would read next. It was the most beautiful of all—*The Golden Bowl*.

Hazel thought perhaps she knew parts of it by heart. Once again the prince from Italy liked his London because it echoed Imperial Rome: "If one wished, as a Roman, to recover a little the sense of that, the place to do so was on London Bridge, or even, on a fine afternoon in May, at Hyde Park Corner."

Hazel shut her eyes and swallowed a lump in her throat along with a mouthful of rice. She saw the Thames as

Henry James had loved it—glittering among its ships under blue English skies that she and James would never see again.

But James had left his words. Laura read them in her musical, low voice, hour after hour of the afternoon.

Hazel listened. Something was wrong. Something wrong had been growing for days, souring sentences she knew by heart. She lay and stared at Laura Pray.

# 24

**B**en wandered around his house waiting until it was time to meet Laura at the theater. He was jumpy, excited. The chase, he supposed—you had to try it. She was so cool, so touch-me-not. The greenroom's couch kept leaping into his head while he got his dinner, and then he started imagining doing it onstage—wouldn't that be something to remember when you directed play after play on those boards, and every time the curtain went up . . .

She'd come to his house, and he'd been to hers. Now the theater. They could play around with costumes—infinite possibilities. The Summer of the Hideout. The August of our Disguise. Maybe she was a little crazy. Finally the sun went down. Finally it started to get dark.

A main highway ran near the theater, and passing cars streaked the Strayer-Wood's expanse of wavery glass like fish going through an aquarium. Cleaners had been in the new building Friday; it was empty. He took a deep breath of its air—dust and sawdust and a breath of burned metal from the welding room. The smell had his ambitions and frustrations in it.

He went over it, floor by floor. Nobody anywhere. He turned on lights that wouldn't show from outside and waited by the back door.

When it was dark she knocked and looked around her before she came in. "Nobody in the whole building," Ben said. "I've checked."

She sighed in darkness and brought hot, damp summer night and her secretness with her, slipping past him into the dim lobby. Her white shorts and shirt glimmered, and silence closed around them until Ben could almost hear the excitement, the secretiveness; it tingled in the air, power switched on. Then she gave a little laugh at his elbow. "When does the next tour start?" she said.

He wanted her right there and right then. He came in that door every day of the school year. What if, there by the wall, he could stop and remember the damp softness of her breasts, her mouth under his . . .

But he said, "Right now," and only dared to grab her hand. "I can't put lights on where anybody can see them."

Holding his hand and following, she said, "I'm sorry about the fibs to Mrs. Nepper at the wedding."

"Never mind," Ben said, close to her in a pitch-dark hall.

She said nothing more.

Ben showed off big control booths with computers spread before plate glass like a starship cockpit. The Colortran, now—look at it! He raised and lowered the lights and pivoted the Super Trouper on its pedestal, changing gels to sweep colored beams across a black stage—he felt as if it all belonged to him, a lowly instructor.

Catwalks were as spooky as an old-fashioned movie, with a houseful of empty seats far below. He unlocked the gridiron door; they climbed steep metal stairs toward the stage-house roof. He'd never seen her in shorts; she was still thin, but not so bony.

"Where the snow falls from in *Lear*," Ben said when they stood on the grid. "Dead leaves for autumn. Confetti for parades." Usually he liked explaining, but not now. He wanted her, and the wanting gave all conversations he'd had with her the same sour colors as he looked back. He'd thought he enjoyed them. He'd thought that kind of talk with a woman was the best thing in the world.

"It's like a cobweb," she said. Wires of hemp-rigged lines and pipes hung before them. She looked through the metal grating they stood on. Motionless scrim and cycs and drapes were festooned below like sails in a calm. He was so close to her he smelled her hair, her skin.

Darkness and fifty-five feet of air under their feet and no make-believe left—it was laid wide open here. Ben's hands itched to touch her.

They looked at mechanics of fantasy below, down to the rail with its counterweights and winch sets. Maybe characters in a play gestured gracefully or kissed or said witty things, but cables and steel hung over their heads and they walked across black mouths of stage traps.

Ben didn't explain much. Space hung between them, and she was asking questions to keep the space there, like a damn tease.

Their shoes rang on iron steps, going down.

"Look," she said, and laughed—a free sound. Somebody had draped a skeleton in a chair with a bottle in its finger bones. No one was watching as the scene shop closed its clutter around them, smelling of paint and glue.

He had saved his makeup room and costume room for last. "Here's my bailiwick," he said, snapping on lights. Headless mannequins stood among sewing machines and cutting tables in *Candide* costumes.

"Oh!" she cried, going from one elaborate dress to another.

"Here," Ben said, and handed her one of the great feathered hats. Laura put it on and posed before mirrors. "Wrong hairstyle," she said.

"Beautiful," Ben said. Bright lights gleamed in his eyes. She stopped laughing, but she stole a look at herself and ran her hand over lush velvets and lace.

"I'll tell you what—if you like living in the past, this is the place," Ben said, opening a costume storage door. She walked up and down aisles, fascinated by ranks of brilliant colors. Fripperies, enticements, make-believe, disguise.

"Look!" she said, lifting a huge black satin bonnet.

"Try it on. Mirrors all over the place," Ben said.

She twirled before them in the bonnet, then tried another. "Go ahead," Ben said, "don't mind me." She was forgetting to shrink back and be afraid.

Her eyes glowed like the satins and silks. She slipped a Renaissance dress off its hanger and ducked behind a storage box. Ben sat down to clap and whistle as she came out and posed before a half-dozen lovely Petrarchan Lauras in mirrors. He supposed Laura had walked by poor old Petrarch with that witchy reserve, that cool.

She knew how beautiful she was; she was laughing, but she knew. A Roaring Twenties gown changed her to a silver trout glittering with beads, flashing with bits of light. It hung on the tips of her breasts and showed her knees, then dipped to a fishtail in back.

Her cheeks were pink and her eyes shone. She played in bright colors of madams and dowagers and maidens, show beauties, flimflam hussies, false wives, disguised mistresses—she wore them all, giggling, her eyes knowing how she looked, though she laughed at herself.

At first the two of them put everything back. There were spotlights; Ben turned them on. Sara's glistening hair, satins, velvets, and jewels sprang out, brighter than real.

"Oh, look!" She had found a blue hoop-skirted dress.

"Go on," Ben said. She went behind the box to take off her T-shirt, and Ben heard a rustling of yards of cloth. She came out at last to look at a tiny-waisted, bare-shouldered beauty surrounded by tiers of ruffles and braid and roses. When she spun around a garden of great skirts swung like bluebells in the row of mirrors. Ben clapped. She stood staring at herself.

"Here's Cunégonde's gown from *Candide*," Ben said. "Eighteenth-century upper-class maiden—before she gets attacked by a few regiments, of course."

Laura went behind the box. He heard her elbows whack it once or twice. "Somebody's following me," she giggled, coming out in the white, lacy, rose-budded, Dresden-china dress; it had immense padded hips and behind. He caught her shoving her hair under her wig. "What a birdcage!" she said, and giggled. "I wonder how they ever sat down!"

"They sort of perched," Ben said. "We have two other

identical costumes for her, each one more dirty and bloody and ragged.''

Now they began to pile dresses and hats and veils in heaps, intent on the next one, and then the next. He saw her stuffing her hair back under the wig again, but couldn't see what color her hair was. He pressed costume after costume on her, draping her with plumes from the Empire, slit sleeves from the Middle Ages. She fluttered fans, fluttered her eyelashes, curtsied.

"I'm crazy!" she cried at last. "I wonder who I am!" She stood beside a heap of clothes, pointing to her mirrored self wearing a Greek chiton and holding a huge Edwardian feathered hat and a flapper's kid slippers. Now she looked grave, watching herself. She didn't look at him or laugh any more, but turned to stare at costumes in heaps.

"Who are you?" Ben asked softly.

Now the frightened look came back to her eyes. She shook her head, then turned her bare back to him, a confection of gauze held around her. "I can't get this zipper down," she said in a toneless voice.

He worked with the zipper, and her glossy, false hair touched the back of his hand. He unzipped the Greek dress and then, slowly, ran his hands over her bare shoulders and tried to turn her . . .

At the first touch of his fingers she jerked away, catching her breath. "Don't," she said, putting space between them, both hands holding gauze against her.

She saw his face. "I shouldn't be here!" she cried.

Some women were like that—Venus on the half shell, cold. Finally he said, "Let's try again. Start all over."

"I don't want you to think it's you," she said, turning her half-bare back to him. "That I don't . . . that I'm just teasing." She rubbed her forehead with the heel of her hand and looked around her at the colored heaps.

"It's okay," Ben said.

She looked at him for a moment, then went behind the box and came out in a few minutes in her own shorts and shirt, holding the dress. They began putting costumes on hangers. They found boxes for hats, lined up shoes.

Neither of them spoke. It was like a movie run backward, so that all the places where they had laughed together were now places where they avoided each other, backed away.

Piles got smaller. Colors were hung away. When Ben snapped off lights the room was neat again. Ordinary.

# 25

**"I** haven't shown you my office," Ben said. He didn't look at Laura. His voice had a businesslike sound.

"Fine," she said. She wasn't looking at him either.

"Here we are," Ben said, snapping on his desk light. "Not much to look at. I'm an instructor and the lowest of the low. And here's my makeup room."

She followed him in. "But I'll tell you what—you *are* in the company of one of the makeup magicians of the Middle West," Ben said. "No crepe-wool beards or mustaches in my plays—and no yak hair either. We ventilate the pieces—real hair. Cost you hundreds to order. 'Hooking a rug,' the students call it. Same process."

Hairpieces were tacked on the wall. She ran a finger along a mustache. "You hook it on net?"

"Gauze net. Simply disappears against your skin," Ben said. "Incredible. Can't see it a foot away. Put it on with mat spirit gum, take it off with remover, clean it with acetone. That's all."

She looked at every hairpiece, then glanced at herself in a big mirror over the tables. "I wonder . . . could you make me look like a man?"

"If you wore a beard."

"A beard?"

"The woman's neck—it gives you away," he said.

"I'm tall," she said. She wasn't smiling. "My voice is

pretty low, but what about my hands?'' She looked at her breasts. "I can flatten myself enough."

"Ace bandages," Ben said. "Wide ones. You wrap them around your breasts a few times and pin them under the arm."

She looked at her hands.

"It's gestures more than anything," he said. "Keep your fingers stiff. Keep the nails real short. Don't wave your hands around. Wear a big ring on each hand so people will look at it and not notice there isn't any hair."

"And that's all?"

"You've got to practice and practice—walk differently, hold yourself differently—everything boys learn. And get your voice down in your chest."

"Would you try that dark beard on me?" Sara wasn't looking at him; she sat down in front of a mirror.

"It's the bearded lady's beard from *Barnum*," Ben said, and went to a cupboard. "You're in luck—it's too small for a man." He dabbed some mat spirit gum on Sara's upper lip and cheeks and chin, his face very close to hers. Their eyes didn't meet. Her chin was soft when he cupped it in his hand. "Watch."

Sara watched a fine, curling beard, nicely trimmed, cover half of her face. Then a mustache feathered around her mouth. Now a young man with breasts sat at the makeup table.

The bearded man with breasts stared at himself.

"If the mustache is bushy and drooping, it covers your lips . . . you can strain your soup," Ben said.

Sara smiled, and saw her own teeth appear and disappear in the black, curling hair that seemed to grow there — the net beneath the beard had faded away. When she touched the mustache with her fingers she saw her familiar hand laid on that strange face.

"You'd have to work on your voice. Pitch it down and practice till you can do it without thinking. Some men have pretty high voices."

"I'm fairly tall," the young man in front of the mirror said. "I'll need to disguise myself and make a trip out of town pretty soon. Can I buy anything like this around here?''

"I'll tell you what—borrow these," Ben said. He asked no questions; he didn't look at the young man. "We can fix you up with costumes, I think, or we can go shopping like two fellows."

"I'd rather wear what you have here."

"There's some contemporary stuff—we'll look. A summer suit that might fit you. Some pants and shirts, maybe. Even shoes. And if you need my car . . ."

"Oh, no," the young bearded man said. "I couldn't do that." But blue eyes met Ben's in the mirror.

"No problem. I won't need it for a while. It runs okay, but you can't lock the door on the driver's side."

"I don't have a driver's license."

"Don't get arrested. And we'll have to thicken the eyebrows." He squinted at the dark young man in the mirror.

"You haven't asked where I'm going or how long I'll be gone," the young man said.

Ben got remover and acetone out of a cupboard, not looking at him.

"I'm going to see my mother," the dark man said. "My father died quite a while ago, and my mother's in a nursing home. She was forty-five when I was born, and she's bedfast now. I'm all the family she's got left."

Ben felt odd for a moment, looking into the strange man's face. He had started to act differently; he couldn't say how.

"She's blind," the bearded man said. "She won't know I look like a man. If I don't come, she might think she's all alone in the world."

Ben put remover on a toothbrush, still feeling the strangeness. Laura had seemed, for a second or two at a time, to be like him. "I'll show you how to take the beard and mustache off every night."

Sara watched as he dabbed at net with the toothbrush. Once she put her hand on his, and he looked at her in the mirror, and she smiled.

She wanted to go home by herself, so they packed clothes and beard and makeup and Ace bandages and acetone and spirit gum and remover in a box. He carried it for her as they walked dark halls without speaking and passed through the lobby to the door he came through every morning. He unlocked it, and she was gone in damp summer night.

Ben went back to his office. He sat at his little, cluttered desk for a long time looking at four walls without any windows in them.

Sara was smiling at herself in her mirror. She'd put on the beard and mustache, and bound her breasts with bandages, and put on a man's summer suit and shirt and tie from Ben's costume storage room. She stood in a corner of her apartment and talked into that pocket, pitching her voice low, hearing her voice bounce back. She'd borrowed a cheap pair of dark-rimmed men's glasses. She'd buy a big man's ring for each hand.

Banana wasn't fooled by the costume and twined around the bearded young man's trousered legs as he went into the living room. It was faintly lit by a shaft of light from Ben's house.

The dark young man knelt on the couch, rested his bearded head on his arms, and looked at the painting of a bullfight on Ben's wall. Now there was a shadow on the wall beside the bull—a naked man. He wasn't dancing. He paced back and forth.

One man watched the other's shadow for a long time.

The shadow on Ben's wall stopped pacing. Suddenly Sara saw Ben come into sight to fling himself in his living-room chair, lamplight glowing on his naked back and legs. He lay like a grieving child, his face pressed against his knees and hidden by his arms.

Sara held her breath, swallowed hard, could not take her eyes away.

Soft wind blew in Sara's living-room windows. There was someone laughing in Seerley Park.

Sara left the couch and took off the man's clothes, mustache, beard; she unwound bandages from her breasts.

In her shirt and shorts, barefooted, she rustled past lilacs and knocked softly at Ben's kitchen door.

The kitchen was dark when Ben opened his door and she stepped inside. He'd pulled on a pair of shorts. "Hi," he said.

"I have to stay away from you," Laura said. "It isn't that I—"

Ben's arms closed tight around her, but not before Laura gasped, threw her hands up to ward him off, and came into his hard grip with the angles of her elbows and wrists and knuckles between them. She felt his hot face—he'd been crying because of her. Their few seconds of struggling left Sara against his kitchen table and Ben in the doorway, both breathing fast in the old wood and cooking and soap smells of Ben's kitchen.

Neither spoke. A car went by. Ben's kitchen clock ticked.

Then Laura came close to Ben and put her hands flat against thick, curly hair on his chest. His hands slid up her arms—the long fingers she knew. He was square and solid; his bare skin warmed her even when she wasn't quite touching it.

"I'm so sorry," Laura whispered, her whisper going high in a squeak because she was crying, her wet face on his shoulder. "It isn't y-you. It's got nothing to do with you."

He said nothing; she only felt his chest rise and fall with a sigh.

"I don't want to be chased. Caught. I've been hurt," Laura whispered.

His fingers tightened a little on her arms, that was all. "I have to live by myself," Laura whispered. "Take care of myself."

"I'll tell you—I've been hurt too," Ben said. He pulled away from her a little; his voice was flat. "You don't know how it was. I loved her, and she'd hardly let me kiss her. God, I hated her."

Laura flung her arms around Ben then. She was tight

against him, her mouth almost on his. "You don't have to hate us!" she cried.

"I don't!" Ben cried, astounded, and kissed her. She was pinned between him and the wall, and he slid both hands under her shirt.

Her face was wet and she began to cry against a rack of wet dish towels. He mumbled words of comfort he didn't even hear and fumbled for the zipper on her shorts, found it, pushed her shorts down, got out of his own.

He kissed her and kissed her, and when they stopped for breath she was trying to get her feet out of her tight, stretchy shorts. He could taste the wine he'd been drinking in both their mouths now, and their bodies were hot against each other. He shoved her T-shirt out of his way until it was around her arms and face and then carried her out of there and through his dark house and up the stairs with her shorts hanging around her feet still. He heard the belt whack on the banister.

When he put her on his bed she was crying softly; he didn't hear it. She curled in a ball, her feet still in her shorts.

"You call this hate?" Ben said, stopping to laugh, to run his hands between her legs.

"Yes," Sara said with a sob.

His hands froze on her warm skin. The dark bedroom was silent.

She was crying. She had her back to him.

He rolled away from her, sat on the edge of the bed. He clenched his fists. He was burning all over.

"Hate," Sara said.

"No!" he yelled.

"But what *are* you feeling?" she said.

"You've got a right to say No," he said in a cold voice, hunching his shoulders and turning his head back and forth in the dark.

"You're feeling hurt. Insulted. Rejected."

"Sorry," he said in the same icy voice. "Can't blame a man for trying."

"Yes," she said. "I can."

"Christ! Come here and talk and smile and kiss me, and then say, 'No, not you, not now—' "

"Makes you hate me, doesn't it?"

"Yes!" Ben cried. "I'll tell you—yes, it does! You want me to say it, I'll say it!"

He felt her leave the bed. Her bare feet whispered on the floorboards. She was putting her shirt and shorts back on. He struck his fists on his bare knees, sat still while she came to stand before him a moment. Faint glow from a streetlight edged her white shorts, the curve of one arm and leg. Then he heard her feet on the stairs. His back door shut softly behind her.

# 26

September was hot in Boston. Martin's house still stank of Sara's burned diaries. Martin walked around the metal wastebasket he'd burned them in; it stood on bricks in the kitchen like a crematorium, like a grave.

Sara could swim.

He drove to work mumbling to himself "She could swim." Every red light on the way to Rambaugh Computer Sales and Service made him swear—he was a fool, pinned to his stupid job like a stuck butterfly, trapped by red lights and his bosses at Rambaugh and not knowing *where* Sara was, *if* she was. When the light turned green he stamped on the gas and squealed away from other cars as if he had a clue, a destination, a clear track to Sara, who ought to be dead—who would be dead as soon as he found her, if she were alive.

Then he started thinking. He should never have let that bitch in the supermarket get away.

Now the wastebasket in the kitchen wasn't like a crematorium or a grave—it stank of lies and hate and getting even. He'd fed and clothed and housed Sara all those years, and bought her a house and furniture and rugs and new refrigerator and stove, and let her work at the library, and she'd made him think she was drowned.

She'd gone swimming off to some man waiting in his car along a beach road, probably . . . stripped off her wet clothes in front of him, giggling, and put on dry, pretty ones. She'd driven off with some man, and they'd laughed at Martin Burney, who was screaming "Sara! Sara!" and diving into Manhasset Bay.

She could swim. She wasn't afraid of the water.

He should have made that bitch in the store tell him everything—hell! She probably knew where Sara was.

So he had to go to the new supermarket in Waltham after work. He sat in his car watching the entrance, watching for a stringy woman with brown bangs and no makeup—he couldn't remember her name.

Sara was off with some man—of course she was—another man who'd buy her clothes and a house and a new refrigerator and stove, the sucker.

Martin drank port or sherry from a bottle, watching the supermarket entrance, swearing, thinking of his .25 Baretta. A pretty little pistol. Make a silencer from an orange-juice can and some steel wool.

He couldn't remember her name. When she told him Sara could swim that was all he'd heard.

Sara was sleeping with somebody else.

He drank wine and hit his new car's wheel with his fist and swore. Stringy Bangs wouldn't ever come back to that supermarket—probably lived miles away and he'd never see her again.

At night Sara started to be in bed with him. He'd wake up and smell her special scent, her perfume, and reach out to find her full breasts and long, round thighs—and they weren't there.

Who cared whether he did a good job at Rambaugh? He knew they were all talking about him, Martin Burney, who had lost his wife and his grip.

One night he tried to wake up when Sara got in bed with him, but he couldn't. He smelled her in his dreams and reached out for her, and she was there all right, but not smelling like Sara any more. Whatever was there smelled worse than the kitchen wastebasket. His hands, feeling for her soft body, found something slimy and swelled up with sea water.

He didn't sleep very well. He sat in his car outside the

new supermarket after work, watching for a bitch with bangs.

All puffy with floating in the ocean. Bones sticking through the mess. He'd seen a drowned dog once that looked like that, half covered with sand on the beach near Manhasset.

He was finished at Rambaugh. Sara had done that to him. He'd get her for it. A little Baretta that fit in your pocket—didn't even make it bulge.

People kept going in and out of the supermarket until closing time. The big plate glass doors slid back and forth until finally the lights went out, and all he could do was go home.

Now he had to sleep with the bedside lamp on, so that when he dreamed of rotting Sara with her bare nose socket and teeth showing in a big grin, he could wake up, sweating, and see there was nothing in bed with him at all. She might have drowned. Maybe she was dead and rotting. Maybe that was what the dream meant.

But the next night just about seven-thirty there was Stringy Bangs, going in the supermarket. Martin was sure it was Stringy Bangs. She was wearing jeans and a halter top; she swiped at her limp hair as she went through the door. He hid his wine bottles and tied his tie, and when she came out again with a bag he was waiting for her.

"Mr. Burney!" she said, popping her rabbity little eyes at him under her bangs.

"You told me about Sara, and I was so upset I didn't remember your name," Martin said, smiling. He could be very warm and friendly when he chose. "I've waited here after work for a couple of days, hoping you'd come back. I wanted to ask you all about Sara."

"Well . . ." she said.

"Your name began with an N, didn't it?" Martin said.

"No—it's Vanessa Shelly," she said. "I really didn't know your wife too well."

"I miss her so," Martin said, looking sad and lonely. "I guess I just want to talk to people who knew her."

"The cat's having kittens, that's the trouble," Vanessa

said. "I feel responsible, you know. I left the door open and she got out, and now she's having kittens."

"I suppose it seems crazy to you—wanting to talk about Sara," Martin said. "Just go to some nice restaurant and have dinner and talk about her—could you do that?"

"It's so sad about Sara, and I know how you feel, but it's the cat," Vanessa said. "I feel so responsible, and Jean isn't there."

"We could go to your place if you're worried about the cat," Martin said. "I have to talk to you tonight because my company is sending me out of town for a couple of months tomorrow." (Big chance he had to be sent anywhere by Rambaugh now, but Stringy Bangs would think he wouldn't bother her again.) She was looking him over, and he was glad he had on a suit and tie. "I work for a computer company."

"That's nice," Vanessa said, looking worried because the bed wasn't made and she'd left dirty underwear in a heap near the door.

"But maybe it's asking too much," Martin said, and started to turn away, looking as lonely and sad as he could.

"No—no," Vanessa said. "No, of course not. Why don't you follow me in my car and give me a minute or two to get our place straightened up? We're in 2 E."

Martin said that would be fine, and Stringy Bangs drove off in an old, rust-gnawed Ford. He followed her in his fancy new car—she'd be impressed with that too. She parked in front of a run-down apartment house, waved to him, and ran in.

Martin followed her in a few minutes. The hall was dark and smelled like cats and dogs, or maybe wet diapers. Feet had kept the stairs clean in a narrow track; the rest was dirt and cigarette butts. "2 E" must mean the fifth floor.

It did. Stringy Bangs had her door open when he got there and was making hospitable and apologetic noises.

Martin stepped in and hit his head on a white garbage bag strung up just inside the door. It was hung with others in a long row and dominoed the rest so that the whole sagging bunch of them rustled and twirled until they hit a wall, bounced back, and started to rustle and twirl in the other direction.

"We don't have any storage space," Vanessa said nervously, shutting the door. Her shoulders and arms were freckled, and there were worry lines on her forehead already. They faced each other in the small part of the room that wasn't filled with a double bed, a bathroom sink full of dishes, a microwave, two bicycles, pictures, dirty cups, cardboard boxes, clothes drying, stuffed animals, straggling plants, and the rows of white garbage bags tied by their tops to ropes overhead like meat at the butcher's, or hanged men.

It was hot. Martin stared at knotted ropes that ran from one curtain rod to another, crisscrossing the room. Dozens of the white bags sagged by their necks from them, each labeled in big black letters: JEAN'S CLASS CRAP, VANNY'S $$$, VANNY'S STINKERS, JEAN'S WINTER STUFF, VANNY'S GOAT FEATHERS, JEAN'S FLUBS, JEAN'S I DON'T CARE, VANNY'S MAN KILLERS, JEAN'S . . .

Martin stopped trying to read what was lettered on the bags and said, "Nice place you've got." The bags hung just above Vanny's head. "Clever idea."

"We don't have places to put things, so Jean hung the bags up—she's awfully resourceful," Vanny said, and crawled under the far side of the bed. She came to her feet with a red face after a moment or two. "Just one kitten so far," she said.

"Congratulations," Martin said.

"Sit down, won't you?" Vanny said, pushing a stuffed pig and wadded-up panty hose off the only chair.

Martin ducked between a garbage bag labeled SALVATION ARMY and one with CLASS STRUGGLE—JEAN on it and sat down.

"Coffee?" Vanny asked.

"That would be nice," Martin said.

"It's her first litter," Vanny said, putting two cups of water in the microwave.

"I just wanted to know if Sara told you about her

troubles and hopes and ambitions—that kind of thing," Martin said.

Vanny perched on the other side of the bed and swiped at her bangs again. There was sweat shining on her nose. "I didn't know her awfully well, I'm afraid. She said she did a lot of gardening and work around the house and that was why she was so br—why she wanted to get exercise, you know—learn to swim." Vanny's face was red again, and she sat stiffly on the far edge of the bed, as if she were staying as far away from Martin as she could.

"Did she talk about the fellow she was in love with?"

"The fellow?"

"She was in love with somebody else. I just wanted to know if she ever talked about him, or if he came with her, or was waiting for her, or anything."

"Well, I—"

"It can't hurt to talk about it," Martin said. "She's gone, you know."

"It's so sad," Vanny said, sitting stiffly on the bed and glancing now and then at the microwave.

"Did you see him?" Martin said.

"Why, no, I never . . . but I didn't know her very well. . . ."

"You can tell me," Martin said, getting up and hitting his head on a garbage bag marked VANNY'S FAMILY. One sack hit another, and away a row of them went across the room to the opposite wall and back again as he walked around the bed toward Vanny.

"I didn't know . . ."

"Yes, you did," Martin said. "You knew her. She told you about this guy, didn't she? Told you she was going to leave me?" His voice was loud now.

Vanny backed under a bag labeled JEAN'S JUNK FOOD and opened the microwave door between herself and Martin. "I'll just make the coff—"

"Tell me!" Martin shouted, slamming the microwave shut again. "Tell me everything!"

"But I don't *know* anything!" Vanny was backed against

a wall now. Her eyes kept going from Martin to the door of the room.

She was expecting somebody to come—Martin grabbed her by her bare arms and shook her hard. "I'll kill you, you bitch—you know where she was going to go!"

Tears of fright popped from Vanny's eyes. "You knew she had a man she was seeing!" Martin yelled. "She told you who he was! She told you where she was going to run away with him and make a fool of me!"

Vanny wailed, "No!"

Martin slapped her once, not too hard, just to sober her up.

Vanny screamed, as if he were going to rape her—unappetizing as she was—so he hit her a lick in the face to make her quit screaming.

She screamed some more.

A small cat shot out from under the bed and into an empty box in a corner, a kitten in her teeth. Vanny kept yelling, backed against the wall under the plastic bags, her hands in front of her face. Martin hit her again, but that didn't stop the noise.

If he had the gun . . . somebody would hear her. . . .

Martin ran, slamming the door so that garbage bags swung and rustled back and forth over sobbing Vanny. He clattered down four flights of dirty stairs, leapt into his car, and gunned it out of its parking place and away.

# 27

"**M**artin Burney! I didn't know what to do!" Vanny sobbed.

"Hold still," Jean Tarkley said. "You've got to keep the ice on it or you'll have an awful black eye."

"Martin Burney! He wanted to come here and talk, and you weren't here!" Vanny wailed. "And Walks-by-Herself was having the kittens—"

"I went for cigarettes, I told you. Then I met Harold and we had coffee," Jean said. "Hold still."

"I should never have said anything to him in the supermarket—should have let him go by and minded my own business. I had to stick my nose in!" Vanny began to cry again. "And I didn't remember the bruises in time—"

"You're all right," Jean crooned. "We'll get you quieted down and then call the police."

"Police!" Vanny sat up. "Call the police?"

"Hold still."

"Have them come poke around here, and then maybe the newspapers, and your folks knowing we're living together again?"

"Well, you can't let crazy men force their way into women's apartments and hit them," Jean said. "You're going to have a real black eye."

"He was waiting for me outside the Quik Shop and wanted to know everything about his wife, Sara, he said— the one who drowned early last month, remember? So I was sorry for him, you know, because he'd lost his wife. And all the time I should have remembered."

Walks-by-Herself was in a box on the bed now, licking two newborn kittens under the plastic bag that said JEAN'S I DON'T CARE. "Maybe I should get some steak, or some whiskey," Jean said.

"Don't go! He might come back! He pushed me against the wall over there and told me he'd kill me if I didn't tell him everything, and I *was* telling him everything!"

"We should call the police," Jean said. "What did you remember?"

"This ice is so cold!" Vanny sobbed. "I should have remembered right from the beginning . . . I always noticed it. I was just so sorry for him, and he's nice-looking. How could I ever guess he'd go after me. . . ." She sobbed and lay back on the bed beside Walks-by-Herself and the kittens, with the ice bag on her eye and her brown bangs wet and stuck to her forehead.

"What did you remember?"

"That Sara was always black and blue." Vanny sat up again. "You wouldn't see it if she had clothes on, but when she was in swimming or taking a shower—on her chest, and her back, and her hips. She swam awful hard."

"So that's why he hit you."

"Why?"

"Because you said this Sara was always black and blue," Jean said.

"No! I told you! I didn't remember in time, not until he was in here and I was making some coffee. If I had, would I have invited him in here? She always said she did a lot of gardening and housework and bruised easily, and she was a blonde, so we thought—"

"I'd better get some steak."

"No! He might come back!" Vanny yelled. "You don't know what it was like, having him come at me like that. He's tall, and big—"

"He won't come back. He'll expect us to report him and get the law on his tail." Jean sighed. "All right. We'll stay at my folks tonight, okay? If you're so scared, we can even stay longer. I don't care what they think any more, and it's close to your work and B.U. We'll put you to bed and give you a good night's sleep. I still think we ought to call the police.''

"I'm all right." Vanny got up. "Your folks won't send you money any more if they find out I'm here, and how'll you pay your tuition?'' The ice bag dripped on Walks-by-Herself when Vanny bent over the box. "He didn't break anything.''

"Couldn't you tell he was crazy—wanting to go to your place and talk about his wife? You better pack up a few things. Put some makeup in. You're going to need it for work tomorrow.''

"He looked *ordinary*," Vanny said. "Nice-looking. Had a new car—drove home behind me and parked right out there. But if I'd remembered in time, Sara being all black and blue.'' She shivered. "He's out of his mind.''

"Go on and pack, and take something respectable to wear.''

Vanny put the drippy ice bag in the sink with dirty dishes and untied a garbage bag marked VANNY'S GOAT FEATHERS. "Sara used her maiden name at the Y . . . at least I think it was her maiden name. I told you that was funny.''

"Didn't want him to know, maybe.''

"But I recognized him from that picture of them in the paper. Maybe I shouldn't have told him anything. He said Sara was in love with another man. Maybe she didn't want him to know about the Y." Vanny was filling a clean garbage bag with clothes and makeup. She sniffled now and then.

"Well, she's drowned.''

"That's right," Vanny said. "Doesn't matter now if he knows." She fingered her swollen face.

"Let's go," Jean said.

Vanny held the box with Walks-by-Herself and the kittens in it while Jean drove. When they got there Jean's parents were stuffy the way they always were, but Jean wasn't going to lie any more. Jean's mother gave Vanny the guest room and stared at Vanny's black eye. Jean supposed everybody wondered why they'd come. They could just wonder.

"You lovebirds have a little fight?" Jean's teenaged brother snickered, going up to bed.

Jean got some hot soup for Vanny, and another ice bag, and stroked her long, soft brown hair until she fell asleep.

The house was quiet. Jean tiptoed down the hall to her own room. Her mother kept it just the way it had looked in Jean's high school days: ruffled curtains and ruffled vanity skirt and dolls cuddled close to each other on the bed, little-girl faces, little-girl arms around each other.

There were pictures of boys she had known still stuck on the mirror above her debate trophy and cheerleader letter and valentines.

Jean didn't touch the bed or the dolls. She put on her nightgown and washed her face and opened Vanny's door softly; she knew when it would start to squeak.

Nobody ever slept in the guest room except a now-and-then relative. It was part of the house, but really not; plants got dusty there, and so did a big Bible on the table by the window, and a neat pile of the best towels beside it. "We have to be ready for guests," her mother always said. "Hospitality. Make them feel comfortable and welcome."

Walks-by-Herself was asleep with her kittens in her box under the table.

Vanny gave a little snort with her stuffed-up nose, and Jean crept into bed beside her. Little by little she slid her arm under Vanny's neck until Vanny's head was on her shoulder and her warm body warmed Jean's. They lay together in the guest room as still as dolls, one with her eyes shut, the other with her eyes open

# 28

**H**e was out of his mind. Martin drove fast, his car windows open to cold September air. Crazy weather for early September. Just went into a red fog—came out the other side and saw what he'd done.

The bitch would call the police. She stood there yelling and holding her face under those crazy garbage bags—she'd call the police.

But he could get home and pack some clothes, shut up the place. He had that much time.

He parked a block away and sneaked down the alley and around to the front door. He dumped clothes in a suitcase and took out his .44 Magnum—now that was a gun, a real cannon—but what he needed was his little .25 Baretta with eagles on the grips. He found the Baretta and a clip for it, knocked both ends out of an orange-juice can, found some steel wool to put in it, and got out of there. He stopped at an automatic teller on the way out of town for plenty of cash and drove fast toward the ocean.

"Damn fool," Martin said out loud, taking two-lane roads toward Manhasset. Into a red fog. That bitch he'd met in the supermarket wasn't going to tell him anything more, so he hit her.

Damn fool. Sara. She'd made him a damn fool and was off sleeping with some man, her beautiful body . . . the truth was like a hot stove he had to sit on whether he wanted to or not. She'd learned to swim. That scared little rabbit. Said she was going to Boston U. for classes every

Monday, Wednesday, and Friday when she was learning to swim or kissing some man, lying under him and laughing at Martin Burney.

When that bitch in the supermarket told him about Sara, he froze; for a while he couldn't think it straight through, and he didn't know any answers yet. Sara lied and sneaked—he could see that—took swimming lessons on the sly. But what else had she been doing behind his back? There had to be a man in it.

Just an hour or so and he'd be in Manhasset. Stevenson never rented his beach house after Labor Day. Hide out there if he wanted to. Park the car in a new place every afternoon in one of the towns, then walk to the house when it got dark. He had to hide. He had to think.

Sara wasn't afraid of the water any more. If she'd fallen or dived into Manhasset Bay that night, she'd had a good chance to get back to the beach house and get the hell out while he was sailing around the bay with John Fleishman, yelling and crying. He'd never doubted she was drowning and going out to sea.

When he got to Manhasset, Martin didn't drive through town; he parked on a dead-end street that ran to the ocean between empty warehouses and walked down the road to the sand hook.

He hid in clumps of scrub pine when he saw lights of a car, and remembered hiding that way with Sara, making love in the dark, laughing. She was laughing now, all right. She'd been somewhere laughing while he dragged out her clothes and cried. She was laughing with some man, while he lost the manager slot at Rambaugh Computer Sales and Service. And now he'd lose his job. Ruined his life. Laughing.

Unless she'd been desperate enough to drown herself.

The ocean pounded toward him in darkness behind the dunes. How could you understand women? They might as well have tails like fish—and so mysterious, pretty, and dirty, even if they had "principles" and talked all the time about being crooked and lying.

Black water pounded toward him. Maybe Sara wasn't

laughing. Maybe she was out there, shredded by fish.
Maybe she was a skull grinning through long blond hair.

Waves thudded and hissed. His thin-soled office shoes
sank in sand. He passed a grass-topped dune that had a
hollow toward the water. He'd talked with Sara for hours
in that sandy half-cave . . . all they wanted had been right
there, with gulls crying over it. And when it was dark Sara
was ready to make love, eager under him on sand still
warm from the sun.

Tears in Martin's eyes turned cold in the wind. He'd
kissed her mysterious, beautiful body afterward, and slept
until he felt a cold touch on his elbow, his ankle. The
ocean was inching up at high tide to find them. They
dressed and went home in the moonlight, hand in hand.

Now icy September wind tunneled up his sleeves and
pants legs.

He had tracked her all the way to Nebraska once, after
he'd broken her toe. She'd run away to her mother. But
you couldn't just let them leave. You couldn't say "Yes,
dear, you can walk out. You made those promises and I
bought you the house and red kitchen and fancy appliances
and you talk about being independent? With your little
two-bit job, checking books out, checking book in?"

He jammed his heels into sand; it filled his shoes. They
put on sexy clothes and all that makeup. It was a damned
battle every day at Rambaugh with McManus watching—
and then come home to Sara. And she wasn't complaining,
not saying anything, but he knew what she wanted. She
wanted to get out. She wanted to shack up with somebody
else, and she'd done it.

Sand in his shoes. He imagined her body down there on
the beach, inched in by breakers, in pieces, maybe, rotted
by more than three weeks in the water, like dead fish in an
aquarium he'd had when he was ten. Like his dream.

He knew the road, even in the dark. Beach lights weren't
on. The wind was cold. Martin ducked into a pine grove in
front of the beach house and listened. No car in the drive.
No lights. He waited in pine scent and wind, then walked
slowly downhill. The house hung above him, beach stairs

descending, locked storage space underneath. No sailboat at a next-door dock. Nothing but constant breaking of waves.

The beach stairs gleamed a little along their sharp, painted edges. A red fog of hate, and then the sound of Sara hitting steps, going down. Nobody had seen it.

His hands were numb with cold. Nobody had seen it. Nobody knew. Loyalty. No blackmail. Just the stinking little salesman's desk at Rambaugh instead of a private one with a secretary. Just watching Al Surrino promoted. Laughing with another man now. Sneaked off. Shacked up. Fooled him.

Martin climbed the beach stairs. It wasn't hard to break in if you knew how the lock had been jimmied once. He thought the dark kitchen smelled like fish.

No electricity. No gas. No water. Closed for the season and dead cold. Dark, but he didn't run into the table with crazy legs or chairs with lumps on their backs.

A dead, dark, cold bedroom. A bed stripped to the mattress. When he sat down on it, it squeaked C, A-flat, F.

You couldn't trust them ever. Martin shivered; cold from the mattress came through his thin pants. That last time she'd been getting dinner, and he'd made her stop and kiss him and take her clothes off and come in there. The noises they made and what they told you afterward. Hell. Nobody knew what they were thinking.

Sara had beautiful breasts. She had a mole exactly between them, and another mole straight through on her back between her shoulder blades. "Shot by Cupid," she said. "That's the myth about moles. His arrow went straight through me."

She read a book a day all the time she was growing up. She never stopped sticking her nose in books, as if she hadn't had enough of them in college. He had. As if she didn't work in a library full of them.

She had such a curve to her hips, even when she began to get thin. Even her toes were pretty. When her tan wore off she was blond all over. She'd shine in the water like a dead fish.

Martin made himself get off the bed and go into the little front room that looked out on pine grove and road. She'd opened the box at that front door and taken out the black silk teddy, and he'd said he was sorry he'd hit her and kicked her. He'd bought her roses and beautiful underwear.

Wave-crash echoed in cold dark. He whacked his head on the front door over and over, tears running into his mouth.

Start at the beginning. If she'd learned to swim, what had she done it for?

To run off. To make him think she was dead, make him cry like a baby, make him lose his chance to be where Al Surrino was now, make him lose his job.

And her brother Joe egging her on. Courage was really just little things, she always said, and then she whined and wouldn't go near any water because Joe had drowned, she said.

That bitch with the bangs. Telling him about Sara swimming so well, and then clamming up all at once. Wouldn't say any more, looked at him funny. Well, the police would be after him now—have his license number, be out looking for the car. But they wouldn't think of this place, out of season and all. Not before he started on the road, looking, with the pistol and silencer—just an orange-juice can and some steel wool. It worked.

There had to be a clue. Maybe it was here. The kitchen was where they'd spent most of their time when they weren't outside. He sat in a dark kitchen and remembered piecrust rolled out in a circle. The sailboat was always his idea, and Sara had been scared—she couldn't fool him—she'd been terrified. Hell. Her hands were shaking, and she'd watched the piecrust, not him—

He grabbed a kitchen chair in the dark, smashed it down on the table, smashed it over and over again until he had nothing but the chair back in his hands, with the stupid bulge still in the center of it.

Waves rushed below the beach house in darkness, rushed back.

Martin didn't know how long he'd sat in the cold. He found he was holding a chair back and was on a bare mattress in a silent bedroom. Where was the rest of the chair? He stuck what was left of it under the bed, and the bed squeaked C, A-flat, F.

Slowly pictures came into his head: a silly bitch yelling when he hit her, a gun small and warm in his hand, cold wind on a beach road. Sara, who had learned to swim, and was laughing. . . .

She couldn't have planned it, even if she had taken swimming lessons. He saw her standing by a low stone wall, not wanting to come, hoping he'd call it off. Unless that was faked. So dumb they wouldn't go out for a good time unless their hair looked just right, but sneaky as hell. Getting in that sailboat and hanging on the way she did. Even fooled Fleishman.

If she'd practiced swimming all that time? There was a full moon the night they started to sail to Bankton, with an onshore wind, smooth and easy. When that first big swell hit he'd been busy with the main sheet. . . .

Her blank, scared-rabbit face, when she'd been planning it, letting him set it all up and never suspect. Stinking, sneaky bitches, creeping behind your back like cats, using their boobs and butts to get what they wanted. Even his mother. Cheat on the grocery bills. Get in the old pants pocket. Hell.

All right. She could swim. She wasn't afraid of the water. Those "night classes" she took in Boston so she'd "get more money on the pay scale"—what a lie. Slipping behind his back to take swimming lessons on Monday, Wednesday, Friday—or maybe jumping into bed with some guy. Laughing at him. Months and months she'd been laughing at him, planning her getaway. He'd think she was drowned. Cry every night, thinking she was dead. Wreck his chances at Rambaugh. Let him sit here and smell her clothes and look at food she hadn't eaten, cry like a baby, and she was—

Where was she?

Near her mother? That's where she'd gone before. But he'd found her, and brought her to the beach house from Fredsburg, and slapped her downstairs.

Martin sat shivering in darkness, listening to waves break. She couldn't stay away much longer. Where would she get money? Anybody could find out she wasn't dead if she used her social security number to get a job. She couldn't do that. Their money was all in the checking account. Not a penny missing.

So she'd have a man to pay bills. A woman like that could always find a man. Both of them living it up somewhere and laughing at poor old Martin Burney.

Fredsburg. The nursing home. Sara wouldn't stay away from her mother very long; she felt responsible, and Joe wasn't there any more, and her mother was so sad that Sara was gone. If Sara were alive, she'd go to Fredsburg to tell her mother she wasn't drowned. Or maybe the man she was shacked up with would go instead.

Martin sat on the bed until four o'clock in the morning, then went to get his car. He parked in the pine grove the way he always had, then took his suitcase into the beach house.

They'd be looking for his car. Assault and battery. That bitch with her mouth all pinched up, not talking. But he could rent a car and be out of the state fast. Let them find his new car here at a dead end.

He sat down on the bed again. C, A-flat, F. Wiggling and saying "Oh! Oh!" and all the time pretending. Planning. Laughing at him with another man, kissing another man and saying "Oh, Oh!" and meaning it, and then coming home to that clown, Martin Burney.

He laughed a little without a sound. He had the pistol in his coat pocket—such a little son-of-a-gun—fitted in the palm of his hand. Plenty of clips. You couldn't kill a drowned woman. Get rid of the body and nobody would miss her. And he'd get that man too.

She could have fallen overboard.

Martin sat there with his face in his hands, listening to

surf thudding. Sara had eaten dinner alone that night, listening to that sound. Hell.

Cold crept into him. You didn't need a boat. You could walk out too far. Just walk out. Choke a little bit and it would all be over. Waves came in. Waves went out.

But he jumped up, walked back and forth to get warm. If they found the car, they wouldn't find him. Gone, they'd say. Drowned. "Despondent over his wife's death."

# 29

Sara lay watching leaf shadows on her bedroom wall. They seemed to flow in the rush of wind, but if she kept her eye on single leaves, she saw that every one was tethered to the tree.

Above her window was Ben's bedroom window; there was a rim of light around his drawn shade. He was awake before dawn too.

Sara turned over, hid her head under her pillow. A month had gone by since she'd first seen Ben Woodward mowing his backyard, leaving too-long grass in green swathes. He had curls like Joe's, and golden-red hair on his chest, and long legs in tight jeans. The way he pushed the mower and pivoted around his backyard trees had seemed to say that he liked Iowa summer afternoons and the smell of cut grass.

She had spied on him when he was secret and naked and suffering, knees under his chin, shoulders hunched, face hidden.

Sara watched leaf shadows on her bedroom wall and remembered the shock when strange lips mixed their breath with hers, and somebody else's eyes filled her world. Trapped between him and the wall, she'd been shivering, and smelled wine, and thought of a fist raised, smashing at her—

She was a poisonous plant, rubbing death off on any man who touched her.

Ben had said, *I hated her*.

Smell and taste of wine . . . angry kisses . . . Sara packed her pillow over her ears but remembered being carried through Ben's rooms where they had laughed and talked. A fern she'd brought from her garden had brushed her dangling foot, a small, sad touch as Ben's feet thudded upstairs and his arms hurt her.

But she'd escaped from his arms and his bed, shut his door behind her.

There in the lilac tunnel outside Ben's door, still breathing hard, feeling his mouth, his hands between her legs, she'd looked up. There was the moon, the same one that—only three weeks before!—had gone into clouds over cold Manhasset Bay. As she watched it through lilac leaves the moon skimmed behind a shred of mist and came glowing from it.

She had run in that moonlight to her own back door, locked it behind her, and stood against the smooth, new paint of her kitchen, feeling it with her trembling hands.

And he hadn't come; he hadn't telephoned. He'd stayed out of her life for almost two weeks. She was safe from hard hands and arms and thighs, and a mouth that groped and bruised and didn't care.

Sara sat up in bed. She wondered if she'd slept at all. The night had been almost an autumn night, chilly, wet with dew.

The owl called from his maple tree in dew-drip. Gardens and lawns were scattered with the first dead leaves of fall when wind rose before dawn.

Sara got up, drank a cup of hot coffee, and dressed for a run, walking softly through her yellow and cream-colored and orange and gold rooms that were the color of sunlight even before the sun rose. She left her doors open. Ben's bedroom window looked down on hers. She took a deep breath of before-dawn air.

Fall was coming—she smelled it and felt its wind on her face the moment she stepped out her front door. If two or three autumns went by, she could be a little like everyone else, maybe. As years passed she might let a man touch her without trembling and crying and running away . . .

Sara took a step in the dark and felt something under her running shoes. What was it? She bent down to pick up the dim object that was soft, like a bunch of flowers.

When she walked out to the streetlight, she saw it was a bouquet of small white roses, with one red rose in the center.

"Ben," she said to herself.

Ben. Suddenly she was lifted by happiness until she seemed to float. She sniffed the fresh, wet spiciness of the flowers.

Autumn air blowing against her face was cool, carrying the scent of still-dark farm fields. How many years since anyone had given her flowers?

Ben. Sara left the roses on her step and ran around the corner and down Seerley Boulevard, keeping up a good pace, solitary in a silent town.

Ben had said "I was in love and she would hardly kiss me. God, I hated her."

A cat ran along a fence and disappeared, alone in the darkness too. Sara crossed Main and the railroad tracks and heard Dry Run Creek talking to itself where it hid in black bushes under railroad ties. Water sounds ran beside her for a little while, then she passed unlit houses, then Peet Junior High School facing the municipal pool across the street. In August afternoons the pool sparkled with color and rang with shouts, but school had begun now in early September. Every weekday the children looked from their classrooms to that blue water, she supposed, and wondered where summer had gone.

She smiled to herself as she ran. Somewhere in dark trees overhead a bird chirped. Sweat began to film her skin.

Then Martin came into her mind, arms above his dim face, alone in their bed. Sometimes his eyes opened and turned her way across all the miles like a lighthouse beam slicing into distance, sending bright hate into cracks, and she pressed back in darkness, terrified, and saw the .25 pistol, and felt bullets hit her . . . hit Ben. . . .

But weeks had gone by—more than a month since she'd

gasped, going down in bitter cold ocean, aiming for two smashed-dark spots on shore. She breathed deeper and relaxed as she ran. Streetlights stood one by one in their cones of light. Ants ran on the sidewalks even before the sun came up; she saw their small shadows moving with them.

Children slept as she passed. Men and women lay in each other's arm.

"It was rough," Ben had said once, leaning back on her old sofa, staring at lighted candles. "Those beautiful high school girls, and they weren't for me. I thought they were angels, another breed, and their motto was 'You don't touch.' "

She could leave Ben, keep him safe, come back after years to find him married, perhaps, a friend who wouldn't know why she'd gone away.

Or she could stay in Cedar Falls and bring her mother to a nursing home just a few blocks away on University Avenue. Let Martin hate, let him come, let . . .

Sara stopped, trembling, before the university library.

Library windows glowed before her; night lights lit a row of magazines here, a rack of maps there. She stood in her own sweat, panting, alone before clear glass. *I want to get a master's degree in library science.*

The campanile sounded its eight half-hour notes. She ran across brick walks and gravel and parking-lot concrete, downhill toward town.

But she'd married Martin, and it had been all wrong.

She took deep breaths as she ran. Sara Burney was rotting in the water . . . in Martin's mind. He would imagine Sara Burney lying open to the sky on some beach, or sinking deeper, breaking apart. That body floated in Martin's mind, unless she had made one mistake, and he knew (Sara thought of a Sylvia Plath poem) and was waiting—like Sylvia Plath's Medusa—to make stone out of what she had now in Cedar Falls. Sylvia said none of her days were safe because a man was somewhere thinking of her.

Sara picked up her pace, paid close attention to the

smell of dew-soaked gardens, the descending, far whistle
of a train, her own blood beating in her ears. Ben had put
roses on her doorstep. She ran down Main Street all the
way to the Parkade's storefronts and globed lights, then
ran back home, happy, panting, soaked with sweat.

Ben's bouquet waited for her on her doorstep. As she
carried it to the kitchen she felt that something dangled on
a ribbon from it—a note? She turned on her kitchen light.
A bit of paper hung from the one red rose at the center of
soft white petals.

Sara untied the note, smiling at the thought of Ben,
looking around her orange kitchen. There was dark black
printing on the folded paper:

> I KNOW WHO YOU ARE, MY LAURA.
> I HAVE FOUND YOU AND I WILL
> NEVER LET YOU GO.

Hand-printed letters writhed beneath Sara's eyes, crawl-
ing out of white petals where they had been fastened to
one rose as red as a drop of blood.

Sara gasped and turned cold. She leapt to shut off the
kitchen light, and even as she did her mind ran back to the
past like a rabbit doubling before a fox: Martin's pistol
against her temple, the first time she had thought of diving
into the bay, her bruises at the Y, but she hadn't used her
name and no one could connect her with drowned Sara
Burney, smashed lights on the shore, John Fleishman for a
witness, nothing in a beach house, nothing in a little Cape
Cod—

She held her breath, ice cold. Martin must be here,
hidden in a dark house that crouched around her and
wasn't safe any more but was like the Montrose house, the
beach house, a shell, a trap. She held her breath, listening
for someone else breathing.

For minutes Sara stood in her kitchen, absolutely still,
roses crushed in her fist. She hadn't even locked the doors.
Fool. Fool.

Sweat ran under her clothes until she was cold and wet.

Martin was in the bedroom or bathroom or living room or study or at the top of the stairs, waiting.

Bullets in the dark—*I know who you are*.

To dive into Manhasset Bay, pretend she was dead—who could forgive that? Her brain skimmed the years as she stood there. Of course he'd kill her, and he'd scare her first, torture her, play with her—nothing could be cruel enough to pay her back. He'd be sure she had a man. He'd hunt until he found Ben and kill him too.

Her nerves pricked at the least sound behind her, ahead of her, above her.

Quiet. So quiet. Ben wouldn't telephone at breakfast time again; Martin wouldn't answer the phone and hear Ben's voice. Ben wouldn't have anything to do with her now. Maybe he was safe.

She stood ready to run for the nearest door, the back-porch door. Minutes went by. A car went by. No matter how fast she ran, he had a gun.

At last she took one step, then another. She crept softly past the empty bath to put her back to a wall beside the bedroom. Light from the park showed that her closet door was open. She didn't know how many minutes she stood listening, one hand feeling smooth yellow enamel she had brushed on hour after hour, thinking she was safe here, could stay here. A first bird called once; dawn was coming.

The floor groaned once under her running shoe as she reached her closet. There was no one in it. She bent to see, in faint light from the park, that there was no one under her bed.

He could be in the living room, or study, or hiding at the top of stairs to the second floor. He knew she was there—floorboards squeaked now and then. He was tormenting her with his silence, a gun in his hand—if he waited there at all.

*I have found you and will never let you go.*

Sara crept into her study. It was empty. She looked into her living room, which was empty too. The cellar door was locked. Climbing the stairs to the second floor step by step, she expected to see Martin against the locked door above her. No one was there.

Sara ran to lock all her doors and pull down every shade. She sobbed and rubbed her wet face, and found she still had the roses and note crumpled in her hand. She lit a kitchen match and looked at dark black printing.

The match went out. She stared through living-room curtains at the park. Martin had been there. His hate was there—it stood along her street like dark houses, like trees, like park swings moving just a little in a breeze before dawn.

Sara crawled into her bed, sweaty as she was, and pulled the sheet over her head and was in a small space again, like the beach house, their house in Montrose, the bathroom of that house in Montrose (with Martin smashing the door). Home was supposed to be the safe place. What if anywhere outside of it was safer?

She packed the sheet against her mouth with her fists, trying to plan, but Martin came close, kissing the mole between her breasts, turning her over to kiss the one between her shoulder blades, and she saw Martin's round forehead, wrinkling when he opened his eyes wide so that they glinted and quivered a little. Hunting with him, she'd felt his warm breath on her cold face, his whisper over a glistening rifle.

She wondered if she should go find Martin. He was somewhere out there in the night, watching from the park, or her backyard. He'd keep her sleepless and terrified, hiding for days, maybe. She wouldn't go to anyone for help. What could she say? She saw Ben lying in his blood, his unbelieving eyes on her.

Sara got out of bed. She'd find Martin, call his name softly out there before it got light, before anyone heard her. She'd tell him she would never leave him again, never.

Standing by her bed, she rubbed her forehead with the palm of her hand and thought how stupid she had been not to remember to pick up the cleaning. She could hang the towels so the fringe was even. Was that so much to ask?

She could remember to take his letters to the mailbox by the library and never be gone from home when he came from work. She could fold his undershirts in three, not two. If she put lots of dollar bills in his billfold, he'd think no money was missing. If he'd had only two glasses of wine he'd be friendly. . . .

Sara ran to her bathroom to vomit until she was weak and soaked with sweat, left with the sour smell of hate she knew was there in deep voices, big fists—she could never go back. She remembered a young mother with a black and blue, swollen face above two wailing children on the Abbey Shelter's doorstep.

Kneeling by the toilet, Sara remembered that the police had been courteous; they had seen it all before. Their eyes went past her to the next assault, the next domestic quarrel. "Lady, you think we can sit outside your house all night?"

She saw her neat library desk with green plants on it, her name on a plaque, her files and notebooks. How could she have left her job to hide at the Abbey Shelter? She had tracked snow into the courthouse day after day. A court clerk had said in a flat voice, "You went back to your husband again."

Sara washed her face and tried to think. Where had Martin seen her go? Through the lilacs to Ben's? She saw Dr. Channing listening to Henry James. Which ones would Martin kill?

Pack. Leave before dawn. Ben would remember only a thin, dark-haired person who wouldn't be touched or loved. Anger made her hot and sweaty again—her job, her house on the park gone. She started to put the few clothes she owned in her plastic bag. At the bottom of a drawer was the black silk teddy; she smelled red roses stuck in a pickle jar on a kitchen table.

Pack? Leave? She was crazy. Sara stopped and put her hands over her eyes. He was out there with a gun, watching—he'd see her leave. He had her trapped in this house.

Flowers, she thought, shivering. Of course he'd leave

roses. Printed words ran through her head over and over—
warnings, sly little paw strokes a cat gives a mouse. She
took the black silk teddy out of her plastic bag and began
to cry, and then stopped, and hung her one dress back in
the closet with hard eyes, as if she already saw her blood
spattered on some sidewalk, floor, wall.

Banana would be at the back porch, crying to come in;
Sara listened a long time by her kitchen door.

When she opened it the kitten's eyes glimmered like
fireflies beyond the door screen.

Sara reached for the knob. There was something soft
where the knob should have been—she snatched her hand
away. Then she felt it again, yanked it off, ran into her
kitchen, locked the door behind herself and Banana, and
stood trembling in her living room with another soft bunch
of flowers in her hand—fresh daisies. The note tied to a
daisy was in the same black printed letters as the note tied
to a rose:

> I DREAM OF YOUR SOFT THIGHS,
>    YOUR BEAUTIFUL BREASTS.
> WILL YOU EVER BE MY LOVER? MY
> LIPS ARE ON YOU WHEN YOU GO BY.

Daisies looked at her with yellow eyes. Banana licked
Sara's salty ankle and looked at her with yellow eyes too.
Sara began to laugh and sob at the same time, rubbing her
wet forehead with the heel of her hand, as if to rub out
nightmares.

"I was so afraid," she told the kitten. She sat down at
the kitchen table and put her head on her arms. "I was so
afraid. But it must be Ben."

She blushed, reading the notes again. Banana jumped on
her lap. They were love notes, that was all.

Banana kneaded four paws in Sara's lap.

"I wonder—are you a woman?" Sara asked.

Banana had no way to answer the question except with a
steady yellow stare. "If you are, you choose, don't you?"
Sara said. "No tom can fool around with you unless

you're willing." She knew she was babbling with joy and relief. Banana didn't mind.

Banana began to purr.

"I was so frightened!" Sara cried, scratching behind Banana's ears. Dawn began to light orange walls and hanging ferns of a kitchen that was safe after all.

Putting the plastic bag away, she took deep breaths of fresh air from her open window. Birds were singing now, but Ben would be asleep in his walnut bed, gold eyelashes, gold-red hair on the pillow.

*If there's a man, I'll kill him too.* Sara stood for a long while looking at the plastic bag in her dresser drawer on top of the black silk teddy.

That angry voice: *I was in love and she would hardly kiss me. God, I hated her.*

Pack up and leave. Move on.

*I thought they were angels, another breed.*

# 30

He was crazy. Ben drove fast, his car windows open to the hot September morning. Laura. He'd just gone into that red fog of love—came out the other side and saw he'd been taken again. He'd had to live with that for almost two weeks now.

Ben whacked the wheel with his fist. Laura let him kiss her, let him carry her upstairs and then froze and talked about hate. Hate. Well, she was right.

Just a tease. (There were worse words for it.) And he was into his third week of classes. His student evaluations were ahead. Members of his department would be watching him teach, then they'd write long letters describing his teaching methods, his testing, his attitude. . . .

And his lawn mower had quit on him. Sears used to have a branch at Black Hawk Village, but now you had to go all the way to the Crossroads if you wanted repairs. He had time enough before a two o'clock curriculum committee meeting.

And he couldn't sleep.

"Damn fool," Ben said out loud, taking South Main. He shouldn't have rushed her, but he just saw red. She wouldn't tell him anything about her, and she wouldn't let him—

Damn fool. Laura. She'd made him feel like a damn fool.

His front yard looked like a hayfield.

He had to park a long way from Sears and carry the

mower, and it was hot. He had to wait in a line. He tapped his fingers on a counter and thought maybe he shouldn't have rushed her. She was crying. He'd just forget her completely. Let her walk out.

A fat clerk took down everything but the color of Ben's eyes and his mother's maiden name when all he wanted was a lawn mower that worked. He watched the clerk scribbling and thought that he hadn't made any promises, hadn't bought Laura fancy presents or taken her to New York. He'd just dreamed about it, thank God, and now he didn't have to be with her any more, hadn't been for almost two weeks now.

He was pretending she didn't exist. Finally he got out of Sears and walked back to his car in the heat. Women who wear sexy clothes and smile and then say "Oh, no, not you" and slide right out of your life. Laura was probably laughing at him because he'd tried to score.

The road home was nothing but four-way stops; he swore. Her breasts were so beautiful. Damn. He could have gone with Laura to New York at Christmas and seen plays and foreign films; he imagined them arguing in their hotel room afterward, hashing over the directing, the acting, the staging, and then making love.

You were supposed to go after them—they wanted you to—and she had such a curve to her hips now. But she cried. And pretty legs—

Red lights at Main and University seemed to last five minutes. He sat and swore in the stink of everybody's exhaust. If they were married and she wanted to go on and get an M.A. in library science, he'd let her; she'd practically be living on campus because his house was so close. If he had a wife, he wouldn't have to take care of all the damn details and could write that book . . . here he was, out of bread and he had to make his own lunch.

Ben swung into the Jack and Jill lot and stopped with a squeal of tires. She wouldn't tell him anything about her. She was probably married. That quiet face of hers.

He had to wait in line again at the checkout counter. He hunched his shoulders and looked around the store. It was full of university students, as usual, because it was only a block or two from the campus. A brunette with pants as tight as skin on a peach was getting to the guy sacking her groceries—the poor guy was putting cans on top of bananas.

A woman like Laura could always find a man. Probably Laura'd been living with some guy and just got tired of him.

Ben got home and was so hungry he fried a hamburger with onions the way Laura had taught him, even if it wasn't lunchtime. He knew enough now to pour the grease off.

"Damn idiot," he told himself every now and then, and listened for her screen door, and was careful not to brown the hamburger too much, and mumbled, "Idiot. Damn." Her white skin would look almost blue when it wasn't tan. He could have a nice, quiet evening by himself or a few hours at one of the joints on the Hill with Hal and Noney Esterbrook or Grant Barney and Jan Dugan. He wasn't going to think about Laura Pray. Maybe she liked women, not men? A cold lesbian.

Laura's back-porch door barely squeaked. When he heard it he might as well have had her plastered against him. He watched hot grease pop in the pan and wanted her in bed and wanted to hit her—

Hate. While he was shaking with what he wanted, he was shaking with what scared him.

And Laura stood where he could see her, white shirt and shorts bright against deep green. She rubbed her forehead with the heel of her hand, an inward-turning, vulnerable gesture. Birds called now and then, but the stillness of late morning was something she could almost touch, the way she touched wet green bushes that stuck through a pile of junk at her backyard fence.

She didn't want to make love. Ben stared out his kitchen window at Laura. Banana trailed after her across still-wet grass, shaking one foot, then another.

Ben turned off the hamburger and leaned his forehead against the cool window. Laura looked at junk piled in her yard: old chair cushions, wire, tin, rotten logs, broken bricks. Banana slid into the jungle it made, and only one nodding daisy told where a kitten had disappeared.

Sara stood thinking that the notes and flowers were Ben's, that was all. She sighed. He was only doing the usual thing men did. *My lips are on you when you go by.*

Mrs. Nepper had said, "You can do what you want with that overgrown mess of a backyard. You can do what you want, yes. That overgrown mess. What you want."

Sara listened. A distant clunk and groan began, no louder than a mosquito's whine, but growing. Before long a garbage truck came down her alley from Seerley. Sara waded into her junk pile. "Hi," she called to men swinging off the truck at her gate, "I wonder—could you take some of this stuff for me?"

One little garbageman had ears that stuck out and a gap in his front teeth. "Sure," he said. "Looks like you *got* enough. Want us to give you a hand?"

Sara said yes and grabbed a soggy chair cushion and he grabbed another. He looked like somebody's grandfather, his shirt already dark under his arms and across his back, but he slung junk through the air. "Catch!" he called to the other man.

Hunks of tin, rusted fangs of wire fence, dead branches, rotten logs went over the fence, and the truck's groaning maw swallowed it. When the truck rolled off to complain at another set of cans, Sara could see bare ground at last from her back door to the alley.

Watching Sara, Ben saw drops of night rain fall now and then from lilac leaves. Each fern frond and grass blade seemed as clear to him as a detail on an artist's canvas, placed exactly for its exact meaning.

Now the ground was clear. Laura stood in yellowed, twisted dandelions that had grown through junk with wild daisies and thistles, knobby plantain, goldenrod. Wisteria and grapevines knotted it together; she'd have to wrestle them to the back fence again, tie them there.

She went to get an old hoe and spade from her back porch. The sun was hot and so was she; sweat ran down her face. For a little while she was in a new town with Joe again, trying to fix up another old house to live in while their mother grieved over what they had left behind.

She hacked at weeds, but left flowers standing: lily of the valley, perennial phlox. Lacy fern meant there would be asparagus in the spring.

Ben watched Laura. Weeds she grubbed out withered fast, their leaves as green as the ones she didn't uproot, their flowers beginning to curl where she threw them in heaps. She chose, foot by foot. She killed green leaves and colored flowers; they died in the sun.

Ben stopped leaning against the window and looked around his kitchen as if he were a stranger in it.

He went out to Laura, slamming his back door behind him.

"Looks like you need a hand with the spade," he said.

Black printed words sprang before Sara's eyes. She didn't look at him, but saw him naked on the edge of his bed, his fists clenched. "Lilies of the valley," she said, standing on the spade handle trying to get roots to let go. "Beautiful green leaves and little bells in the spring, and the rest of it cast-iron roots in all directions. Look what they've done to that clump of flags."

"Look what you've done to that kid next door. He's at his window with binoculars," Ben said.

Her head turned so fast her dark hair ruffled. She looked at the red house on the corner, its back turned to them, the one white eyebrow raised over its back door. Above the round bed of chrysanthemums a curtain in the corner house was yanked shut. Ben thought he saw anger and fear in Sara's eyes for a moment before she began spading up lilies again.

"He's an odd one, Mrs. Nepper tells me," Ben said. "He's a junior at U.N.I., but the minute university classes are over every day, he locks himself in and plays music." After a few minutes, as if to answer him, music began to blare from the red house.

Sara grabbed lilies as Ben forked them loose; she shook off dirt, threw them away. "Mrs. Nepper told me I could do what I want out here," she said after a while.

Ben was very close to her, his eyes level and aware of her. Somebody was shouting about hot love and fire in the song from next door. Sara straightened her back, wiped mud across her forehead with the back of her arm, and remembered Ben's cheek still hot with tears. "So much to kill," she said, looking at heaps of wilting green.

Ben spoke softly. "I'll tell you what—how about dinner Monday night, my place?"

She looked at him for a second, and he thought he saw happiness in her eyes. Then it went away.

Sara felt sharp edges of the words he had printed. "I hurt your feelings, and I didn't mean to," she said. "I'm not good company for anyone." She looked away, looked at an upstairs window.

Music blared from it—beat-heat-beat. Had the curtain moved there? "Thanks for the roses and daisies," she said, and stepped away from him. Her face grew pink.

"Roses and daisies?" Ben said. "From my yard? You're certainly welcome. Help yourself anytime."

Laura stared at him. "Thanks," she said. She was dirt-smeared now, but still pretty with her long brown legs; her white, tight shorts rode up from her hips in back, and her shirt hung half out, half in.

Music blasted from the window overhead. "Air polluter," Ben said. "Listen to that."

"We'd better quit. I've got to get dressed and go to work. Thanks for all the help." She took the spade from him and shouldered it with her hoe.

"You won't change your mind about Monday night?"

She smiled and he saw relief in her eyes as she hesitated there looking at him. "Yes, I will," she said. "When it gets dark?"

Ben nodded and grinned and rubbed blisters on his palms. The music kept up its hot beat. She climbed her porch steps, sun on her hair and her white-shorted bottom, the kitten leaping from stair to stair behind her. Its tail just missed getting caught in the screen door.

Sara left the old spade and hoe in a corner of her porch.

Her kitchen was cool still. Green backyard ferns hung in the windows, feathering sunlight.

A bunch of daisies wilted in a glass by her sink.

The notes weren't from Ben.

The notes weren't from Martin.

But somebody faceless watched her, sneaked to her back door, her front door—Sara grabbed the daisies, threw them in the wastebasket and yelled. Banana shot under the stove.

"Never mind," Sara told Banana and herself. She washed her hands and arms and knees, and then found notepaper and envelopes. She sat down in the green light of the ferns with a cup of coffee and began to write upside down and backward, a neat handwriting that looked nothing like hers. She'd always been able to do that. No one would recognize her writing. She addressed six envelopes to her mother at the Craigie Court Retirement Center.

Dear Chloe:

It has been so long since you've heard from me, but don't think I've forgotten the many good times I had when I lived with your family for a while.

I'm working for a professor now, traveling and doing research, and this gives me plenty of time to write, so you'll be hearing from me often from now on.

Perhaps I can come see you someday. I remember how your family moved every year or two, and you and Sara and Joe fixed up the houses you lived in. Remember making screens for windows out of scrap lumber when you lived near that farm with all the flies? Remember the time you and Sara made living-room curtains by hand?

Those were good days, though. Stay well and happy. I travel for the professor, so I will mail these notes from wherever I am, and write again soon.

With love,
Larry Day

Tears rose in Sara's eyes. Her mother thought both her children were dead. She lay in a nursing home where no one ever came to see her and no one ever called. Ben's car was in his barn. She could jump in it, drive to Nebraska—

But it was planned. Dr. Channing had to find someone else to come in while Laura Pray was gone. She had to wait.

She wiped her eyes on the back of her hand. Joe had found a red velvet stage curtain at a pawnbroker's, and they'd made living-room curtains by hand because they didn't have a sewing machine.

Her mother worked so hard when they had to live in a little trailer in South Dakota one winter. She had washed dishes and clothes and children in a filling-station bathroom, and somehow sent Joe and Sara to school looking as nice as anybody there. She'd made it seem like a game. It didn't look like a game to Sara now.

Sara stared at her pen and listened to a cardinal's click-click-click in her backyard. She couldn't write about the trailer—someone would have to read these letters to her mother. She didn't mention the ramshackle apartment house in Manhasset either. They had lived there free for two years because her father was janitor and stoked the mon ster furnace in a dirt-floored cellar. She wrote instead about a cricket in the cellar that sang like a canary, almost, and ate slices of raw potato . . . and the garden they'd had. She didn't write that the garden was among cars in a junkyard.

Joe had drowned in Manhasset Bay. When she wrote his name a redheaded ghost ran behind her sentences.

She couldn't tell about living with relatives when they didn't have any money. She wrote about the night her mother called the police because they heard noises. "Remember?" Sara wrote. "The noise was only buttons on old Aunt Jennie's long underwear, racketing down the clothes chute."

Sometimes she laughed. Sometimes she cried, thinking of her mother's blind eyes staring at the rest-home ceiling, her name above her head on a card. The women who worked in the rest home were kind, most of them, but they shouted at all old people because some patients were deaf.

They called old people by their first names, as if they had never been hardworking members of the community, as if they'd lost their right to be Mr., Mrs., Dr., Miss.

Sara wrote her notes upside down and backward, hunting for a code that would tell her mother "I'm Sara. I'm alive." She found it in the name of an iris, the color of a front door, or a secret way they'd found to keep rabbits out of a pea patch.

Six notes. She slipped them in their envelopes and stamped them, put them in a paper sack, and looked around her kitchen. How bright the orange looked in morning sun.

But there were daisies and a wad of squashed roses in her kitchen wastebasket. Someone was watching her, thinking of her: *Will you ever be my lover? My lips are on you when you go by.*

Someone was crowding her in where she had felt free to dance by herself, and laugh, and hang green ferns in an orange kitchen.

# 31

Ben hunched his shoulders and looked up and down the hall while the department secretary ran student evaluations in Ben's Introduction to Theater class. "Rate your instructor on the following qualities influencing teacher effectiveness. This is a seven point scale with '1' indicating the *lowest* score and '7' indicating the *highest* score."

He stared at a hall bulletin board without seeing it. His students were marking little circles from one to seven: "Knowledge of subject matter (content and supporting material). Preparation for class (daily as well as total). Organization of course. General attitude and concern for students (interested, sympathetic). Accessibility outside class (office hours, approachability). Explains and illustrates clearly. Interest and enthusiasm in subject. Fairness in testing and grading (clear criteria for grading). Stimulated my learning (challenging questions aroused intellectual curiosity). Makes purpose and objectives clear. Give your instructor an overall letter grade for teaching effectiveness: F,D,C,B,A."

Ben gritted his teeth. These were kids just out of high school, grading him on "knowledge of subject matter" and "teaching effectiveness." He'd had his hair cut that morning and he itched all the way down his back, but he couldn't rub against the bulletin board and scratch it. And the department head called you in and read your student evaluations out loud. There would be little scribbled notes at the bottom of them: "Writes on the board too much. Doesn't write on the board enough. Ought to grow a beard. Should wear a suit jacket."

"All right, Dr. Woodward, we're through." The secretary came out of his classroom door.

Ben wished he could scratch, but he had to walk to his desk in front of ninety students who had just decided whether he was prepared, organized, sympathetic, accessible, enthusiastic, fair, stimulating, and clear enough; they had written it down for his department head to read. Luckily it was almost time for the bell; he took pleasure in making a very long assignment and announcing a test for next week.

Of course he wasn't the best teacher in the world, he knew that. Ben walked back to his office feeling thin-skinned and freshly evaluated, but he remembered a girl in a white shirt and shorts, grubbing up weeds in sunshine. He lived through lunch and committee meetings, impatiently waiting for the night to come: "She lingers my desires, like to a step-dame, or a dowager, long withering out a young man's revenue." Laura knew he wanted her, and maybe she wanted him—he'd seen the happy look in her eyes for a second when he said, "How about dinner Monday night, my place?"

Walking home, he thought he was heading for an evening (and maybe bed) with a beautiful woman, and he was in love, but it was confusing.

And yet, wasn't it simple? He thought about her breasts while he was taking a shower.

He thought about the way she smiled when he started frying hamburger and onions. Her skin would look almost blue when she didn't have any tan.

Her back-porch door squeaked softly.

Ben held his breath and thought of kissing her . . . her beautiful mouth with the full upper lip. . . .

Lilacs rustled.

Ben swallowed hard, remembering her breasts against his hands. . . .

"Larry Day," a man's voice said at Ben's kitchen door.

Ben stared. Larry Day was about his own age, dark-bearded, and wore a summer suit and tie.

"Larry," the man said.

He opened the door and seemed at home in Ben's kitchen; he shut the screen door behind him and leaned against a wall under two masks, one smiling, one frowning. "Spaghetti?" he said in his warm tenor voice. He was short and walked with his body stiffly held, as if he expected a fight.

"Yes," Ben said.

"I have to practice," Larry said. "For the trip tomorrow."

There weren't any breasts for Ben to look at (or try not to look at). He'd been sweaty at the thought of Laura. Now he tried not to stare at the man in his kitchen, and got out carrots and lettuce and cucumbers and green peppers, and felt angry. "I'll tell you what—you look good," he told Larry Day. "That beard fits. Looks as if it grew on you."

"I've got to practice," Larry said. "The real test comes when I walk on the street. Hope nobody will pinch me or whistle at me or say 'How about some fun, baby? How about a little fun?' or words to that effect."

"One of the prices we men have to pay," Ben said.

Larry grinned, then frowned. "And I don't have to smile. I still forget. I go grinning away like a damn woman. It's a tic."

There was silence in the kitchen for a while. Ben started chopping carrots. (Larry wasn't helping with the dinner.) He knew who Larry was. He didn't have to figure out when he could kiss him.

"My brother tried to get me to stop," Larry said. "But I found out that people feel uncomfortable with a woman who doesn't smile a lot."

Ben laughed.

"They do. My friends started asking what was wrong with me. Why was I so cold and unfriendly?" Larry walked back and forth from Ben's plastic-covered table to the chipped refrigerator, his hands stuffed in his pants pockets.

"Men don't talk about themselves much," Ben said.

"I haven't," Larry said, and glanced at Ben, who scowled, golden-brown eyebrows jutting over his blue gaze.

"Invisible," Larry said after a while. "Now I'll be able to go places by myself, late. I've got change in my pockets! Lots of pockets, and wonderful, wonderful, comfortable shoes I can wear even to parties, and stockings that don't snag. And I can run."

Ben mixed salad in a bowl. He'd dreamed of Laura all day. He could yank off that beard—

Larry's blue eyes shone under his heavy brows. "Even when I'm dressed like this, I'm comfortable, except for the bandages, and they're not so bad when you're used to bras." He carried the salad to the table; Ben brought the spaghetti and got garlic bread from the microwave. He poured wine, and they sat down.

"Nice," Larry said, and smiled. Larry's blue eyes were Laura's—friendly, not flirting. He said he liked the spaghetti and could he have another piece of bread? Ben had expected their love scene in the kitchen to hang over them all evening, unmentioned, always there, and he'd been right.

Larry had Laura's quick, engaging way of drawing Ben out to talk and talk and talk. He'd brought over a funny article comparing Norman Mailer with Alfred Lord Tennyson. Then Ben said Browning was boring, and Larry pounded on the table; plates and coffee cups rattled.

"Boring," Ben said.

"You haven't read him for years. You admitted it! How can you say he's boring when you don't know 'Childe Roland to the Dark Tower Came'?" Larry yelled, then asked, "Am I getting my voice down low enough?"

"Fine," Ben said. "Keep your elbows out a little when you eat."

"Do you notice a difference?" Larry asked.

"From what?"

"From . . ." Larry stopped. Laura was doing a pretty good job; sometimes Ben thought there wasn't a woman there for a moment or two. "From the way you talked to me when I was a woman?"

"You're still a woman underneath," Ben said, and was afraid some of his anger got into his tone of voice.

"I dressed like a man to practice, but I wondered if it would make you feel better. About my saying no all the time." Larry helped Ben carry dishes out to the kitchen.

"I know you're Laura," Ben said, and felt mad. Nobody in the kitchen was showing breasts through a shirt or crossing pretty legs. He knew who she was. He put soap in the dishpan.

"I'm sorry about the other night," Larry said. He finished scraping plates. "You'd be the one I'd choose if I could . . . but I can't."

Ben didn't look at the dark-bearded young man. "I'm sorry too," he said. Their eyes met. Then, for a few moments, two men put their arms around each other, Ben with soapsuds still on his hands, Larry with his dish towel. They stood for a while by the sink, the dark-bearded young man's head on the taller man's shoulder. Ben scowled at clean dishes on the kitchen table. He knew her breasts were there, pressed against him, and her pretty legs under the pants.

"It's a theory of mine," Larry said, letting Ben go. He picked up a wet dish.

"What is?"

"I'm here but I'm not, right?"

"You're not?"

Larry Day's teeth were white between his dark mustache and beard when he smiled; he straightened his tie once, jerking his chin forward, the big rings on his hands flashing. "I'm here," he said.

"Laura?" Ben said. "Larry?"

"Neither." The bearded young man stacked clean plates, put them in the cupboard. "That's my theory. Most of what we are isn't male or female at all."

Ben dumped the soapsuds down the drain, wiped off the table's plastic cover.

"That's what I think." Larry walked into the living room. "How do I sit down?"

"Don't wiggle your hips. Just sit. The main thing you

don't do is cross your legs. That's only for women and old men. Put your ankle on your knee if you want to.''

Larry sat down on the couch.

Ben couldn't sit down; he wandered around. He'd imagined love scenes with Laura on the couch and every chair and even the rug. He picked up Banana and stroked the kitten for a few minutes in silence.

Larry watched him from a lumpy, sprung armchair. "Do you *feel* what I've been talking about at all? Isn't it kind of nice?''

"I keep wanting to find Laura under that hair and suit," Ben said.

"But isn't there a sense of richness because I'm not just Laura. I'm somebody else too.''

They sipped Ben's after-dinner wine. "We don't even have to talk," Larry said. "You don't have to say how nice I look, and I don't have to say I'm glad you like whatever it is. I don't have to ask how your teaching day was.''

"I'll tell you—it was pretty bad," Ben said. "Student evaluations in my classes. Little freshmen get to tell you whether you're a good teacher or not, and then the department head calls you in and reads all their little scribbles to you, as if you ought to care.''

Larry smiled, then stopped and took a sip of wine. "Maybe you can dress like a woman for me sometime— raid the costume department.''

"Me?''

"You'd be a woman and a man. Both. Neither.'' The bearded young man stared at Ben and rubbed his forehead with the heel of his hand, a gesture Ben recognized. "I'd feel . . . strange. It would be like a double exposure—you and a woman superimposed. Where they overlapped the image would be solid, and that would be your core.'' Larry's eyes were glowing. "It might fascinate you—change your ideas of what's natural—change your view of your work.''

They sat in silence, two men stroking a kitten.

Ben took a book from the old coffee table. "The two of us are book fiends—we live in them, carry bits of them around in our heads. We're crazy.'' He found a marked page. ''Listen to this. 'With one foot already in the stirrup, and with the agony of death upon me, great lord, I write to you. . . . My life is drawing to a close. . . . A time will come, perhaps, when I shall knot this broken thread and say what should be said but which I cannot say here. Good-bye, thanks; good-bye, compliments; good-bye, merry friends.' ''

''An old voice,'' Larry guessed. ''Shakespeare's time?''

''Died in the same year!''

''Cervantes,'' Larry said.

''Right.''

They sat in silence for a little while. ''It's raining,'' Ben said.

''That wonderful smell of summer rain,'' Larry said. He sighed. ''Hope city folk don't find out about small towns.''

''They won't,'' Ben said. ''They're looking for excitement. Beaches, crowds . . .''

''Stores full of expensive goodies. Mountains. New films.''

''Celebrities in dark glasses.''

''We're safe.''

''Yep. I'll tell you what—how about watching *Swan Lake?*'' Ben asked. Larry nodded, so Ben switched on one hall light and settled with Larry on the couch to sip wine in television glow, two men and a spotted kitten.

Waiting for the ballet to begin, Larry opened the book to the marker. '' 'A time will come, perhaps, when I shall knot this broken thread and say what should be said but which I cannot say here,' '' he read in his tenor voice, and looked into Ben's blue-green eyes, and put a hand on Ben's cheek.

Tchaikovsky's beautiful music began. Long-legged, muscular Prince Siegfried danced to his youth that was slipping away; he'd have to find a wife. He'd go hunt swans to cheer himself up. (The prince and his friends disappeared jauntily, toe-and-heel the way male dancers walked, guns at the ready.)

''If we were in the theater, we'd be watching tiny

figures," Ben said. "About an inch high, far away on a doll's stage."

"And nowhere to prop your feet," Larry said. He had his shoes beside Ben's on a hassock whose seams had burst in several places.

"Intermission in yakking crowds. Cigarette smoke."

Larry stretched and leaned back again. Odette, Queen of the Swans, shed her disguise between midnight and dawn, became a woman, and Prince Siegfried swore his eternal devotion.

"When figures are so far away their tragedies seem tiny too," Larry said. (The sorcerer was threatening the lovers and plotting to make Siegfried break his vow.)

"But *we* can see them sweat," Ben said. "Did you ever think what you'd have to be doing to get the same picture we're seeing?"

Larry squinted at the screen. "Flying like some kind of crazy bird? Back and forth, close to the dancers and then far away."

"Makes you dizzy."

"Never thought of that."

Tchaikovsky's music wrapped them in magic. Odile was pretending to be Odette. Siegfried was fooled.

Larry smoothed his beard.

Ben scowled, TV light sparkling in his blue-green eyes.

Siegfried broke his vow, sure that Odette was Odile. Nothing could be done. The swans would never be human now unless Odette and Siegfried died.

Larry looked fixedly at death, danced beautifully by the black swans.

"It's perfectly unrealistic," Ben said.

"But haven't you ever broken a promise or done your best and guessed wrong?"

"And then had to do your best again and save the other swans, who weren't responsible for the catastrophe?" Ben asked. "Luckily, no. I haven't met very many swans lately." The last chords of *Swan Lake* faded. He reached to shut off the set; it was an old one and crackled afterward. The two men looked at each other in the dimness.

"Who else would have ever tried this with me?" Larry

said. His bearded face was calm; his blue eyes met Ben's, direct and still.

Ben poured a little more wine for them both. There was silence in his living room for a while. Banana lay on the couch next to Larry, nose under tail.

"I'd better get to bed." Larry yawned. "I leave for Nebraska before it gets light tomorrow morning, thanks to you. I appreciate the disguise and help and car. I'll be back in time for work at Dr. Channing's Friday noon. Ellen's found a friend who can come while I'm gone."

"Glad to help," Ben said.

A car went by on Tremont. A park swing squeaked back and forth, back and forth.

"I don't want to be anybody's helpmeet," the bearded young man said. "I don't want to be kept."

Ben held his breath, staring at him.

"It's pretty easy to find someone to support you," Larry Day said, stroking his beard. "You don't want to live on somebody else's money, do you—let them tell you how to spend it?"

"No," Ben said. "But I'm not a woman."

"And do you want to live in somebody else's house, even if it's supposedly yours because they say it is?"

"I've got my own," Ben said.

"You want respect," the young man said. "Your own job, your own house, your own money."

"Yes."

"That's what I want first." Larry put one ankle on his knee, lifted his bearded chin, and fixed blue eyes on Ben under heavy black brows. "Respect. Not the kind we 'give' women. I want the kind men *get*."

When Larry went out Ben's kitchen door Ben stood near his stove, remembering that he'd jammed Larry against that wall, run his hands under his shirt, pulled his shorts off.

# 32

Five weeks now," Larry Day told the cat, and ran a finger along thick eyebrows, scowling into his mirror in the half-dark bedroom. "I'm going to see my mother!" His deepened voice bounced back from a corner.

Banana purred.

Larry put Banana out and locked doors. When he stepped from his back porch there was a small package on the top stair.

Larry snatched it up, went through back gates into Ben's yard, and drove Ben's car out of the old barn and down Seerley Boulevard in darkness before dawn. A box of candy lay beside him on the seat with a note stuck to it:

> YOU BELONG IN MY BED UNDER
> ME. I WILL MAKE YOU BEG.

Boulevard lights came and went on the young man's jacket and jeans, low-heeled boots.

He scowled as he drove. The notes were all alike and showed up every now and then. There was no guessing when they'd arrive, so there was no way to wait and catch whoever it was. One note had said:

> IT'S GOING TO BE AWFULLY HOT
> FOR YOU WHEN WE'RE IN BED
> TOGETHER. THAT'S A PROMISE.

Under his dark mustache and beard Larry Day's white teeth showed suddenly, almost like a smile.

YOU WILL KISS MY FEET AND BEG
ME TO DO IT AGAIN.

There was no woman in the car. Larry Day ripped the note in pieces as he drove, threw it out an open window with the candy.

Mile after Iowa mile went by.

When the sun was up Larry turned into a gas station, shut off the motor. Unsmiling, he told a station attendant to fill it up.

The door said "Men." Larry pushed it open to find a dirty urinal and a booth with a toilet in it.

When Larry Day came from the booth he read "Up em all" scratched into the door's paint. There was no soap, no towels. A dark-bearded young man looked back at him from a dirty mirror.

LAURA—
I KNOW WHAT BABIES LIKE, AND
THAT'S WHAT YOU'RE GONNA GET
FROM ME.

A mechanic came in and looked Larry over, then glanced at him again. He unzipped his pants at the urinal.

Larry paid for the gas, took the highway out of town. Trees in farmyards had patches of yellow leaves; September sun grew hotter.

Larry drove steadily until it was lunchtime, then stopped at a highway restaurant. He walked in his comfortable boots to a table and ordered the cheap special and remembered not to smile or tip his head. He raised his chin and propped his fists on the table edge. He'd arrive in Fredsburg late and get a motel room when no one was around.

"There you are," the young waitress said, bringing his order. She leaned her breasts a little closer to Larry than was necessary.

"Thanks," Larry said. The waitress teetered off on high heels, glancing back at him in a mirror before she went through swinging doors.

Larry Day forked food between his beard and mustache, but Sara ate it carefully, slowly. She watched the restaurant's ordinary room from under her bristly eyebrows, and did not need to wear anything like a friendly expression, and no one stared.

When she opened her car door again heat poured out. She turned on Ben's air conditioner.

Miles of farm fields and little towns . . . about seven Sara stopped for dinner. Darkness fell.

Trucks passed Sara now and then on the narrow road, rocking her car. She passed grain elevators, small town parks with moths beating at their lonely lights, and billboards lifted only a little above wind-blown corn.

Then, at last, there was Fredsburg. Lighted streets gave a pale shimmer to the sky ahead as Sara began to recognize every road curve, every clump of trees.

"Joe," she said, alone in dashboard glow. She started up the hill to home.

She didn't stop when she saw the farmhouse they had rented for three years on the edge of town. She didn't even cut her speed. The barn had fallen into a pile of timbers. Faint light struck boards nailed over a window. The house was empty, abandoned.

Before she even passed it she was running through ditches with Joe on a rutted track to the west field. She didn't have to see willows to know they were there. A green lawn sloped past her with the tenderest curve, she smelled a musty front hall, her mother laughed, her old brass bed threw its shadow on the wall, and then it was all gone in a rearview mirror and she was driving downhill to the Craigie Court Retirement Center.

She didn't stop there—she looked for Martin's car in every lot and along Fredsburg streets. It wasn't much of a town. There was the courthouse on the square, and Andy's Candy Store across from it, where high school boys braced skinny hips against a stone ledge after school, exhaling cigarette smoke, their eyes narrow. You wanted so much to be pretty, with power to make boys come off that ledge and throw the right insults after you, the way smaller boys threw snowballs, singling you out for the choicest nastiness, four-letter words like spit, the smack of ice on the back of your head.

Fredsburg was bright, and she drove through it, watching for Martin's car. She was like a stupid moth drawn back to the one place Martin might be waiting with a gun to kill her. Thousands of miles of safe country in every direction, and she drove through Fredsburg late at night and parked at the only motel or hotel in town, the one across from the Craigie Court Retirement Center.

Sara looked down the road to a grove of trees where she'd hidden all night the summer before. Small lights shone above motel doors after midnight. Martin had shouted there, beaten with his fists. She remembered. His car wasn't at the motel or in the Craigie Court lot.

Now a dark-bearded young man got out of his car below Martin's motel window; Martin watched him as he slammed the door on the driver's side and tried to lock it, slammed it again, and rang a bell at the motel office. A sleepy clerk showed the young man a room. A click of a door, and Martin saw nothing from his motel window but cars in a lot, and Craigie Court Retirement Center with night-lights here and there.

Sara looked from her motel window at the Center across the road. Martin had always wanted her to run in and see her mother and then leave; he never went into Craigie Court. It gave him the shivers, he said. Lights shone here and there in Center windows.

And had this been the motel room she'd crouched in, terrified, while Martin beat at the door?

A bearded man stared at Sara from her mirror. She shut the window's venetian blind, then peeled off her beard, mustache, thick eyebrows. A person neither male nor female watched her now. Its chest was almost flat; it wore a pair of jeans.

Sara took off heavy men's shoes, jeans, shirt, bandages,

dark wig and saw a young woman in the mirror who was freeing her heavy braids of hair. No one beat at the door or burst in to yell, knock her down. . . .

She looked at her bed, her closet, her bathroom; she turned on the TV low and stretched on her bed to wiggle her toes in the faces of television gangsters shooting each other in an alley. There would be no notes at her door in the morning:

> BEAUTIFUL DOLL:
> YOU CANNOT ESCAPE MY LOVE. I
> WILL TAKE YOU AND YOU WILL
> LOVE IT.

Hot water soothed her; she stood in the shower for a long time. Her beard and mustache and the summer suit she had packed were by her bed, waiting to keep her safe one more day, until she was back in Cedar Falls.

Yawning, Sara turned out lights, then opened the motel blind enough to see her mother's nursing home across a narrow highway. The dark parking lot was almost empty, but a man walked from car to car there, scribbling on a pad in his hand. A policeman, probably. She hadn't left anything in her car; the door on the driver's side wouldn't lock.

There was no light in her mother's room over the entrance.

Sara pulled the blind shut, lay down, sighed, and dreamed of Cedar Falls. Then she dreamed of a great presence, a woman who came and went as she pleased, filling the sky above Sara with that huge woman's face. And then there was Ben in her dream, and she lay smiling in her sleep beside the suit and shirt and mustache and beard.

Martin walked quietly past Sara's window and eased another car door open. His flashlight was small; it barely lit the registration: "Benjamin Woodward, 2309 Tremont Street, Cedar Falls, Iowa 50613." He left the car door slightly ajar.

The next car was unlocked too. "Harley Fendstrom, 18905 Strawberry Lane, Omaha, Nebraska."

Martin never slammed a car door, but walked on soft-soled slippers to his own motel room on the corner. Cars came in late sometimes. He sat by his window until dawn every day and scratched and scratched at his two-week beard that was growing fast. It itched like hell.

For almost two weeks Martin had copied the license number of every car parked at the motel or the Craigie Court Retirement Center, fool that he was. Maybe Sara had learned to swim, but that didn't mean she made it to shore from the sailboat. She was probably drowned and had the last laugh after all.

His new beard itched. He'd dye it to match his dyed-brown hair. Sara would never recognize him if he wore sunglasses—not until it was too late. He swore and watched everybody who came to the Center or the motel, and felt like a ghost. He didn't have a wife, he didn't have a job, the pigs were after him and here he sat watching for somebody who was drowned. He followed people who were new in town—saw them park their cars at the motel or Craigie Court and followed them. Sara might have somebody come see her mother—maybe the man she was shacked up with. She'd want her mother to know she wasn't dead, but she didn't dare telephone. Chloe never got calls. Sara wouldn't dare write either.

If people left a car unlocked overnight, he copied the registration. He had quite a list now, and he was sick of a motel room and hamburgers. Mostly he drank wine. But the police hadn't found him yet. Maybe that grocery-store bitch hadn't reported him. Maybe they thought he'd drowned.

He wrote a description of everybody who came into Craigie Court. The nurse at the infirmary desk told him Sara's mother hadn't had a letter or a telephone call from anyone since Sara drowned, and nobody had visited her.

Every day he checked to see if anyone had called or come to see Chloe Gray. Sara would come there or send somebody, he knew that.

Martin watched and waited and swore and talked to

himself and drank wine until his head felt bigger and bigger, like a pumpkin.

As weeks went by he started seeing Sara all the time: Sara under the big tree at the corner . . . Sara sitting in the corner of his room. Sometimes she was in bed with him, swelled up and stinking, and when he tried to make love to her, her bones slid around in slime. He slept with the light on.

He could wait. She'd come. He had money, and time, and a gun.

# 33

Sara couldn't sleep, though her motel room was cool and still. Her mother was just across the street in her narrow bed. Perhaps she was dreaming of her daughter Sara, who had drowned.

Sara lay awake for hours until it was almost light, wishing she could simply get up and go out, run to her mother and put her arms around her, tell her she was alive. But she couldn't get into Craigie Court so early—it wasn't even dawn.

She got up and put her beard and mustache on and wrapped bandages around her breasts again. Eyebrows. Wig. Shirt and tie, suit, socks and shoes. When she looked in the mirror a man's reflection frowned at her in yellow lamplight; he was her shell, her camouflage.

The young bearded man carried his suitcase out and put it in his car trunk. The driver's-side door wasn't shut tight; he stood for a moment looking at it. He checked every car in the parking lot and crossed the street to look at cars at Craigie Court—that was funny, Martin thought. Martin watched him from his window as the bearded man went in the motel office. Probably paying his bill.

The bearded man came out of the office and walked to a twenty-four-hour restaurant down the street. Martin watched him go and scratched his new beard and yawned.

"No," the restaurant waitress told the young man, "you can't even get in the door of Craigie Court until seven-thirty." So Sara ordered breakfast and read a paper, and then the waitress watched the short young fellow with the beard walk toward the dark highway.

Martin watched him go too. What the hell, he thought. He could take a little walk and follow that bearded guy, see where he was going. He stuffed his feet into his shoes.

Sara turned on the highway, recognizing every faint rise in farm fields, every grove of trees, though their shapes were only blacker shapes against black sky. Sand and gravel made a brisk crackle under her shoes. She walked fast now. Martin kept far behind the bearded fellow: he could barely see him moving like a shadow along the gravel shoulder.

Sara topped the hill. There was the farmyard! She cried out to herself and ran down the old lane between trees, passing what was left of the barn. She didn't need light to see the porch roof she'd crawled on, following Joe . . . she knew its shape against stars, and the larger mass of the old maple tree they had climbed down while their mother's light shone from the living room.

Two boards nailed across a back-porch window had one nail apiece; when she swung them aside it was easy to push the window up and climb through.

Sara had brought matches; she struck one. Her mother's familiar kitchen leapt at her, a ghost place. Memories swarmed like motes in match light, until the match went out.

Martin climbed the hill, scratching his new beard. The fellow was hidden from him on the other side, he supposed.

Sara tiptoed through dark silence. Floors were sticky under her shoes; the tacky sound of her steps went ahead of her into a back hall where Joe had kept his hamster in a cage. When her steps halted at the living-room door, she heard nothing but dark, stale silence.

Something scraped in the wall near Sara. A mouse turning in its sleep?

Martin started down the hill. There was a sharp curve ahead. The bearded fellow was out of sight already.

Sara remembered a windbreak of firs grew on the north, pressed against every window. The house had always been dark, even on summer afternoons when cornfields across the road melted and blurred in the heat like reflections in water.

Stairs to the second floor creaked under Sara's shoes. Each step had a different voice, and she knew them all. An upstairs hall was narrow and black, but dawn was coming— its first faint light fell through her bedroom's open door.

The bedroom wall was cool and rough under her hands. She could see a cheap child's desk in one corner; tears came to her eyes. She pulled out one small, flimsy drawer. It was empty, but she pulled it all the way out and bent to look in the hole, then lit a match—there was something stuck at the back.

Before the match went out she had an envelope in her hand. It was small, the corner of a used envelope; she and her mother had stored garden seeds in them. Seeds made a small mound in this one; she put it in her pocket. Match scent hung in the dawn air.

Martin rounded the road's curve in the growing light. There was no one in sight; the highway lay in a silent glow from the sky, empty as far as he could see. Martin said, "Hell!" and stopped, looking around him.

Sara walked through other bedrooms, then went back downstairs. There had always been a row of hooks by the kitchen door for coats and scarves and hats. She felt for them along the wall. They were gone now.

Brightening light showed under the dining-room door. Sara pushed the door open.

This room wasn't empty or dark—it was like a stage, a room within a room, lit by green-fir light. The first slight glow of dawn filtered in; no one had put boards over those windows. Windbreak firs, dense and still, flattened themselves against the glass, their needles glistening with dew.

"Hell!" Martin said again, stopping, turning to walk back around the curve toward town. He came to the hilltop. A muddy farm lane straggled between trees to a boarded-up house. No sign of anybody there at all. He went down the lane a little way. There were prints of a man's shoes in mud.

Sara took a step inside the dining-room door. It was a child's playhouse in the middle of the empty room, she could see that. There were acorn dishes on an orange crate, and tin-can saucepans on a cardboard-box stove. Silverware on a board table was twigs. The bed was an old quilt folded between boards. Two battered dolls lay in the bed; one had its eyes shut, but the other's wide-awake look was painted on.

Sara almost smiled. Some little farm kid had made a playhouse for herself in the middle of the floor, away from cracked walls and spiderwebs and the silent watch of the firs. Dawn light filled acorn cups and tin cans and a bookcase-crate that had newspapers torn and folded into make-believe books.

Out in the farmyard, Martin looked at a sagging porch roof, a maple tree, and boards over doors and windows. He walked around the house on weedy grass until he came to a thick fir windbreak on the north. He turned back, went around the other way. There was only a back porch there. Boards were loose and open over a window there; he could climb in, look around.

A bird chirped so close that Martin turned toward the sound and saw sunlight pierce hilltop trees—yellow fingers of brilliance ran through green corn. He yawned and felt how tired he was. He ought to be in bed. The bearded fellow had taken some side road he knew about or cut across some field.

In the dining room, Sara held a make-believe book in her hand, smiling. Martin walked the highway toward town. When Sara crawled out of the kitchen window and shut it behind her, pulling boards back in place, Martin was only a speck far down the road; the speck turned a corner and vanished as she came down the rutted farmyard path.

Sara walked back to the motel, a young man out for a stroll along the highway.

At seven-forty she crossed the road to the Craigie Court Retirement Center. Smells of the infirmary met her at the door; they hadn't changed. Sara walked past a nurse's station in her summer suit and black beard, glancing at name cards beside doors. One said, "Chloe Gray," and under it "Lila Rainey."

"I'm a long-ago friend of Lila Rainey's," the young man said, coming back to a nurse behind the counter. "I wonder if it would be possible to see her early. I have to leave town soon."

The nurse checked her card file. "She isn't scheduled for her bath just yet," she said. The nurse was young, and she smiled at the bearded man. "You can go right along to the Sunshine Room, second door on your left."

The dark young man walked to the Sunshine Room, which had names above its two beds: "Lila Rainey" in blue crayon with red X's around it, and "Chloe Gray'" in green crayon with yellow daisies.

Chloe Gray's bed was empty.

"Come on, Marie," a nurse bellowed from the hall. "Time for your bath."

"Listen to that. They shout all the time here, but do they listen?" A dry, small voice startled Sara. The bed next to her mother's had a quilt-covered mound on it, and the mound was twitching now. "You can tell them you're a murderer—done it twice—and they don't listen." The quilt twitched again. "Think you're deaf and stupid and couldn't kill a fly."

"Hello," the man with the beard said.

"Hello," the mound said in its paper-thin voice. "I thought there was somebody there. At least you don't yell. I'm Lila Rainey, and I been yelled at enough. You should have heard my husband. And you should have heard Roke Pritcher."

"Are you all alone here?" Sara said in her deep voice.

"Nope," the little voice said. "Chloe's having her bath."

Sara leaned over Lila's bed and turned the quilt down to find a woman as small as her voice staring up. "I bet you don't remember me," Sara said.

"Slide down in this bed all the time," Lila said. "They

moved me in this room yesterday, and I think I been lost under here ever since. No, don't remember you at all.''

Lila Rainey was as light and bony as a paper kite. When the man propped her on her pillows there she lay, all nose and flyaway white hair and indignant black eyes. "I've changed a lot," Sara said. "I wonder if you can guess where you knew me."

"Des Moines?" Lila said.

"Right!" Sara said. "I was just a little kid neighbor of yours you used to give cookies to."

"The Brownings, maybe?" Lila said.

"Right! Jimmy, the youngest one."

"Can't remember," Lila said. "But I always liked kids. I never had a baby but once. She was my daughter and heir."

Jimmy Browning went to the window and looked at the front walk and the motel across the street. After a while he asked in his low, man's voice, "Who was Roke Pritcher?"

"He was a raper," Lila said. When Jimmy Browning sat beside Lila the old woman smelled like lavender among the assaulting smells of the nursing home: urine, floor wax, and the last (or next) meal.

"I wouldn't have liked this Roke Pritcher," Sara said, trying to keep Lila talking so she could watch from the window and look out the door. Martin hovered over her here; she was sweating in her man's hair and man's clothes.

"You would've if you were a woman," Lila said. "Roke was bee balm to the ladies. He'd go into town and smile with those picket-fence teeth of his, and they'd hover round, hover and buzz just like bees. He was mean from the first time he wet a diaper. Sharp white teeth, and how he would laugh, rubbing some little fellow's face in the gravel on the way home from country school. I knew Roke Pritcher real well. We were poor and I was just sixteen, and Roke Pritcher hired me to cook for him and his hired hands 'cause he was a bachelor.''

Her mother would be brought back soon, Sara thought. She couldn't stay away from the window. She was watching for Martin. "What happened?" she asked.

Lila's fingers were nothing but joints and bones covered with papery skin; they picked at her quilt's yarn ties. "Roke was bigger than me, and he jumped me. Gave his hired men the day off for the state fair and jumped me. I got pregnant. The worst of it was that those men, they thought it was natural. Roke wanted me, he'd marry me, and I'd be living on a good farm, and what more could I want?" Her bright black eyes snapped at the young man who wouldn't sit still but roamed to the window, the door, and back to her bed. "You don't listen! You men get together and tell each other what women are like, but you never listen to find out. Shut up in your heads like clams."

Sara said nothing. There wasn't anything to say. Lila's bright black eyes glittered at the television set. There was a get-well card with shamrocks and green elves on the TV beside a picture of somebody's smiling family with a dog and their split-level house. If her mother came, how could Sara talk to her? She wasn't supposed to know her. She'd come to visit Lila Rainey.

"In a minute," an attendant said loudly, pushing a thin old man down the hall in his wheelchair. "We're going to have a nice cake-and-coffee party in the lounge."

"That old man doesn't want cake and coffee," Lila said in her crackling whisper of a voice. "He never does. He'll piddle on the floor. You watch. They're shut up in their heads. They don't listen."

The sound of the wheelchair had died away. Sara was listening for Martin's voice as she huddled inside her man's clothes and hairy face.

"I had to get rid of the baby or marry Roke," Lila said. "I married a feed salesman I met in Des Moines years later, but I never could have another baby."

Her old hands were picking, picking at the quilt. One tear slid down her wrinkles and gave a calico daisy a dark eye. "I had to leave my little girl in the trap to spring myself loose. Just like a fox that gnaws its paw off."

"C'mon, now, Lila," an attendant said, coming in the door briskly. "It's time for your bath. Your friend can wait in your room." She smiled at the bearded young man and whipped off Lila's quilt and sheet. There wasn't enough of Lila in her hospital gown to give the gown shape; it seemed to inhabit the bed by itself.

"Here we go," the attendant bawled, scooping up Lila. Lila stared from the attendant's arms, an old face in a bundle of flower-sprigged flannel. Thin voices were singing a hymn in the lounge down the hall.

"She was my daughter and heir," Lila said.

"There you go," the attendant said, loading the nightgown and Lila's face into the wheelchair.

Lila's big nose and flyaway crown of hair bobbed over the attendant's shoulder; her bright black eyes glared at the young bearded man. "Murder—two murders—and nobody cares!" she hissed. "See?"

"Let's get our pretty pink slippers on," the attendant bawled, down on her knees by the bed.

"Murder!" Lila yelled in the attendant's face that was only an inch or two away.

"There we are," the attendant said, getting to her feet. "Lila will be back in just a little while. You can sit in the lounge if you like," she said to the young man.

Lila's eyes glittered. Borne away out the door, she left a last, whispered "They don't listen!" behind her in the air.

# 34

Sara was standing by the window when they brought Chloe Gray back from her bath. Two attendants rolled her from a high cart to her bed, tucked her in, and smiled at the bearded man. "Clo, there's a young man here waiting to see Lila," one of the attendants said in her loud, cheery voice.

The young man waited until they left, then shut the door softly. Sara crept to her mother's bed. It was covered with a quilt like a garden—there were poppies and narcissus on it, and fruit, grain, and green leaves spilling from baskets.

Her mother's eyes were shut, and she might have been dead, she lay so still. The face on the pillow seemed as gray as the thin hair spread around it. Her breath rasped in and out.

Hot tears sprang to Sara's eyes. "You fought, Mom," she whispered softly. "You always fought, don't you remember?" Her mother's face, the same hands, and all the years. "Oh, Mom," she whispered, "don't be scared."

Her mother jerked. Her blind eyes opened and stared up.

"It's me, Mom," Sara whispered. She smoothed her mother's thin hair on the pillow and grabbed the wrinkled hand that had a scar along the thumb and over the wrist. "It's me . . . it's Sara."

The blind eyes had no expression. The wrinkled hand lay in Sara's, unmoving.

"Did they tell you I was gone? That I'd drowned?"

The scar on the hand—Sara remembered her mother smashing a window, throwing a rug down in the shattered glass, helping a small Joe and Sara to climb away from a fire that was bursts of smoke and ash behind her. "Do you remember the fire at Uncle Ronald's? You got the scar on your hand saving Joe and me at Uncle Ronald's. . . . Oh, Mom . . ."

The hand was still dead in Sara's hand, as if no one remembered what she remembered any more.

Sara began to sob. "Remember the Halloween costume you made for me from remnants? I was supposed to be a rose. And somebody threw hot chocolate at the party I went to, and we could never wash it out?"

Her mother's blind eyes showed Sara nothing. Her mother's hand lay unmoving in hers. The other hand moved a little from a cloth poppy to a cloth narcissus in the quilt's overflowing basket, that was all.

"Mom," Sara breathed in her ear. "Mom—I'm Sara. Feel me!" She lifted the scarred hand to her hair, but the hair wasn't hers—it was coarse and false. Her beard covered her face.

Only her mother's labored breath showed she was alive.

Sara slid her arms around her mother, holding her tight, burying her face in the remembered scent of her mother's hair and skin, crying. She whispered, "I'm Sara. Mom . . . I'm here!"

Her mother's rasping breath caught in her throat. She gave a sigh. Her voice was so faint it was hardly a whisper; her lips were dry and worked to form words: "Sara's dead."

"You know my voice, don't you? I had to make them think I was dead."

"Sara's dead," her mother whispered.

"I'm not! I've come back as soon as I could!"

"They said she fell out of a sailboat in Manhasset Bay." Blind eyes stared at the ceiling; when Sara sat up her mother said nothing more. Her breath made its way in and out, hardly moving the quilt. Sara stared at the shut door. A nurse might come at any moment. Martin might come.

"Mom . . . I couldn't live with Martin. I tried. I'm hiding from him, Mom. He thinks I'm dead."

"Sara drowned like Joe," her mother whispered. Her thin fingers wandered over the quilt's poppies and apples, ears of corn, green leaves.

"I never told you how Martin beat me up. He broke my toe, and after I came to see you last time he knocked me downstairs and ruptured my spleen, and broke my wrist." Sara sobbed. "I'm afraid of him, Mom. He has a gun and he said he'd kill me if I left him, and kill any man I was with."

"She tried to save Joe," her mother whispered, "and she couldn't, so she wouldn't go in the water ever again. That's how I know."

Tears spilled from Sara's eyes, and she sobbed, remembering how screams had worn her throat raw. She felt beach sand sticking to her as she crawled out of the water. Lights blinked on in beach houses while she screamed, and boats went out on a moon-slick bay. Her father's face when they woke him up; the stern policeman and a twelve-year-old girl, soaked and gibbering. "Why didn't you tell me you knew, Mom? I couldn't tell anybody, ever. I tried to save Joe. . . ."

"Sara tried. I knew she tried. But we couldn't talk about it. We never could talk about it."

Her mother's voice was so low; Sara hovered over her. "He dared me to swim across to Bankton, and he'd had pneumonia, remember? Halfway there he screamed that he couldn't breathe, and when I found him he pulled me under. I had to get away from him, l-let him go d-down. . . ." Sara sobbed, her face against her mother's. She dug her arms beneath the old body and hugged it tight.

After a while her mother's hand reached up to feel her hair, her beard. Sara lay still, her tears soaking her mother's pillow.

"My Sara?" her mother said.

"Mom!" Sara was laughing and crying at the same

time. "I'm dressed like a man, Mom," Sara whispered. "So Martin won't know me. Has he come here?"

"Sara," her mother whispered.

"I drove here to tell you as soon as I could. I'm making a new life for myself where Martin can't ever find me. I'm afraid of him, Mom. Don't ever tell him I came. I wonder, has he been here? Has he telephoned to ask if you've had calls or letters or visitors?"

"I thought you were gone. Sara." Tears began to run from the corners of her mother's eyes to the pillow. After a while she said, "No. Nobody ever comes. Nobody calls."

Sara squeezed her mother's thin hands. "As soon as I can I'm going to get you and take you home with me."

"I didn't want to be a bother when you were married," her mother said.

"But now I'm free."

"Sara!" Her mother said her name over and over: "Sara! Sara! I won't tell anybody."

"I'm afraid Martin might think of finding me here if he ever suspects I'm not drowned. And I didn't have any money. That's why it's taken me so long to let you know. I said I wanted to see Lila Rainey, not you. Remember— *nobody's* visited you. Martin thinks I'm dead, Mom. He's got to think I'm dead. He said he'd kill me if I ran away again."

Her mother's hands tightened, holding hers. "He's mean," her mother said. "I always thought he was mean."

"Remember the good times with Joe?" Sara said. "Remember the vegetable gardens you always had, and all the canning? I could get my hands in the pickle-jar tops for you, remember? And the sweet corn you grew—best in town? I've got a garden now, a whole garden all to myself!"

"You're really here," her mother said.

"You've got a beautiful quilt on your bed. Did you know? It's covered with baskets of poppies and narcissus— spring and summer, I suppose—and fruit and corn ears and wheat for fall," Sara said. "Remember I had a light table for African violets in Montrose? There wasn't any yard in back, and Martin wouldn't let me put flowers in the front yard, but even when I was living in that hell with him, I had the violets you and I used to grow—Twilight Princess and Pomegranate and Saturn and Autumn Honey . . . and I've got them yet!''

''It's you. Sara.''

''I've got to leave now, because I'm scared. But don't you ever think I was a dream, Mom. Look, I'll give you this cheap ring I'm wearing. Keep it right on your hand. Every time you think I was a dream, you just feel that ring and tell yourself that Sara's alive, and that pretty soon we'll be together, when I can get a good library job somewhere.''

The big man's ring with the oak tree on it would stay only on her mother's thumb. Her mother closed her bony fingers over it and breathed, ''You're not dead. You're not drowned!''

''That's right,'' Sara said. ''Tell yourself that every time you feel that ring. Do they take good care of you, I wonder?'' She lifted her mother's covers. The hospital nightgown was split down the back, and clean, and so were the sheets. Sara could roll the thin, light body on its side so easily. No bad bedsores. Her mother had a plastic-backed diaper on, and it was dry. ''Yes,'' her mother whispered. ''Real good care.''

Sara rolled the light body back, pulled her mother's flower-garden quilt up, and tucked the sheet over the top. She smoothed her mother's long, gray hair.

When a nurse opened the door and looked in, the black-bearded man bending over Chloe Gray had tears in his eyes. She shut the door again. Sara squeezed her mother's thin fingers a last time.

''Sara,'' her mother said, ''I thought you were gone. I thought nobody cared about me anymore. Nobody ever came.''

Sara wiped her mother's wet eyes and her mother clung to her hands.

''I've got to go,'' Sara said. ''I was so lucky there was nobody in your room but us. I'm living in my own apartment in a nice little town and I'll just stay there until Martin's sure I'm really dead. I've got a job. Don't you worry about me."

"I won't," her mother said. "You're not gone." She began to cry again.

"That's my ring I gave you, and I'm not gone," Sara said. "I can't write you any letters with my own name on, but if you get a letter from Larry Day, you'll know it's really me. Can you remember that Larry Day is going to start writing you lots of letters, and only you will know he's really Sara Gray?"

"Yes," her mother whispered. "Larry Day."

"That's me," Sara said. "Don't you forget. And don't you ever, ever tell anyone I came today to see you. Martin could find me that way, maybe, and kill me."

"Oh, be careful," her mother whispered, hanging on to Sara's hands. "I won't tell anybody."

"Good-bye," Sara whispered. "I came as soon as I could. I wish you hadn't thought I was drowned. I couldn't help it."

"It's all right," her mother said. "It's all right now."

Sara went to the window and looked into the street, then bent over her mother lying under the quilt's poppies and narcissus and ears of grain. "I'll mail you a letter to-night," she whispered to the pale face on the pillow. "So you watch. You'll hear from me tomorrow or the next day. You make them read it to you. Say it's from a distant relative. But it'll be me, Mom. It'll be Sara. Good-bye, my love," Sara said, and smoothed her mother's hair and kissed her.

"Good-bye," her mother whispered, kissing her back. Her blind eyes stared at the ceiling; her fingers picked at the flowered quilt. "My Sara. Good-bye."

The dark-bearded young man came out of Chloe Gray's room and nearly ran into Lila Rainey's wheelchair. He stopped and knelt beside her in the hall. The nurse at the desk looked at him. A nice-looking fellow, but pretty short, she thought. Nice suit.

"I can't stay longer, Lila," he said, taking Lila's hand

that was as light and dry as balsa wood. He glanced up and down the hall as if he were looking for someone. "But I'll try to come again. What happened to Roke?"

Lila's black eyes stared at the bearded young man. "Once Roke and me were alone in a hog house, and Roke was on the top rail of a pig pen—he was just climbing over, a foot on each side, with a stone floor down there to bust your skull right open, just like a nice ripe pumpkin."

"Uh-huh," the young man said, kneeling beside Lila.

"They said I was brokenhearted when they found what those hogs left of Roke Pritcher," Lila said, her eyes glittering like black coal in their wrinkled sockets.

An attendant in white polyester came to the young man's rescue. "Are you telling your story again, Lila?" she said sweetly, and the young man stood up then and said he'd try to come back again and good-bye.

"They don't listen!" Lila yelled after him.

It was cool outside yet, and night dew was still on the grass. Sara hurried past two cleaning women coming in and a laundry truck backing up the drive. She hurried to her car. The door on the driver's side hadn't been closed when she went out to put her luggage in the trunk before dawn. She couldn't lock the car.

Sara pulled out of the parking lot and aimed for the highway. Only when she was miles away from Fredsburg could she unclench her hands from the wheel. She smelled the sweet summer morning air and took a long, sighing breath.

An attendant lifted Lila Rainey into her bed again.

Craigie Court Center had shining white floors that an old man polished every morning. Fran, the tall, skinny nurse, watched him push the polisher back and forth. She brought the patients' cards up to date, sorted the mail, yawned through the morning hours.

When Martin came about eleven-thirty Fran gave him a strange look. They all wondered about him, a Mr. Baker who said he was a friend of Chloe's but never would go to see her and wouldn't believe that Clo hadn't had any visitors. When he'd started coming more than a week before, he just had beard stubble, but his beard had grown fast and was a dark blond, not like his hair.

"No point in telling Clo about this Mr. Baker," the night nurse had said once. "He's been coming for maybe two weeks but he never goes to see her."

"I think there's money involved," Fran told her. "Some kind of inheritance." And the night nurse had said maybe this Mr. Baker was crazy?

"Good morning," Fran said to Mr. Baker.

"Nobody was here yesterday afternoon to see Chloe Gray, were they?" Mr. Baker asked. That's what he always said, day after day.

"No, but there was a young man here this morning who seemed to know her. He came to see Lila Rainey, but he talked to Chloe for quite a while, and she was so happy afterward," Fran said. "A short young fellow about thirty with a dark beard. He left a few hours ago."

"He what?" Mr. Baker shouted.

Fran stepped back. "He left a few hours ago," she said.

"Did you tell him I wanted to see him?"

"No," Fran said. "He didn't really come to see Chloe—"

Mr. Baker ran past the amateur paintings show, the large calendar with flowers pasted on each day, and Mr. Maunders in his wheelchair by the drinking fountain. He left black heel marks on the white floor. The door closed slowly after his headlong rush. "Well," Fran said.

"Crazy," an attendant said, standing near the desk with an electric shaver for Mr. Maunders. "What did you tell him?"

"I just said a young bearded fellow had been in early this morning to see Lila Rainey."

"Crazy," the attendant said, looking out a window. "He's running around the parking lot at the motel."

"He never did go see Clo, did he?" Fran said.

"No. He's driving off now—look at that—he drove right over the curb twice!"

"Crazy," Fran said.

Martin hardly saw the road or the town. He was watching for a blue car. He'd seen a short, dark-bearded man get out of it the night before. There was only one way out of town to the highway.

"The blue car—the blue car—the black-bearded, short guy," he kept saying to himself, driving on the wrong side of the road because he wasn't looking for anything but a blue car. "Followed him this morning past that boarded-up house."

He came to the highway and squealed to a stop in the middle of the road. If the man was gone, he was long gone. But he might still be in town someplace.

Martin drove back and forth, looking in parking lots and driveways and open garages for a blue car with an Iowa license plate. Finally he stopped in the shade outside of town. He'd missed the bearded guy, but he could find him. He got the notebook out of his pants pocket. "Benjamin Woodward, 2309 Tremont Street, Cedar Falls, Iowa 50613."

# 35

Sara mailed her first printed note to Chloe Gray in a town forty miles from Fredsburg. Her mother would get it the next day. Watching the long miles pass, she sang a little to herself, thinking that in her mother's mind she was alive now. One person knew there was a Sara Gray.

Sara stopped to eat at a restaurant close to the Nebraska line. Her waitress was a friendly-looking older woman with straggly hair in a net.

"Here's five dollars for you if you'll mail these letters to my mother, one every week," Sara said to the waitress in her tenor voice. "I want them to be postmarked from Nebraska for old times' sake." The waitress said she sure would mail one every week, and it was so nice that a son cared about his mother. She waved and smiled at the nice dark-bearded young man as he left the restaurant.

It was after two in the morning when Sara drove down the alley and into Ben's old barn. Backyard grass was wet with dew. Banana leapt through it, long-legged and mewing.

Ben had a key to Sara's kitchen door. When she turned on her kitchen light there was a note on the table: "Snack and your breakfast in the refrigerator. Welcome home." She opened the refrigerator door. Cookies, milk, a coffee cake, orange juice, and eggs waited for her in cold light.

"Ben," she said to Banana, shutting her eyes, thinking of him sitting naked on the edge of his bed, fists clenched, dim streetlight glow edging his angry face. Martin had never come to Fredsburg—he thought she was drowned. She felt too free, too happy to sleep. Maybe she was safe. She could go out with Ben now . . . perhaps even love . . .

A hot bath, and then cookies and milk.

Banana sat on a kitchen chair, blinking at the man who went into the bathroom and the woman who came out. Sara hid the beard, mustache, eyebrows, and bandages in her dresser's bottom drawer, hung up the man's clothes. "I've seen my mother!" she told Banana. "She knows I'm alive!"

Banana settled in Sara's lap when she sat at the kitchen table, and was sprinkled with cookie crumbs. Ben was asleep next door. Perhaps he was curled up, his face hidden by his arms and his red-blond hair. More than five weeks since . . . was she safe enough to go out with a man, to stop hiding? Sara yawned, put Banana down, crawled into bed, and was asleep at once.

Then the telephone rang. She stumbled out into the living room to answer it.

"It's Ellen." A whisper hardly made its way to her ear.

"Yes? Ellen?"

"It's Ellen." The whisper had a sob in it. "Can you come and stay with Dr. Channing? I just got a call from Waterloo. My aunt there is awful sick and she hasn't got anybody else. I have to take a taxi to her house right away."

"I'll get there as soon as I can," Sara said.

There was one more sob and the line went dead.

Sara put Banana out, packed some clothes in her plastic bag, put on a shirt, slacks, and running shoes, and ran down Tremont, down Eighteenth, down Clay.

Dr. Channing's house was dark except for Ellen's window upstairs. Sara opened and shut the kitchen door quietly and stood for a moment in the dark, listening. Someone was crying upstairs, crying softly and steadily.

Sara knew where Ellen's room was. She went up wooden stairs that seemed to be wet. "Ellen?" she said, and knocked.

No answer. The bathroom keyhole glowed across the hall. "Ellen?" she called softly, and knocked there. No one answered. She opened the door a crack, and saw blood on the tile floor.

There was blood on the floor and sink; Ellen's legs and feet were smeared with it. There seemed to be no blood in Ellen's white face. She lay with her head propped on the sill of the shower.

"Ellen!" Sara cried. "Oh, Ellen!" she knelt beside her. Ellen held a bundle of towels in her arms.

Sara whispered, "Oh, my dear!" She smoothed Ellen's wet brown bangs. "What's happened? You're bleeding. . . ." She looked again at the room and Ellen's legs and feet. Could she lift her, get her on a bed?

Something moved in the bundle Ellen held in her arms. It made a mewing sound like a kitten. Tears were running out of Ellen's eyes. She pulled the corner of a towel back, and Sara looked into a small red face. An unbelievably small human hand beside the face made a fist, then spread its fingers wide. "It's a girl," Ellen said.

Sara stared into Ellen's opaque brown eyes. "Your *baby?* You've had a baby?"

Ellen stared at her. "You'll tell," she said. "I couldn't get to the hospital—it went too fast. And now you'll tell." Tears began to fall to the bundle of towels and the small red face whose mouth opened and shut, mewing.

"Oh, n-no!" Sara said, stammering with her shock. "I'm very good at not telling anything to anybody. But are you all right? Is she—"

"I left the afterbirth on," Ellen said. "I think she's all right. She's fine."

The baby waved her hand and made her mewing cry. "My father mustn't know," Ellen sobbed. "He'll leave my mother again—"

"*Nobody* will know," Sara said.

"Listen," Ellen said. "My name is Ellen Dehlstrom. I was just hitching a ride through Cedar Falls and went into labor, and you found me and called a taxi . . . if anybody at the hospital ever finds out I came from here and calls."

"All right," Sara said. "Ellen Dehlstrom."

"Can you telephone for a taxi? Dr. Channing won't hear us, the air conditioner's on," Ellen said. "The hospital won't know I have anything to do with Cedar Falls, and I'll have them call my aunt. She'll come to the hospital right away. She'll take care of everything."

"I'll call," Sara said. "I'll be right back." She telephoned for a taxi and came again to find Ellen on her side trying to mop the floor with a towel.

"Don't!" Sara cried. The sight of fat, quiet Ellen trying to clean the floor twisted her heart inside out. "Let me do it afterward. I'll have everything back to normal before anybody sees."

"I had it all planned," said Ellen. Her pale face was drawn and sad.

"I can take care of Dr. Channing. You just go right along and don't worry about a thing. You've gone to be with your sick aunt in Waterloo." Sara found a clean washcloth and wiped Ellen's face and bloody hands, then cleaned her legs and feet.

Sara put the baby on the bed and helped Ellen stand up. They pinned two towels around her under a clean nightgown, and put her dark raincoat over it. Ellen lay on her bed while Sara put on Ellen's ankle socks and shoes.

"You'll tell," Ellen moaned softly, rubbing her face against her pillow. "People always do." She began to cry, a hopeless sound. Her brown bangs were wet and stuck to her fat face.

"Don't cry," Sara said, leaning over her. "Don't cry!"

Ellen couldn't stop crying. Sara looked into Ellen's sad face, looked away, looked back. "Here's my secret," Sara said. She pulled off her wig. "And my name's not Laura Pray. Now you know something about me that nobody else here knows, and I know something about you. And neither of us will ever tell."

"No," Ellen said, staring at her. "We never will. Ever."

"Of course not," Sara said, pulling her wig over her thick blond braids again.

"My suitcase is all packed in the closet," Ellen said, rubbing her eyes. "I'll be back here. . . . I don't know how many days it will take."

"You'll bring your baby?"

"No," Ellen said in her flat voice. "I have to give her up."

Sara smoothed Ellen's bangs on her forehead, then carried her suitcase downstairs, looked through the kitchen window, and saw a taxi come around the corner. She closed the door softly behind her and went to tell the driver they'd be right out.

"The taxi's here," she said, leaning over Ellen. She put her arms around Ellen then and kissed her white face. Ellen's eyes were still full of tears. Then she kissed Sara back.

"I'll come see you," Sara said.

"No—don't!" Ellen said. "Please. Don't do anything. Don't even telephone. Just pretend I'm at my aunt's. If anybody calls there, she'll say she's sick and I'm taking care of her."

They went down the stairs slowly. Sara held Ellen's baby wrapped in a blanket and felt the small body squirm against her. There were no lights in neighboring houses when Ellen crawled into the taxi and took her baby from Sara. "Good-bye," she whispered, and Sara shut the door and watched the taxi turn the corner toward Main Street.

It would be dawn soon. Ellen had gone to take care of her sick aunt in Waterloo. Trees rustled around the corner streetlight as if they knew secrets; Sara thought she smelled blood on her fingers yet.

The bathroom had to be cleaned. She found cleanser and a rag and began. One more secret to keep. None of her secrets were happy like Ellen's—a baby that was a new life in the world.

Down on her knees on the tile floor, Sara thought of Martin's hair that was thinning on top, and his brown eyes, and the feel of his body against her, and all the years.

Then she remembered kicks on the back of her legs—heavy kicks, big, heavy shoes, purple-red bruises.

Blood smeared the tile pink. She wiped it away. You kept secrets and survived with your mouth shut, as strong as Ellen, who wasn't even twenty years old. *I had it all planned. You'll tell. People always do.*

Sara finished the bathroom floor and hall and steps. She stripped Ellen's narrow bed and looked around a small room that had so little to say, like Ellen. There were two children's crayon drawings with ''Beverly'' and ''Art'' scrawled in the corners and the usual sun, twig-tree, and box-house with a door.

The houses in the drawings were surrounded with crayon-blue sky. Free. Sara took a deep breath in the small room. Free

Sara's eyes were hard as she took bloody towels downstairs to the washer to soak. You kept secrets and survived them with your mouth shut.

# 36

Long before dawn came Martin found 2309 Tremont. Lights from a city park dappled Ben Woodward's old house. Martin cruised past. No blue car in sight.

He parked a block away and walked back, keeping in shadows away from streetlights until he stepped into an alley. Backyards strummed and peeped with insects; no dog barked. Four o'clock in the morning.

Gravel crackled under Martin's shoes. He tried the door handle of what looked like a barn behind 2309 Tremont, pushed it open. A flicker of his flashlight lit a blue car with the right license number parked next to a lawn mower and a pile of junk.

Woodward's back gate was open. No lights showed from the house. Sara was asleep there, maybe—sleeping with somebody named Ben, who'd been in Nebraska telling her mother Sara wasn't drowned . . . *talked to her quite a while, and she was so happy afterward.*

When he had been in the dark for a while, Martin could see backyards that had no fences except along the alley. He crept through Woodward's gate and felt fallen fruit under his shoes—apples.

It was very dark under Woodward's apple tree, but light from a house next door showed lawns that ran to the corner house's big round flower bed.

Martin tiptoed across grass. The lighted window belonged to an old frame house with a screened back porch:

Woodward's neighbor. Suddenly a cat startled Martin—it leapt from porch steps hidden in bushes. Martin felt his way to the window and looked in.

Just a kitchen. Nobody there. Lamplight against an orange wall made a cozy, framed picture of a coffeepot, a cup and saucer on the table, flowers in a vase.

Martin made his way back to his rented car and drove to find a motel, seeing nothing but Sara, her long, light hair spread on Ben Woodward's pillow, his dark-bearded face on her rising and falling breasts.

Cars began to appear on Cedar Falls streets.

Milkmen stamped up porch stairs; newspapers thudded beyond railings. Trees caught the first sun and gave back a chorus of birds.

High in their high-rise dorms, students slapped alarm clocks, stumbled down halls to showers, thought of Friday classes and then the weekend. By noon lucky ones pulled out of campus parking lots on their way home.

Sounds of passing cars hardly reached Dr. Channing's dim bedroom; the cleaning lady's vacuum droned in the hall. Sara carried a lunch tray in. "Macaroni and cheese for lunch," she said to the face on the pillow. "Green beans."

There was never any answer but silence. Sara slid her arms under Dr. Channing and turned her on her back, the heavy body familiar to her now. Dr. Channing could do nothing about that familiarity; she had to suffer hands putting her on a bedpan, washing her, wiping her, looking at her old flesh. Sara listened to the vulnerable, helpless silence. "I'm glad to be taking care of you until Ellen's aunt is better," she said after a while as she scraped up another spoonful. "Maybe we can go on reading *The Golden Bowl*."

Dr. Channing's stillness replied, yet it seemed changed, as bedroom light changed from noon to evening. Sara glanced at her. Now somebody lived behind that lined face. The large lips had expression, and if the eyes still seemed wounded and grieving, they had other expressions too.

"You're stuck with only me all weekend, I'm afraid,

until Mrs. Eaker comes Monday to give you your bath,'' Sara said, spooning in macaroni and cheese. ''I wonder if you'd like me to put on one of Chopin's sonatas, or an etude? I think she's done with the vacuum cleaner.''

Dr. Channing nodded.

''A sonata?''

She nodded again.

The hi-fi was a new one, with speakers hidden in living room and dining room and bedroom. Cascades of Chopin began to fall through silky, curtained-away sunlight; all shimmered together.

Sara looked around a bedroom that her voice had filled for hours with the words of Henry James. James knew why a woman might hide. Chopin knew. Sad, liquid cadences of sound said so.

So live alone.

Sara spooned macaroni and listened to a truck go by.

The truck went down Clay to Seerley and turned toward the campus, passing a white car.

''Hell,'' the man in the car said, keeping his eyes on an old house on Tremont. He chewed on a fingernail that was down to the quick already and wished he could go to the motel and sleep.

''Hell,'' Martin said again, and looked at his fingers. ''Chewing nails again?'' his father always said—what a damned silly joke.

Hell. Sara rotting in the ocean somewhere, and he was in a little Iowa town he never heard of, looking for a short, bearded man who probably never heard of Sara Burney.

His thumbnail was bleeding. But Sara could be there in that wreck of a house—found herself some man. They'd planned the fake drowning together, maybe . . . this Ben Woodward had waited for her near Manhasset with his car or even come to the beach house. Now they were at 2309 Tremont laughing at Martin Burney. He kicked the car door, kicked it again, closed his fingers over the .25 pistol in his pocket, watched children playing in the park.

Leaves fell here and there through the sunshine, though most trees were still green. Children called beneath Dr. Channing's window, ''All-ee all-ee in free!''

*Live alone,* Sara said to herself, and looked up at what seemed like a bird's flight across the sunlight in the room—a falling leaf.

How sad Chopin could be. Her throat felt tight, but suddenly, spooning green beans, she was sure Martin would never find her and almost laughed, hard-eyed and straight-backed, feeding Hazel George Channing her lunch. Even dogs had sense enough to be happy when nobody kicked them any more.

Sara watched cars going past Dr. Channing's kitchen window as the afternoon crept by. Sometimes she saw her mother's blind eyes or felt how light and thin her mother's body was, rolled over in bed, the eyes staring and sightless. Her mother's knobby legs looked as if she'd never used them, never worked so hard to keep poverty off, beating at it with brooms and mops as if it were a stray dog, joking about its smell, its ugliness, its sharp teeth.

Sara washed and dried towels Ellen had used and put them away. Ellen and the baby were safe in the hospital now; Sara had called to ask. "I'm just a friend of the family," she said.

She called Ben Woodward too. "So you're home. The car was in the barn, but I went through the lilacs and couldn't find you anywhere," he said.

"I tried to call you this morning. I should have left you a note," Sara said. "Ellen telephoned in the middle of the night and asked me to come take care of Dr. Channing. Ellen heard that her aunt's very sick, and she had to stay with her in Waterloo.

Ben's voice was velvety, deep, subtly changing. When he said "Are you coming home?" the "home" had a yearning that Sara felt on her skin like a warm hand.

"I can't," Sara said. "There's no one to stay with Dr. Channing until Mrs. Eaker comes on Monday."

"The four of us are leaving in a university car for that Chicago conference. I'll be gone all weekend until Sunday night late, but the car will be in my barn. You know where the car key is if you need it. I can leave food and water out for Banana. Your kitchen lamp is on. Should I turn it out?"

"Leave it on, will you?"

"You'll be ready to get out by Monday. So will I," Ben said. "I'll tell you what—maybe Mrs. Eaker could give you Monday afternoon off. Think about meeting me at Cattle Congress after my eleven o'clock." He asked nothing about her trip, nothing about her disguise. He offered his car, his help, that was all.

"I wonder—can I get a bus on the Hill?" Sara asked.

"Right. In front of the president's house on College." She heard a smile in his deep voice now. "Best show in the Midwest, and who knows when it'll go the way of high-button boots and whalebone corsets? Ought to get there about twelve-thirty, and I'll watch for you at the gate."

"Don't come here. It's better if you don't," Sara said.

"I won't," Ben said. Their good-byes echoed in her ears with his courtesy, the space and air she thought he was learning to leave between them.

She put the telephone in its cradle and covered her face with her hands. The tips of her fingers felt her coarse, fake hair. She shouldn't be seen with any man, not anywhere. She had been with Ben Woodward in his backyard, at his door. She'd used his car.

But Martin was at work at Rambaugh Computer Sales and Service this afternoon. He had never even called the Craigie Court Retirement Center. She had drowned and come out of deep water to land and was safe—her mother knew it. Yes! Sara smiled, her sudden happiness as vivid as the sunny geraniums in Dr. Channing's window.

But when Sara found clean sheets, made up Ellen's bed for herself, and lay down for a little while, her eyes wouldn't close. She felt the road under the car wheels, smelled blood.

Lying in Ellen's bed, Sara stared at a crayon drawing of a house surrounded by nothing but scribbled blue sky.

# 37

"**L**ate September, and this hot," Edna Grant said to Helen Tyler while they stood at the corner of Walnut and Seerley. Edna wiped her forehead with a wadded-up tissue. "See that man with dark hair and dark glasses in that white car?"

"What about him?" Helen said, looking down Seerley.

"He was parked there yesterday."

"Quit that," Helen said to her spaniel.

"You ever see that car before?"

"Maybe it's Clara's new renter."

"You rent an apartment, you don't sit in a car in front of it," Edna said.

"Moving van's coming, maybe, and he's waiting for it," Helen said.

"On Sunday? And she rents furnished."

"You know those two men Alice has?"

"The salesmen."

"She kept hearing rain on the roof in the morning. When the sun was shining." Helen unwound Brownie's leash from a telephone pole.

"Rain?"

"Them."

"For heaven's sake."

"Wouldn't wait to get in the bathroom, I guess," Helen said.

They passed the white car, looking in to see a dark man at the wheel. He turned his face away, but Helen let go of

Brownie's leash and chased the dog around the white car so she saw the man's face before he had time to duck.

"Dark and youngish," Helen said at the next corner. "Big nose and kind of sulky-looking. Type that goes bald early. Brushes his hair over the bare spots like your economics professor. Growing a beard."

"Why sit in a car when there's a nice park?" Edna said.

Martin sat in his car and drank wine and scratched his chin. Damn itchy beard. Damn drugstore dye all over his hands when he tried to get it on his head and chin.

Friday night. Saturday night. No lights at Woodward's and his car in that barn. Nobody in the old house next to Woodward's toward Seerley, just a light in the kitchen. On the other side an old couple sat on their front porch until nine.

There was no connection to Sara but Ben Woodward, who had only been kind to Chloe Gray, probably . . . no connection to Sara at all. Sara could be in Fredsburg right now, and here he was, chasing some stranger. Martin sat in his car and drank sherry and port. He couldn't remember when he'd had any food. He didn't want food.

By eleven at night all the wine bottles were empty. Martin was almost asleep when he jerked awake and saw a car drop off somebody at 2309 Tremont; the car drove away.

Ben Woodward. Martin fumbled for his car key, dropped it, swore, couldn't find it on the floor of his car, found it, pulled out on Seerley. When he turned the corner, swearing at the dark, all he saw was a man coming down front stairs of the place next to Ben Woodward's. The man went through deep shadows around the old house.

Martin parked around the block, closed his car door softly, and ducked into Ben Woodward's alley again. He was wearing a dark shirt and jeans—hard to see at night—and he knew where to go now.

Lights were all out at Ben Woodward's—had been for days. Woodward's car was in the barn. Martin thought he heard someone calling a cat: "Kitty . . . here, kitty! Here, Banana!" Then a rustling, as if someone were pushing through leaves. Tall bushes hid back doors of both houses from Martin, but there was a click as Woodward's door shut. One light went on in his house, a bathroom window, probably; there was only a border of light around a closed blind.

Martin waited, flattened against the barn wall because he was dizzy and half sick. Sara hadn't gone in or out when he'd been watching the house. No lights. Maybe they thought someone might be looking for her? Sneaky bitch.

Martin swayed and hung on to the barn wall. Break in. Get them both. But maybe this Woodward never heard of Sara Burney—he just cozied up to a blind old lady in a nursing home, and Martin Burney was a fool.

Martin Burney wasn't a fool. Martin Burney needed a toilet. Hell. Martin Burney stood in the dark on one foot and swore to himself. The last light went out at Ben Woodward's.

Nearly midnight. He hadn't learned anything all weekend, except that Woodward was home. Martin peed into bushes in the yard, and a cat shot out of the bushes fast—scared Martin so he watered Woodward's barn, too, for a minute.

Zipping up, Martin looked at the house next door. Ben Woodward had gone up the front stairs there. Martin tiptoed over the grass to the kitchen window. He was wobbly in the knees—all that wine.

There was the cozy room again with the orange wall and cup and saucer on the table. The coffeepot's handle was in the same position; flowers in a vase were beginning to wilt. Nobody had been there all weekend.

At the old house's back-porch door, rays from a park streetlight stabbed through leaves to show a kind of path between houses; its trampled, pale dust made a white smudge on the dark. So Woodward had rustled through those bushes. Why had he gone up on a neighbor's front porch? Maybe to get mail or newspapers—Sara's?

Martin peered in the porch's back door, put his hand on the knob. Something soft was hanging there; it squashed under his fingers. He stuck whatever it was in his pocket and tiptoed away on soft grass.

He had to drive carefully because he kept seeing two highways, two red lights, two green lights. The motel parking lot was almost empty on a Sunday night. Cedar Falls was dead. Sara might be close to him, sleeping under some roof in town. She'd be too smart to use any of her own names, but he'd looked for Sara Burney and Sara Gray in telephone books anyway and called the operators in Cedar Falls and Waterloo.

One more motel room. He shut his door behind him. He was Jim Baker with a rented car. "Ben Woodward," he said to the empty bed. Ben Woodward would know where she was.

There was some brown-haired man in the mirror with a beard that still showed his chin through it here and there. Martin stared at the man in the mirror, trying to focus his eyes.

Maybe Sara was at Woodward's . . . she was hiding out, having a good time in bed while Martin drank wine in a hot car and peed on a cat.

Or was she somewhere else? In the ocean, maybe.

The man had walked up the next-door steps as if he belonged there.

Martin took the pistol out of his pocket. Something soft came with it—a bunch of flowers.

Martin squashed them in his fist. They'd been stuck on that back-porch doorknob with a rubber band.

A note fell out of the flower lump. After a while Martin focused his eyes enough to read the black, printed letters:

> MY GORGEOUS LOVE:
> EVERY HALF HOUR ALL NIGHT
> LONG, AND YOU WILL LOVE IT,
> YOU WILL BEG FOR IT.

# 38

"**WELCOME CATTLE CONGRESS**" said a red and white banner buckling in hot wind. Sara leaned close to the bus window and saw a Ferris wheel revolving, silvery, airy as a dandelion's halo of seeds.

A policeman directed traffic before the gate; crowds waited at a ticket booth where Sara got off the bus. She was early; Ben wasn't in sight. She bought her ticket and stood by a fence to wait. Behind the fence were kiddie rides: pink plastic elephants with seats in their backs, small airplanes with machine guns that children aimed as they circled. A knee-high train rattled along a buckled track, ringing its bell.

Crowds of people—Sara felt hidden in them, anonymous like them. Her green dress fluttered around her legs in the breeze; the sun was hot. No one knew her here.

Then a tall man came from the entrance, ticket in hand. He saw her and strode past a corn-dog booth, bent forward a little as he came, his red hair glowing above the glow of his blue eyes, all of him intent on her, seeing nothing but her, and Sara held both hands out to him, as if he were a warm fire on a cold day.

"Hi!" Ben said. One man among so many of them—his red hair and blue eyes shone for her. She said, "Hi," softly, and smiled, and took his arm.

**WELCOME CATTLE CONGRESS.**

Martin read the banner as he turned into mud and crowds

of a parking lot. He'd lost sight of the fellow with red hair—followed him all the way from Seerley Boulevard—saw him drive that blue car out of Ben Woodward's barn, then lost him. He wasn't Ben Woodward. Woodward had a dark beard.

Martin snarled, "Hell!" and shot into a parking spot ahead of a fat farmer with a carful of women, jumped out, and ran toward the gate of whatever it was—looked like a carnival with that Ferris wheel.

Lines at a ticket window. Martin stamped and fidgeted and had to wait. Sara might not be there at all. He had to find Woodward. Follow Red Hair and see. Follow him. All the time.

Children jumped up and down in line; a baby stared over its father's shoulder at Martin. Martin bought a ticket and went in past kiddie rides and food booths. There were three or four directions Red Hair might have gone.

"Blood pythons, sungazers, green tree vipers, horned adder, fat-tail geckos . . ."

Ben and Sara stepped into Estel Hall, hearing a voice drone, "Water moccasin, Gila monster, gaboon viper . . ." Cool air and a blast of sound met Ben and Sara; people closed around them, each face wearing the preoccupied, self-effaced look of those who have come to see.

There was nobody interested in sungazers or fat-tail geckos; a bored-looking young man sat at the booth door. Chants of "Rattlesnake, eyelash viper . . ." joined polkas from the next booth. Sara and Ben gave up conversation.

"Multiplan Combination Bar-Fireplace," said a sign.

"Keeps you warm, serves drinks, and plays music!" Sara yelled over the "Beer-Barrel Polka," and Ben yelled back, "Newest thing for the home!"

"Water Conditioning for Car Washes, Restraunts," said a large red sign.

"Are you interested in a water conditioner, ma'am?" a polite young man shouted to Sara over polkas and snakes.

"No," Sara yelled back, "I'm interested in your spelling!"

The polite young man jerked his head back to look at his

sign. "I spelled it that way to get attention," he shouted. As Sara and Ben walked away he yelled after them, "I know how to spell it, honest!"

"Cow Pregnostic: Tells You If Your Animal Is in the Family Way." "Teli-trone Company." "Barry Jackson for Senate." "Help Prevent Child Abuse." "Hand-blown Glass." Tired people lolled in recliners on display. Half-moons of bunting looped from rafters above an expanse of booths.

"Old Times Portrait Studio. Your Picture Taken in Five Minutes." Sara and Ben stopped before rows of sepia photographs in oval mounts: a saloon girl, an ace in her garter and her arms around a gunslinger, watched Ben and Sara beside a framed Indian maiden with her brave. There were Victorian brides and grooms, and couples in deerskin and calico from a wagon train, and Southern belles with their Civil War officers in blue or gray.

The pictured lovers stood together, faces close. Ben put his arm around Sara, and Sara leaned against him, lit by a row of lovers' eyes. Costumes and guns and feathered hats lined the walls of the booth; a photographer was posing a Davy Crockett and Annie Oakley before gold-tasseled red curtains.

Crowds, dust underfoot, loud music. Martin got to Estel Hall  he'd thought he saw a red-haired man at the door. A wall of people met him with a blast of polkas and somebody chanting about blood pythons. He started down the first aisle, smelling popcorn, watching for one face, one body that belonged to him and would never get away from him, if it existed at all.

Sara and Ben left Estel Hall's crowds and noise for warm sunshine outside. "A farmers' circus," Ben said. "Judging going on. All kinds of animals." In a smaller building there were caged pigeons; they made a double row on each long table.

"Such names!" Sara said, and read from tags as she and Ben walked along the aisles: "Komorner Tumbler, La Hore, Jacobin, French Mondain, Indian Fantail, Silver-laced Starling, Oriental Frill, English Carrier, Berlin Short-faced Tumbler, African Owl, Saxon Swallow, Frillback, Ideal American Giant Homer, Giant Runt—Giant Runt?'' Brown and white and buff birds crouched in their little cages; a cock watched her from an enormous ruff, like an old man in a shawl. There were wood shavings on the floor, and the air smelled like feathers and hot skin.

''You look so happy,'' Ben said.

''I am,'' Sara told him.

''You look so beautiful,'' Ben said.

A man reached in a cage for a pigeon, brought it out to fold it in a neat package, as if it were a piece of cloth or a newspaper. He turned it bottom-up on his sleeve. The pigeon's pink feet hardly moved; one patient eye stared at the man's coat.

''We've got to go on some rides,'' Ben said. ''And have hot dogs! Cotton candy!''

Martin left Estel Hall. Food concessions faced each other under a Ferris wheel. Martin bought a corn dog—a greasy, coated weiner on a stick. He could have had French Fried Eggplant or French Fried Cauliflower or French Fried Nuggets or French Fried Onion Rings. Sun baked him, but he'd get the man and he'd get Sara, if she was alive. Carmel Apples. Sno Cones. Elephant Ears.

A hot summer day. As Sara and Ben walked they touched—her hand in his, or Ben's arm around her, or her arm around Ben. It seemed to Ben that he could walk that way the rest of his life under Iowa sky and flags snapping in that hot blue.

Sara stopped to watch cobwebs of candy wind upon a spindle in a woman's hand.

Martin came to a bingo tent where rows of people sat in sun and shade, sliding plastic covers over numbers on their cards, tense with the craving to win. Sara. Ben Woodward.

Ben bought Sara a hot dog, and ate two himself. They stood in the shadow of a barn where a family was intricately braiding colored ribbons in a horse's mane and tail, whispering to the horse, murmuring in its twitching ears.

Ben had some mustard on his chin. Sara wiped it off with her napkin. Her face was so close to his and her eyes looked into his so long above her soft mouth that he knew she'd kiss him if no one were watching. They shared a Coke with two straws, and didn't say a word; they sipped and almost touched, or touched, beyond speaking.

Martin jammed his heels into dirt and squinted against sun, looking up with the crowd—an animal was at the top of a ladder of steps. It looked like a donkey, and it put one hoof over the edge of its perch, then the other. "Cheer for the little lady!" a voice bellowed over a loudspeaker. "She's about to jump!" The animal fell, making a brown center for petals of water that bloomed from a tank. Wet streams surged at the feet of the crowd; people hopped and laughed and yelled.

The Sky Dipper car was just big enough for two. Ben helped Sara climb in, and they pressed thighs, hips, and arms together under a transparent parasol. Sara braced her feet on the dusty floor as they rose fast behind other cars whose couples shouted and grabbed each other as they shot toward blue sky, dipped fast, swooped—Sara didn't grab Ben. She only shut her eyes, and he, squinting, saw her long, pale eyelashes coated with dark mascara, her thin hand holding her wig tight.

Martin's eyes hurt from sun and his constant scanning of crowds; he squeezed his eyes shut as Sara and Ben sailed over his head, rising and falling on the rim of the Sky Dipper wheel. Martin opened his eyes to see couples strolling before him: men with an arm around their woman's shoulder or waist or holding her hand.

"Ferris wheel next!" Ben said, and they ran for the last car and were just in time. A man clicked them in with a heavy bar and the wheel lifted Sara and Ben skyward.

"How did the beard and mustache work for you?" Ben asked.

"They worked fine," Sara said. "I've been so worried. But my mother's all right. Someday I'll tell you . . ." Her voice trailed off. She looked far, far down at the crowd-clogged fair—a distant, multicolored world. She started to speak again, but once over the top she sank fast with Ben, descending to noise, music, glances of people passing . . . then rose again, fell again, rose. . . .

The wheel carried them up, the car rocking. Sun poured over them; Sara put her head on Ben's shoulder, and then the great machine stopped as they dangled at the very top, too far for any sound or sight to have meaning except the sound of their own breathing, the sight of each other's faces. Hot sun, hot wind. Their mouths were hot, meeting; their eyes shut against the brilliant, bare sky, and they kissed closer and closer until it seemed to them they had melted together at the top of the world.

But then their car, rocking like a cradle, started down. Sara's lips opened against Ben's and she said "Oh" once. He blinked like an owl in daylight. They hurried to sort their own lips and hands and arms from the other's, and came down to the fair as two separate Ferris-wheel riders, but dreamy-eyed, as if being so close to the sun had shown them something new. They climbed from the car without a word.

Dirt was gritty between Sara's toes, black dirt that wasn't like beach sand—it stuck. There was no smell of the sea in that heat, only hot-dog and hamburger smells, reek of gas from the tractor pulls, and a breeze from counties of corn on every side.

"I'll tell you what—we ought to have our picture taken," Ben said. "To remember." So Sara went back with him to Estel Hall and the "Old Times" photo booth.

"I have to leave at three," Ben said while the photographer fastened a white ruffled shirt over his T-shirt and tied a fancy velvet coat in back so it fit him like skin. "It's too bad. A department meeting was called at the last minute, and I can't miss it."

"That's all right." Sara was in the curtained corner of the booth near Ben; her voice was muffled. "I'll just wander around here. It's fun. I can get a bus home."

The photographer fastened a string tie on Ben's shirt and slipped sleeves with ruffled cuffs up his arms under the velvet coat. Holsters, and two real guns. A broad-brimmed hat pushed back on his head. Ben looked at himself in a mirror: the Wild West Kid, Wizard at Poker, Devil with the Ladies, Death with a Gun. The mirror was painted like a poster that said "WANTED" under his gunfighter face.

And here came a gorgeous saloon floozy. Sara had taken off her dress, and what there was of the new one was red velvet and braid and lace, just a corset, and low. Ruffles and ruffles on her petticoat, and bare leg above her black stockings and her garters when the photographer told her to put one foot up on Ben's stool. He put a little pistol in her garter and a bottle in her hand. A feather boa wound around her bare neck, and a foot-long feather sprang from the headdress on her short, dark hair. She had gloves to her elbows and one elbow on Ben's shoulder.

She'd ask for the pictures, Sara thought, and hide them.

"Both your chins up a little," the photographer said. "Get closer to him, miss. Put your arm around his neck . . . that's right. Keep your leg so the gun shows."

The photographer disappeared under his red velvet cloth, and there was a brilliant flash. Then he came to take the pistol from Sara's garter and put in an ace of spades instead. "Now look at me and don't smile."

Martin came around a corner. In the depths of a photographer's booth a couple posed in brilliant light. Martin's glasses turned their bright colors dark.

A red-haired, ruffled-shirt gunman, pistol in each fist, stared at Martin past camera and booth pictures. Martin felt for the pistol in his pocket.

Around the gunman's neck were the pretty, gloved arms of a brunette. She was almost bare to the waist and had the ace of spades stuck in her garter. Lights flared, etching gunfighter and saloon girl in Martin's mind in sharp, unmistakable detail. She was, Martin could see, Sara.

# 39

$S$ara got her clothes back on in the narrow space behind the curtain. When she came out Ben held the pictures up for her; they were still wet. There she was, a bare-shouldered brunette hugging a redheaded gent in ruffles, velvet, and six-guns.

"Like them?" Ben asked.

Sara nodded, looking at the prints. Neither gunslinger nor saloon girl had smiled, so the picture's sepia-brown pushed them back in time to nineteenth-century folk who could not keep a grin on their faces for the long minutes a photograph took. They did not smile at each other or the camera's black hole. Guns were something they lived with, their calm eyes said.

As Ben paid for the pictures a brown-bearded man in dark glasses watched. He saw Sara take the envelope of portraits and walk away, Ben's arm around her.

Beautiful Sara should be dead, rotted.

There she was, plump and smiling in a green dress he'd never seen, walking away with a man's arm around her.

Summer breeze ruffled Sara's short, dark hair as Martin followed them outside.

Martin walked in a dream. She had a wig on, or else she'd cut off her hair and dyed it. That dark hair told him what he wanted to know—she had tricked him, and she was in hiding.

Martin narrowed his eyes, watching her say good-bye to Red Hair at the gate. Sara's thin green dress blew against her beautiful breasts and legs that were his—she was his own wife. And she walked in the world without him, and was happy.

Martin kept her in sight. She was happy . . . while he fell over electric cords and dodged a little kid who had a cheeseburger oozing mustard in one hand and an ice-cream cone in the other. Martin felt as stiff and cold as a machine, its metal head chattering "Sara, Sara, Sara." He had the gun in his pocket. He'd kill her now—catch her alone and kill her.

Her short, dark hair was a wig, he thought—it glinted in the light. Martin knew that body, but not the way it walked aimlessly, dreamily, at peace and by itself. And yet every movement of it was Sara's. She walked back to Estel Hall as if no one had ever paid for her food and house and clothes year after year. She left him behind like the paper cups and Popsicle sticks people were kicking around in dust and sunshine.

But he followed her, his hand in his pocket and the gun in it. Halfway down one noisy aisle, Sara stopped in front of a mirror to try a necklace on, and then another one. The man behind the booth counter handed them to her delicately; Sara took them in her cupped hands, bent to fasten them at her nape. Her half-smile met its twin in the mirror as she kept a small gold heart on a chain around her neck, and paid for it, but never turned to a man in dark glasses behind a sign that read "Will Your Dog Be Cut Up for An Experiment?"

Sunlight shone on her when she was in open air again; she swung her arms lazily. Sometimes her short, loose sleeves fanned wide in the breeze. Martin felt sickish—it was the corn dog he'd gulped down, and two bottles of root beer. He walked on in a dream, his eyes on a body back from the dead. It raised its arms to a barricade, leaning to watch a bronco machine pitch men and boys into an inflated rubber sea. "Ride 'er, cowboy!" the crowd yelled, because there were long eyelashes and a lipsticked mouth painted on the bucking machine. A kid pitched off headfirst. Martin could shoot Sara, drop her where she leaned against the barricade, smiling. She'd fall in the dirt. He'd be lost in the crowds. But there were people around her.

Martin followed a body that had been drowned. It walked under patchwork quilts hung over high ropes. It strolled in dusty sandals where rows of crocheted baby bootees and knitted toilet-paper covers wore their blue, red, or gold prize ribbons. He saw men turn to look at dark hair, a green dress.

Then Martin lost the green dress. He ran wildly in and out of doors. Finally he found Sara in a covered arena watching a six-horse hitch and a shouting driver. They made smaller and smaller figure-eight turns while the audience clapped. He kept his eyes on Sara, who sat alone in a front row with her hands in her lap staring at great cart horses cramped to a standstill.

Then it was saddle horses and adolescent girls in jodhpurs. Judges picked the winners, one by one. Losers trailed by Sara. "Horses on the rail are now excused!" boomed a loudspeaker. There she sat, watching horses.

Martin's stomach churned. He could walk down to her row, shoot her, jump off the stand under the railing, and run into crowds outside.

He started to walk to her row where she sat alone, her back to him. He had to go slowly, as if in no hurry to get anywhere, and while he was strolling the act ended and she was on her feet, leaving.

So he had to follow her outside. Afternoon sunlight blinded him; the green dress disappeared in a press of people. Martin ran behind it to big brick buildings labeled "SADDLE HORSES," "CHAROLAIS," "BEEF," "POLLED HEREFORD." "SHORTHORNS," "ABERDEEN ANGUS," "HALL OF BREEDS." . . .

Stink of dung and straw met Martin as he followed Sara under low rafters. Cattle lay with noses to the wall, and up against their rumps sat farm families on folding chairs or big painted boxes, visiting with each other, kicking the straw, drinking pop, holding babies.

He couldn't get too close to Sara's fluttering green dress and the long legs she'd had to cover up when she'd been with him. Martin swallowed against sickness in his throat. Between long brick barns men hosed down animals; tan puddles reflected sky and clouds. Cows chewed cud in the shade.

Sara walked slowly through the Hall of Breeds, stopping to read signs. Martin kept behind her with other people, signs sliding past his eyes unread: "White Park, imported to U.S. from England 1941. Found in Rome before 55 B.C."

He was sick with the hot dogs he'd eaten, and hate. He wished he were alone with Sara—he'd stalk her from building to building. She'd think she'd lost him and then . . .

"Red Angus," a sign said. "Pinzgauer." She'd jumped in Manhasset Bay. She could swim. She'd gotten away, laughing, and let him cry and hold her clothes and yap to his father about beating her up.

"Limousin." "Chianina." "Brangus." "Beefalo." "Blond d'Aquitaine." Calm cows watched him, chewing. He'd get her by herself and make her beg, and then shoot her.

Light grew at barn's end and half blinded him as he followed her out to where immense toy dogs hung in rows, three freckles beside each black nose, one red tongue, one red collar, two black ears. "Stand Up Bottle. You Win. Game Ends When Bottle Falls. Take a Chance. Win a Prize."

Sara walked with a half-smile on her lips, completely herself and alone. Sometimes she talked to a child or a mother. She won some small toy by hooking it up in a glass case and gave it to a girl in rompers. She waited in line at a women's bathroom while Martin ducked inside the almost empty men's and lost his corn dog and some of the root beer in a toilet booth made of raw lumber, with sunshine running under the door. He thought maybe he was beginning to believe Sara was alive.

She was happy. Her dress blew in the Iowa breeze. And he had smashed mirrors, quit his job—he was wanted by the police. His hands were sweaty on the gun in his pocket, and when he looked the design of the eagle on the gun grip was printed on his palm.

"Throw a dime!" a girl yelled at Martin. "Take a chance!"

Fake gun went pock-pock-pock at booths in a row. Martin followed Sara, keeping back in the crowd. He could shoot her here. They'd think it was just part of the pock-pock-pock.

Sara stopped to look at racks of Halloween masks for sale. There were hideous rotted faces with fangs for teeth, and the traditional ghosts, witches, and skeletons. They watched Sara with their empty eyes as she stepped around the rack and was, for a moment, alone with the sound of guns going pock-pock-pock and the gaze of a man in sunglasses. He came closer, came to stand by the rack of rotted faces, his hand emerging slowly from the pocket of his coat—

"Hi!" Sara heard someone say close to her ear. She turned to see a blond man of nineteen or twenty wearing a T-shirt with a nude woman stretched out under the words *Heavy Metal*. "You're sure beautiful," he said, throwing his head back and giving her a hard glance—the gunfighter riding into town. He stared at her, but something made her think he was horribly embarrassed and didn't have enough courage to say one more word.

"Thanks," Sara said, as sparing of words as any cowboy.

"I like that green dress," he said, running his eyes over it as if it were a horse he might buy. "And that necklace."

What could Sara say? She turned back to the skeletons and cadavers; they grinned at her as she passed, and the reflection of her green dress rippled over their mottled surfaces and empty eyes. The young blond man stood in the hot sun, watching her; a man in sunglasses watched them both. Before Sara disappeared around a corner Martin saw the kid's eyes go over her greedily.

She was out in the crowds again—Martin had to follow her, passing dogs hitched to a wagon. They crouched in the sunshine, tongues out. "Hell," he said to the dogs— look at Sara talking to men, strolling along in her green dress as if she didn't belong to anybody. She was alive, picking up men! Martin almost laughed at the joke on him—but he'd kill her. Any time now he'd kill her.

He watched Sara from behind a turkey-sandwich stand. He had to back out of the way when the six-horse hitch came rumbling along—hot brown horse flanks, twinkling spokes.

Martin followed Sara through the gate. She stood at a bus stop in the narrow shade of a telephone pole, eating an ice-cream cone, licking it the way a kid would as Martin passed in a crowd of people . . . enjoying it with half-shut eyes.

Down Rainbow Drive half a block, Martin waited and watched her. She was cut off from him, from all their years, not even using a name he knew . . . he didn't even know her name!

Traffic streamed both ways along Rainbow Drive. He watched Sara. She was plumper. Sunshine caught blown folds of her dress. She swung one foot idly back and forth and licked her ice-cream cone, her eyes half shut, a little purse and the "Old Times" photos in one hand. When the bus came she popped the end of the cone in her mouth and disappeared up steps.

It wasn't hard to follow a bus to Cedar Falls. Sara got off on Clay Street and never looked once at a white car across the street. She climbed to a green house high on a bank and went in the side door as if she belonged there.

"Hello," Mrs. Eaker said as Sara shut the kitchen door. "Thought you'd be back about now. Miss Parrish called and said she'll come about ten this evening to stay so you can have the night off if you want it. And you can come back at noon tomorrow."

"That's nice," Sara said, washing her hands at the sink. She was awfully pretty in that green dress, Mrs. Eaker thought. It did her good to get out.

"I've been to Cattle Congress," Sara said.

"Quite a show. I been going ever since I was five, and it never changes much. See the tractor pulls?"

"No," Sara said. "I saw the six-horse hitch, and beautiful saddle horses, and the Hall of Breeds—"

"A real Midwest show," Mrs. Eaker said, looking at herself in a kitchen mirror. "Dr. Channing certainly is perked up. Now that she's eating, her color looks a lot better." She said good-bye and shut the door behind her.

Sunshine all afternoon. Sara sang softly as she got Dr. Channing's dinner. Her dress smelled like fresh air when she bent over Hazel to tuck a napkin under her chin.

Sara smiled, warm and tired and peaceful, and thought of her plan. Perhaps now. Perhaps it might happen. She told Dr. Channing about Cattle Congress, talking to all she was used to: silence, curtained-away light, the never-changing gleam of a dresser handle here, a mirrored panel there. But when she was almost through spooning applesauce she gave Dr. Channing a long, measuring glance and went to get *The Golden Bowl*.

Hazel Channing watched Laura open the book and felt uneasy. Something had been wrong for a long time now. She dreaded the first words.

Then Hazel sighed and rolled her head fretfully on her pillow. Who cared about Henry James? Who cared whether he had called this novel his "blest good stuff" and said his characters had made a bargain with him: "Actively believe in us and then you'll see"? James had believed in the Prince, the Princess, Mr. Verver and Charlotte—seen them, real as Laura Pray was, sitting beside her bed reading.

But who cared?

Yet Hazel opened her mouth for applesauce, spoonful by spoonful. She listened. Henry James began to weave her in his exactly spaced, deceptively silky strands of long, long, roundabout, in-and-out, tightly knotted sentences. They shone around her in milky window-light, making spaces that let the whole world show, yet framed it.

But something was wrong, and had been growing for days, snagging the sentences. Hazel stared at Laura Pray.

*"What a pair of insane ladies!"* Laura had said. How could she? Hazel trusted Laura. Ellen Garner never could understand, but Laura knew differences. She distinguished.

Hazel watched Laura, hardly needing to hear familiar words. Laura had said that Miss Tita and Miss Bordereau were insane ladies! Couldn't she understand two women and such a man?

Beautiful, convoluted sentences Hazel knew so well wove their silvery net in the room. Hazel hardly heard them. Laura had laughed when Catherine shut her *Washington Square* door on the lover who jilted her—Laura said Catherine was cold, unfeeling! And now Laura's soft, subtle, flexible, eloquent voice droned on, indifferent, as if she didn't understand . . . as if she hated the words! The greatest of Henry James—*The Golden Bowl* that was Hazel's golden bowl, too, because she had devoted so much of her life to it—gold, gold!

Hazel glared at Laura and was filled with hate suddenly—hate for the world that smashed things, hate for Laura, who was smashing Henry James with her good reader's voice. Faint mockery tinged every word; Laura didn't like the book. Didn't like Henry James!

Laura went on reading, not spooning any more applesauce. Her thin face was without expression. Last light of a summer day was a pale shimmer through the curtains; it fell on Hazel Channing's twisted mouth and Laura's inscrutable face as her voice condemned and mocked.

A beautiful, raped, insulted chapter came to an end. Laura stopped, not looking at Hazel Channing.

Silence was as thin as the light in the room. Finally Laura met Hazel's glare with her own. "Why doesn't he write what he means? Words, words, words!" Laura cried. "The Prince and Charlotte are still in love, I *think*. I *think* Maggie's such a cold fish, and her father's no better, I *think*. But it just goes on and on! The greatest novel of Henry James!"

There was only a second after she finished her sentence. Surely it wasn't long enough to hear a bird sing outside the window, but Laura thought afterward that she had.

The sound she was sure she heard was Hazel George Channing's voice yelling, "No! No! He writes *exactly* what he means! He's the only author who does!"

Silence came back to the room, a changed silence that made Hazel and Laura looked at each other like strangers. "He *can't* say what he means!" Hazel cried. "It's got to be between the lines! The things we learn about each other are like that!"

Then Laura laughed, a happy, warm laugh. She dropped *The Golden Bowl* and ran to yank glass curtains back with one cord, drapes with another. She hauled at the window until at last it shot up with a clatter.

"He's got to *represent* those delicate things that are ruining lives! And he does! He does it all the time!" Hazel cried, squinting against the glare.

The last of the day's sunshine fell over Laura now; hot wind blew into the room. Laura ran to the bed, circled Hazel with her thin arms, and laid her cheek against the old one on the pillow.

Wind ruffled Laura's green sleeve. Hazel smelled fresh-cut grass, a spicy, almost rank scent of damp earth, and wind blown over farm fields for hundreds of miles.

# 40

Martin pulled around the corner and parked where he could see both doors of the house Sara had gone into; he pretended to read a newspaper. A bony old lady came out of the house in a few minutes, and a bus picked her up on a corner.

He still felt as if he were dreaming everything. Could have killed Sara a dozen times—her in her fancy dress with the bare leg and garter, smiling at Red Hair, talking with a blond kid as if she'd never heard of Martin Burney, or cared, or knew he was going to find her and blow her head off. Hell.

He had three bottles of sherry and port on the backseat.

A window went up on the side of the house toward Martin. He thought he saw Sara's green dress, but only for a second.

Cars went by. Now and then somebody walked past, looking at him. It began to grow dark. He finished a bottle of sherry and started on port.

Then a fancy car pulled up at the house. A stylish middle-aged bitch with a fancy suit and fancy gray hair got out of it and went up the walk. Lights went on. He could see the fancy old bitch talking to Sara in the doorway. Then she threw her arms around Sara. The door shut.

So tired. Dust on his shoes from the damn Cattle Congress, and dust in his nose and throat too. Go back to the motel. Martin's head felt sick, like his stomach. He wanted to go to sleep. He wanted to kill them both and get it over with. He wanted a shower and a bed. He wanted to wake up and find Sara beside him and everything a dream.

Two little kids bicycled by, shouting I did, too, and no, you didn't.

Sara came out the door and down the walk and turned the corner.

He followed Sara, keeping a block behind; he could see her running under streetlights in her white shirt and shorts and running shoes. She was aiming for Red Hair's, he thought. She could walk around that carnival all day and then run! He spit the sickly sweet taste of port out his open car window and waited until she turned on Tremont Street. The bitch. He'd shoot her from the car. Perfect. Couldn't kill a drowned bitch.

He drove behind her and slipped the safety catch off the gun. It was dark enough so nobody would see much, but he could aim at her white shirt. She didn't even look around as he pulled closer.

Then Martin swore and braked. A procession of what looked like college students turned a corner and came toward Sara. They were up to some fool stunt—half the men had the other half on their backs and staggered along. They shouted and laughed and then yelled at Sara when she passed them, and Martin had to go around the block.

When he caught sight of her again he saw she didn't go into Red Hair's; she climbed stairs of the old house next door. Maybe she worked at one house and lived at the other.

She unlocked the door and went in. So the note on the door had been for her: *Every half hour all night long*.

Martin parked on Seerley across from Sara's alley, then dodged into its twilight shadows. Red Hair's note with the flowers had been on Sara's back-porch doorknob. It was burned into Martin's head now, back of his eyes: *My gorgeous love . . . you will love it, you will beg for it.*

But she wouldn't find Red Hair's flowers. She wouldn't find his note. She was like a bitch followed around by sniffing dogs—red dogs and dark dogs and blond puppies. *My gorgeous love*. She was living next to Red Hair, with no idea Martin Burney was any closer than Montrose, Massachusetts, crying over her because she had drowned. *You will love it, you will beg for it.* Sara in bed with Red Hair, begging for it—hate made Martin dizzy, made him feel blind—where was he? In the backyard of some old house in some Iowa town, following Sara to shoot her.

Lights went on in other houses. Somebody across the street yelled, "Mike-ee! Mike-ee! Time for bed! Come on!"

A summer night, though it was late September. Sara thought it might rain; the air seemed heavy. Trees were losing their leaves. A leaf stuck, stem first, in Sara's bedroom screen, catching the light.

Sara knocked the leaf off from the inside, pulled shades down partway, shut off lights, and undressed her new-feeling body in the dark, a body that had brought her to the surface again without thought. Warm air slid over it as she ran free and secret and naked into her bathroom for a shower; she stepped into water with a feeling that was almost awe, rubbing and soaping and rinsing her body that was mysterious and had power.

She shut her eyes, soaping her hair, and saw Ben's freckles crowding each other over his nose and cheeks as if they'd been sprinkled and baked on him and run together. His eyebrows were golden brown, not red, jutting over his eyes like thatch. He had small ears close to his head, and a freckled neck, and was square and solid, and they had melted together at the top of the world.

People in Boston and Montrose were forgetting her. Once in a while they might remember and say how sad it was—Sara Burney had been so young.

She had dirt between her toes: dust from Cattle Congress. Her skin had a joy of its own, wanting to touch Ben again; her lips opened, feeling pouring water like kisses.

Sara laughed. Hot water softened the ache in her tired legs. Hot kisses in hot sun . . . Ben pulling her across him, his hand on her breast. She remembered Dr. Channing's outraged voice. Georgia Parrish hadn't believed it when Sara told her Dr. Channing had finally decided to talk. Georgia ran her red-tipped fingers through her silver helmet of hair and said it was a miracle. Hazel Channing, her old voice soft and embarrassed, said it was a trick and smiled.

Even the weight of her hair or a towel moving over her made Sara remember Ben's hands, Ben's kisses. He didn't know she was home for the night. If she picked up the telephone and said, "Hello. I'll be home until tomorrow noon. . . ."

Bare and clean and dry from her shower, Sara looked at her body in the long bathroom mirror. No bruises. She was plumper, and pretty. Ben was next door. She ran into her dark bedroom and groped for lace under her everyday clothes. There in the shadowy room she pulled on the black silk teddy. It was the nicest thing she had, and she shut her eyes and thought of Ben seeing it, of Ben sliding it off. . . .

Sara went to open her refrigerator a crack and look at her own good food. Cold milk—Sara reached for the carton.

When Martin looked under her half-pulled bedroom shade, he had the pistol in his hand with the safety off. He saw in refrigerator glow for a second, like a memory, a smiling Sara in the black silk teddy she'd drowned in. She was half covered in her lost, long, shining hair.

"Oh, hell," Martin whispered. The safety catch was off the gun. He raised it and aimed at the black silk teddy, the shining hair.

"Hell," Martin whispered. His eyes filled with tears until he couldn't see, and he leaned against the house, his face pressed to its still-warm boards.

Sara drank cold milk and smiled to herself. Her mother knew she was alive. Martin knew she was dead. She could wait a little while, then slip through the small space between lilacs and fence. . . .

Sara put on her robe, turned on her kitchen light.

"Here, kitty, kitty!" Martin heard her call from her dark back porch. The one voice in the world that was Sara's hung over evening gardens like a ghost. "Come here! Come on!"

Martin stood swaying under her bedroom window and couldn't focus his tear-filled eyes. If everything had been different . . . he dug his heels into dirt to steady himself. The little pistol was wet with sweat in his hand.

Somebody would come before long—what's-his-name with his red hair. Ben Woodward? *Every half hour all night long* . . .

Martin went to Sara's kitchen window. There was the cozy room again—orange wall, flowers in a vase. Kitchen light spilled over Sara's clean hair and pink robe. A small cat licked a paw under the kitchen table.

Sara poured herself more milk and looked for crackers in a cupboard. Her canned food was stacked three cans high; some of the labels were facing front. She had walked through the Cattle Congress like anyone else, and gone in women's rest rooms where women smiled at each other. They let the children use toilets first, and held babies for their mothers.

She had hidden the pictures of gunman and saloon girl. Hazel Channing's voice, and her shamefaced smile . . . it was as if someone had told Hazel, "I know you've got a lover."

Sara sighed and stretched and drank cold milk. The blond young man had said, "You're sure beautiful," his eyes never meeting hers.

Sara smiled. Her happiness had spilled over on the embarrassed blond fellow—she had still been feeling Ben's mouth on hers high over a fair in hot sun. . . .

Night noises came through her open kitchen window: crickets, a passing car, wind in wind chimes at a house on the next street.

Ben's lights seemed to be out now. Maybe he'd gone to bed early in his funny old bed under the bunches of grapes. If she crept up his stairs . . .

"Ben," Sara said, all by herself in her kitchen. Martin heard her through the open window: "Ben."

Fury dug Martin's hand with the gun in it out of his

pocket. Smiling, Sara sat drinking milk at her kitchen table not ten feet away.

"Ben," she said softly, and laughed.

The name froze Martin's hand halfway to the window-sill. *My gorgeous love,* he heard inside his head. *Every half hour all night long, and you will love it, you will beg for it.* Hatred made Martin shiver and burn at the same time. Kill the man first, while she watched. Make her beg. Make her see what she'd done.

A group of teenagers slammed their cars to a stop along Seerley and shrieked after each other in a race to the merry-go-round in the park.

Their shouts reached Martin as he went into the lilac tunnel at Sara's back door. He felt the eagles on his pistol's grip. He wouldn't kill her until he killed the man. She could see the man dead first—dead because of her. He had meant to do that all along.

He felt sick. Drunk. Wine on an empty stomach. Red Hair would come, and he'd get it over and sleep. Through the lilacs—he'd come between the lilacs and fence.

Martin cradled a bottle of port in his arms. His feet hurt from those miles at the Cattle Congress; his legs ached. Nobody in her house but Sara. He'd looked in every window at her lighted rooms.

Martin left the tunnel and sat down with it at his back. He took a swallow of port. Red Hair couldn't come through the lilacs without making noise. Or Ben Woodward. She'd see the man dead first. She'd beg for the man's life, maybe. Let her.

"Faster!" somebody yelled in the park. Somebody else was stamping at the top of the slide; metal clanged. Two swings began a grating counterpoint.

Sara trembled at the thought of Ben's warmth in his big bed. Arms around her, kisses, whispers, not being afraid—

"No!" she said to her kitchen. "Keep him safe." She covered her mouth with her hands and shut her eyes. Leave Ben Woodward alone. Only a month and a half since cold black waves, a high moon, gravel crackling underfoot on the road to Grenville. She had meant to be alone for months, years. A man with red hair shoving his old lawn mower around trees in the sweet scent of cut grass . . .

Sara's kitchen light was a golden shaft in the air before Martin. He finished the port fast and half fell on the grass to watch that yellow shimmer in the dark backyard. There wasn't a star in the sky—it was black. He could wait. When Sara's kitchen light went off and her house was dark, Martin lay curled up like a child under the lilacs.

By nine-thirty the teenagers had left the park, but a few younger children made the swings squeak and groan. A boy rode his bicycle at a trapeze, grabbed it, and his bike spun off alone to fall on its side near a curb, wheels spinning.

# 41

Midnight. Martin was asleep near Sara's back-porch door when rain began to fall.

He twitched in his dreams and the rain. He ran after Sara down street after street, opening one door, another door, until she was behind one of them, naked and laughing in bed with somebody.

Martin yelled and rolled over in his sleep to grab the .25 pistol in his pocket. Beautiful Sara's arms were around another man's neck, and she didn't care if Martin saw her. Martin found the pistol; he found the safety catch.

Sara held the man close and laughed, and a photographer's lights flared like lightning.

Thunder cracked in Martin's ears, but all he heard was Sara's laughter. His dream was all around him as he opened his eyes and saw a man coming from Sara's back-porch door.

The man ran through Sara's yard toward the corner house. Martin came to his feet and was after him, firing his pistol as he ran.

Martin's head felt like a huge throbbing pumpkin. Sara's house was dark. A man yelled in thunder and soaking rain, and it seemed to Martin that Sara was still laughing as the man fell in a big round bed of flowers that were yellow in a flash of lightning.

Martin ran to the man, turned him over. Rain fell on open blue eyes, a young face, blood, and hair as light as

Martin's had been once. Wet chrysanthemums stank, strong and green, smashed under the young man's body.

A voice called, "Who's out there?"

Martin stood up, swaying, then ran back from the corner-house yard to Sara's. He slipped in soaked grass and mud.

Sara, jerked out of her bed by gunfire, stood against her back-porch door, her nightgown already stuck to her body by the downpour. She saw Martin coming from the yard of the corner house; he stared backward over his shoulder and slid in wet grass, but she knew him. Martin! Sara ducked out of sight in the lilac path just as Martin fell at her porch steps.

A light went on at the arched back door of the corner house. "Who's there?" somebody shouted.

Martin was on his hands and knees now, pawing among lilacs so close to Sara that she never breathed, never blinked. She saw by lightning that his hair was dark brown and he had a short brown beard, but he was Martin.

Now there was more than one voice next door by the chrysanthemum bed. Martin got to his feet and stumbled through Sara's gate to the alley.

No one else ran like that, toeing in, shoulders raised. Sara thought, Martin. Here where she was. *Martin.*

So she ran behind him in the dark between lightning flashes. Once in the alley behind her house, she saw a car parked on Seerley Boulevard etched clear by lightning—its make, its color. She saw Martin throw himself in it; he squealed tires and was gone.

"Who's there?" someone yelled from the red corner house.

Sara had run to the alley in the dark between lightning flashes, her soaked nightgown flapping against her legs. Thunder split the air overhead. She crouched in high alley bushes, waited for lightning, then ran in the blackness after it, hurting her bare foot on something hard and cold in the grass.

She felt for whatever it was—a small pistol. When she crept up her porch steps there was something soft on the doorknob.

Sara ripped the soft thing off the knob, closed porch and kitchen door behind her without a sound and stood shivering and dripping in her dark kitchen.

Lightning blinked like a strobe through her kitchen window; bushes, trees, and fences came and went. Sara's yard was empty, but a fat man and a young woman bent over someone lying in the bed of chrysanthemums by the corner house. Sara had seen the fat man mowing that lawn. The young woman sometimes sunbathed out there by the flower bed with music blaring from the window above.

Now they hoisted a man to his feet—a young man with blond hair, his mouth open.

In a brilliant flash Sara saw notes at her door, blood splotching a white shirt, wet blond hair lit by lightning. *You're sure beautiful. . . .*

And she stood dripping on her kitchen floor, a .25 Baretta in her hand. Familiar eagles on the pistol's grip pressed their sharp claws into her palm. Martin had shot a man, and lost his gun in the lilacs when he fell, and driven away in a white car.

Thunder cracked and rumbled. Nothing was a dream. Sara was holding Martin's gun. Softness in her hand was a bunch of flowers and a note. Martin had shot the man who brought them. *I'll kill you, and the man too. You're sure beautiful. I like that green dress. And that necklace.*

She lit a match and read the familiar printing:

BEAUTY IN GREEN—
MY HEART IS AROUND YOUR NECK
ON THE CHAIN.
I AM ALL YOU NEED BETWEEN YOUR
LOVELY LEGS.

A wailing ambulance came down Seerley. It stopped at her corner like a scream strangled.

The small pistol fitted Sara's palm. The eagles on the grips spread sharp claws, their beaks open. She checked the clip in the butt of Martin's pistol. He had shot a man. He would come back for the gun and her.

Sara rubbed between her eyes with the heel of her hand, staring around her dark kitchen as if she didn't recognize it. *He was here.*

Once again Sara wiped out wet footprints, her jaw set, her blue eyes hard and glittering. She dried herself, put her wet nightgown in soapsuds in the bathroom sink. Police would be there soon, tramping through backyards in the rain.

She saw a poinsettia broken in snow, and a bloody hand worming through smashed wood.

Her fingerprints belonged to a drowned body. She would take her ordinary clothes with her—one more disguise. She stuffed her shorts and shirt and running shoes in a bag.

His car would be at one of the motels; there weren't many nearby.

He had been in town long enough to find her house, follow her there. Follow her! She pounded with her fist on a wall; she had thought she was safe, had been a fool. Dressing fast, she kept her eyes on the pistol on her dresser and felt her heart pounding.

It was after midnight now. Rain poured, making leaves dip and rise, soaking the Cattle Congress banner, pounding roofs on the cattle barns. A police car drove down University Avenue, where lights turned red, yellow, green—swords of light on wet concrete. One white car crept along those blades of color.

Police. Martin drove the half mile from Sara's house to his motel, following the squad car. Rain on his windshield poured too fast for wipers; motel lights swam through water. There were several spaces in front of the Holiday Inn; Martin pulled into one and sat where he was, tasting vomit in his pumpkin of a head. No small pistol weighed his pocket down. He only had the juice-can silencer, and he hadn't even thought to use it.

Martin sat slumped in his car for a long time with rain beating above his head. His hands went into his pockets and out again. After a while he found they were playing with the wheel, measuring off its shape by so many finger spaces. He began to count finger spaces. His head felt better when he counted.

He counted spaces for a long time while a young man with a dark beard crept from Sara's back-porch door to Ben Woodward's barn and drove Ben's car away in drenching rain.

Finally Martin's fingers searched his pockets again. He knew what they were after—the pistol with eagles on it.

Hell. They wanted it. He'd have to go get it, and kill her.

"I love her," he whispered to his hands, and felt Sara in his arms, smelled her hair.

His fingers didn't listen—they found car keys and drove him back, parked him on Franklin Street. His feet walked him through middles of dark blocks, through strange yards and around clothes posts, trash cans, hedges. He crawled through when he couldn't go around or climb over, his clothes heavy and wet, and dug his heels into mud to steady himself, and carried his head on his neck like a big pumpkin that could be broken.

The university campanile rang through the rain.

Finally Martin was in Sara's backyard, where his pistol was.

His feet took him to her back-porch steps. His hands began to feel over concrete there, clever as animals. They knew what they had to have.

The pistol wasn't there. His hands climbed steps and ran through lilac bushes and wet grass. He kept his head up as much as he could, balancing it. His clever fingers opened her porch door and felt along the floor. They were after the pistol, and Sara. They went in and he followed.

Martin's hands felt over furniture. They opened doors. His hands found his little flashlight in his pocket, and the small beam wandered over a bed with empty sheets, and a closet with Sara smells in it. He pressed his face to her clothes in the dark, but his hands didn't care. The flashlight showed a bathroom, and when his clever hands found a toothpaste tube, they tightened the cap. They folded every towel on towel racks into threes while his pumpkin head seemed to grow bigger.

The flashlight wobbled through a living room to a kitchen and cans in a cupboard. Martin's clever hands put all the cans one deep and turned their labels to the front.

"Not here," he told his hands. "Nobody's here."

But he had to take his hands into a cellar anyway so they could feel along damp stones, a tub fastened to the floor, shelves full of cobwebs and splinters. His pumpkin head wobbled on his shoulders.

His fingers wanted to go upstairs, so Martin climbed steps to a locked door, until he heard voices, stumbled downstairs to see lights in Sara's front yard, and ran with his clever fingers out the back door, through back lots, into his car, and drove back to the motel.

Martin never noticed a blue car parked in the motel lot or the dark-bearded young man watching from its driver's seat as Martin roamed the motel balconies trying to find his room. He couldn't read the number on the key. Soaked with rain, he tried every door until the key worked, then stumbled in and sat on the bed.

Martin's clever fingers knew what he needed. They found a bottle of port.

He had left his door open. Rain sheeted down beyond the balcony; thunder cracked. His hands didn't care. They wanted the pistol and they wanted Sara. His head bobbled around on its stem.

His hands felt over the woven bedspread when they weren't letting him drink. "Not so clever," he told his hands. "Messed it up Killed somebody and don't know who."

His hands turned on a bedside lamp. Moths came in and whacked against the lamp shade. "Stupid hands," he said, so the hands caught moths, rubbed them into the bedspread. "Messy," he told them.

When Martin looked up there was a man in the motel-room doorway. The man said, "I'll kill you."

Martin tried to focus his eyes. He thought it might be Ben Woodward—the short fellow with the dark beard he'd followed from Nebraska but couldn't find. "I don't exist," the bearded man said. That made sense, Martin thought—he had never been able to find Ben Woodward. "So I can't kill anybody, can I?" The man pulled gloves on and shut the door softly.

"Hell," Martin said over a thunder crack. "Ben Woodward?"

Ben Woodward was short and skinny. "You'll chase me forever," he said. "You'll kill men I don't even know. I wonder why you ever thought you owned me."

Martin didn't think he was dreaming, and yet Ben Woodward sounded like somebody in a dream. "I don't own any guy," Martin said. "I have to take orders from McManus." He thought maybe Ben Woodward had tears running down his beard now, but he couldn't see him very well—just a man with a bushy black beard and mustache.

"I loved you," Woodward said.

There wasn't a man who had ever said that to Martin. His father's sour face rose in his mind, and faces of McManus and Chuck Jenner and Al Surrino. He almost laughed at the funny sound of *I loved you.* "Aw, come on," Martin said.

"You'll follow me and kill me," Ben said. "And yet we're just the same. You don't want to beg someone for money, do you?"

"No."

Ben Woodward stepped a little closer. "You want respect, right?"

"Yes." Martin kept answering questions. He saw two Ben Woodwards—they were both talking. He tried to concentrate on one to see if the other would go away. "I got my own job—" Martin said, and then stopped, because he didn't. He didn't have any job any more. He looked around for a wine bottle. "I haven't got a job," he said. "I haven't got a wife." He thought maybe he was dreaming, because suddenly he couldn't remember where he was or what he'd come there to do.

"You want your own money, your own job, your own house—you don't want to live in somebody else's house?"

Martin shook his head. The man was asking so many questions. Maybe he was a policeman.

"And clean up after somebody else?"

Martin shook his head and remembered now—he was afraid of the police.

"How about a nice part-time job that you can keep as long as your wife says you can?"

Martin keep staring at two Ben Woodwards.

"I wonder if you'd like to live with a man bigger than you who hits you every time you don't write a weekly letter to his parents on time or let moths get into his cashmere sweater."

Martin remembered he'd had a blue cashmere sweater once. Sara had forgotten it when she sent clothes to be stored. He'd found it, and stood in front of their bedroom mirror seeing white shirt through moth holes, and then he had slapped the hell out of Sara and thrown the sweater away.

Martin's hands were twitching; he knew what they wanted—the pistol.

"I loved you!" Ben Woodward whispered. Martin's head felt like a pumpkin again, bobbing on its stem. "You would have killed me," the man said.

Ben Woodward was short and skinny.

Martin watched Woodward's gloved hands shake.

Ben Woodward's voice wasn't loud; it got softer and higher and sweeter. "Remember communion at the church, kneeling with me at the altar rail, and walking through snow near Harvard Square to see Christmas wreaths on the Tory Row houses, and reading *A Christmas Carol* to music on Christmas Eve?"

Ben Woodward's voice, soft and high and sweet, made Martin's head wobble. "Remember plays at the Brattle Theatre? Borrowing records from the Montrose library? How beautiful the Charles River was with rowing shells on it on a summer afternoon?" Ben Woodward stuck his hand in his pocket, and when it came out it had a pistol in it.

"I'm sorry," Martin said, getting up. "They want it."

His hands were running up and down the sides of his pants.

Ben Woodward had a black beard and mustache, heavy eyebrows, black hair, but his eyes—Martin was sure of it now—his eyes were Sara's. Woodward was close now. There was only one of him, and Martin squinted to see Woodward's eyes. He thought they were Sara's eyes.

"They want it," Martin said. He was talking about his hands.

"Could you make love to someone who beat you?" Sara asked. She spoke from a man's body, so she was a man, but she was a woman remembering what Sara knew, what he knew. Who did he think she really was, she asked—a human being like him or a wife?

"I can't help it if they want it," Martin said, taking a step toward Ben Woodward. She was a man who had the gun, and his hands were after it. Martin heard Ben Woodward slip the safety catch off the pistol—a small sound between claps of thunder.

Martin stared at Sara, listening to Sara, who was a man and had tears running down his beard, and hands that shook, holding a .25 pistol. He took two more steps. "I'm sorry," Martin said, because his clever hands were going to grab the .25 pistol they wanted.

"Unless I kill you, I'll never be free," Ben Woodward sobbed.

Martin's clever hands had been rubbing moths into the bedspread because they couldn't find a bottle of wine. They'd already killed the man in the chrysanthemums, the man with Sara. They wanted the gun. "You'll kill men I don't even know," Ben Woodward said, rubbing between his eyes with the heel of his gloved hand.

Martin leapt for Ben Woodward. His clever hands grabbed Ben Woodward's hand holding the gun. "They want it," Martin tried to explain.

Woodward still had the pistol. He fought to keep it, and Martin stared into wide, desperate, hate-filled blue eyes under black eyebrows—they were an inch from his, so familiar, so strange, and the mouth under the black mustache panted against his cheek.

"I loved you!" the man in Martin's arms whispered. Martin sobbed for Sara's long, fragrant hair, round breasts. Martin's clever hands twisted Ben's wrist, a skinny little wrist—twisted it until the dark-bearded face moaned.

Now Martin's clever hands had the pistol. It was his own pistol—he felt the eagles on the grip. His hands had what they wanted.

Then he smelled Sara. A man panted and struggled in his arms, but Martin smelled Sara, drowned Sara in her green dress that blew against her lovely legs, with a mole between her breasts, and her long, soft hair—Sara, who would never come back.

For a second Martin shut his eyes, his pumpkin head swelling on its stem. He saw police. He'd slapped a woman around and killed a man, and the pigs would be after him. A woman screamed against a wall. A man sprawled in chrysanthemums. Machines shone in neatly ruled sunshine through plate glass. Sara was falling and falling as thunder thudded down the sky now from stair to stair.

Martin's head was a pumpkin blown up. It wobbled around on its little stem.

"They want it!" he sobbed in Sara's arms. His clever hands had the gun. They broke the pumpkin.

# 42

Moth wings and moth bodies were rubbed into the bedspread, and it was pulled half to the floor where Martin lay, his arms over his head as if in sleep. The hole in Martin's temple sent a small stream of blood in a crooked path toward his ear; a .25 pistol gleamed in his hand. Martin watched the motel ceiling with a thoughtful stare, as if his mind were on something else and he waited for an answer. A bus passed on Highway 218; the far-off sound of its gears shifted through to high.

A short man with a dark beard bent over Martin, sobbing and whispering, "Martin," saying, "My love," saying, "Oh, God, oh, God, why did you shoot yourself, why did you kill yourself, Martin? Martin?" and trembling, listening to no-sound in Martin's chest, feeling for the no-beat in a still-warm wrist.

Sara let his hand drop. She recognized his shirt—she had taken in the underarm seams for him. She remembered her sewing machine humming in their small bedroom on a spring day full of leaves and mist.

Sara's eyes widened above the black beard. Martin watched her with his preoccupied eyes, as if she must make the next move. "I could never have killed you. Why did you kill yourself?" she whispered.

Martin's eyes were on her. "My God," she whispered, stretching her hand toward Martin. She pulled it back, flattened her palm against her forehead above her heavy, fake eyebrows, then looked around her.

There was a bathroom, dim through an open door . . . a luggage rack, an open closet. There was a TV squatted on a brass stand, and a desk with a telephone on it. A sign saying "Please Do Not Disturb" dangled from a desk knob over Martin.

Thunder had been pounding overhead. She tiptoed back and forth—a black-bearded man wringing his hands. Had anyone heard a gunshot through thunder? Martin looked up at Sara thoughtfully, as if he were thinking of that too.

The short man ran to the motel door and opened it softly with his gloved hand. He shut it behind him, softly, and ran through thunder and rain to a blue car parked on a back street. He was gone down the highway before a last moth fluttered to the lamp beside the motel bed, dived into its bowl of light, and sputtered above Martin's open, wondering eyes.

A shivering, dark-bearded young man drove along Seerley Boulevard. He was alive—blood beat in his head and his throat and his chest. His wrist was bruised and ached.

"They want it!" Martin's voice echoed in the car's small space, as if his breath weren't gone, pushed from his lungs a last time.

No police cars or ambulance were on Seerley now, but the young man drove into Ben Woodward's barn from Twenty-second Street. He hung Ben's car key in its hiding place, then listened, trembling a little, in the barn doorway. No lights showed in Ben Woodward's house, or Sara's.

Backyards dripped with rain where Martin must have looked in windows. He had dropped a pistol by a back-porch door. Leaves brushed against Sara's cheek like a hand. She had called the kitten across dark backyards. A man who could hear nothing now must have stood here listening, his hair and beard dyed brown, a .25 pistol in his hand.

Rain dripped from every leaf above Sara, not caring that a man sprawled on a motel floor, staring thoughtfully at nothing.

Sara had her shirt and shorts and running shoes in a

paper bag in her hand; she took a few steps toward her own house across wet grass. Suddenly a door opened at the corner house; she heard voices.

A bearded young man ran noiselessly under an apple tree to Ben's kitchen door. It was unlocked, and closed quietly behind Sara. She crept to Ben's kitchen window.

Two men came around Sara's house corner. When they followed flashlight beams into her garden, she saw dim shapes of their uniform caps—police. Bushes, flowers, her alley fence leapt from dark in sweeps of light; now policemen came to her back-porch door. She heard them knock.

*He was my husband. He broke my toe and my wrist. . . .* Sara's mind ran back and forth from present to past like a mouse through a mousehole. She held her breath.

Policemen knocked at her kitchen door again. Flashlights threw yellow circles on the side of her house; policemen went up stairs to her front porch and knocked. A train whistled through town and over the Cedar River, as lonely as if it were a human voice not expecting an answer.

Sara tore beard and mustache and false eyebrows from her face and stripped off a man's trousers and shirt. She unwound bandages from her breasts with shaking hands, dumped the contents of her paper bag on Ben's dark kitchen floor, and stuffed in what she had taken off, quickly, quickly. She hid it on Ben's lowest kitchen shelf, far back.

Now she was only a naked woman wearing a wig. She wiped footprints from Ben's floor and heard men talking on her front porch, but she was wondering, too, if it had been Martin at the motel in Fredsburg, walking in darkness from car to car.

Knocking on her front door stopped. They would come back. *Where were you at the time of the shooting? You must have heard . . .*

Why had he suspected she hadn't drowned?

She waited for Ben's doorbell to ring.

How had Martin known she wasn't dead?

Sara rubbed her wet face. Blood would drip to the shoulder of the blue shirt.

Martin shouted and laughed in her memory. He ran into sparkling surf at Manhasset, sunlight on his yellow hair.

Sara picked her shorts and shirt and running shoes from Ben's kitchen linoleum and piled them near his back door. Now there were voices in the alley—Ben's downstairs bathroom window, open a crack, let them leak through.

Was Ben still asleep? He'd heard only thunder, perhaps, or the heavy beating of rain.

Martin would still be looking at the motel-room ceiling. Blood might find its way to his shoulder, run into his shirt pocket, pool there, ooze to the bedspread in quiet lamplight.

Sara listened to voices. Brilliance flashed into Ben's kitchen from a spotlight in the alley; she held her wrist in that glow and saw red fingermarks. It seemed to her she stood in shadows of a honeymoon beach house again—she was looking in a mirror that was losing its silver, and Martin's caressing hands had made her breasts and shoulders pink.

She waited to hear Ben's doorbell. Her house was dark and empty.

Ben's doorbell never rang.

Stairs whispered under Sara's bare feet as she crept upstairs to Ben. Sharp edges. A long fall . . .

No waves pounded below. There were voices in the alley, but they were only low murmurs through Ben's half-open bedroom window. Listening to them, Sara pulled her wig off, unpinned her braids. Her long hair, rippling free, brushed warm against her cheeks and breasts as she turned back Ben's sheet softly, slowly.

She knew how to crawl into bed so gradually that a sleeping man would never wake. At last, smoothly, holding her breath, she stretched out at the edge of Ben's wide mattress. His breathing had never changed.

When she shut her eyes she saw Martin finding her— how had he found her—stalking her, striking almost exactly where she was, but swerving, swerving at the last possible moment to die in her arms and fall. *I'll kill you and the man too.*

She clenched her hands into fists—they had slipped the safety catch on a gun. *Unless I kill you, I'll never be free.*

"I hated him. I went to kill him." Sara's lips moved soundlessly. Ben's breathing kept its slow, steady rhythm.

Sara shut off the memory of Martin's heavy body slipping through her arms, kicking her leg with its heavy shoe as it fell. She kept from trembling by listening to a small chorus of insect voices through an open window. They said a storm was gone.

Ben. She listened to his slow, measured breathing from another world that she would seem to belong to when he woke.

Small chirpings and tickings measured off the night. Summer was over. Tears ran from Sara's eyes to a pillow. Only three years since she and Martin hadn't been able to keep their hands off each other in the Blue Lobster's back booth. Once they'd run back to their honeymoon beach house before dinner was over, passing the waiter bringing their dessert, his mouth open a little in astonishment.

Autumn. A car went by, its tires sounding sticky on wet concrete, and suddenly Sara was herself and alone—she bared her teeth and gritted them, like an animal that has caught what it wants and grips it tight in its jaws.

Without moving, listening to Ben's quiet breath and voices in the alley, Sara remembered a cramped house that was like a rabbit hole, a mouse burrow, dense with crowded bodies of women and children who hid.

The battered woman shelter . . . she remembered she had slept there on the floor with women who cried in their sleep, or wept softly, lying awake. Those who had stopped crying crawled in the dark to put their arms around those who hadn't, and sometimes they talked over the small mounds that were sleeping children.

Sara listened to Ben, who breathed so softly, so regularly, and she wanted to fit herself close to him. He had slept through an ordinary night, never hearing a gunshot, never seeing a face settle into glazed, detached thoughtfulness as if to say, I have stopped here. How will you go on?

*With lies*, Sara told the small stream of blood running down Martin's neck. *I'll go on with lies. The way someone will kill if she's cornered,* she said to the bullet hole.

Martin watched her with his brown, wide-open, little boy's wondering eyes.

# 43

Rain dried slowly on leaves and grass.

Before the streetlights dimmed and darkened, Seerley Boulevard and the highway had dry patches; the first cars trailed wet tracks behind them.

Schoitz Hospital's facade grew clearer, taking its colors back for another day. A maternity-ward nurse came to give Ellen Dehlstrom ice water.

She pulled up Ellen's shade. "You're going home with your aunt today!" she said. Ellen turned her plump, expressionless face to the window.

Sun filtered through clouds in Montrose, Massachusetts. The Montrose library janitor let Pam Fitzer in the library's side door. He always did that at eight on weekdays.

"Good morning," she said. He said good morning. She was wearing her black cotton dress again. He watched her click past the checkout desk on her high heels. She was skinny and wishy-washy and had been wearing black for weeks. Somebody she knew had drowned, she'd said, when he got up nerve to ask. He turned on the lobby lights.

First sunshine tipped the trees above Hazel Channing's old house. "Dinner in that Venetian restaurant under the bridge, with the water slapping right at our feet," Georgia Parrish said, buttering another croissant for Haze.

Hazel laughed. "Gondoliers under our bathroom window."

"No hot water for a shower," Georgia said. "But the Duke's song from *Rigoletto* while you froze."

A cleaning woman opened a motel door, took a few steps inside, yelled, turned, ran.

It was raining in Nebraska. Water dripped from roof to grass at the Craigie Court Retirement Center—gutters were clogged with a night's fall of leaves.

"Listen to the rain," Chloe Gray said to Lila Rainey. "It'll be good for gardens going into winter." Her blind eyes turned to the water sounds.

"Those nurse's aides are out the door halfway through a sentence," Lila said. "Never mind. I'll read your nephew's letter to you again . . . maybe you'll get another one this morning."

The Holiday Inn's office chair creaked under the police captain. "Suicide," he said to someone on the telephone. "A Martin Burney from Massachusetts. Dyed his hair."

The motel manager looked glum. "Bad for business," he said to his wife. "Local business."

"How about that shooting on Seerley?" the police captain said. "When do we get the report on the bullet? That kid says a prowler took a potshot at him—out for a walk and came back home and found some guy at the back door trying to get in, right? Well, it could have been this Martin Burney. Rented car." The captain twiddled a pen and stared at the motel manager's wife as he talked. "We checked on Burney, and he was supposed to have drowned in Massachusetts somewhere three weeks ago. The kid says he saw him pretty close, so bring the kid to look at the body, will you, when he's patched up and calmed down?"

The motel manager looked at his wife and shook his head.

\*    \*    \*

After a while morning sun brightened Cedar Falls streets and sparkled in crab apple trees on Seerley Boulevard, but at the Abbott house there was nothing but crying, fighting children. Mrs. Abbott was braiding Sandra's hair. "Go out and play if you're not going to eat your cereal," she told Markie. "Go on."

Markie's wagon squawked and groaned, pulled along Tremont Street in early sunshine.

Sara heard it. She had hardly moved for hours, her eyes open and full of questions, like Martin's. She didn't think she was herself. "Hello?" she said to the silence inside her. "Hello?"

Ben Woodward's bedroom was dark, except for one half-open window. Shades were drawn, and so was a heavy curtain. Ben half woke to squeaking and groaning, half opened his eyes in his dim bedroom. He found the way to his toilet, hardly bothering to look, and then crawled into bed again. He'd been exhausted the night before—home late Sunday from the conference, classes Monday, Cattle Congress, and then the damn committee meetings. He'd been so tired he hadn't even eaten dinner—took a couple of sleeping pills too. . . .

Then he remembered. He saw Laura in her beautiful green dress. "Blood pythons, sungazers, green tree vipers . . ." A pigeon's patient eye against a man's coat. Cotton candy winding and winding on a spindle. The Sky Dipper's swooping car. Laura's lips under his in hot sun, high on a Ferris wheel. A saloon girl, and a garter with the ace of spades . . . joy exploded in Ben; he laughed softly, all by himself with such happiness.

Back and forth went the creaking and squawking. Ben lay listening . . . but wasn't there something else? He opened his eyes, sat up, and his hand traveled the distance between himself and warm skin, warm, long, slippery hair that clung to his groping fingers. "Deborah," Ben said under his breath.

Someone lay in his bed, turned away from him. He reached to raise a window shade, and she sat up.

It was Laura—he saw her dim flower-mouth and narrow nose.

Light from the window glistened on her hair—it was pale as moonlight trailing across her shoulders, dividing across a bare breast.

He wanted to roll across the wide space between them to hold her so tight she couldn't breathe.

"Ben," she said.

Sheets rustled between them as Laura brought her knees up to her chin and watched Ben from the rippling hood of her hair.

Ben said nothing. He lay naked and still.

"About midnight I had a terrible dream, and I was lonely," Laura said. "I wondered if your door was open."

"Yes," Ben said. "I never heard you."

She turned on her side now and came closer. "We both slept."

Ben held his breath, afraid to say a word. He felt her hair brush across his arm, then smelled its perfume, felt its weight as her lips closed on his and her slenderness fitted itself to him.

Ben heard the Abbott children from the corner wheeling their squeaky wagon down the sidewalk, and the sound was so sweet to him with Laura's soft breasts in his hands that he thought he would cry. He was here, not dreaming—a wagon squawked and groaned along Tremont toward Seerley, and the scent of September's wet gardens came through an open window.

"Laura," Ben whispered. "Laura." Heavy blond ripples fell over his face in a wonderful, slippery, pale shimmer. He turned his face into their perfume. Now a woman called Laura was under him, her wet face against his, her bruised wrist behind his back. There were no other bruises on her body, but she cried as if there were, and sobbed and shook in his arms.

"Laura," he whispered, wiping tears from her face, kissing her so sweetly she could hardly stop crying with the comfort, the warmth of his careful, gentle touch.

Tuesday morning in Cedar Falls, Iowa, closed over Ben

like warm hands folded together. When he stopped breathing heavily at last and lay still, the squeaky wagon was going the other way, from Seerley down Tremont.

"My love," he said, floating in happiness so wide he couldn't see the end of it. He smoothed long, shining hair, hidden hair, fragrant now against his cheek. His heart swelled, it seemed to him—he could feel it expand with happiness. "You were here all night, and I didn't know?"

Laura's eyes were close and blue and dreamy, with fine lavender lines in them. She pushed her silvery hair aside to kiss him. The world went away once more, like a squeaky wagon.

"Beautiful . . ." he murmured after a while against Laura's breast. He sat up beside her and stroked her hair. "I love you! You haven't said you love me, but I'll tell you—you do!"

"I love you . . ." Laura began, not looking at him. Tears began to run down her face again, and she didn't even wipe them away. She put her arms around him, her wet face against his.

"Don't cry," Ben said. He stroked her hair. "You're so beautiful . . . beautiful blond—"

"No. I'm not," Laura said. She sat up in his bed then, and rubbed between her eyes with the heel of her hand, her breasts shifting in the window's greenish light. She began to braid her hair. "Not yet," she said. When her hair was braided she grabbed hairpins from his dresser, grabbed for the dark wig beside them. "Someday." She pulled on the wig and all her long, lovely hair was gone.

"All right," Ben said. He hunched his shoulders and looked around for his jeans. "Tell you what—I'll make us some breakfast."

Sara watched Ben buckle his belt. He snatched up a shirt. Golden hairs on his chest shone. He smiled at her, came to kiss her, then thumped barefooted downstairs.

Blinds in the kitchen were open. Ben took a deep, happy breath and found eggs in the refrigerator. A woman of his own. His body was lit up like a theater marquee.

He'd make scrambled eggs, bacon, toast, coffee, juice,

the works. Dr. and Mrs. Benjamin Woodward, together in this house. Fancy stuff with flowers and white satin and veils and organ music and women running around chirping. She'd marry him. When it was this good, she'd marry him. He could wait.

Ben hummed a music-hall tune, cracking eggs, hearing the shower running upstairs. Laura in his bed. Laura in his shower. Laura coming downstairs in one of his big bath towels, not looking at him much. Then she met his eyes and laughed at herself a little, tossing her head back. Now he knew why she did that, tossing her long, soft, hidden hair. She was cool and soap-smelling under the towel, and her lips were cool, too, until they opened to his like tulip petals.

When they got their breaths back Laura put on the shirt and shorts she'd left in a corner of his kitchen. They ate breakfast in sweet almost-silence, their eyes meeting over buttered toast, a jam pot, cups of coffee. Halfway done, they met at the stove and kissed for a long time, swaying a little together in fresh garden breeze, bacon smells, early sunlight.

They had just finished the coffee and a kiss when Ben said, "There's a policeman poking around your backyard."

Laura left breakfast dishes she was gathering and stood beside Ben at his kitchen window. Green grass and leaves sparkled in sunlight after rain.

"Tell you what—I'll go talk to him," Ben said. "Maybe he's lost his badge. Maybe he's lost his shoes. Maybe he's lost." His voice had a lilt in it; he grinned, trying to make Laura smile, and slammed his kitchen door behind him.

Laura watched Ben come from the lilac tunnel to stand with the policeman on her back sidewalk. Ben's body was relaxed as he asked his first question; then she saw it stiffen. He looked around him, turned back to the officer. The officer pointed here, then there.

Laura was stacking cups in Ben's dish cupboard when he came back. The policeman was with him. "A shooting at the corner house," Ben said.

"Sorry to bother you folks." The policeman was young

and awkward, running his cap around and around in his hands. "We're just doing a routine check with the neighbors."

Laura seemed to be in a dream, Ben thought. Finally she asked the policeman, "Would you like some coffee?"

"No. But thanks anyway."

Laura sat down at the table, and the men sat down too.

"The Coreys' son was coming home late last night and caught a prowler in their yard," Ben said. "The prowler shot him in the shoulder and ran. Just nicked him, really."

The policeman took out pad and paper. "You're renting Mrs. Nepper's apartment next door, I believe," he said to Sara. "Did you hear or see anything suspicious last night?"

"No," Laura said.

"You sleep on this side of your house?"

"Yes," Laura said, not looking at Ben.

"We'll be examining yards around here, although we've got the gun," the policeman said, getting up. "If you see or find anything that might be significant, let us know."

Laura followed him to Ben's kitchen door, then turned. "I should be getting back," she told Ben. "But I'll leave your lunch ready for you. I'll probably be at Dr. Channing's tonight."

"Give me a call," Ben said. The policeman closed the door behind him, and Laura came into Ben's arms, a dreamy, almost stunned look still on her face. She came back to him twice before she finally shut his kitchen door and took the lilac tunnel. Banana was yowling by her back-porch door.

A group of people in the next yard never saw Sara come from the lilacs. There was no bunch of flowers on her porch doorknob. She had wiped up her wet tracks. . . .

Sara gasped, then shut her porch door softly and quickly behind her. Muddy footprints, dried gray now, ran across her back porch and clean kitchen floor.

A prowler. Call the policeman—he was with the group of people in the next yard. No. Sara went from room to room. No one was there.

She grabbed a rag from under the sink, wet it, and was

on her knees scrubbing while busy voices chattered under her window. She cleaned the porch floor, and the kitchen floor, and the hall, the stairs to the second floor—

Her doorbell rang.

Sara wiped up the last footprint in her bathroom before she answered her bell.

"I came as soon as I could," Mrs. Nepper said, white hair nodding above her brown face. "Heard it from Mary Harris. She cleans at the Holiday Inn. Came as soon as I could."

"Come in," Sara said, and held her screen door open.

"Heard it from Mary Harris." Mrs. Nepper stepped into the living room and looked around. "My, doesn't your woodwork look nice? She cleans at the motel, but she didn't find the body, thank goodness."

"What body?" Sara said.

"I came as soon as I could. Wanted to see was everything all right, because I called Hazel Channing's and you weren't there. Did you hear the shooting? She didn't *find* the body, but the police talked to her and everybody."

"Where?" Sara said.

"At the Holiday Inn. It was the prowler. You've heard about the prowler, haven't you?"

"The police came," Sara said.

"Yes, well, I came as soon as I could, because Mary Harris knew about it. She works at the motel. He's dead."

"Who?"

"The prowler! I came as soon as I could, because I thought you'd be so scared, being here all alone with the Corey boy getting shot next door. Did you hear anything? I said to Mary Harris, 'I'll go right down and tell Laura Pray so she won't worry. He's dead.' "

"No, I didn't hear anything except the storm," Sara said. "Can I get you a cup of coffee?"

"He shot himself. That *would* be nice," Mrs. Nepper said, sitting down on the couch. "Crazy, I suppose, if he did that. It'll be in the papers tonight, but I thought you'd want to know. All of us are nervous with somebody out there shooting." She got up and came to stand in the kitchen doorway. "Never thought you could get those ferns to grow."

Sara's kitchen floor was almost dry now; water was on for coffee. They sat down again in the living room. "Crazy, I suppose," Mrs. Nepper said. "Mary said he did it with a little pistol, and still had it in his hand. Nobody even heard it, there was such lightning and thunder. Did you ever hear such thunder? My porch roof leaked, and my porch roof never leaks. But I told Mary Harris I'd come right away and tell you so you won't worry, because he's dead."

The water was boiling. Sara went to get instant coffee from the cupboard. Mrs. Nepper came to the kitchen door and said coffee was so expensive now . . . she could remember when it was fifty cents a pound.

Reaching into her kitchen cupboard for the coffee, Sara saw canned food she had stacked up. But now . . . she stared at neat rows of cans, one deep, facing front.

"I don't suppose you remember such nice low prices for things, do you?" Mrs. Nepper said.

Sara didn't hear her. She didn't answer.

"He was somebody from the East. Boston, I think. Had a white rented car," Mrs. Nepper went on. "Edna Grant and Helen Tyler saw him sitting on Seerley in front of the old Atcher house, but they didn't know it was him, and I suppose he had that gun with him too. Somebody out there shooting—makes you nervous, I told Mary Harris."

Sara touched a can that faced front with the rest. She found a spoon in the silverware drawer. "Yes."

"That's what I said—I imagine she's nervous, and I'll just go over and tell her he's dead. Not too much . . . just a level teaspoon is plenty. How's Hazel Channing?"

"Fine," Sara said, handing Mrs. Nepper her coffee. "A friend stayed the night with her. I have to be there at noon."

Mrs. Nepper finished her coffee in a hurry. "That's what the friend told me when I called. And I've got to go. When's Ellen Garner coming back?"

"She hasn't let us know yet," Sara said.

"And you didn't hear a single thing last night?"

"No."

"Well, I can't stay, but I told Mary Harris I'd just come by and tell you they found the body. She works at the Holiday Inn, but she didn't find it. It'll be in all the papers tonight, and people will be talking about it for weeks. We don't have shootings and suicides much. Thanks for the coffee."

Sara watched Mrs. Nepper go down her front-porch steps saying, "At the Holiday Inn. Mary Harris."

Sara shut her front door. She went to her kitchen and opened the cabinet again.

Every can of food faced front, showing its label; not one can was piled on another. They stood in ranks, holding their names for her inspection as if called as witnesses: peas, peaches, apricots, green beans.

Sara looked out her kitchen window . . . *sitting on Seerley . . . I suppose he had that gun with him.* A knot of people stood by trampled chrysanthemums. No music blatted from the red house above them. Twenty feet of sunlight and green grass separated her from the others. She was only a neighbor looking from her window.

She searched her rooms and wiped every doorknob, every place on doors or sinks or cupboards a hand might touch, careful that nobody saw her open and shut her back-porch door. She cleaned up after him one last time.

When she went to brush her teeth in the bathroom, the cap on the toothpaste was too tight for her to turn.

Then she saw that each towel on her towel racks was folded in thirds. She reached out, almost touched them. She left them as they were.

# 44

Sara's telephone rang. "Hello?" Georgia Parrish said in her light, high voice. "Are you all right? We heard about the prowler on the radio, and Hazel wanted me to call you right away."

"I'm fine," Sara said.

"What a world we live in—mad people shooting college boys at their own back door. But the man who did the shooting killed himself at the Holiday Inn. You probably know that already."

"Yes. I'll be coming at twelve—"

"That's the thing—I've got a few days free to spend with Haze, now that she's talking. Is she talking! There's no getting in any words of your own. Haze says you can stay home and have a good rest. We're going over pictures of our travels together and reminiscing—"

"Can't I come cook or wash—"

"No. I'm good at things like that, and I know what Haze likes. You've worked the miracle here. You enjoy yourself, with pay, of course. I'll call you before I have to leave. Maybe Haze will have said everything she can think of by then, but don't count on it."

Sara thanked her, put the phone receiver down, and saw the look of a confused child in Martin's eyes, the small trickle of blood . . . the sight came to her over and over without warning. She went in and looked at towels folded in thirds on her bathroom racks, and saw the look in Martin's eyes, but what she felt on her skin and along her spine was Ben—Ben at noon, coming home for lunch, for two hours . . . she put her hands over her eyes and whispered, "Martin!"

No one answered her but Banana, scratching at the kitchen door. Sara let the kitten in, put out some cat food, and saw what she could do—she could walk to College Hill stores. She could talk to people. She could go to the university library. . . .

Her towels hung in a row. Ben's body was square and hard. His hair was soft and springy, and once in a while, at delicious places, he moaned "Mmm," to himself, to her. . . .

"Banana!" Sara cried. The kitten, crouched over a saucer, looked back at her, chewing. "Martin's dead," she whispered, "I'm free."

Banana stopped eating and sneezed, then started again. "I'm thinking about sleeping with Ben," Sara whispered. "Martin's in some morgue and I'm thinking about making love to Ben at lunchtime. He's got two hours at lunchtime!" She sat down beside Banana, her face in her hands.

After a while Sara whispered to the kitten, "I'll have to be Laura Pray for a long time. I'll have to lie to Ben and everybody, but I'm safe!" Banana licked the saucer, then sniffed all around it delicately. "I can telephone my mother in a week or so and say I'm somebody else. Maybe I can wear my black wig and glasses and go see her." Sara flung her arms in the air, free, free—she was free!

Banana climbed into Sara's lap and looked at her with crumbs of food clinging to a whisker. "Some women don't have social security numbers, and they lose their birth certificates, don't they? I can say I don't know where I was born. I can lie," Sara whispered to Banana. "I can lie," she said again, and buried her face in her arms.

The cat licked its whiskers and looked at Sara, who whispered, "I'm a widow." Banana licked a paw, then curled nose to tail in Sara's lap.

"Ben's got two hours," Sara whispered in a little while, and rubbed between her eyes with the heel of her hand, a shamefaced look on her face. "It's delicious."

Now Sara could walk through her yard to Ben's back door in the morning sunshine. Ben had gone to his classes after a last cup of coffee—his cup was beside the sink. Sara touched her lips to brown drops on the rim, closed her eyes.

Then she found the paper bag in the lowest cupboard and went back home to put mustache and beard and man's clothes away. The bag was damp still with rain; she tore it up. When she hung up the coat something rustled in its pocket.

She reached in to find the old piece of envelope from the farmhouse, folded and taped over its mound of seeds. "Marigolds" was written on one side in her mother's handwriting.

Sara looked at letters her mother would never write again: "Marigolds." She felt hot sun on her back where she knelt in her mother's garden behind the farmhouse. She smelled windbreak firs, and heard her mother and Joe talking in the kitchen; their voices came to her on that lost air.

She found a flowerpot and some potting soil, and took one marigold seed from the envelope. It lay in her palm— its black body, its fuzzy tuft. It wouldn't have much chance to bloom. Winter was coming. But it could have the sun of her kitchen windowsill. She covered it over, watered it, and set it there.

Her violet leaves from Montrose listened along the sill, their green ears alert. They had grown roots. Sara lifted pots to see how nearly every leaf had small leaves sprouting under its furry roof. She needed to build a light table. By the new year she might have every one of her lost Montrose violets blooming again.

Sara ran back to Ben's house, climbed his stairs, lay across his unmade bed, her mouth against the sheets. She said out loud, "I'm alive."

After she made the bed she cleaned Ben's bathroom—it needed it. What should they have for lunch, if they ate it at all? She leaned against his stove with pleasant lightning playing along her spine, and laughed to herself, and heard herself laughing.

Chicken pies—her special ones—he had a whole chicken in the freezer. His microwave defrosted the chicken fast, and she set it to simmering slowly on her own stove. They could have lunch at her place for a change. She rolled out piecrust while Martin's narrow brown eyes watched her sometimes, or she stood again in Ben's closet, her face pressed to his clothes in the dark. Her kitchen was filled with sunlight. If the doorbell rang, she could answer it, answer any questions.

Her bed. She ran to change it, smooth it. At the bottom of a dresser drawer was the picture of the gunslinger and the saloon girl; it could stand on her dresser now for anyone to see. The saloon girl looked calmly into her eyes. Martin had been alive then. The saloon girl's lips looked soft from kisses at the top of a Ferris wheel, and her arms, tight around the man with the guns, looked as if they'd been there before. Sara felt breathless. She put a little perfume on the sheets and pillows, then stood in that fragrance half asleep, unbelieving, seeing a wound and blood.

Now the doors of her house stood open. She sang softly to herself, then stopped, her mouth open a little, her hands hovering over piecrust bits she had cut off with a sharp knife. Martin sat on the motel bed, his eyes fixed on her.

The campanile struck twelve just as she took the chicken pies from the oven; their fragrance filled the house. She was groggy, she thought—she hadn't had any sleep the night before. She ran to her bedroom and opened a dresser drawer to look at a black silk teddy. She put it on under her shirt and shorts, her whole body tingling with the thought of Ben.

The doors of her house were open; it smelled of her good cooking. She'd cleaned Ben's bathroom and kitchen too. . . . Sara suddenly stopped by her bed, her eyes blank. She looked around her bedroom that smelled of perfume and the lunch that was almost ready. The saloon girl stared at her, not smiling, the ace of spades under her garter.

"Hey!" she heard Ben call, and found she had run to her front door and out on her front porch. "You're here!" he said, coming up her walk.

"I-I don't have to be at Dr. Channing's for a few days," Sara said, staring at Ben. "Georgia Parrish is staying with her—"

Ben was inside her door kissing her before she finished. He hadn't even put down his briefcase; she felt breathless, held close against him in the midst of chicken pie, peeled oranges, and coffee smells. Ben ran his hands under her wig and kissed the back of her neck and she shivered; he chuckled and ran his hot mouth down her back as far as he could, and she shivered again, and said she'd made chicken pies and—

"I'll tell you what—they can wait," Ben murmured, and pushed her T-shirt up. She didn't have a bra on, but she had a gorgeous black silk teddy under her clothes. "Hey!" he said, and saw her nipples under black lace. "Just for me?" She giggled and got her arms out of her T-shirt, and then he could push down all that lace. She got her feet out of the teddy and her tight shorts, but Ben pulled her T-shirt over her head while she was still bent over. Then she was naked in the dim green light of her living room, the wig knocked sideways. "Take it off!" Ben cried, and pulled at it.

"Wait . . ." Sara said. "It's all braided and pinned—" but he had the wig off and her hair half down already, hairpins falling out.

"C'mon," Ben said. She heard a hairpin hit a living-room chair leg, then another fell on her bedroom floor. She slid under the sheet and in a minute he was there where she'd dreamed him, making her cry out and finally lie with her hair in her eyes and mouth, cobwebbed with it, eyes shut, lips open. They lay for a while without a word, his kisses mixing with the web of hair over her mouth, until she pushed her hair away, and he said, "More?" and she said Please Oh Yes Please. . . .

After a while her afternoon house and the scents of summer air came back to her. Children were yelling in the park. A gunslinger and saloon girl watched her from the dresser. "I've got to get to that goddamned meeting," Ben murmured against her lips.

The chicken pies were only warm, and her special salad wasn't cold. Who cared? Ben asked, so they ate the lunch the way it was, and kissed between bites.

He had to find a folder of notes in his study; they went to his house and kissed in his study, kissed at his front door. "Curriculum committee again," Ben said. How beautiful Laura was, smiling by his old sprung-cushion armchair, the bust of Shakespeare looking over her shoulder. He could tell her about department fights and rehearse his strategy. When he came home he'd smell dinner at the front door, and there'd be a glass of wine.

Sara watched him go down his front walk, then remembered there were dirty dishes. She washed them and put them away, looking out at Ben's barn door through lilac leaves. A blue blur inside it was the fender of Ben's car.

"Dinner at my house," she'd told Ben as he lifted handfuls of her hair, braided it, unbraided it, let it fall on her breasts again.

"When are you going to tell me where you come from . . . everything?" Ben had asked, kissing her hands, kissing behind her ears and under her chin. She answered him by pulling his face down to her breasts and long hair.

Sara pounded steak with the side of a saucer and watched red meat turn white with flour. Her head felt light with a rising Ferris-wheel car, blazes of lightning, a bedspread smeared with moth wings.

Could she sleep? she wondered, rubbing her tired forehead with the back of a floury hand.

"Right about here." A man's voice drifted through her kitchen window. Breeze blew in with laughter and voices. Half asleep, Sara leaned on the sill and met, for a second, eyes in the yard next door. Then a blond young man in a T-shirt that said *Heavy Metal* pretended not to see her. "Smashed the damn chrysanthemums," he said to two college girls. His door behind him raised its white-painted eyebrow.

"Wow," breathed the dark girl, swinging a book bag from her wrist.

"Scared the bastard, that's all," Mark Corey said. "Thought he was going to break into our house, and then he saw me." His jeans were very tight; he slung his thumbs in the pockets and grinned at the other girl, who had long, brown-blond hair and a U.N.I. shirt hanging over her short shorts.

"I got to get to class," the dark girl said. They started walking toward the street. "It must have been scary, getting shot at."

"Not really," Mark said in a voice that was a little too loud. "I could see he didn't have the guts to do the job right."

"Wow," the dark girl said.

Sara looked around her kitchen. Everything was ready for dinner. Maybe she could sleep a little while. She pulled her bedroom shades, set her alarm, and washed her face at her sink. Reaching for a towel, she saw Ben had been there before her—he'd grabbed at towels on the rod, and only one was still folded in thirds.

But it was folded in thirds—it watched her leave the bathroom and take off her shirt and shorts and teddy and lie down bare on her tumbled bed. "Oh," she breathed to herself under the sheet, stretching her arms out, thinking she felt the warmth of their bodies yet, shivering at the thought of the night, and Ben.

Forty-six days since she'd walked across a Manhasset street with Martin, making "a nice pair." She was so tired. The bed was still warm.

Sara shut her eyes. In a moment or two she was asleep. Dreaming, she wondered why nobody up and down a street in Montrose, Massachusetts, happened to be looking out windows when a taxi stopped at the Burney house—then realized it was very early in the morning. No one saw Sara Burney pay the taxi driver and carry her bag up the sidewalk and put her key in the lock. She stood at the door of the little Cape Cod house thinking that dead leaves on her lawn would kill the grass if she didn't rake it.

Dreaming, she turned the key and the smell of her own house took her in—the individual, one-of-a-kind scents of year after year. She shut the door behind her and put down her bag in that still, secret smell of the past.

Pine furniture. Sara took one step into the living room to see guns shine behind glass in a gun cabinet, an empty space among them.

In her dreams a clock was ticking. She had forgotten she'd put their wedding candlesticks on the mantel. There they were. And there were slipcovers she'd made, and the curtains.

A hall mirror glimmered, but it wasn't beautifully beveled any more. Without light from that glass the little hall would be dark. Their bedroom seemed dark when she opened the door.

Dreaming, she found her clothes in the closet; dresser drawers were full of her underwear, her sewing and patterns; Sara opened them one by one. Fluorescent lights on her violet tables still worked; she switched them on. When she opened the hall linen closet she found the two new pairs of blue top sheets she'd found on sale, and flowered fitted ones to match, and pillowcases too.

The hall floor creaked under her; she knew that exact sound. Sara stood in her kitchen doorway, then put her hand on her new refrigerator, her new stove. The red kitchen should be painted green.

Her dishes were clean in the cupboards. There were the glass nut chopper and her plastic butter dish.

Dreaming, she found the car keys in the dish on the desk that had been Martin's. She opened her garage door.

The car gleamed when Sara turned the light on. She got in and sat behind the wheel, then started her car and listened to its motor roar. After a while she turned the key, took it from the ignition, put it on her key chain, and dropped it in her purse on top of the savings account book from the bank.

It was so quiet; dry leaves rustled along her drive and shoved dry fingers under the garage door.

Dreaming, Sara climbed out of her car, sliding her feet from gas and brake pedals.

She felt a faint grit of beach-house sand under her shoes.

A late-afternoon breeze fluttered shirt and skirts and flags on campus. Ben Woodward came from the curriculum committee meeting, yawning discreetly without opening his mouth. Off he went past students sunning themselves on thick grass—the young professor who walked heavy-footed, curls over his ears.

Late sun streaked and dappled the campus walk with shade. Sara opened her eyes, sat up in her tumbled bed, and stared around her at an Iowa bedroom, a saloon girl hugging a gunman in a picture on her dresser.

Loud music came from the Union as Ben walked by; he hunched his shoulders, turning his head this way and that. He whistled past the president's house, whistled along College Street, whistled through Seerley Park, thinking of nothing but Laura, her long blond hair lifted by a summer breeze. He laughed out loud as he opened his door, laughed for the joy of it—Laura in his bed all night long.